WHEN SHE LOVES

A DARK MAFIA ROMANCE

GABRIELLE SANDS

THE FALLEN

THE FALLEN SERIES

When She Unravels

The story of Valentina & Damiano

When She Tempts

The story of Martina & Giorgio

When She Falls

The story of Gemma & Ras

When She Loves

The story of Cleo & Rafaele

"Rafaele wouldn't do that," I say. "You know how traditional his family is."

My sister shakes her head. "Don't be naive. In our world, they only respect the traditions that serve them. Rafaele won't raise another man's baby." Her lips tremble. "I don't know what to do. I never should have left Ras. You're right, Cleo. I should have been brave and stayed. Ras loved me, and I broke his heart because I was so damn scared that one day he'd regret sacrificing so much for me. I was so insecure and worried about the future that I completely missed what was right in front of me."

My heart clenches. That's how people act when they've never been allowed to put themselves first. They self-sabotage because they believe they're not worthy of happiness.

Oh, Gem. Her whole life, she's been molded by our parents to be the perfect daughter—obedient and self-sacrificial. They've succeeded spectacularly.

She drags her nails down her cheeks. "Ras and I could have had a family together. We would have been happy. Instead, I fucked everything up." A tear slips out of her eye, followed by another. Her heartbreak is so clear, so devastating, that I feel an echo of it inside my own chest.

She doesn't deserve to suffer like this.

I'm a shithead, but Gem is good and kind and loyal. She's spent years protecting me. While I was sneaking out at night to kiss boys who'd never understand my world and going to parties where I'd never belong, Gemma was covering for me and getting beaten up by our father.

How many bruises have I earned her? How many tears has she shed on my behalf?

I never even knew Papà was abusing her until a few weeks ago. He had hurt her for years, and I never noticed it. Honestly, what kind of a person does that make me? It's like I had blinders on to everyone's suffering but my own.

Hot shame prickles over my cheeks.

I have got to be better than this. I can't keep failing my sister. That stops right now.

I walk over to where she's sitting and kneel in front of her. "Is that what you want? Do you want to be with Ras?"

Her eyes swim with tears. "Yes. More than anything."

Finally. There's real conviction in her voice. This might be her chance to break free from Papà's shackles and do what's right for her. But she can't start a new life with Papà and Rafaele on her back. As long as they need her for this marriage, they'll never let her go.

A heavy weight settles in the pit of my stomach.

I can make them stop needing Gemma.

After all, she's not the only Garzolo daughter around here.

Fucking fuck.

I brush my curls off my neck, feeling a nervous heat creep up my skin. Can I do this?

I have to do this.

Yes, it's time to grow up. I've spent years dreaming of moving to LA, working as a music manager, rubbing shoulders with the talented and the famous, and having the freedom to do whatever the hell I wanted, but I'd never enjoy it if the price is Gem's happiness. She deserves to live her life with someone who loves her the way Ras does.

She's always had my back. Now, it's my turn to have hers.

I wrap my palms over her knees and look into her eyes. "Are you willing to fight for it?"

Gemma sniffs and wipes her cheeks. "I'll do whatever it takes."

My chest tightens.

And so will I. For her, I'll do anything. She deserves no less than that.

"Gem, I'll take your place."

Confusion flashes over her features. "What do you mean?"

I take a deep breath. "I'll marry Rafaele."

A day later, I'm sitting in an Italian restaurant in Chelsea owned by the Messeros.

This was supposed to be an intimate dinner with Rafaele's immediate family and ours, so there are just seven other people scattered around the large dining table.

It's quiet enough to hear a pin drop.

Rafaele's mother and uncle have barely said a word since we sat down. So far, the conversation's been dominated by Papà, but even he's got his mouth shut now. A drop of sweat rolls down his pockmarked temple, and the sight of it fills me with satisfaction.

Nervous? You should be.

Gemma asked to speak with Rafaele alone just a few minutes ago, and now they're talking in his office. Everyone can sense something is wrong. My sister's supposed to be getting married in three days, but if their conversation goes well, it won't be Gemma walking down the aisle.

It will be me.

Mamma is staring at her plate, her jaw tight. Beside her, my brother, Vince, is swirling the wine in his glass, a notch between his brows. I glance to my right, over Gemma and Rafaele's empty seats, and lock eyes with Nero De Luca, Rafaele's consigliere. For once, that annoying mountain of a man looks a bit uncertain. He lifts his brows, like he's asking me if I know what this is all about.

As if I'd ever tell him. He's just as bad as his tyrannical boss.

While it's a bit thrilling to be the only one here in on the secret, what's *not* thrilling is knowing that the best-case scenario ends with me walking out of here as an engaged woman.

I vowed I'd never marry a mobster.

But for Gemma, I'll break that vow without any regrets.

Footsteps sound, and a moment later, the two of them reappear.

My heart jumps into my throat. I search Gemma's expression for a hint of how it went, but she's looking at the ground as she hurries over. As soon as she slips into her chair beside me, I take her hand and give it a squeeze. She squeezes back twice.

Is that good or bad?

Before I can ask her how it went, Rafaele stops at the head of the table like he's about to announce something.

6

I turn my attention to him.

Sculpted cheekbones.

Jaw line carved into a firm, decisive line.

Muscular build that even the sleek tailoring of his black suit can't hide.

In another universe, Rafaele Messero could have been an underwear model, but in this one, the only thing he's modeling is how to be the most intimidating man in a room full of killers.

At twenty-seven, he's the youngest don New York has seen in decades, but he's already gained a reputation for being the most brutal.

A shiver slithers down my spine. I might be marrying this guy.

I should probably be more afraid of him, but I'm not. I've long since trained myself not to think too hard about the consequences of my actions. Papà and Mamma have spent their lives trying to keep me on a tight leash, and if I worried about how they'd punish me every time I broke their stupid rules, I'd never have any fun.

Of course, back then, I didn't know Gemma often paid the price for my indiscretions.

Rafaele drags a tanned hand over his black silk tie. "The engagement is off."

For a second, my lungs seize.

Holy shit. It's done.

"What?" my father barks, his gaze darting between Rafaele and Gemma.

"Take a breath, Garzolo," Nero warns, sensing the impending meltdown.

"You promised me a virgin bride," Rafaele says. "And Gemma is not a virgin."

Papà's face turns red. "Nonsense."

"Garzolo, she admitted to it herself," Rafaele says.

"She's unwell. You know how she's been ever since she returned to us. She doesn't know what she's saying."

"I know exactly what I'm saying," Gemma says firmly as she stands up.

Nero clicks his tongue. "It seems to me like she's quite in control of her mental faculties, Garzolo."

Papà rises, his chair skidding out behind him. "This is a misunderstanding. Let me talk to my daughter in private."

No way in hell. He's not going anywhere near her again.

I move to put myself between my father and Gemma, but my brother beats me to it. Vince stares down Papà, his jaw a hard line.

"I'm done talking to you," Gemma spits out, peering around Vince. "It's already been decided. I won't be marrying Rafaele."

Papà tries to come closer, but Vince blocks his path. "Sit down," my brother snaps.

"Get out of my way," Papà snarls at him. "Gemma, what the hell is this? How dare you—"

Gemma slams her fist against the table. "How dare I? How dare *you* demand anything from me after what you've done?

8

I spent my life trying to keep you happy, only to get beaten by you and emotionally abused by Mamma. You've never loved me. I don't think you've ever loved any of your kids. I'm through with you. My only regret is that it took me this long to get here."

Let him hear it, Gem.

"And by the way, I'm pregnant," she says.

Our parents' reaction is priceless. I wish I could take a picture of their shell-shocked expressions so that I'd have something to look at on the days I'm feeling down.

"Like I said, Gemma is no longer qualified to be my wife," Rafaele drawls, cutting through the stunned silence with his cold voice. "The stipulations in our contract were very clear. I've already delivered what I promised. I got you out of prison, and I got your charges dropped. This isn't how I do business, Garzolo."

"What do you want me to do?" Papà rasps. He's really panicking now. "I had no idea—"

"You owe me a wife." Rafaele's gaze falls on me. "So I'm taking your other daughter."

Our eyes clash together. His are so cold that most people are repelled by their icy scrutiny, but right now, there's something else swirling inside all that ice.

Something vaguely possessive.

My blood chills in my veins as my surroundings fade. I don't break eye contact even though it feels like a noose is slowly being tightened around my neck.

In our world, marriage is never an equal partnership. It's a prison.

And I'm not the kind of person who does well in captivity.

Just ask my parents. I've disobeyed them my whole life. The more they tried to control me, the more I rebelled. I was going to find a way out of this life. I would leave New York, build a career, and become independent.

That dream is all over now, isn't it?

I tear my gaze away from my future husband and look at my sister.

Gem.

That's right. This isn't about me.

I'm doing this for her. Because I love her, and I want her to be happy with Ras and her baby. My dreams have always been just that—dreams. But her happy ending is real and ready for the taking.

"Everyone knows that girl is a slut."

The voice of Rafaele's uncle pierces through the pounding in my ears.

I flinch even though it's not the first time someone's called me that.

One of my recent attempts to piss my parents off included lying about going all the way with an outsider. They bought it, given Papà was the one who walked in on us in bed. The truth is all we did was some heavy petting, but I encouraged the rumor to spread. If it helped me avoid marriage, I didn't care what anyone thought of me.

But right now, the word bothers me. If it's what stops Gemma from getting away from here, I'll never forgive myself.

Rafaele turns to his uncle. "I'm aware there are rumors floating around about my future wife. Good thing they're completely unfounded. From now on, anyone who speaks a word of them will lose their tongue. Have I made myself clear, Uncle?"

My future wife. My mouth goes dry. Jeez, he's adjusting quickly to the change.

And already doing damage control. He needs to clean up my reputation, so I guess he may as well start now.

Rafaele's uncle pales. "I didn't know. I apologize."

Nero grins and claps his hands. "The matter is settled then."

"Go, Gemma," I urge her, giving her hand one final squeeze. "It's done."

She gives me a nervous smile, hope shining in her eyes.

Rafaele nods at Gemma to signal that she's free to leave. Papà starts shouting in protest, but Rafaele's men block him from interfering as Gemma slips out the door.

The dinner appears to be over. Rafaele walks around the table to where I'm sitting and grabs me by the arm. "Let's go," he says in a low voice. His hold on me is firm but not painful. I let him lift me to my feet and lead me out of the restaurant.

An SUV is waiting outside. He opens the door, shoves me inside, and slides in after me. His scent washes over me, spicy and masculine.

Nero takes the driver's seat and starts the car, his eyes briefly meeting mine in the rearview mirror.

My head spins. I press my temple against the cool window and try to come to terms with what just happened.

"Your sister said your father beat her. Did he do the same to you?" Rafaele asks, a strange lilt to his voice.

I glance sideways at him. "No," I say. "Only Gemma."

He rolls his shoulders, not looking at me. "I'm taking you to my home. You will stay there until our wedding, because your father is clearly incompetent when it comes to over-seeing his daughters. There won't be any further change of plans. You will walk down that aisle in three days and become my wife. Do you understand?"

He's right. My father is incompetent in many ways.

But Rafaele isn't.

Something tells me there won't be any sneaking out of *his* house.

When I don't say anything for a second too long, he takes my chin in his hand. His touch burns against my skin, but his blue eyes are pure ice. "Do you understand?"

Dismay drips into my blood.

By marrying this man, I'm signing my life away.

I swallow and give him the smallest of nods. "I understand."

CHAPTER 2

2 DAYS LATER

CLEO

THE DOOR behind me opens without a single knock.

That's a first. The maid usually knocks before she brings in my meals.

I tear my gaze away from the view of my fiancé's garden through the arched bedroom window and turn. A strange woman I haven't seen before stands in the doorway.

Black button-up shirt, gray knee-length skirt, and a sensible pair of Mary Janes. The outfit screams uniform, but it's different from the one the maid wears.

She gives me a cross look, her gaze critically scanning my body, and her lips curling at my two-day-old clothes.

I'm still in the same dress I wore to the dinner where Gemma announced she's pregnant. I would have loved to change into something else, but for whatever reason, the maid only brought me Rafaele's T-shirts.

No thanks.

The woman closes the door and chucks a black garment bag onto the unmade bed. "Go shower. You need to get ready for your rehearsal dinner. The Messeros will all be here to see you, and you will not embarrass the don by looking like something the cat dragged in."

Wow. Sounds just like Mamma.

When I don't move, she scowls at me. "Are you deaf?"

Mild indignation coasts over my skin. Who the hell is she? She's got a mean look and a mean mouth, but what she doesn't realize yet is that I can be far meaner.

I march over to her until I encroach into her personal space. Her eyes widen. When I grab her wrist and squeeze hard, she gasps.

"Where is my sister?" I demand.

She jerks her wrist out of my grip, anger flashing over her face. "How should I know? You ever touch me like that again, and you'll regret it. I've worked for the Messeros for two decades, and this is the first time I've been tasked to take care of a *whore*." She spits out that last word as if it's poison on her tongue.

I scoff. Does she think she can intimidate me? It'll take a lot more than a few cruel words. "I need to know what happened to my sister. Can you find out while I get dressed?"

The woman's scowl becomes even uglier. "Ungrateful slut. I serve at the don's orders, not yours. The guests are arriving

14

in an hour, so you better go wash up now." Her eyes narrow at my hair. "It'll take ages to tame that red mop you've got on your head."

If I hadn't bitten off all my nails while being locked alone in this bedroom, I would have raked them over her face, but in their absence, I have to settle on just glowering at her. "My sister—"

"If you want to know so badly about your stupid sister, you can ask the don at the rehearsal dinner," she snaps.

Red bleeds into my vision. She can call me any name she wants—I've heard the same and worse from my own parents for years—but if she says another word about Gemma...

I count to three in my head so that I don't fly off the rails. Until I know Gem's safe, I have to play this carefully. It's why I've sat quietly in this room for two whole days, not causing any trouble, waiting and hoping the man I'm supposed to marry in my sister's place kept his word and let her go.

When I can't stand to look at the old woman's hateful face any longer, I whip around and grab the bag she threw on the bed.

Inside the bathroom, I lock the door behind me and look in the mirror.

I don't recognize the girl staring back at me.

I've barely slept, I haven't showered, and there are dark bags under my eyes. My worry is a churning mass inside the pit of my belly.

Gem, where are you? Did you make it? Did you manage to escape?

When Rafaele brought me here, I didn't expect him to keep me cut off from the world until our wedding. He took my cell phone. He also must have instructed the maid who's been bringing me food not to answer any of my questions.

Well, that bitch in my bedroom is not going to tell me anything either, so I guess I have no choice but to hope I can find out more at this rehearsal dinner.

I shrug off my old dress and step into the shower.

The wedding is tomorrow. It still doesn't feel real.

This is like a nightmare I can't wake up from.

At least I can sort of imagine what the celebration will be like, given I sat in on a few of the meetings Gemma had with the wedding planner.

But what happens *after* tomorrow?

That's where I draw a blank.

Me. A married woman.

My vision grows fuzzy, so I brace my palms against the shower wall. If I knew Gem made it to Ras, I wouldn't give a fuck if I fell and snapped my neck, but I've got to stay alive until I'm sure she's safe.

It's about the only reason I've got left to live.

I can hear an echo of Gem's voice inside my ear. *Stop being so dramatic, Cleo.*

How can I not be dramatic when my life is a fucking tragedy?

I dry myself off and peel open the zipper on the garment bag. Inside is a dress.

It's pretty. Cream-colored, smooth satin fabric with capped lace sleeves, and a V-cut neckline. I stare at it while I pat my hair dry by the bathroom sink. It looks vaguely familiar.

Hold on. Is this the dress Gem was going to wear tonight?

I put it on. It's short on me and tight around the chest, just like all the clothes I've ever borrowed from my sister.

Nostalgia wraps around me.

I grasp the neckline and pull it up to my nose, searching for a hint of her scent, but it doesn't smell like Gem. My heart clenches. She has to be okay, or I don't know what I'll do with myself.

When I come out, the woman is scowling by the dressing table. "Sit down. I need to do your face and hair."

"I can do it myself."

She holds up a hairbrush like she's about to smack me with it. "*Sit.*"

I heave out a sigh and slump in the chair. Again, none of this treatment is new to me. Mamma never let me get ready for events she dragged me to, and I always had to wear the itchy, frilly dresses she picked out for me. I hated how I looked in them—just like an obedient mafia wife.

Good thing I learned a long time ago I could ruin that perception as soon as I opened my mouth.

The woman sweeps on my makeup in a precise and efficient way, and then she prods and pulls on my curly, copper hair. I accept her rough treatment without a single complaint, but I remember every time she pulls on me harder than she needs to.

"Cleo," she says, testing my name on her tongue with a scowl. "What kind of a name is that? It's not even Italian."

Oh, she'll love this story.

"My mamma was carrying me when she walked in on Papà fucking another woman in his office. She gave me a non-Italian name out of spite."

The brushing stops abruptly. I meet the woman's appalled gaze in the mirror and raise a brow. "She preferred he kept his whores far from our home."

What's sad is that my name was my mother's only act of rebellion against her husband during their twenty-plus years of marriage. Sometimes, when I made Mamma really angry, she'd say I was her punishment for that rebellion. *I put that rotten streak in you with your name.*

The woman recovers from her shock. "I hope you're not stupid enough to talk that way around the don's relatives."

"What's your name?" I ask. I like to know the names of my enemies.

"Sabina," she says. "I'm the house manager. I was hired by the don's grandmother, the late Signora Costa. She was a real lady. Pure class." She leans down until her lips are hovering beside my ear and whispers, "This used to be a respectable family, and now look at the trash they've brought in."

Miserable woman. "Take it up with your don. This trash would be happy to take itself right out if he no longer wants it."

She straightens out and sneers. "The don is making a mistake marrying you. Everyone knows it. If only you knew how the family's been arguing about it, you wouldn't dare to show your face tonight."

I purse my lips as I process this information. Interesting. So the Messeros aren't happy about the bride swap, huh? Well, it's good to know I won't be the only miserable person at the wedding.

"You really overestimate the number of fucks I give about the feelings of Rafaele's family," I retort.

Sabina sprays something over my hair. "With that mouth, you won't last very long."

Maybe she's right. Rafaele doesn't know what he's getting here. I'm not an easy person to live with, and once I know Gem's safe, he won't have anything he can use to keep me in line. Even if he threatens to hurt me, I won't care. I'd rather die than become a submissive shell of a human like my mother.

"You're ready. Let's go." Sabina wraps her palm around my elbow and hauls me to my feet.

"Where are you taking me?"

"To the don, of course."

Heart hammering, I let her lead me out of the room and do my best not to stumble. My legs feel like jelly.

I am so damn fucked.

CHAPTER 3

RAFAELE

MY FIST CRASHES into the man's jaw with a sharp crack. "I have somewhere to be, Joshua. Stop wasting my time."

He moans, blood and saliva leaking out of his mouth and onto the polished concrete floor.

The old white clock on the wall ticks past six thirty. I need at least a few minutes to get myself cleaned up before I head down for the rehearsal dinner.

"Pffease," Joshua bleats through a mouth full of broken teeth. "Pffea—"

I punch him again. A few drops of blood land high on my forearm.

Fuck. I'd hoped this wouldn't turn into such a fucking mess.

"The next time you say a word, make it one I want to hear."

Behind me, Nero lets out a loud sigh. "Maybe he really doesn't know anything. He's a vain bastard. I don't think he'd let you pummel him like this if he did."

Joshua's chin bumps against his chest. Did the fucker just pass out?

I kick him hard in the shin. Nothing.

Annoyance crawls up my spine. Joshua's father, Conor Paddington, owns one of the biggest cement-pouring businesses in New York, and he's been paying his twenty percent dutifully for over a decade. Then last week, he disappeared. Joshua took over in his stead, but the guy's a certified idiot. He's already fired their VP of operations, and it won't be long until he runs the business into the ground.

If Conor is alive, we're going to get him back, and my hunch is that the only person who knows where he is, is the son of a bitch before me.

"Get me the adrenaline."

There's a rustling sound behind me. A moment later, a syringe is placed in my open hand. I take off the cap and jab it into Joshua's thigh.

The man intakes a sharp breath, his eyes springing wide.

I've really got to wrap this up. I pick up a serrated knife off the tray, grab Joshua's hand, and start sawing off his pinky finger.

His screams fill the air.

I raise my voice so that he can hear me. "I hope you have an assistant to help you answer emails. You won't be typing any time soon. Or ever, if you don't start talking, right. Fucking. *Now*."

When I reach bone, Joshua breaks.

"He's at the house in Poughkeepsie! Jesus, fuck!"

I stop moving the knife. That's an hour and a half from here. "What did you do to him?"

"He's alive. Or at least he was when I checked on him a few days ago."

I glance at Nero. My consigliere raises his hands in acquiescence. He'd thought Conor ran, but I told him there's no way. Paddington's not the kind of man to run away from his own problems. It's why I've always liked him. He pays his protection money on time and in full. And we're not the type of outfit that takes cash and doesn't deliver on our end. That's the kind of shit Stefano Garzolo used to pull, and look where he is now.

"Send a few guys to check it out, and tell them to take Doc with them. Conor might need medical treatment on the spot."

Nero nods and leaves the interrogation room to make the call. I grab a towel and do my best to wipe my hands clean of Joshua's blood so that I don't leave bloody fingerprints all over the house once I head upstairs.

We have guests coming. My whole family is probably arriving upstairs right now, and while showing up with blood on my hands would certainly send a message to those who've questioned my judgment in the last few days, tonight is not the place or time.

Everyone is eager to get a glimpse of the woman I'm supposed to marry.

Especially since until two nights ago, they thought I'd be marrying her sister.

"Messero." Joshua's voice is no more than a low rasp. "Not everyone is as lucky as you. Your father croaked all on his own. Some of us have to take our fate into our own hands if we ever want to get to the top."

I crack my neck. My father would have preferred it if I'd been the one who ended him. He loathed dying slowly, rotting like a vegetable in his bed while his kingdom slowly slipped through his fingers. In his last few days, he begged me to do it. To end his pain.

I smiled at him and repeated a line I'd heard him say very often. *We can't rely on anyone to save us but ourselves.*

"You got impatient." I throw the towel to the ground. "The plan you concocted was sloppy."

Joshua shakes his head. "I was tired of sitting on the sidelines. I deserve more."

Entitled piece of shit. I lean forward until we're face-to-face. "You deserve *nothing* until you learn to not be a slave to your emotions."

Joshua lets out a pained moan and starts mumbling something, but I'm done with this conversation. I turn away from him and head for the door.

I exit the room and lock the door behind me. Nero's standing just outside, making the necessary arrangements over the phone. The hallway has low ceilings, so he has to hunch slightly to make his six-five frame fit. He glances at me and gives me a nod. There's no need for me to stick around to make sure Nero carries out my orders. There

23

aren't many men I trust completely, but my consigliere is one of them.

I'm about to take the stairs when Nero calls out my name.

I glance over my shoulder. "What is it?"

Nero presses his palm over the phone's receiver. "You sure about this?"

He's not talking about Conor.

He's also not the first person to ask me that question over the last few days.

I'm a man who likes to be in total control, and yet I'm about to marry a famously uncontrollable woman.

Cleo Garzolo has done everything in her power to make herself unattractive as a marriage prospect, including lying about losing her virginity to some kid. A lie that will hang over me until I display our bloody wedding sheets as proof that she was pure.

She's erratic, has no sense of self-preservation, and drinks enough to qualify as a barely functioning alcoholic.

It's understandable why my very traditional Italian family disapproves of her.

When Gemma, the Garzolo sister I was originally supposed to marry, said she was pregnant and that Cleo was willing to take her place instead, I agreed to the outrageous proposition before I even realized the words were out of my mouth. On paper, Gemma was the perfect woman to marry. But for some fucking reason, I found myself looking at Cleo whenever I was supposed to be looking at her sister.

"I'm collecting the payment Garzolo owes me."

Nero snorts. "You're so full of shit."

"Watch it."

"You wanted that girl long before she got served to you on a silver platter."

I give him a warning look. Nero's been by my side for nearly a decade, and he's the closest friend I've got, but that doesn't change the fact that he's my subordinate. We're close, but not so close that I'd ever jeopardize my duty as don—to do whatever it takes to protect and grow my family's power—for his sake.

That duty is why I'm marrying in the first place.

"Stefano Garzolo bargained his family away to stay out of jail. I can either get what he owes me through force, or I can marry his daughter. The latter is the logical choice for more than one reason. It avoids bloodshed. It also gets me a wife. At my age, I need one."

Nero looks amused. "Right. Very logical. Tell me, what's the logic behind all the times I've caught you staring at her tits?"

I purse my lips. Sometimes I forget how observant my consigliere can be. "She's a beautiful woman, and I'll enjoy having her in my bed," I say dismissively.

"She's not just beautiful, is she? She's *unhinged*. And yet, you still said yes to marrying her. All that for a lay who'll likely try to bite your cock off on your wedding night." He barks out a laugh.

"She won't bite anything off."

"She'll drive you fucking insane with her behavior."

"Most of her misbehavior was aimed at avoiding marriage. She failed. Why would she continue to act out after she's married to me?"

"Don't think she'll see it that way. She's not pure logic like you are. She's marrying you because of her sister, not because she likes you, and based on what we've seen of her, Cleo isn't one to suffer in silence."

I arch a brow. "Good to know you think she'll suffer being married to me. How have you survived all these years by my side?"

"I often ask myself that question," he says with a grin before his expression turns serious. "I've seen how she gets under your skin."

Sometimes Nero overreaches. Nothing gets under my skin. Unlike Joshua, I'm not ruled by my emotions. My own father made sure of that.

I fold my arms over my chest. "You know what does get under my skin? My consigliere doubting me."

Nero laughs. "I'm just trying to do my job and watch out for you. Keep an eye on your drink. She might try to slip poison in it."

"You think she can conjure some out of thin air?" She doesn't have access to anything remotely dangerous in the bedroom I've kept her in.

"If I had to bet on any woman being a witch, it would be Cleo Garzolo."

"You overestimate her." I turn away from him and head for the stairs.

"I think you're making a big mistake by *underestimating* her," he calls out after me.

I shake my head. Cleo's erratic behavior is a product of her father's incompetence. Stefano Garzolo is a fool. Cleo must have sensed his weakness and exploited it.

But there's no weakness to sense in me.

I'll give it a week before she falls in line.

CHAPTER 4

RAFAELE

Bloody water runs down the white ceramic sink in the bathroom attached to my office. I didn't think Joshua would hold out as long as he did. He's a civilian, not used to violence, but greed is a powerful motivator for weak men like him. I scrub my forearms clean, dry my hands on a towel, and go to sit at my desk.

My work stares back at me. The boring kind, anyway. A bunch of documents need my signature, so I get started on them. Might as well make a dent in the bit of time I have left before I'm due to collect my fiancée.

I'm two signatures in when the door opens, and Elena enters with Fabi close behind her. Their dresses swish around them, and their heels click-clack against the hardwood floor.

That's the end of my productivity.

I haven't seen my sisters in a while. Elena's dyed her hair blond, which is throwing me off. Fabi looks the same, with her dark, wavy hair loose around her shoulders. They both look tired. They must have just gotten in from the airport.

Fabi shuts the door behind her and gives me a gentle smile.

Elena scowls.

My sisters are fraternal twins, but their characters couldn't be any more different.

I put the cap back on my pen just as Elena stops in front of my desk, her arms crossed over her chest. "I can't believe this. What the hell, Rafe?"

"Is that how you greet your don?"

Elena narrows her eyes. "You've been our brother far longer than you've been our don. We have a right to be angry at you. You switch the girl you're going to marry days before your wedding, and you don't think to even call to bring us up to speed?"

"When was the last time you called me, Elena? I barely hear from you when you're abroad." You'd think my sisters would be a bit more grateful about the fact that I've allowed them to live in Geneva even after they graduated from college, but there's nothing remotely grateful in Elena's expression.

Her cheeks redden. "I've sent you texts."

"And I've responded."

"Your one-word answers to my questions hardly clarified anything. How did this happen? Rumors are that the other Garzolo girl fell pregnant with another man's child."

I twist the pen between my fingers. "And for once, the rumors are accurate."

"And you decided to take her sister instead?" Fabi asks, her brows moving up her forehead.

"A debt is owed to me, and I'm collecting on it."

Elena scoffs. "How simple. So you're forcing this poor girl into marriage?"

"I'm not forcing her into anything," I say, annoyed that she would assume that of me. "For someone who just admitted to having no knowledge of the situation, you're making a lot of assumptions. Cleo offered to take her sister's place, and I accepted."

Elena's narrowed gaze drills into me. "Is it true what they say about her?"

"What do they say about her?"

"She's troubled. She's a nightmare to be around. She lost her virginity to an outsider."

"Her virginity is intact," I say evenly. "Send anyone who says otherwise my way."

My sisters exchange a look. "We heard you killed some guy that was after her," Fabi says after a moment. "Is that true? In front of everyone at your club?"

That I did. Ludovico Rizzo, the last made guy Garzolo tried to set up Cleo with.

Nero's words come back to me. *I've seen how she gets under your skin.*

Bullshit. I just had to enforce a certain level of civilized behavior at one of my establishments.

I shrug. "He deserved it."

Fabi swallows. "How come?"

"He came to my club and acted like a baboon. It was an important night, and I thought I'd send a message."

"What message?" Elena demands.

Do not fucking touch what's mine.

It's what I said to Ludovico right before I killed him, although Cleo was far from mine when I saw the bastard trying to force himself on her.

But in the moment, that didn't matter.

I wanted him to die.

A prickling sensation appears at my nape, and I run a finger under my collar.

I must have drunk too much that night to snap like that. That would explain why I lost control for a brief moment.

Long enough to murder someone.

But it all worked out just fine, didn't it? It served to remind everyone about my reputation, and that never hurts.

"To not behave in my club the way one would in a cheap whorehouse," I say.

Fabi sighs and smooths her hands over her dress. "Should we talk to her before you're wed? Offer words of encouragement?"

"You mean offer our condolences?" Elena snipes.

"No." I don't want Cleo talking to anyone but me and Sabina, the house manager who's been with the family for decades. She's seen it all, and she's loyal. I know nothing

Cleo says will ruffle her. Until there's a wedding band on Cleo's finger, I'm not taking any chances.

Elena shakes her head. "Have you even had a conversation with your future wife?"

"A few." None of which have gone too well, but I've replayed each one of them in my head more times than I care to admit.

Fabi tucks a strand behind her ear. "Do you like her?"

Yeah, I like her. I like her full pink lips, and her green almond-shaped eyes, and the way she looks at me when she's angry. I like her sweet ass and her round, plump tits.

I know I'll *definitely* like having them in my mouth.

It's like I said to Nero, Cleo is a bombshell. It's been a while since I wanted to fuck someone as badly as I want to fuck my future wife. But I'm not about to say that to my sisters.

"This is a business arrangement. Cleo is as good as any other woman as far as I'm concerned."

Fabi's face falls. "Rafe...she's going to be tied to you for life."

She says it with pity, and if I had to guess, it's not me she's pitying.

There's a light knock on the door, one I immediately recognize as our mother's. "Come in," I call out.

Mamma shuffles in, dressed in a light-blue outfit, and when she notices Fabi and Elena, her steps falter. "Am I interrupting anything?" she asks softly.

I spin my pen again. "Not at all."

She meets my gaze, but as usual, she only holds it for a second before she looks away. It used to bother me how after all these years, she still can't look at me. It's like she sees the shadow of my father inside my eyes. But I've made peace with it.

"Maybe you can help us talk some sense into him," Elena snaps.

"Regarding what?"

"This parody of a wedding! Mamma, do you really think this is a good idea?" Elena implores. "Rafe changes the woman he's marrying days before the ceremony, and we're all acting like it's no big deal?"

I groan. "Trust me, no one is acting like it's no big deal." Since I made the announcement, my phone has been ringing nonstop with calls from the family. I swear, I forgot some of these relatives even existed. Aunt Eliza went as far as to show up here in person, all to say I'm bringing shame to the entire family by marrying someone with a reputation like Cleo's. Uncle Philip had to drag her away when he saw the look in my eyes.

"It does seem a bit rushed," Fabi says, trying to be more diplomatic than Elena. "Why not wait a bit?"

"The wedding has already been planned," I say. "Caterers scheduled, church and venue booked."

"So what?" Elena demands. "It's not like anyone would argue about the extra work they'd have to do if you wanted to reschedule."

"I delivered on my part of the deal with Cleo's father, and now it's time he delivers on his. After what happened with

Gemma, I'm not taking any more chances. I want this squared away as quickly as possible."

I also feel an incessant *need* to see my ring on Cleo's finger, but I'm not going to waste a second trying to figure out why that is.

Elena scoffs. "Deliver this, deliver that. She's not a FedEx package, Rafe. She's a human being. I get we're all about arranged marriages around here, but to force her to marry you on two days' notice? It's ridiculous!"

My anger spikes. "I already said I am not *forcing* her into this. How many times do I have to repeat myself for you to get it?"

Elena grits her teeth.

"Mamma?" Fabi asks. "You haven't said anything. What do you think?"

Mamma wraps her arms around herself. She doesn't like being put on the spot. "I think you should trust your brother's judgment. He is our don, and he knows what he's doing."

Elena groans, her cheeks turning a deep red. "You always take his side. I don't understand why you never question him. Aren't you at all concerned about this?"

Mamma shoots me a pleading look, asking me to save her from answering.

I clench my jaw and turn to my sisters. "I suggest the two of you save your concern for all those starving kids you've been trying to save by working at the UN. They appreciate your bleeding hearts far more than I do."

Hurt flashes in Fabi's eyes, and for a moment, there's a vague tightening inside my chest, an echo of a feeling I used to experience before I taught myself to feel very little.

Elena comes to her rescue, the way she always does. "Charming," she bites out. "I can see that you already can't wait to send us back to Geneva."

I don't refute that statement, even though my sisters are dear to me. They're my flesh and blood. I protect them and I care for them, but we're not close like some siblings are. I've always sensed their resentment, especially Elena's. We all know one day I'll have to summon them back home and make them marry. And when that happens, they'll have to leave the life they've built in Geneva behind.

I straighten out my jacket and round the desk. "I'm leaving. My fiancée is waiting for me." There's no need for me to entertain any more of this female disapproval, especially when everything's already been set in motion.

Tomorrow, Cleo Garzolo will become Cleo Messero, and there abso-fucking-lutely nothing anyone can do about it.

CHAPTER 5

RAFAELE

VOICES from the dining room trickle down the hall, but I ignore them and make my way to the sitting room where Cleo is supposed to be waiting.

I pause in front of the French doors and drag my palm down my tie.

My skin buzzes with something that feels vaguely like excitement.

Strange. I don't get excited very often.

I definitely wasn't excited about getting married to Gemma, but I would have gone through with it. It was in the contract, my name and hers signed on the bottom line. She was perfectly acceptable, a woman raised to be a wife of a high-ranking capo or a don, someone I wouldn't have had to worry or think too much about. She knew what was expected of her. But as the date of our wedding neared, I couldn't stop thinking about her sister, with her insolent mouth and reprehensible manners. A girl completely unsuitable for the role.

Cleo's narrowed green eyes taunted my dreams. I woke up hard, desperate to know what it would feel like to have that mouth wrapped around my cock.

I give my head a shake and grasp the door handle. Tomorrow, she'll become mine, and then I'll be able to move past this bizarre fascination. Cleo will no longer be a beautiful temptation, but a woman who's tied to me for life.

Familiarity breeds boredom, right?

I pull the door open and step inside.

Cleo is perched on a black velvet sofa, her back angled to me. Beside her is Sabina, but I barely notice the house manager.

My fiancée turns and when our gazes clash, a current sparks through me.

Her expression is carefully guarded, her spine is welded straight, and her hands are folded primly in her lap. This is the most demure I've ever seen her.

I slide my hands into the pockets of my trousers. "Good evening."

That's when the demure illusion breaks. Anger flashes inside her gaze, and then she's on her feet, stomping across the room until she's standing right in front of me.

Amusement crackles through me at the fierce expression on her face.

Yes, this is the Cleo I recognize.

"What happened to my sister?" she demands.

Her scent fills my nose. No perfume, just clean skin, and a hint of floral shampoo.

My pulse picks up speed. Her hair is all pulled back in a bun and my hands itch to loosen it. I want to bury my nose in that magnificent copper hair and wrap it tight around my fist.

Why the fuck did Sabina hide it all away?

The old woman rushes to Cleo's side. "Don Messero, I apologize—"

"Leave us."

Cleo holds my gaze as the house manager scurries out of the room.

"I asked you where my sister is," she says in a low, hostile tone. "I need to know if she's okay."

I should have known that would be the first question out of her mouth. After all, she's doing all of this for her sister's sake.

"I don't know. She is none of my concern anymore."

Her nostrils flare like she's unhappy with my response, but it's the truth. I made sure Gemma was allowed to leave without any interference from her father, but that's where my goodwill ended.

"Can't you find out? I'm going crazy with worry. It's been days since she left, and I've gotten no news."

"You'll get news tomorrow at the wedding."

Hope flashes in her green eyes. "Will Gem be there tomorrow?"

"She's not invited." I am not so charitable as to let the woman responsible for our broken engagement attend my wedding.

"My other sister?"

"If Valentina and De Rossi decide to show up, they will be welcomed. Your mother and brother will be there. Your father will walk you down the aisle."

Red spreads over her cheeks, and she takes a small step back. "No. I'll walk on my own."

"It's customary to be given away by a male relative." If I ignore another of my family's traditions, someone is going to suffer an aneurysm.

"Then I'll walk with Vince. I don't want anything to do with my father."

I study her. She said Garzolo never lifted a hand to her, but she could have been lying. If her father hit her like he hit her sister...

A sudden wave of anger makes me clench my fists.

"Are you afraid of him?" I ask.

She scoffs. "He would like that, but no. I just don't want to walk with him."

It's a simple enough request, and I don't care about Garzolo's stance on the matter, so I nod. "I'll talk to your brother."

The dress she's wearing is modest enough, but it stretches tightly over her tits, drawing my attention to them. There's a dusting of freckles over her skin. The fact that I'll get to unwrap her like a present in twenty-four hours and see how far those freckles go sends a jolt to my groin.

39

"How long will this dinner take?" she asks.

Reluctantly, I drag my gaze back up to her face. "As long as necessary."

I can tell she's trying to keep herself from mouthing off to me, which is a first. Given what I know of her, she's being surprisingly cordial. What will happen once she's sure Gemma is safe?

"I hope I don't need to remind you that you've signed up for this willingly."

Her eyes narrow. "Don't worry. Tomorrow, I'll walk down the aisle, say I do, and let you put a ring on my finger. I know if I don't, you and Papà will do everything in your power to hurt Gemma to get back at me."

I have no intention of harming her pregnant sister, but I don't correct her. After all, I want this wedding to go smoothly.

"I'm confident you'll quickly adjust to your life here."

She gives me a blank stare. "Right. Because I'm generally so well-adjusted."

My mouth twitches. I've noticed she can be very funny at times.

"I hope you realize I'm not your papà."

"You might be worse."

"How so?"

"You'll want everything he wanted from me, plus so much more."

She's right about that. I want to bury myself in her and fuck her so hard she'll forget her own name.

I take a step closer. "Like what?"

Her body jerks, but she holds her ground. She tilts her chin up, meeting my gaze, a blaze inside her eyes. "Don't try to intimidate me. It won't work."

I lift my hand to her cheek. "I'm very good at intimidation. I'm also quite good at other things."

She swipes my hand away, the pulse in her neck speeding up. "I'm good at a few things too."

I move even closer. "Do tell."

This time, she shuffles back. "Coming up with creative insults, cooking inedible food, spending absurd amounts of money—"

I take another step toward her.

Her eyes narrow. "Making grown men suffer—"

"Don't stop, you're turning me on."

Her mouth parts in shock. "Jesus, there's something wrong with you."

"Did you really think that pathetic list would scare me off?"

Her back hits the wall. "Can you stop moving into me like a freight train?"

I bracket her with my arms, placing my palms on either side of her head. Her chest rises and falls with quick breaths, and she's giving me a startled look, like she's not sure what to make of me.

Did she think I'd be as cold to her as I was to her sister? Her sister didn't make constant appearances in my R-rated dreams the way she does.

Cleo swallows. "I'm also excellent at ruining parties. In fact, I strongly suggest you leave me behind tonight and go on your own."

"It's not a party. It's a rehearsal dinner." I press my nose against the crook of her neck and inhale.

"What the *fuck* are you doing?" she asks, sounding panicked.

"Don't you ever smell your food before you taste it?"

She starts beating her small fists against my chest. "If you don't take five steps back right now, I'll scream and knee you in the balls so hard you can forget about procreation. I can't believe no one told me you escaped from a lunatic asylum."

I bite my lip.

"I mean it," she says angrily.

I take another second to compose myself and then back away. "Save the screaming for our wedding night."

When I see her grow pale, I feel a tingle of regret. Maybe that wasn't the wisest thing to say for someone with my reputation. Is she scared about tomorrow? She doesn't need to be. I might be a killer and a feared fighter, but I'm not like my father. I don't get off on inflicting pain on those who are weaker than me. I'm about to clarify I meant she'd be screaming in pleasure, but I don't get the words out fast enough.

"I hate you," she spits out. "God, how I hate you."

My gut tightens. Nero was right, she definitely doesn't like me. But hate? That's a strong word and one I don't feel like I've earned.

I clear my throat, disturbed by how much what she just said bothers me. "You'll get over it. After all, you've got a lifetime to warm up to me."

She looks at me like she wants to burn me at the stake.

The antique clock on the wall makes a sound, drawing both of our attention to it. It's seven.

I remove all traces of emotion from my expression and peer down at her. "My family is waiting for us."

Cleo nods and purses her lips, refusing to meet my gaze. I offer her my arm, and after a moment of hesitation, she slips her hand into the crook of my elbow.

We walk out of the room with her anchored to me. Tension crackles around us.

I can't resist studying her. She's got one of the most striking faces I've ever seen, and yet I didn't really notice her the first few times we met. It was after an encounter at her oldest sister's wedding in Ibiza that my mind seemed to latch onto her.

Nero and I picked her up off the side of the road. She was walking—no, stumbling—with a half-empty mickey of vodka at eleven in the morning. Nero was the one who recognized her. I told the driver to stop the car, knowing she must have snuck out without her father's permission. Even that idiot Garzolo wouldn't let one of his daughters do something so reckless.

I can still remember the shock in her eyes when she saw us. She tried to run. Didn't get very far, but she caused quite a scene. Vehicles slowed down to see what was going on, so we grabbed her and tossed her inside the car. When she nearly clawed my eyes out, I slid a zip tie around her wrists. When she wouldn't stop arguing, I slapped a piece of tape over that brazen mouth. She glared at me the entire ride back, and when we returned her to her parents, she threatened *me* and called me a jerk-off. I couldn't remember a woman ever speaking that way to me. I became very, *very* aware of her in that moment.

And that awareness has stayed with me ever since.

Her body stiffens as we walk through the arch leading into the ballroom. She must be nervous, but when I look down at her, her expression is a guarded mask.

Thirty or so Messeros sit at one long table, awaiting our arrival in a room where we've celebrated countless birthdays, anniversaries, and engagements, and where we've grieved more than a few deaths. This was my parents' house before it was my own, and before that, it was my grandparents'. Our history is in these walls.

The conversations fall silent as people notice our entrance. I wonder if Cleo is attentive enough to notice their poorly concealed sneers. The position of the wife of the don is a coveted one, and Cleo is not the woman they wanted for me. No one would risk openly insulting her in my presence after I made it clear I wouldn't entertain it, but still, their true feelings about my future wife are obvious on their faces.

I'll have to fix that. The moment Cleo takes on my last name, she becomes mine, and disrespect against her is disrespect against me.

Nero lifts himself out of his chair and everyone follows his example.

When everyone is on their feet, I glance at Cleo. "I'd like to introduce my betrothed. Cleo Garzolo."

There's a murmur of unenthusiastic greetings.

Pink spreads over Cleo's cheeks, and her expression turns downright hostile.

I should walk her around the table and introduce everyone to her one by one. Instead, I take her straight to our seats. I'm not going to risk someone who's had a glass too many saying something they shouldn't. I didn't clean the blood off my hands only to get them dirty again before the appetizers are served. My relatives will have plenty of time to get to know Cleo once she becomes my wife. They know better than to test my patience by being anything but civil after that.

I lead Cleo to the two chairs at the head of the table and pull one out for her. Her lips are pursed into a tight line as she slides into her seat.

I take the chair beside her and nod at Nero and my mother. Elena and Fabi are sitting to Cleo's left. My sisters' expressions are strained as they study her. Both of them seem unsure if they should say something or not.

Maybe it would have been better to just bring her out tomorrow and scrap the whole rehearsal dinner idea, but it's too late now.

I signal for the staff to start bringing out the food and lean toward Nero. "Anything I should be aware of?"

"Mario and Arturo were running their mouths before you came," he says, tipping his head in the direction of my uncles. "I put a stop to it. The women are gossiping, but there's nothing I can do about that."

Their opinion of Cleo aside, even my harshest critics in the family know this union will make us stronger. If you're not getting stronger, you're getting weaker. By joining our family with the Garzolos, we stand to take control over their existing cocaine operation, which would be a new business line for us.

Racketeering and construction are our bread and butter, but adding cocaine, along with the counterfeits deal Garzolo helped arrange with the Casalesi, will put us on par with the Ferraro family. No matter how much their patriarch hated my old man, he'll quickly see it's better to have us as friends instead of enemies. There's no point in letting the fact that my dead father killed one of his uncles over a decade ago destroy the potential of establishing a mutually beneficial relationship.

Still, looking at the disapproving faces of my aunts and uncles, I wonder if I've underestimated the blowback I'll receive for taking Cleo as my wife. But is that blowback going to be enough to stop me?

I take a deep pull from my wine.

Not a chance in hell.

CHAPTER 6

CLEO

I TWIST the emerald engagement ring on my finger. I wish I could stop fidgeting, but you try sitting still while being scrutinized by thirty-plus fucking people.

Sabina wasn't exaggerating. Rafaele's entire family does hate me. They all think I'm a whore who's unworthy of their precious don.

They can all go to hell. As far as I'm concerned, Rafaele is not worthy of me. At the end of the day, Rafaele must care more about his deal with my father than his family's opinion, since he's still marrying me.

Of course, unlike them, he knows I really am a virgin.

I accidentally blabbed the truth to him while I was drunk. He and Nero kidnapped me off the side of the road and stuffed me into their car when we were at Vale's wedding in Ibiza. I was so angry that I wasn't thinking straight. Until then, I'd managed to convince everyone who mattered that I was disgraced and unsuitable for a wife, which suited me just fine.

It used to make me mad that Rafaele knew the truth, but if he didn't, he may have never let Gemma off the hook.

I bet his family wishes Gemma were still the one marrying their don. After all, my sister didn't spend a lifetime trying to ruin her own reputation in every way possible.

I blow out a breath. I thought I had a chance to break free from all this. How naive of me. Instead, here I am, sitting beside a man who thinks of me as nothing more than a piece of meat.

Goodbye college. Goodbye moving to LA. Goodbye summer internship at a talent agency. See ya never to all my hopes and dreams.

I glance discreetly at Rafaele. I can't believe this is the man I'm about to tie myself to.

For life.

At least he's easy to look at. Okay, not just easy to look at. Rafaele is fucking *hot*. Far better looking than the last guy my father tried to set me up with—Ludovico. He was over forty, balding, and always had bad breath.

Rafaele is twenty-seven. That's still eight years on me, but it's the kind of age gap that nobody even blinks at in the mafia. His dark hair is shiny and smooth, longer at the top and shorter on the sides, and he's got a clean shave. Young made men often grow out their beards to make themselves look older, but not him.

There's no mistaking that he's the don of this family, even though he's far from being the oldest person in the room.

He's got an air about him that practically screams, "Do. Not. Fuck. With. Me." Maybe it's because of his serious expression, or the kind of perfect posture I thought wasn't a thing in the age of smartphones, or those damn eyes of his.

Gemma called him the ice prince because of his cold blue gaze, but I don't know if that's accurate. I've seen him rage.

I'm not sure what was more traumatizing, Ludovico trying to grind his crotch against me, or having his blood splattered on my shoes when Rafaele just casually *murdered* him.

The memory sends ice down my veins. Rafaele's brutality is his brand. His civilized exterior is a mask he puts on to make himself palatable in public, but he can remove it just as easily. And besides an affinity for casual murder, I'm not totally sure what else is hiding beneath.

"I'm very good at intimidation. I'm also quite good at other things."

What was *that*?

I thought he'd lecture me on how to behave at this dinner. What I didn't expect was to be blasted with all that sexual energy and innuendo. I mean, he backed me against a wall with that powerful body and *sniffed* me for fuck's sake.

The back of my neck heats. I hadn't anticipated him being interested in me in *that* way. This is a political marriage, nothing more.

He never even kissed Gemma, and they were engaged for months. I assumed that like some men in the mafia, his wife would be there to pop out babies, but beyond that, he'd entertain himself with whores. That sort of arrangement is common.

Now, I'm not so sure.

Even now, he's studying me like I'm something fascinating.

I swallow.

I haven't thought much about what he'll expect of me beyond the obvious on our wedding night, and now I'm getting the sense he definitely has certain expectations.

Anxiety fans through me. My life has done a one-eighty in the span of a few days, and I'm still coming to terms with all of this.

When the servers come out with the appetizers, the blond woman sitting to my left leans closer. "I'm Elena Messero." She extends her hand.

I eye it with suspicion, half-expecting her to jerk it back and say "Gotcha."

But she doesn't, so eventually, I take it. "I'm Cleo."

Her grip is firm, and her smile is friendly. She gestures at the woman beside her. "This is Fabiana, although everyone calls her Fabi."

The other woman also offers me her hand. "We're Rafe's sisters."

Sisters? I didn't know he had sisters. I never saw them at any of the Messero family events Gem and I went to.

"I didn't realize Rafaele had siblings."

I don't know much about him at all. Rafaele is stingy with words. His annoying consigliere talks about ten times more than him.

"We live in Switzerland," Fabi says. She twists her bracelet around her wrist like she's nervous. Maybe she's not supposed to be talking to me?

Rafaele doesn't seem to care, but some of the other people at the table are watching us with disapproving expressions.

My irritation bubbles to the surface. Fuck them. If they don't want me talking to Rafaele's sisters, that's exactly what I'll keep doing.

"My brother, Vince, also lives in Switzerland."

Fabi arches a surprised brow. "Vince Garzolo? I don't think we've met. Is he in Geneva or Zurich?"

"I think Zurich, but he may move around a bit. I'm not sure." My brother's life abroad is a mystery. I get the sense Vince likes to keep it that way.

"We're in Geneva." Elena takes a sip of her wine.

"How long have you been there?"

"Our mother sent us to boarding school there at eleven. We went to college afterward for undergrad and masters. Now, we both work at the UN."

My eyes widen. "The UN?"

Beside her, Fabi laughs softly. "I know. Believe me, the irony isn't lost on us. We keep a low profile, and no one there has any idea who our family is."

I wonder how they manage to do that. They must use fake names. "So, you're there on your own?"

"We have bodyguards with us, but they're good at staying hidden. And at work, we're as safe as it gets."

I nod. I can't imagine the UN offices would slack on security procedures.

"You look surprised," Elena notes.

"I am. I didn't think you'd be allowed to do something like that in your family. Based on what I've heard about Messeros, your men sound like a bunch of Neanderthals." I glance at Rafaele, who's still looking like a beautiful Roman statue, but I know he's listening to every word.

His sisters stifle their laughs. Am I imagining it, or did Rafaele's lips just twitch?

"Our father wanted us back after our graduation from uni, but then he got sick with cancer, and all of his plans for us went on hold," Elena says, her voice dropping lower. "And when Rafe took over, he told us we could stay for a few more years if we wanted to."

"So we'll stay in Geneva until time comes for us to marry," Fabi says, a note of resignation in her voice. She doesn't sound too excited about the prospect.

Trust me, I know exactly how you feel.

The servers come out with the main courses and signal an end to our conversation. A plate of steak appears before me.

I frown at it. I'm a vegetarian, but I suppose the maid who brought food to my room over the last few days didn't care enough to notice that I've avoided eating any of the meat. I pick at the mashed potatoes while everyone else digs in.

Rafaele's sisters seem nice. It's hard not to be jealous of the freedom they get. I would have done anything to be allowed to leave New York, but there's no hope of that now.

I scan the faces of other people sitting nearby. There's Rafaele's mom. I've spoken briefly to her before, but now she seems to be avoiding my gaze. She's a frail woman—thin and pale. Beside her are two women who bear a resemblance to her. Are they her sisters? One of them meets my gaze and sneers. I sit up straighter.

Fuck you too, lady.

"Do you not like the food?"

I nearly drop my fork, startled by Rafaele's question. I glance in his direction. His own plate is nearly clean.

"I don't eat meat."

He frowns. "Why didn't you say something earlier?"

"Didn't think you'd care," I mutter.

"Do you think I want to starve you?"

"Maybe you want me famished as a precaution so that I won't have the energy to run away tomorrow."

He arches a brow. "I already know you're not going to run away. You care too much about your sister to do that." He leans closer, brushing the tips of his fingers over my wrist and making my skin tingle. "But if you try, I'll catch you," he says, his eyes locked on mine.

I swallow. That shade of blue really is something. It feels like he can see right through me.

Rafaele pulls back and waves down one of the staff.

"Get her a vegetarian meal," he says to the young server before moving his attention back to me. "Tonight, I want you to write down a list of all of your food preferences and give it to Sabina."

"Fine." There's a high likelihood Sabina will toss that list right into the trash, but whatever.

"This is your new home. I want you to be comfortable."

I bite down on my lip. Comfortable? I'll never be comfortable here. Why is he trying to act nice to me? This place is my new prison. It doesn't matter how pretty it is.

A cage is still a cage, and he will always be my jailer.

CHAPTER 7

CLEO

My new food arrives quickly. It's a vegetable curry over jasmine rice, and it's so fucking good that I inhale it in minutes. I immediately feel better.

Now, if only I could get some wine.

There's a bottle sitting on the table right in front of me, but the servers pointedly ignored my glass. If I had to guess, I'd say Rafaele told them to keep the booze away from me.

So what if I like to indulge on occasion? I'd like to see him living with Pietra and Stefano Garzolo for nineteen years without developing a vice.

I huff out an annoyed breath and glance around the table. Two ancient nonnas are giving me the evil eye from behind their plates of steak. If I was sitting any closer, they'd probably try to spit on me.

Does Rafaele really expect me to sit through the rest of this dinner sober? He's drinking, so what gives? The air in this palatial ballroom is suffocating enough to clog my throat. It's like I'm being tried for a crime I didn't commit, and his relatives are my jury.

Fuck it.

I reach for the bottle, but Rafaele beats me to it, snatching it from under my fingertips.

Frustration prickles over my skin. "Oh, come on—"

He fills my glass and tops off his own.

"Drink," he commands.

My brows arch up. What's this? Has he decided to take pity on me? Or maybe he can tell I need something to take the edge off or I'll explode.

I don't care about the opinions of other people. Never have. But normally, I wouldn't just sit here quietly, letting their judgmental gazes skewer through me. I'd cause a scene, embarrass my parents, find a way to be sent home.

Only now *this* is my home.

I drink the entire glass in three gulps and I swear I feel a light buzz right away. Some tension leaves my neck.

Rafaele pushes his chair back and stands. "Come with me."

My gaze slides up his huge body. He must be at least six-two. "Where?"

He opens his hand, like he wants me to take it, and doesn't answer. His entire family is watching us, their conversations quieting. I sigh and slide my hand into his. At this point, I'd rather be anywhere but here.

His hand, warm and rough, swallows up my own as he leads me out of the ballroom.

Touching him is not entirely unpleasant, which gives me pause. Whenever Ludovico got too close to me, I got the strong urge to hurl, something I communicated to him quite often. It kept him away from me for a while.

We turn down a wide hallway and walk toward the door at the end of it. Behind it, a narrow staircase leads downstairs. Rafaele flicks on a light and gestures for me to go first.

I swallow. This is starting to feel ominous. "Want to tell me where we're going?"

"You'll see."

I narrow my eyes. "Any reasonable person would want to know why you're taking them to a creepy dark basement."

"They would, but we both know you're not a member of that group," he drawls.

Wow. "So you expect me to follow you around like some lapdog?"

He crosses his big arms over his chest. "I don't like dogs."

I scoff. "You don't like dogs? Well, that explains a lot. Is it because you're deathly allergic?"

His eyes spark. "Wouldn't you just love that."

"If you have any serious allergies, you should probably make me a list. I wouldn't want to accidentally kill you, would I? That would be very unwifely of me."

His cheek ticks. "You can either take the stairs on your own, or I can throw you over my shoulder and bring you down there myself. Your choice."

"Jesus, I got it." I brush past him. I should probably keep my mouth shut, but I'm brimming with nervous energy.

Getting down is a challenge due to the narrow skirt of my dress. The air gets colder and colder with each step I take.

The chill fills me with foreboding. Seriously, what the fuck is down here? I mean, he wouldn't kill me the night before our wedding, right?

I finally reach the bottom landing and take a few steps into the darkness.

Rafaele flicks on another light, illuminating the space.

It's a cigar room.

Four leather armchairs are arranged in a circle with a small coffee table in the center. Behind them is a large glass case filled with cigars.

Rafaele opens the case, touches something, and then closes it. A second later, the entire wall starts moving.

My eyes widen. "Holy shit."

A passage opens. I'm so stunned that I follow Rafaele down it without another peep. The passage isn't very long and we stop in front of an armored door with a biometric lock.

Now, I'm genuinely curious. What is this place? A panic room? We have one back at my parents' place, but it's not nearly as high tech. And why would he take me here?

Rafaele walks up to the lock and allows the sensor to scan his eye. I can hear the lock disengage. The door pops open, and Rafaele holds it, gesturing for me to go in. I take a tentative step inside.

Oh. *Oh.*

It's a vault *brimming* with jewelry. Three full wall cabinets, four shelves each. On each shelf, jewels glitter. Sapphires, rubies, emeralds, and diamonds—*so* many diamonds.

Some are loose, but most are set into diadems, necklaces, bracelets, earrings, brooches, and rings. Stunning. One shelf even has a row of extravagant watches bobbing on watch winders. I have to scrape my jaw off the floor.

Rafaele stops by my side. "My family's hundred-year-old collection."

I'm speechless. Rafaele could have told me this was the jewelry collection of some dead king and I would have believed him. It must be worth hundreds of millions. I knew the Messeros were richer than my family, but I never thought they were *this* rich.

I walk around the vault, taking it all in, and my shock only deepens. I might hate Rafaele, but this...

This, I like a lot.

I'm a sucker for pretty, expensive things. Jewelry has always been my weakness. I had my own small collection back home, but it's a joke compared to this.

"Pick something to wear for the wedding tomorrow."

I glance at Rafaele. He's leaning against the wall, watching me with an intent gaze. I probably look shell-shocked. My heart pitter-patters in my chest.

"I can pick whatever I like?" My voice comes out as a breathless whisper.

"Yes."

Is this a test? This must be a test. But what is he testing exactly? Am I supposed to act all modest?

I nibble on my lip, trying to read him, but he's not giving anything away with that indifferent expression.

Bah. Screw it.

I don't know what he's expecting, but modesty isn't in my DNA. I head straight toward the shelf with the biggest, most over-the-top pieces.

What to choose, what to choose... Everything is gorgeous. I eye a pretty brooch in the shape of a butterfly. It's made with dozens of diamonds and some ruby accents on the wings. It would look nice in my hair.

Rafaele walks up to the case and points at the showstopper diamond necklace in the center of the shelf. "That was my grandmother's. Magdalena Caruso. She wore it to her wedding."

Magdalena Caruso... Is that the Signora Caruso that Sabina is obsessed with? The one she said was pure class? What will that miserable hag think if she sees those diamonds on my neck? The neck of a trashy whore?

Oh, she'll hate it. She'll hate it so much.

"It's perfect," I breathe.

I'm half expecting Rafaele to refuse me, to say I'm not worthy of a piece *this* grand, but he simply nods, opens the case, and carefully lifts the necklace.

He turns to me, an expectant look on his face.

"What?"

"Turn around so I can put it on you. Don't you want to see how it looks?"

"Oh. Right."

I give him my back, and a moment later, the cold gems land on my upper chest. Rafaele's fingertips brush against my nape as he secures the latch.

"There," he murmurs. Big hands wrap around my shoulders, spilling heat over my skin.

He steers me to stand in front of a mirror before letting his hands drop away, and some illogical part of me misses the warmth.

Relax. It's just because it's cold as fuck down here.

I look at my reflection and a gasp falls out of my mouth. The necklace is stunning and...outrageous. Forget Signora Caruso—this is a piece that could be worn by actual royalty. It's definitely going to make a statement tomorrow.

The fact that Rafaele is on board with this... I meet his gaze in the mirror. Maybe it's a statement he needs to make to his family too. It's clear they're pissed about this marriage, about *me* being brought into the Messero fold. Is this a way for him to say "fuck you" to all of them for questioning his judgment?

Probably. I guess I'm helping his cause but given the treatment I've received tonight from his relatives, I'm happy to do it.

I walk back to where the necklace was and point at the matching earrings. "Those too."

He takes them out and hands them to me.

"And the bracelets," I say as I put the earrings into my ears. When I'm done, Rafaele slides the bangles onto my wrists, three on each.

This is a lot, but that butterfly brooch...so dang pretty. It really would look nice pinned in my hair. Would I be pushing it if I asked for that one too?

I shoot Rafaele a cautious glance. "And this one."

Mild amusement passes over his features. "Why not just ask for the whole shelf?"

I scoff. "Are you crazy? I'm going for subtle."

His lips twitch. He reaches inside the glass case and gets the brooch. "Where is this one going to go?"

"My hair. I'll put it there tomorrow." I slide the brooch into the small matching purse that came with the dress.

His gaze brushes over the bun on my head, and his lips tighten like he's displeased. "Wear it down."

"Sure, whatever," I mutter as I move back to the mirror. I want to see how I look now that I've got everything on.

Oh my God. A laugh bubbles out of me. I'm practically a disco ball with how much light I'm reflecting and the effect is only going to be amplified with all the natural light in the church. "It's perfect."

Rafaele comes up behind me, stopping close enough for me to feel his presence against my back. My skin tingles with awareness that narrows to a point when he raises his hand and lightly presses a knuckle to my nape. My breath hitches. He drags his knuckle down the length of my spine and I have to consciously suppress a shiver. I swallow, forgetting about the jewels.

Forgetting about everything as I register how he's looking at me.

There's a dark possessiveness in his gaze that chills me all the way through to the bone.

His eyes rise to meet mine in the mirror.

"I agree," he says in a low voice. "Perfect."

And that's when the spell lifts, and I remember exactly what I am to him. A thing to own, just like these jewels. A butterfly he's got locked in a glass cage.

And tomorrow, he'll break my wings.

CHAPTER 8

CLEO

THE NEXT DAY, I arrive at the church in my sister's wedding dress.

Gemma has impeccable taste, so the ivory gown is perfection. It's strapless with a built-in corset and an A-line skirt with a train. No embroidery, no complicated details. Just minimalist and classic and a perfect complement to the over-the-top diamonds that hang around my neck and sparkle on my wrists and ears.

When I climb out of the limo with the help of the bodyguards, my brother is smoking a cigarette as he waits for me at the bottom of the church steps.

I frown. I don't remember Vince being a smoker. The stress of having his three sisters pissed at him must be getting to him.

I haven't forgiven him for the part he played in brokering this entire deal with Rafaele. Because Vince didn't want to become Papà's successor, they had the bright idea of offering the position to Rafaele. Rafaele wouldn't have agreed to get Papà out of jail for anything less than that. But a successor can't be just some outsider, which is why Rafaele has to marry into our family.

I stomp toward Vince, grateful that I'm wearing flats beneath the dress instead of heels. The skirt was tailored for Gemma, so it would be too short on me if I added a few inches of height.

Vince watches me approach and takes another puff of his cig.

Nervous?

I stop in front of him and knock the cigarette out of his hand. It falls to the ground, the red cherry flashing against the concrete before it turns to ash.

"I'm not doing this so that you can die from lung cancer."

His lips twitch, even as something pained flashes in his eyes. "Never change, Cleo."

Vince is on my shit list at the moment, but he's not all bad like Papà. Until this whole thing with Rafaele, I saw my brother as a kindred spirit. He hated living at home, and he found a way out, something I admire about him.

Of course, it was far easier for him to convince Papà to let him work for the family from abroad because he's a man. That opportunity would have never been offered to me.

He scans me. "Are you all right?"

"What do you think? Feels like I'm walking to my funeral."

He frowns. "I wish it didn't have to come to this."

"Whatever. Can you tell me if Gem made it to Ras? I've been asking everybody, and no one's been able to give me an answer."

"She did."

I close my eyes and let out a relieved breath. *Thank fuck.* "How?"

"Ras was in New York when the engagement was called off. She rang Vale and managed to find him quickly. She wanted to be here but..." He glances inside the church. "You know how it is."

Don't I ever. Will Rafaele let me see my sister again? I don't imagine it will be anytime soon.

I drag my palm over the satin fabric of Gemma's dress. The important thing is that she's safe and her baby is safe. We'll figure out the rest later.

The music inside the cathedral changes.

"I think that's our cue," Vince says.

I blink at him, my thoughts still on Gemma. Then it dawns on me what he means. It's time for us to walk down the aisle. Suddenly, my lungs seize. This is it. My face plummets, and Vince pales.

"I know there's no excuse for what I've done," he says, his voice harsh. "I was... Fuck, I don't know what I was thinking. There are things you don't know about my life in Switzerland. I'll explain it all to you one day if you'll let me."

The remorse in his eyes seems genuine, but I'm not like Gemma. I don't forgive easily. Still, he's my brother, and even though he's an ass, I love him.

"Okay," I croak. "We'll talk later. Help me with the damn veil."

The music gets louder, as if imploring us to move or else. A man appears behind us—one of Rafaele's—and nods toward the entrance of the church. "Go."

"Jesus, we're going," I snap.

Veil in place, I take Vince's arm. We climb the dozen or so steps, moving slowly because of my dress. Someone lifts the train behind me, probably the same guy who rushed us along, but I don't even bother looking to check.

My pulse is racing. I can't believe I'm about to get married.

The massive doors to the cathedral are propped open. Inside are rows and rows of people I've never met with the occasional flash of a familiar face. My family is somewhere here, but I don't seek them out.

The sheer volume of witnesses to my downfall is staggering. I keep my gaze focused on the ground and count my breaths.

The world is a blur, and I'm a tiny speck being propelled through it. Sweat collects at the small of my back, seeping into the fabric of Gemma's wedding dress. My mouth is bone dry. I wish I'd asked for some water on the ride over instead of spending it silently pondering my bleak future as a married woman.

I clutch Vince's arm tighter, and he shoots me a worried look. He can't see my expression beneath the veil. If he could, he'd look far more worried.

My horror builds with every step I take. This is what I've always feared. The complete surrender of my autonomy to a stranger.

I'm living through my own personal nightmare, and there's a demon waiting for me at the end of the aisle, ready to tear the thing I've always held most dear to me—my freedom—to shreds.

I might throw up.

Maybe it doesn't have to be forever. I have to hold out hope that somehow I'll convince Rafaele to eventually let me out of my cage. But how long will that take? Weeks? Months? Years? Years of living with the enemy.

Rafaele may have helped Gemma, but he's still *my* enemy. He's looking forward to owning me. I could see it in his eyes last night when he looked at me like I was another one of his possessions.

What will he do to me? Whatever he wants, I suppose. That's the point, isn't it? Starting with our wedding night. Whatever I don't give to him willingly, he'll take by force.

My breaths are coming quickly now. A pressure appears on my forearm. I look down to see it's Vince's hand.

"Cleo, you're shaking," he says in a low voice.

Yes, I'm about to have a panic attack, I want to say to him, but I can't speak.

Dark spots appear in my eyes.

And that's when I notice the flowers. Bouquets of blue lilies at the end of every aisle.

Gem's favorites.

I was at the meeting with the wedding planner when she picked out that exact arrangement.

Something about the flowers cuts through the panic, and I manage to suck in a single deep breath. Then another.

Gem isn't here, but there are glimpses of her everywhere in this cathedral. She planned this wedding. She chose the flowers, and the music, and this dress, and this veil, and all the other little details that used to be so insignificant to me.

Now, I latch onto them. I claw my way out of my panic and remember that I'm doing this for my sister.

She'd want me to walk down this aisle with my head held high. She wouldn't want me to fall apart in front of all of these fucking Messeros. I won't give them the satisfaction of seeing my misery.

The tightness in my throat loosens. "I'm good," I say to Vince.

When he and I are mere steps away from the altar, I come to a halt.

Everyone in the church quiets, and I can practically sense them salivating. They're waiting for a sign of weakness, the fucking vultures. But they won't get one.

I straighten my spine and pull back my shoulders. I let go of my brother's arm, signaling I've got it from here. He gives my arm a squeeze and moves aside.

I take the last few steps toward the altar on my own.

When I'm standing before him, Rafaele reaches over and lifts my veil.

It's funny how you can hate someone and still find them attractive. Rafaele's high cheekbones and strong jaw feel like an affront. I don't want to like a single thing about this horrible man, but I can't help appreciating the sharp angles of his face, his broad shoulders, and the way his muscular body fills out that bespoke tux.

His jaw clenches. He sweeps his gaze over me, and when he returns to my face, there's heat in his eyes that burns across my skin.

I look away, disturbed by the intensity. For the first time, I allow myself to face the audience. I find my oldest sister, Vale, standing in the front row beside her husband Damiano De Rossi.

She gives me a broken smile, her eyes swimming with tears. Those aren't tears of happiness. My heart squeezes.

In the fourth row, I spot Sabina in a gray dress and drab black hat. I guess I'm not the only one who thinks of this wedding as more of a funeral.

A flicker of satisfaction appears in the pit of my belly at the outraged expression on her face. She must have registered that I'm wearing her old mistress's diamonds. I lift my hand and pretend to brush a strand of hair behind my ear, making sure she also sees the bangles.

Her eyes narrow, and she slowly shakes her head as if in warning.

Does she really think she can scare me?

She's wrong.

After all, there's a far bigger monster in this church, and I'm about to marry him.

CHAPTER 9

RAFAELE

THE PRIEST IS SAYING SOMETHING, but I can't hear a word. My pulse is loud inside my ears, a hard and steady drum, and a vein in Cleo's neck ticks to the same damn beat.

An image of my teeth marks framing that vein flashes in front of my eyes.

This ceremony will take a half hour. I asked the priest as soon as her silhouette appeared at the end of the aisle. I wanted to know how long I'd have to wait to taste that luscious fucking mouth.

His answer irritated me.

Then I became irritated at my irritation.

I'm a patient man. I'm good at waiting. At biding my time.

A half hour is nothing. And yet it feels too long.

Too. *Fucking.* Long. Especially when my bride looks like *this*.

Cleo's copper curls are pulled back from her face with two small braids. The rest of it cascades down her back. My grandmother's jewels glitter around her neck and dangle from her ears.

She thinks she chose those diamonds, but really, they chose her. If she didn't have the body or the character to wear them, they would have looked ridiculous on her. It takes a certain kind of woman to pull off wearing fifty fucking carats.

She does it effortlessly, like she was born to be dripping in diamonds and gold. My Aunt Maria tried to give me an earful about letting Cleo wear the prized family jewels, but I told her that if anyone is worthy of wearing them, it's my future wife.

Her skin glows in the light streaming through the stained glass of the church. And her lips have never looked more inviting.

The things I want to do to this woman. I can't fucking wait to exhaust that tight body, to push her to her limits, to make her come until she's no more than a whimpering puddle on my bed.

A jolt runs through me. Fuck, if I let myself go down that train of thought, I'll get a boner in front of the entire church. I'm already halfway there just from looking at her.

The priest drones on and on. How much longer? Impatience pulses at my temples.

I've seen how she gets under your skin.

If only Nero knew the direction of my thoughts, he'd laugh at me. Fuck, this is ridiculous. I need to get a grip. I take a slow, deep breath.

Cleo chooses that moment to peer at me from under her lashes and bite on the corner of her lip. I tug at my collar, suddenly too hot. My watch says it's only been five minutes.

That's when I decide, *fuck it*. "Skip to the end," I order the priest.

The man's clearly taken aback, but he knows better than to argue. "To the vows?"

"To whatever the fuck is the important part."

Cleo pales. She glares at me, an undercurrent of something dangerous inside her gaze.

I stare right back. Not like I have a choice—I'm unable to take my eyes off her. She must want to get this over with as much as I do, even if it's not for the same reason.

Last night, her relief had been palpable when I took her out of that dining room. And when I saw her face light up in the jewelry vault, I knew I'd done the right thing bringing her there. She doesn't hate me. Last night, she was just angry and still adjusting to the situation. But she'll adjust.

Garzolo women are strong. It can't be easy for Cleo to stand here in front of everyone and go through the motions of a wedding her sister planned, but she looks perfectly composed.

The priest clears his throat again. "Do you, Rafaele Messero, take Cleo Garzolo as your lawfully wedded wife?"

"I do."

He asks the same of Cleo.

"I do," she says sourly.

Nero brings over the rings. I pick up the smaller one and take Cleo's hand. There's a slight tremble in her fingers, the only hint that maybe she's not as composed as she seems.

I slip the ring on and let her do the same to me.

"On behalf of God and his church, I now pronounce you husband and wife. You may kiss the bride."

Finally.

I tug her against my chest and slam my lips down on hers.

Cleo gasps against my mouth.

Her body is so warm, almost burning, and the thought of sinking inside her heat tonight pulls an illicit groan out of my chest. She's rigid at first, refusing to grant me entrance to her mouth, but when I pull her closer, she finally relents.

I slide my tongue between her lips and let out a low moan at her taste. Exquisite. My hands roam over her waist and the flare of her hips, and fuck, I'm having a hard time letting her go.

Especially when her body finally starts to melt against me, and her tongue starts rubbing against my own. Her fingers curl around my lapels, and she tugs me closer.

And then she whimpers.

It's a small sound that only I can hear, but it awakens something so intense inside me, that I let her go suddenly.

When we break apart, we're both panting. Cleo gapes at me, her eyes wide and nearly all black. Her lips are bright pink.

She presses her hand to her chest and tears her gaze away from me toward the cheering crowd. I do the same, only now becoming aware of the noise. My heart is racing.

Cleo's sister glares at me from where she's standing by De Rossi. I give him a small nod, almost daring the Don of the Casalesi not to return it. He does. He knows he's my guest here, and that I could crush him easily on my turf.

They didn't want this for Cleo, but there's nothing they can do about it now.

A sense of triumph sweeps through me.

She's finally mine.

We spend an excruciating hour taking pictures, but at least I have Cleo in my arms for most of it.

The photographer instructs us to kiss, but she won't give me what I want. Her lips remain tightly sealed.

That moment at the altar proved to me what I've suspected all along. There's chemistry between us, and it's the kind I've never experienced before. I'm going to clear my entire fucking calendar this week, because I plan on exploring it in full.

I'll get her out of my system, and then this madness will end.

After all, I've never allowed myself to get distracted by a woman for more than a brief spell.

I rush the photographer along the same way I did with the priest. My right hand is glued to Cleo's hip. She shoots me looks filled with a simmering, defiant heat, and she doesn't smile at the camera even when the photographer pleads with her.

"I'm self-conscious about my teeth," she barks at him.

Little liar. She has perfect teeth. She has perfect *everything*.

When we're finally inside the limo, I pull her toward me, intent on getting my fill of that mouth, but she hisses at my touch and jerks away. "My God, can you stop pawing at me?"

"Why would I? You're my wife." I reach for her.

"Don't remind me," she snaps, slapping my hand away. "Do you think just because we're married you can manhandle me whenever you want?"

"Yes."

She glares at me. "You're horrible."

She's in denial. She enjoyed that kiss as much as I did.

"You didn't seem to think so when I kissed you at the altar."

Her cheeks turn bright red. "I was pretending."

"You're not that good an actress. Few people can make their pupils dilate on command."

She scoffs. "You're delusional if you think I enjoyed even a second of that kiss."

What happened at the altar wasn't an act. She's lying.

"Why don't we try it again and see?" I challenge.

She purses her lips. "I don't think so."

"Is that why you refused to give me a real kiss in front of the photographer? Because you were worried he'd capture how much you enjoyed it?"

"I don't enjoy anything about you."

I reach out and grab her chin, forcing her to look at me. "Prove it then."

She wrenches her face away from my grip and glares.

I arch a brow. "Or are you scared?"

She scoffs. "Of you? Hardly."

"Then what's stopping you?" I challenge her. If she wants to play games with me, we can play, but I'll win.

Her eyes flicker with a mix of defiance and something else. Something I can't quite place. "Fine," she says. "I'll prove it."

Before I can even register what's happening, she crashes her lips against mine in a bruising kiss. My hands instinctively grip her waist, pulling her closer to me, deepening it.

She doesn't wait a second before she slides her tongue into my mouth. Fuck, she tastes incredible. My hand moves lower, cupping her ass through the layers of her wedding dress. I can't remember the last time I've been this eager to cop a feel. When she tugs on my bottom lip with her teeth, I groan into her mouth. I'm on fire. I need to be inside of her.

The limo swerves, and we break apart, gasping for air. She rips her body away from me, slides to the other end of the seat, and faces the window.

"Let me see your eyes," I demand, my voice breathless.

She can't deny it now. Her jaw clenches. When she doesn't turn, I slide over to her and wrap my palm around her neck. Her pulse flutters beneath my touch.

"Will you admit you lied?"

She swallows, her elegant throat bobbing against my hand.

I stroke it with my thumb. "We shouldn't start our marriage with a lie."

Finally, she turns to me, her lips inches away from mine.

Her pupils are blown wide, but it's not just arousal swimming inside of them. She's furious. I frown.

"I will never like your kisses or your touch," she whispers harshly. "You're my jailer. Do you think I'll ever forget that?"

The car pulls to a stop, and she's out of it before I can tell her to wait.

I rake my fingers through my hair and watch her hurry toward the hotel, the sunlight winking against the butterfly brooch pinning her braids.

Stubborn girl. She's too proud to admit the truth out loud, but it doesn't matter.

She's mine.

And she'll surrender to me tonight.

CHAPTER 10

CLEO

THE RECEPTION TAKES place in a mansion on the Hudson River that was converted into a luxury hotel.

From the moment Rafaele and I sat down at the sweetheart table, the walls of the lavish ballroom have been pressing down on me.

I'm itching to sneak out and talk to Vale, but all these people I don't know won't stop giving toasts to Rafaele. My name is mentioned a few times too, but I don't pay attention to their fake flattery.

How can I when I've just discovered my husband kisses me like he wants to devour me?

My heart beats quickly inside my chest. It beat even quicker when Rafaele's tongue was in my mouth and his hands were on me, possessive and demanding.

He's supposed to be the ice prince, but there was nothing cold about his touch. A shameful heat pulses between my legs at the memory.

What is wrong with me?

Rafaele is the enemy. He is single-handedly ruining my life. I'm supposed to be repulsed by him. But my mind and my body don't seem to be on the same page at the moment. Kissing him again in the limo was a mistake. I shouldn't have let him provoke me like that.

What have I gotten myself into?

I grab my glass of wine and drain half of it in one gulp.

An old, creepy-looking man approaches our table and offers his congratulations. "It's a fine day to get married, Don Messero. And look at your beautiful bride." He gives me a lecherous look. "She looks ripe for the taking."

I nearly choke on my wine. *Excuse me?*

He stares at my breasts. "I still remember how Clarissa bled on our wedding night. She was too embarrassed to look at the sheets the next day."

His words are like a bucket of cold water. Whatever effect kissing Rafaele had on me disappears in a blink.

Forget it. These people are disgusting, and so is Rafaele for following this sick tradition. I can't ever let myself forget that.

"Maybe I can share a few tips—"

"That's enough, Uncle Julius," Rafaele interrupts, his voice cold. "I don't need any tips, and if I were you, I'd reconsider the direction of your gaze."

The creepy uncle's eyes jump to Rafaele. "Don Messero, I wasn't—I mean, I meant no disrespect."

"Your daughter is calling you over. You better head back to your table."

No one was calling him over, but Rafaele must have noticed me reaching for my steak knife.

The old man hobbles away, and Rafaele puts his hand on my thigh. "Ignore him. He's practically senile."

I shove his hand off me. "Something tells me he wasn't any less disgusting when he was all there."

Rafaele turns to me, but I pointedly look away. I don't know how I'll make it through the evening. I'm not afraid of having sex. In fact, I think I'd enjoy it very much under the right circumstances. But what's supposed to happen tonight is sick.

I hate the idea that I *owe* my virginity to Rafaele. That I have to *let* him take it. And that I have to *be okay* with displaying the evidence of the act to his entire family.

Does Rafaele think he can make me forget all that just because he knows how to kiss? I said I'd marry him, and I did. But I never said I'd just accept my new life with no questions asked and no resistance.

If he wants to make me into his obedient wife, he better be ready for me to fight him at every turn. Let's see who throws in the towel first.

Vale gets out of her seat and tips her head in the direction of the bathroom. I stand up to go meet her, but before I can even take a step, Rafaele grabs my forearm.

I glare at him. "What?"

"Where are you going?"

"I need to use the restroom."

His gaze jumps between Vale and me.

If he tries to stop me from talking to my sister, I swear I'm going to lose it. I'm already on edge. Maybe he sees that in my eyes, because after a moment he lets me go.

"Don't take too long."

I march out of the room. Vale is waiting for me just outside the bathroom. I rush over to her and give her a tight hug. "How's Gem? Is she feeling okay?"

My sister presses a kiss to my cheek before she pulls away and looks me over. "She's fine. We took her to a doctor as soon as she and Ras got to Italy, just to make sure everything is alright."

"Ras and her are good? He forgave her for leaving him in Greece?"

Vale smiles. "Of course, he did. He's completely smitten with her. Can't stop talking about how excited he is to be a father."

A grin pulls at my lips. It's the best thing I've heard all day. "Thank God. Fuck, Vale. I've been so worried about her since we said goodbye. No one would tell me anything. It wasn't until I met Vince to walk me down the aisle that I heard Gem got away all right."

"God, it must have been awful being kept in the dark." Vale squeezes my hand. "But you don't need to worry anymore. Gem is safe with us, thanks to you."

We step inside the bathroom, and I lock the door behind us.

Vale's expression falls. "Cleo, I wish there was something we could have done to prevent this from happening."

"There wasn't," I say. "What's done is done. I'll take care of myself, but you have to promise you'll take care of Gemma."

"Of course we will. She's got me, as well as Ras. But I'm worried about you. You have no one here to support you."

"It's fine. Maybe I'll convince Rafaele to let the two of you visit."

"Are you going to be okay living with him?" She brushes her palms down my arms, her eyes filling with tears. "You've always craved independence and now..."

And now I'm a prisoner. Expected to serve at the will of my tyrannical husband.

I hide my devastation from Vale because there's no point in upsetting her. What's done is done, and most importantly, Gemma and her baby are safe.

I force a casual shrug. "You know how I am. Rafaele doesn't know what he's gotten himself into by marrying me. I'll drive him up the wall. I bet he'll be sick of me soon."

"Be careful with him. Please. He's clever and dangerous. Far more than Papà. Don't push his buttons."

Oh, I'm planning on giving his buttons a serious workout, but I don't want to worry Vale, so I say, "I'll be careful."

She gives me a wary look that says she doesn't quite believe me. "If you need anything, just call me. Gemma and I are only a phone call away."

We hug again before she goes to use the toilet, leaving me alone with my thoughts.

I stare at myself in the mirror. A bride is supposed to feel beautiful on her wedding day. My hair is shiny and bright. My wedding dress is flattering. My jewelry is impeccable.

But I don't feel beautiful.

I feel trapped.

~

The rest of the reception is a blur.

I pick at my food until it's time for the first dance. Rafaele stands and helps me to my feet, his touch warm and steady. I move through it all in a trance. It doesn't feel real. I'm someone's wife.

Someone's *property*.

More couples appear around us. There's a flash of Vale and Damiano before they disappear behind other bodies.

My new owner stares down at me as he leads me across the dance floor.

I spend an entire song pressed up against his strong body, inhaling his crisp, masculine scent. His hand is low on my back, his pinky finger resting on the curve of my butt.

I think back to how he grabbed me in the limo, like he couldn't help himself, and I swallow hard.

He wants me.

Despite knowing that I only married him to save my sister, he expects me to give myself to him willingly.

I frown. He could have taken whatever he wanted when I refused to kiss him in the limo. Physically, I don't stand a chance against him. But for some reason, he didn't.

He wanted me to admit that I *enjoyed* it. That I wanted him too.

I won't give him that. Not tonight and not ever.

We finish the dance and return to our seats. It's getting late. I eye the clock, sweating in anticipation of what's to come. The wedding gown sticks to my skin. I lift my hair off my neck and hope for a breeze. It never comes.

I try not to look at my husband, but he's impossible to avoid. He reaches for his wine, his thick, tanned fingers curling around the stem of the glass, and brings it to his lips. Veins run over the back of his hand and disappear under his shirtsleeve.

An image of him pushing those sleeves up his corded fore-arms flashes before my eyes. Something nervous and hot curls in the pit of my belly. I scrape my nails over my cheek, suddenly convinced I shouldn't have drunk all that wine, because it's wreaking havoc inside my mind.

He's your enemy. Your jailer. Don't give him what he wants. Don't melt for him.

I shiver as he trails a hand down my back.

"We'll leave in five minutes," he says in a low voice.

I nod, my blood running hot inside my veins. I focus on my breathing and drink a full glass of water to cool down.

My resolve to resist him strengthens when we get up to leave and Rafaele's men start jeering. "Bed her! Bed her! Bed her!"

Rafaele's grip on my arm is tight as he leads me out of the reception hall and toward the large staircase. I keep my chin up and try to tune out the catcalls and the wolf whistles from his men.

We take the stairs to the second floor and stop before a bedroom at the very end of the hall. Rafaele opens the door and motions for me to enter.

I step onto a plush, blue carpet and move toward the center of the room. My gaze lands on the perfectly made bed with its crisp white sheets and a...red accent pillow.

The door closes behind me.

I stare at that mockery of a pillow as Rafaele's hands land on my hips. He pulls my back against his front, and he's all hard muscle beneath that suit. His lips fall to my throat, soft and teasing.

The sensations that follow momentarily stun me. My body comes alive, buzzing at each careful stroke of his tongue against my flesh.

I'm also quite good at other things.

My nipples tighten.

Push him away.

He palms one of my breasts and makes a satisfied sound at the back of his throat that makes a pulse appear between my legs. And then he closes the tiny bit of space left between our lower bodies and lets me feel every hard inch of him against my ass.

Oh fuck.

His fingers slide into my hair. He turns my head sideways, leans down, and claims my lips, pushing his tongue inside my mouth. There's a tug on the top button of my dress as he begins to undress me.

This is moving very fucking quickly.

I jerk out of his grasp. "Enough."

He's breathing heavily, his dark, lustful eyes traveling over me.

Slowly, I wipe my lips with the back of my hand. "You don't get to kiss me."

The arousal in his gaze flickers.

I reach behind my back and undo the remaining four buttons at the back of the dress. "And you don't get to undress me." I let the dress fall off my shoulders into a puddle at my feet. Next, I shed my bra and panties and stand before him, my body naked except for the diamonds.

I keep those on. They're armor. The hardest gem in the entire world, and a reminder for me to be just as unbreakable.

Rafaele is frozen as he drags his hungry and slightly baffled gaze over my naked body.

He wants his stupid bloody sheets? I'll give them to him. But that's *all* he's going to get.

I walk over to the bed, climb onto it, and lie down on my back.

"Do it," I say, my gaze on the ceiling and my fists clenched. "I want to get this over with."

A beat passes. And then he's on me, his hand wrapped around my neck.

I suck in a shaky breath. His hold on me is firm but not so tight as to make breathing difficult.

His lips brush against my own. "Have you forgotten that I'm your husband and that I get to do whatever I want with you?"

I swallow. "Go ahead. Rape me."

When his expression turns to stone at the word, I know I read him right. What he wants is for me to come to him willingly. Triumph swells inside my chest. For the first time, I have the upper hand. He has to do it. We have to consummate the marriage.

But he won't enjoy it.

And if I deny him long enough, he'll understand he made a mistake marrying me. As long as I never give him what he wants, I'll have power over him. One day, I may even find a way to use that power to convince him to let me go.

"That's not what this is," he growls. "You knew the terms of this marriage. You consented to them."

"I know I have to give myself to you, but I don't want you. I won't enjoy a second of it. Call it what you want."

He stares at me for a long moment, searching my eyes for a hint that I'm bluffing.

He won't find it.

When I don't flinch or look away, his gaze narrows. I expect it to harden as he comes to terms with what he has to do, but instead, it turns uncertain.

That can't be right.

This is Rafaele Messero, a man whose dark reputation is a living, breathing companion that follows him everywhere he goes. I have a lot of questions swirling inside my head, but whether or not he's capable of forcing himself onto me tonight isn't one of them. That's a given. We have to consummate this marriage, or his family won't accept it. They'll be happy to have an excuse to annul it.

He can't take that risk. Not when his ability to inherit my father's empire is on the line.

He pushes off me and stands at the foot of the bed. The fabric of his slacks brushes against my bare knees. Seconds tick by. My heart is a tribal drum inside my chest. He doesn't move.

"What are you waiting for?"

Is he trying to draw it out? To let me sink deeper into my fear?

My fists clench.

Finally, he starts taking off his jacket.

A ball of dread solidifies inside my belly. Despite my best efforts, my thighs squeeze together and my lips begin to tremble. Adrenaline and fear pump through my veins.

I wait for him to climb on top of me, to take what he believes is owed to him.

I count my breaths, readying myself.

But seconds pass and nothing happens.

CHAPTER 11

RAFAELE

This is all wrong.

What's even worse is that I can't figure out how the fuck we ended up here. I rewind the past twenty-four hours, trying to decipher the mystery that is my wife.

What's behind her fierce resistance? Is it fear? I didn't think she was scared of me, but maybe I read her wrong. No matter how badly I want her, no matter how desperately I want to sink inside of her, it can't be like this.

Never like this.

My stomach roils at the memories that come flooding back. The hardwood floor beneath my bare feet. Dim light coming from the bedside lamp. My mother's muffled cries amidst my father's groans. I push off the bed, suddenly feeling horribly exposed even though it's Cleo lying bare beneath me.

I want her to be willing. An enthusiastic participant, not trembling prey.

She opens her eyes. "What are you waiting for?" No matter how she tries to hide it, I can hear the wobble in her voice.

Rape me.

A shiver goes through me. I don't know my wife. But if she thinks I'd ever do that to her, she doesn't know me either.

"No."

She sucks in a surprised breath. "No?"

I chuck my suit jacket at her perfect naked body. "*No*, I'm not going to fuck you like this. Not when you're lying there like a sacrificial lamb."

Her mouth falls open. She jerks into a sitting position, clutching my jacket against her chest. "Oh, I'm sorry, I didn't realize you needed me to make my rape more palatable for *you*!"

I anchor my hands on the upper part of the bed frame and stare at her. "For your information, I've never raped a woman, and I have no intention of starting tonight."

I expect her to look relieved, but instead, her anger only burns brighter.

She really thought I'd do it.

Perhaps then it would be easier for her to hate me for the rest of our marriage, and to wallow in that hate. She'd rather hate me than let herself feel pleasure at my hands. To do so would be her admitting defeat.

I file that realization away. "Here's what's going to happen. I'll give you a few days to adjust to your new life and come to your fucking senses. In those few days, I want you to meditate on how wet you got when I kissed you."

She makes a sound of pure outrage and scrambles off the opposite side of the bed. "You're delusional."

"Don't deny it. Trust me, it'll feel even better when my tongue is deep inside your pussy instead of your mouth."

Her lips part in shock.

She's so fucking innocent beneath all that bravado. "When I finally fuck you, you won't be trembling like a leaf. You'll be begging me for it."

Her lips waver for a moment before she presses them into a tight, determined line. "If you think I'll ever beg you for *anything*, you need to get your head checked. I'm starting to see why you let Nero do all the talking. Clearly, the things you spew out of your mouth make no sense. I will never want you."

"I'll make you eat your words the way I did earlier."

"Screw you," she hisses, still holding my jacket against her chest.

"Trust me, you will, once you get over this ridiculous fear."

"What fear? I'm not afraid of you. I'm *disgusted* by you. There's a difference."

I walk around the bed and corner her against one of the thick wooden bedposts. "Disgusted?"

Cleo tilts her head back, giving me perfect access to that lush, pink mouth. Her eyes drift to my lips. She swallows. "Yes."

"You're a horrible liar."

Her eyes flash with defiance, her mouth ready to fire off another snappy retort, so I cut it off with a kiss. My tongue slips between her lips, and the taste of her sends me reeling. She's still holding my jacket, using it as a barrier between us, but I can feel her every curve as I press my body against hers. Blood rushes to my dick.

I wrap my arm around her and let my hand rest just above the swell of her bare ass. Her fingers curl into my shirt, and she starts to return the kiss.

She's sure as fuck not pushing me away now, is she?

I tug her closer, my erection growing against the zipper of my slacks. The kiss is messy, and our teeth clank. She has no technique to speak of, or maybe she's purposefully trying to make me think she doesn't know what she's doing. If she thinks that will serve to repel me, she couldn't be more wrong. I feast on her mouth and her taste, and the feel of her body against mine makes me groan.

She grows stiff for a second as she tugs on my bottom lip with her teeth.

And then she bites it. *Hard.*

Copper floods my mouth. Cleo sucks on the wound, the fucking lunatic, drawing out my blood. Before I can get my bearings, she pulls away, looking triumphant as *my* blood drips down her chin.

She turns and spits onto the bed. "There. Your fucking bloody sheets."

Her eyes blaze.

My dick couldn't be harder.

"You can show that to your creepy family tomorrow, all while knowing that it's your blood they're looking at instead of mine. Now, get out."

I peer behind her, at the red stain, at the false evidence of the consummation of our marriage, and in that moment, I realize my mistake.

I own her, but I haven't tamed her.

I haven't even tried. I've been so absorbed with my raw desire for her, I didn't stop to think about how today must have made her feel. It was a victory for me, but a loss for her.

She'd been playing a game for a long time, and today she lost that game. Her plan to stay unmarried failed spectacularly.

She called me her jailer. Her captor. She wants to make me pay for making her lose. And I just spent the entire day showing her exactly what I want for my prize. Is it really a surprise she would deny me what I want?

I brush my thumb over my lip. It comes away coated with my blood. She glares at me, impossibly beautiful, stubbornly fierce.

If I want her, I'm going to have to seduce her.

No woman has ever made me work for it. My position and looks ensured a steady stream of women in and out of my bed whenever I had time for it. Cleo is different. She's going to hold out on me for as long as she can. But I am a patient man, and there's nothing more I love than a good challenge.

Especially when the reward is her.

She shouldn't have shown me her perfect, untouched body if she didn't want me motivated to conquer her.

I rip the stained sheet off the bed, roll it up, and tuck it under my arm. "You'll get the pleasure of seeing my family deceived tomorrow, but I don't mind being the only one who'll see your virgin blood. I've never liked to share."

Her cheeks turn pink with anger. "The only way you'll see it is if you force me, and it looks like you don't have the stomach for that."

I take a backward step toward the door. "We'll see about that."

I feel her gaze on me as I leave the room and close the door behind me. Then I press my back against it. We're playing a new game now, and she just won the first round. But she's shown me something today that I will use against her. There's a fire between us. She might not like it, but it's there. And I'm going to do everything I can to make sure it burns brighter and brighter.

Until the day it melts her resolve.

CHAPTER 12

RAFAELE

THE SHEETS ARE PRESENTED in front of my capos, soldiers, and a smattering of family and friends at just past ten a.m. in one of the rooms on the ground floor of the hotel. My sisters and my mother are missing, but Nonna is there, as well as a few other old crones who feel it is their duty to ensure the traditions of our family continue to be respected.

Nero comes up beside me. "Should we remove it before Cleo comes out? If someone jokes about it, she'll probably try to claw their eyes out."

Unlikely, given it's my blood everyone is whistling at.

I turn to him. "We'll take it down in ten minutes."

"What the fuck happened to your lip?"

Fuck.

I didn't think the swelling was that obvious when I checked this morning in the mirror.

"We need to have a word. Let's go talk in the library."

Nero gives me a curious look. "You all right?"

"Not here."

He follows me inside. I close the door behind him and lock it for good measure. I don't want anyone interrupting us. Nero takes one of the leather armchairs, but I don't feel like sitting. I walk over to the large window facing the back garden and link my hands behind my back.

I didn't sleep much after I left Cleo in our wedding suite. Thankfully, we rented the entire hotel, so there were more than a few empty suites available. I grabbed the closest one and spent the rest of the night trying to come up with a plan to seduce my wife.

I didn't get very far.

I'm good at many things, but understanding the psychology of women isn't one of them. Good thing it's something my consigliere excels in.

Nero clears his throat. "So...?"

I turn around.

Whatever he sees in my expression makes him laugh. "Seriously, what the fuck happened?

When I stay silent, the amusement in his expression melts away. "Did it go okay?"

"No, it didn't go okay."

He frowns. "Is she...hurt?"

I walk over to the bar cart and splash a bit of whiskey into a glass. "I didn't fuck her. Barely even touched her."

Nero shakes his head, confused. "Whose blood was that then?"

"Mine."

Nero stares at me for a split second before he bursts out laughing. "What did I tell you? Did she bite the whole thing off or just give it a nibble?"

"She didn't get close enough to my cock to even breathe on it." I point at my face. "She bit my lip." I take a swig of the whiskey, and it burns the shallow wound inside my mouth. "She sucked my blood and spit it on the sheets."

"Holy shit." He's taken aback. He didn't expect her to pull something like that. "So what happened after?"

"Nothing. I left. Before she gnawed on me like a fucking piranha, she made it clear she wants nothing to do with me."

"She's your wife."

"She is," I mutter. "But like you said, that doesn't mean she likes me."

Nero blows out a breath. "What are you going to do?"

I take a seat across from him. "You're my consigliere. I was hoping for a little advice."

He rubs his jaw. "Sorry, I'm still processing. Maybe she just needs to warm up to you. Take her out to dinner."

"It's not going to be that easy. She called me her jailer. She's determined to hate me."

Nero looks thoughtful. "She's got a rebellious spirit. Look how she lied to everyone about not being a virgin just so that she could ruin her father's plans for her. Now, she's going to rebel against you."

I frown at my glass. "Rebelling to what end? What's done is done, and no amount of rebellion on her part will undo our marriage."

He shrugs. "Maybe she just wants to feel in control. She chose to marry you in her sister's place, but since making that choice, she hasn't had any say in anything. This could be her trying to assert herself, making it clear you won't get to dictate all of the terms of this marriage."

"And she'll do this by denying me her body?"

He nods. "To start. But I suspect it won't be the end of it. She lost her freedom when she married you. That will take a while for her to process, and I think it's safe to say she won't do it quietly."

My thoughts turn inside my head. "Maybe I can pacify her by giving her an illusion of freedom. She thinks I'll restrict her even more than her father. I can prove her wrong while still keeping the situation under my control."

Nero nods. "That's good. She won't expect leniency from you. It'll lower her defenses."

"But I can't allow her to do whatever she wants."

"Give her a leash so long she forgets it even exists. If she crosses any real lines, you'll have to remind her of it. There's no way around that. If she can't come to terms with it, I don't know how this will work out."

"She will come to terms with it." She has to.

"Pick your battles carefully. She'll want to get a reaction out of you when she acts out, so don't give it to her unless she's really pushing it."

Cleo won't hold back. She lacks any sort of restraint. "It's a good thing I've had a lot of practice not showing my emotions," I mutter, dragging my thumb over my sore lip.

Nero knows better than to say it, but I can see the thought reflected in his eyes. *I told you so.* He crosses his ankle over his knee. "By the way, Joseph Ferraro called this morning. Wanted to offer his congratulations."

My brows rise. Big Joe is Gino Ferraro's consigliere. This is the first time someone of his seniority has reached out to us from the Ferraro family in years. "Did he say anything else?"

"Just some small talk, but you know what this means."

"Big Joe wouldn't have called without getting Gino's blessing."

Nero nods. "It seems like they might be interested in putting this feud behind us once and for all. We should try to arrange a dinner with you, Ferraro, and the wives."

"I don't know if it's a good idea to bring Cleo to an important meeting. Her presence will significantly increase the risk of bloodshed."

Nero snickers. "I don't mean you do it tomorrow. These things take a while to arrange. We'll do it when things warm up between the two of you."

I appreciate that he seems to think it's a matter of when and not if.

I finish the whiskey and rise. "All right, go take down the sheet. I'm tired of everyone staring at my fucking blood."

Nero slaps me on the back. "One day, you're going to look back at this moment and laugh."

He leaves, and when I come out onto the back patio, the post-wedding brunch is in full swing. My wife is sitting at a table with Valentina and De Rossi. De Rossi's sister, Martina, and her husband, Giorgio, are there as well.

Cleo meets my gaze. For a moment, I debate what to do. It's clear she wants to spend time with her family, so I shouldn't drag her away from their table, but at the same time, I have no desire to sit anywhere but beside her. And I sure as fuck don't plan on letting her forget how her body responds to me.

I start toward them, and Cleo's eyes narrow in warning. I ignore it. When I'm just a few feet away, she rises from her seat, and I'm treated to a full view of her body.

Fuck.

She's wearing a silky slip dress that molds to her breasts and hugs her hips. That dress would look even better in a puddle on my bedroom floor.

Cleo's mouth parts. "Raf—"

Before she can finish her sentence, I slip my arm around her waist and silence her with a kiss. She gasps against my mouth, clearly taken aback.

Better get used to this, sweetheart.

I'll wait to fuck her, but she's going to have to come to terms with giving me that mouth whenever the fuck I want.

She makes a low sound of protest. Her palms press uselessly against my chest before she curls them into fists. I slip my tongue past her lips and pull her even closer, ignoring the dull throb of pain inside my mouth.

I'm half expecting her to start bucking against me, but she doesn't. Instead, she grows very still, and when I open my eyes, she's looking right back at me. I break the kiss but hold her close to me. She's panting, her breaths coming out in small puffs against my lips.

"I hope you've been pretending you're as sore as your bloody artwork would imply." My voice is low enough so that only she can hear it.

Her green eyes narrow. "Let go of me."

I do, but not before I stroke her bare upper back with the pads of my fingertips. She shivers. Her body's involuntary reaction makes her glare at me and blush.

I take the seat beside her and throw my arm around the back of her chair. "Good afternoon," I say to the rest of the table, letting the tips of my fingers brush over Cleo's shoulder.

Her sister frowns at me, and De Rossi shoots me a dark look.

"We should talk business before we leave," he says. "Given what happened with Gemma, I'd like to propose some changes to our partnership with Garzolo. I have no desire to do business with a man who's harmed my wife's sister."

I nod. He wants to cut Garzolo out of our counterfeits deal? Fine by me.

"We can talk after brunch," I say.

I should spend the rest of this brunch thinking through how I want to approach that impending conversation, but instead, my awareness stays firmly on my wife. And every time my fingertips brush over her flawless skin, I notice her breath hitch.

CHAPTER 13

CLEO

MY HUSBAND WON'T STOP TOUCHING me, and it's driving me insane.

This morning, I woke up feeling on top of the world. The balance of power had shifted. I had something Rafaele wanted—my body—and I was determined to never give it to him willingly.

If I have to be miserable in this marriage, he'll be miserable right there with me.

That made me happy.

But that happiness turned out to be short-lived when he appeared at brunch, swaggered over to me, and reminded me of the weapon he has against me.

Our incomprehensible, undeniable chemistry.

Last night, I was surprised he didn't force me. Even though I suspected he wouldn't enjoy it, I was sure he'd just get it over with quickly so that he'd have the bloody sheets to show his relatives.

If he had done it that way, it would have been the end of whatever physical attraction I felt for him. As I lay there naked on the bed before him, I thought it was a price I was willing to pay if it meant my body would stop reacting to him.

But he didn't.

Now, we're talking to his sisters, and his arm is wrapped securely around my waist. My body responds to his touch like a puppet on strings. I hate myself for it. I'm hyperaware of every absentminded brush of his thumb against my waist as his manly scent envelops me in a dizzying cloud. Since he's only wearing a black dress shirt and dress pants today, there's no hiding from the heat emanating from his muscled body.

I finally get a break from him when it's time to say goodbye to Vale, Dem, Mari, and Giorgio. I take turns hugging all of them and get a bit teary when Vale's turn comes. She holds me tightly and presses a kiss to my cheek. "Call us, okay? Whenever you get a chance. Gemma is desperate to talk to you."

"I will." I'll probably have to ask Rafaele for permission to call my sister. I don't even have a phone anymore. It was taken from me when Rafaele first brought me to his house.

My stomach tightens. I can't believe that this is my new reality.

The next to leave are Fabi and Elena. They congratulate me and make me promise them that I won't hesitate to reach out if I ever need anything.

"Did you get a chance to meet Vince yesterday?" I ask them, remembering the Switzerland connection between them and my brother. He's not here today, and neither are my parents. I hadn't asked why they couldn't make it, since I've had other things on my mind.

"We did, briefly," Fabi says, smiling. "Turns out we have a few friends in common. Maybe we'll see him around when we return to Geneva."

Rafaele says goodbye to his sisters next. I'm surprised to see him slip on his impenetrable mask as he embraces them. Fabi gives him a smile, but Elena only leans into his ear and whispers something that makes his gaze grow cold. What happened between them to make their relationship so strained?

By the time the festivities wrap up, it's late in the afternoon. Rafaele and I get into a black car that I presume is taking us back to his house.

Five minutes into the ride, I can feel his attention on me. His gaze has the uncanny ability to make me heat up from the inside out.

If he tried to kiss me right now, would I pull back?

Yeah, that's something I don't want to test.

I decide to break the tense silence. "So how is all of this going to work?"

He arches a brow. "What do you mean?"

"We're married. What am I supposed to do now?"

"Whatever you want."

I roll my eyes. "Yeah, right. Papà recited the rules your women follow to Gemma on more than one occasion, so I'm well-versed in them. I can't drive on my own, can't leave the house without guards, can't go to college or hold a job, and I can't be friends with outsiders."

He stares at me, looking as if he's trying to choose his words carefully. "All of those rules are for your own safety," he finally says.

I sneer. "All of those rules are there to control me. Do you get off on it? Keeping me under your thumb?"

His jaw hardens. "I am a don, Cleo. I have many enemies. Enemies that are always looking for cracks in my defenses. As my wife, you are now a target. The guards and the driver are there for your protection, whether you believe it or not."

"Okay, but why can't I be friends with whoever I want?"

"Because outsiders are the easiest people to compromise. They have no protection against someone in our world who wants to turn them into an asset. You can't trust any friendship you make from now on. If anything, I'm saving you from heartbreak."

"Heartbreak? What do you know about that?" I grumble. "You allowed your sisters to go to college. The rules don't apply to them?"

"It was my father who allowed them, not me. But yes, they have stayed in Geneva with my blessing because until they're married, it's far safer for them to be there than here. Abroad, my enemies have far less power than they do here. I have contacts on the ground that keep Fabi and Elena under constant surveillance."

"Do they know that?"

He doesn't answer. I scoff. Unbelievable. His poor sisters probably don't even know that they can't take a bathroom break without it being reported to their brother.

My chest falls. I can't live the rest of my life like that. No way. There has to be a way for me to reclaim my independence.

Is divorce an option? Unlikely. At least not until Rafaele becomes don of my family too. But there are men who don't live with their wives. Papà had a capo whose wife and kids lived in a home upstate while the capo had an apartment in Jersey with his goomah.

If I live apart from Rafaele, my life would undoubtedly be better. Maybe I need to be such a pain in the ass that he decides keeping me around isn't worth the trouble. That shouldn't be that hard.

"I want my own cell phone," I say as we speed down the highway.

He stretches out his legs and crosses them at the ankles. "Fine."

Oh. I didn't expect him to agree so quickly. "And a credit card."

He nods. "It's already waiting for you at home." He stretches out his arm. "Any other requests?"

"I'm sure I can think of a few..."

He removes a cufflink and rolls up his sleeve. My gaze latches onto his tanned, tatted forearm. Fuck, he's got sexy forearms. Muscular with thick veins beneath his skin.

"Go ahead."

I glance up. "Huh?"

He arches a brow as he repeats the same ritual with his other arm. "What else do you need?"

"I need some more time to think about it," I mutter.

For the first time since I've met him, he smiles at me. A real, full-blown tilt of the mouth. How can that tiny movement take him from sexy to undeniably devastating?

Suddenly, the car feels too hot. I wrap my palm around the side of my neck and squirm in my seat.

"Take your time," he says. "Like I said to you at the rehearsal dinner, I want you to be comfortable. And I think in time, you'll find that my rules aren't as restrictive as you think."

That is my cue to argue with him, but I can't seem to get my thoughts straight right now. I wrap my arms around myself and turn to face the window. I need to stop looking at him.

We get to Rafaele's house just before dinner. Sabina greets us, shooting me a hateful glare when Rafaele isn't looking, and then corrals us into the dining room where a feast awaits.

I'm not that hungry after the drawn-out brunch, but I try a few things anyway since the cook went out of his way to make a bunch of vegetarian dishes.

His name is Luca, and he's around fifty years old. I like him immediately. He introduces himself with a warm smile and apologizes for preparing me steak at the rehearsal dinner even after I tell him it's all right.

"As soon as they told me you don't eat meat, I went online and bought a few new cookbooks," he says. "You will have to give me your feedback so that I can prepare things you like."

"Thank you, I appreciate it," I say.

He dips his head. "Enjoy your meal, Signora Messero."

I freeze at the name. It's going to take a while to get used to being called that.

When I truly can't eat another bite, Rafaele stands up and gestures for me to follow him. We take the stairs to a room on the second floor, a few doors down from the guest bedroom where I was locked up until yesterday.

I peek inside. "What's this?" I suspect I know the answer.

"Our bedroom."

The room is twice the size of the guest bedroom. It's decorated in cool blue tones and contains a big bed, a sitting area by the window, and a fireplace. Masculine, but not obnoxiously male. I slip my shoes off and curl my bare toes against the plush carpet. "I want to sleep in the other room. The one I stayed in earlier."

Rafaele throws his jacket over the back of a chair. "What's wrong with this one? Do you not like the decor?"

I give him a pointed look. "Yes, there's this awful talking robot that grates on my nerves."

His eyes spark. "He's a permanent feature, so you better get used to it."

I'm not planning to get used to shit. I also have no intention of letting him touch me. Does he think I'll soften up to him because he didn't hurt me last night?

I cross my arms over my chest. "I'm not sleeping with you."

He takes off his tie and places it on top of his jacket. "We're married, so we're going to share a bedroom. If you don't want to sleep in the same bed as me, you can sleep on the floor."

The floor? Even with the nice carpet, that option doesn't seem particularly inviting.

I glance around. There's an ottoman by the window, not exactly large, but big enough for me to fit. I walk over to the bed, snatch a pillow and the duvet, and carry them to the ottoman. "I'll sleep here."

"Suit yourself," he says calmly as he begins to unbutton his shirt. "I'm going to go shower."

I watch him disappear behind one of the doors. He's playing it very cool today. If I want to get on his nerves, I'm going to have to figure out exactly what makes him angry.

While he's in the shower, I explore the rest of the room.

There's a huge walk-in closet with freestanding cabinetry in the center and two armchairs. On one side of the closet are Rafaele's clothes, and the other side is sparsely filled with what I realize are some of my clothes from home. He must have asked Mamma to pack me a bag at some point, and of course she packed my least favorite outfits.

I wander back into the bedroom. I find a black credit card with my new name on it on one of the nightstands.

Cleo Messero.

God, this is so weird.

I run my thumb over the raised letters. I'll have to put this thing to use soon to buy clothes I actually want to wear.

The bathroom door swings open.

I turn in time to see Rafaele come out in a pair of black boxer briefs, his hair tousled and wet. A choked sound escapes the back of my throat at the sight of all that tattooed skin.

Holy shit.

He's covered in ink from his collarbone down to the waist-band of his boxers.

And he's fit. Eight-pack abs, well-defined chest, and broad, muscled shoulders. My eyes follow the V that disappears behind his waistband along with his ink. A wave of heat crashes through me.

Slowly, I lift my gaze back to his face. There's a challenge in his eyes. Is he trying to play dirty? I realize my jaw is hanging open, and I quickly close it. Fuck. I need to keep my poker face around him.

He walks toward the closet, giving me a view of his muscular back and the intricate snake tattoo on it. He looks even more lethal without his clothes on. I can't stop staring at the way his body moves, confident and powerful, like a predator.

He returns with another duvet in his arms and dumps it on the bed. "This Friday, I'm taking you out for dinner."

My gaze lingers on that damn V. "I'll pass."

"It's not a request."

I blink at him, struggling to formulate a sentence that doesn't end with me drooling on myself. I must be tired. It's been an exhausting twenty-four hours.

"Okay, whatever," I mumble.

It's not until I'm in my pajamas and lying on the hard ottoman in the darkness that the haze induced by his naked body lifts. I rub my eyes and let out a sigh. I can't let my insides turn to mush every time he comes out of a shower. Now that he's seen my less-than-ideal reaction, he's going to keep doing it.

I stare at the star-speckled sky outside the window and try to ignore the sound of Rafaele's deep breaths from where he's lying in his comfortable bed. The bastard's already asleep.

Sleep doesn't come as easily to me, so I stay up for a while longer and slowly piece together my plan.

CHAPTER 14

RAFAELE

"Conor's going to make a full recovery," Nero says when I meet him the next afternoon for lunch at one of my restaurants in Yonkers.

I spent the morning driving up to Albany to go over the books with a capo I've got there. My territory sprawls from Westchester County all the way through Upstate New York, but I've also got a number of restaurants scattered throughout Manhattan, as well as a club in Harlem. It's a lot of area to cover, and I like to see my capos face-to-face frequently, so I'm often on the road.

"Good. What did he want to do with Joshua?"

Nero shrugs. "Nothing. Told me he's going to send him to live with his mother in Chicago for a few months until he cools down."

"Joshua kidnapped him and nearly killed him."

"He's his son."

He's an idiot, and a dangerous one at that. "He's making a mistake. Son or not, Joshua needs to be put down."

"How many times do I have to remind you not everyone thinks like you, Rafe?"

"You don't need to remind me of anything. I already know most people lack all semblance of rationality."

Nero chuckles. "Good thing you've got enough for all of us."

I shake my head, feeling a lick of annoyance at Conor's shortsightedness. "Tell Conor the next time Joshua steps out of line—and he will step out of line again—we won't give him a choice. His son used up his one strike."

"Noted," Nero says. "I'll make sure he gets the message. How was your meeting with Mad Dog?"

"Mad Dog's numbers were fine." Our income from Albany has been dropping over the last six months, and I've been working on figuring out why. "But he lost a few of his regulars recently. I told him to go talk to them and politely invite them back." Mad Dog runs a popular gambling den and has been one of my top earners.

Nero shakes his head. "There's nowhere else to go gamble that kind of money up there."

"I have a feeling that's no longer the case."

A waiter comes around with a bottle of wine and fills our glasses.

"You think it's Ferraro?" Nero asks once he leaves.

"Possibly. It's more likely Bratva. They've been getting more and more bold in the recent weeks." I spread a napkin over my lap. "I want you to ask around. Have you made progress on setting up that dinner with Ferraro?"

"I'm waiting on Big Joe to give me a few dates." Nero eyes the caprese salad on the table and spears some onto his fork. "What about your wife? Did you manage to pacify her?"

I drag my tongue over my teeth. Cleo was still asleep on the ottoman when I left, her copper curls splayed across her pillow. I spent a few minutes studying her flawlessly smooth skin and the elegant arc of her throat before I left. Elena's words from yesterday were on my mind as I walked out the front door. *"Don't hurt her."*

Don't hurt her? Well, if I needed any additional confirmation that my sister thinks I'm a monster, that was it. I have no plans to hurt my wife, but I do have extensive plans on how to make her writhe in pleasure. If only she'd stop being so fucking stubborn.

My hunger for her is occupying a significant part of my mind, but it no longer feels as overwhelming as it did in the church. Now that she's mine, it's only a matter of time before she realizes resisting me is futile.

"I gave her a cell phone and a credit card. As long as she obeys the rules that are in place to keep her safe, she can do as she likes."

"That's a good sta—"

The door of the restaurant flies open.

Nero and I reach for our guns just as Garzolo barges in with the force of a hurricane.

A few of my men are already standing, their weapons drawn. They glance at me for instructions. I tell them to stand down with a small shake of my head. Garzolo prowls over, his cheeks red.

Nero sighs and puts his gun back into his holster. "What now?" He reaches for the bottle of wine on the table and tops off our glasses. "We weren't expecting you, Garzolo."

Cleo's father looks like he's on the verge of exploding. How can someone be a don and be this fucking emotional? It's disgraceful. No wonder Garzolo is the worst don this city has seen in generations.

"I came to see why you were out there talking to De Rossi yesterday when we never discussed you having a direct line to him," he snaps.

I press my napkin against my lips. "Sit down."

"This is the kind of shit that will fuck this whole thing up, you know. The kind—"

"Sit the fuck down, Garzolo," Nero growls. "Don't make us ask you a third time."

Garzolo glares at Nero before he dumps himself into the chair beside me. "Why wasn't I allowed to attend yesterday's event? It was my right as Cleo's father."

"Cut the shit," Nero says. "We all know your relationship with your daughter is nonexistent. She didn't even allow you to walk her down the aisle, and you seemed a lot less angry about that than this. The only reason you're pissed we didn't let you come is because you didn't want us talking to De Rossi."

He doesn't bother denying it. "I got a call from him an hour ago, telling me I'm getting cut out of the deal. I'm the one who brokered it! Without me, you'd still be shaking down restaurant owners and getting your shoes dirty in cement. I *gave* you this!"

I pick up the wine bottle and read the label. "Chateau Du Soleil, Cotes du Rhone, grenache grape. Your daughter likes wine, doesn't she? Maybe I should bring a bottle of this home."

Garzolo stares at me, his outrage emanating from him. "Did you hear anything—"

I toss the bottle into the air, grab it by the neck, and smash it over his head.

The glass shatters, the wine spattering everywhere. Garzolo howls and raises his arms to protect his face. Nero jumps out of his seat, muttering something about getting his new suit dirty.

I'm still holding the broken bottle by the neck. I grab Garzolo's tie and jerk him toward me until I'm right in his face. I press the sharp edge of the glass against a vein in his throat. "You ever come talking to me like that again, I'll decapitate you with this fucking bottle. Do you understand?"

He sputters, wine dripping down his forehead and cheeks.

"This isn't a partnership. We own you. You're lucky I'm giving you five more years to enjoy being a don. That was a favor, or have you forgotten that already?"

"This is why we don't like giving favors," Nero grumbles as he wipes himself off with a napkin. "No one seems to understand how those work."

"I understand," Garzolo bleats, his fury replaced with fear. Pathetic.

Now that I know how incompetent this man is, it's shocking his family has lasted this long. The foundations laid down by his father must have stood the test of time, but even the greatest of empires can be brought down by one man's idiocy.

I let go of his tie and shove him to the ground. "If I want to deal directly with De Rossi, I'm going to deal directly with De Rossi. Did you really think he would still want to do business with you after you raised your hand to the woman carrying his consigliere's child? Your own daughter? You're lucky you've never touched Cleo, because if you had, I would have put you ten feet under as a wedding gift to her."

Garzolo pales. "I *never* touched her."

"Get out of my face. You've still got a business to run, remember? Focus on that, because the last thing you want is to make me inherit a depreciating asset. Do you understand?"

He pushes himself off the ground and nods. "Understood."

"Now leave."

He hurries out of the restaurant.

Nero watches him leave and swears. "Unbelievable. He really thought he could come here and tell you what to do?"

"He's not thinking at all. That's the problem." His power has been significantly diminished, and he's not handling it well. I don't mind him making a fool of himself—it'll make my transition easier when it comes to it, because no one wants to follow a weak man into battle—but I have to make sure he doesn't run his family into the ground first.

A server and the manager run out to clean up the mess, and a waitress rushes over to Nero with a wet cloth. She looks uncertain for a moment, but then the owner hisses something at her, and she starts to dab at the stains on Nero's chest.

The lines between my consigliere's eyebrows melt away, and he grins at her. "Hello, beautiful. I don't remember seeing you here before. Where did you come from?"

The girl mumbles a response and blushes.

Nero spreads his thighs and beckons her closer. "Come stand over here. You can reach better."

I watch him shamelessly flirt with the waitress, and my mind goes back to my wife. Does she really think I'm at all like her father? Just because we're both the dons of our families, it doesn't mean we're the same. I have as much in common with Garzolo as I do with a fucking turnip.

Nero says something to me.

I blink. "What?"

Somehow, he's now got the waitress on his lap while she's scrubbing the wine off his tie. She doesn't seem to mind. Annoyance simmers beneath my flesh. He can get just about any woman to eat out of the palm of his hand, the charming bastard.

"I said, if outbursts like this become common, this isn't going to work," he repeats, wrapping his hands around the waitress's waist to keep her steady.

"We'll talk about it later," I say, suddenly eager to finish our meal so that we can get back to work. The sooner we're done, the sooner I can go back home to my wife.

Nero senses my annoyance. He whispers something in the waitress's ear that makes her smile and get off him. Before she leaves, he takes her phone and puts his number in it.

"Send me a text when you get off work," he says, giving her ass a light smack.

The waitress blushes and disappears into the back. Fuck. I wish my life were that easy. But I don't want an eager waitress. I want my fucking wife.

And I'm going to have her, so help me God.

CHAPTER 15

CLEO

RAFAELE IS GONE when I wake up around ten a.m. I crawl into the empty bed and nearly weep at how comfortable it is compared to the ottoman.

The sheets smell like his bodywash. I recognize the scent from last night when he walked out of the shower in just his underwear. Fuck, he looked so good. I had no idea he was that ripped.

Okay, this is a dangerous line of thought.

I give myself another minute to enjoy the cozy bed before I haul my ass into a cold shower and rinse the traces of him off my skin.

Hot or not, Rafaele is keeping me caged, and I'm not about to go all Stockholm syndrome on him. All of those rules that are supposedly for my protection? The only reason I need that protection is because he's a murderer who's got other murderers after him.

Ah, the life of a mob wife.

My only chance at not going stir-crazy is to get him to send me away from here. I know he's got a massive mansion in the Hamptons—Mamma used to talk about it all the time. I could live there.

And then what?

Okay, there's not that much to do there, but at least I wouldn't have to see *him* every day. That would already be an improvement.

I dry myself off, pull on some clothes, and sit down at the small desk in the corner of the room. Time to write down my ideas.

Cleo's plan for ruining Rafaele's life:

- Bankrupt him
- Redecorate his house
- Get a dog—a big and scary one who'll keep him away from me
- Identify all of his hopes and dreams
- Ruin them
- Never, ever, under no circumstances, even if there's a gun to my head, sleep with him

The plan is as chaotic as my personality, but I feel good about this. Really good.

The things on it definitely play to my strengths. Rafaele is an uptight control freak, so I'm going to do everything I can to make him realize he brought a loose cannon into his life. The only thing he really seems to want from me is my body, so if I never give it to him, he'll eventually realize keeping me around isn't worth the hassle.

Since I need to get more clothes anyway, I decide to hit the first bullet point. Time to put that black credit card to use.

I head downstairs and search the house for a member of staff so that I can get someone to drive me to Manhattan. I bump into Sabina lecturing a maid in the dining room.

She stops mid-sentence when she sees me and dismisses the maid. "What do you want?"

"I need a driver."

"Where are you going?"

"Manhattan. I need to do some shopping."

"What—"

"What's with the twenty questions?" I snap. "Just get me what I asked for."

Her eyes turn to slits. "You little brat. You just got married, and you're already going off to spend Don Messero's hard-earned money."

Oh, if only she knew.

"What did you think of the wedding?" I ask innocently. "I felt so beautiful in all those diamonds."

She sneers at me. "You're a disgrace. Signora Caruso's necklace should be scrubbed with soap after touching your filthy neck."

"You go do that. Right after you get me my driver."

"Don't boss me around."

I narrow my eyes. "My husband told me I had to have a driver in order to leave the house. What do you think he'd say if I told him you wouldn't get me one?"

This drains the blood out of her face. Ah, so she's scared of Rafaele. It dawns on me Rafaele would probably take issue with how she's speaking to me, but I don't need his help handling the maid.

"Fine," Sabina grinds out. "I'll get him." She stalks out of the room, muttering something in Italian, probably more nasty things about me. Not that I care. After all, being around people who vehemently disapprove of me isn't anything new. Try living in the Garzolo household for eighteen years. I can't remember the last time I heard a kind word from my parents.

I'm lounging on the living room sofa when a young dude walks in five minutes later. He's got a head of curly auburn hair, a nose piercing, and a grin that takes up half of his face. He looks like he's in his early twenties.

"Sandro," he says as he extends his hand. "I'm your driver."

"That was quick." I shake his hand. "Were you waiting in the garage or something?"

"Tiny and I were playing cards with one of the guards," he says.

Just then, an older man walks into the living room. And by man, I mean a giant. He's probably the same height as Nero, but twice as wide. Each one of his steps shakes the pictures on the wall. His worn leather jacket looks like it could be a tent.

"That's Tiny," Sandro says, pointing his thumb at the giant.

I let out an incredulous laugh. "Right. Cute nickname."

Tiny shakes my hand with his big paw, and it's unnerving. He could snap me in half if he wanted to. Unlike Sandro, he doesn't seem like he ever smiles. "Nice to meet you, Mrs. Messero. I'm your new bodyguard."

"Anyway, I won," Sando says. "In case you were wondering."

I tear my gaze away from Tiny and turn to Sandro. "Won what?"

"The card game with the guard. Won a hundred bucks." He winks.

"Kid, what are you doing?" Tiny mutters in a low voice. "Don't wink at the boss's wife."

Sandro's cheeks redden. "Oh, sorry. I'm just excited." He rubs the back of his head. "This is a big assignment, you know? Driving you around. But don't worry, I'm the best driver the don's got. I've been racing since I was fourteen."

I raise my brows. "Where were your parents?"

He shrugs. "Dead. Nero and Rafaele took me in. I'll always be grateful to them." He bumps his fist against his chest. "It's an honor that the don trusts us with you, Mrs. Messero. Right, Tiny?"

The big man nods, his face very serious. He looks like the consummate professional. This is strangely uncomfortable. I know how to handle Sabina's scorn, but I'm not sure how to respond to *this*. They're excited to be around me? Sandro is bouncing on his feet like a puppy. And Tiny, well, he doesn't exactly seem excited, but he doesn't seem upset about the gig either.

I settle on giving them a smile. "Call me Cleo."

"What would you like to do today?" Sandro asks cheerfully as we make our way to the garage.

"I need to buy some things."

Tiny pulls a brand-new cell phone out of his jacket and hands it to me. "Our numbers are in there, as well as the don's and the house line. Your sisters' numbers too."

Oh.

Rafaele actually did as he promised? Something warm unfurls inside my chest. I can call Gemma on the drive. I thought I'd have to beg Rafaele for her number. I feel a tiny pang of premature guilt for what I'm about to do to his bank account. But no, one good deed doesn't change anything.

I take the phone from Tiny. "Thanks."

Sandro unlocks a black SUV and holds the door open for me. "Where would you like to go? The Westchester?"

"Take me to Fifth Ave." I'm not going to waste my time in a nearby mall. I need the help of my trusted sales reps for the damage I'm hoping to do. "Hope you're ready for a long day, gentlemen."

An hour later, I'm inside the Dior boutique, buying up their latest collection. Afterward, I pop into Chanel for a handbag and a few pairs of shoes, followed by Hermès, where my rep gleefully offers me a limited edition Verrou handbag. I use the opportunity to order two stunning marble coffee tables and a few lounge chairs from their catalogue. The lounge chairs are thirty grand each.

"They'll look great in my backyard," I croon to the rep.

I dip into Bergdorf Goodman next and ask the sales associate to bring me a bunch of things she thinks I'll like. I spend at least an hour there before going to a few more stores.

By the time five p.m. rolls around, the trunk of the SUV is nearly full. There's a running tally in my head, and it's well into high six figures.

I pull out the black card and look at it. I swear it's looking a bit worn from the workout I've given it. The goal is to get Rafaele to send me away, not to murder me.

Then I remember the jewelry vault beneath his house. He's filthy rich, and I want this to hurt.

To put the final nail in the coffin, I go inside Cartier. When the sales rep sees the glint in my eyes, he takes me to the back and shows me their newest collection. A thick choker that's studded with emeralds and diamonds catches my attention. When I try it on, it looks incredible, the green contrasting beautifully with my hair.

"How much?"

"Three hundred thousand dollars," the rep says.

I grin. "Perfect. I'll take it."

Tiny, who's been keeping a great poker face all day, turns a little pale. "Mrs. Messero—"

"Cleo," I correct him.

"Cleo. The don might not be happy about this."

"You know, I think you might be right." I lift my gaze from the display case.

Tiny looks relieved. He pulls out a handkerchief from his pocket and wipes his forehead.

I sigh. "I've been buying things for myself all day, and I haven't gotten Rafaele anything. How thoughtless of me. I should get my husband a gift." I turn back to the rep. "Show me your watches."

Fifteen minutes later, we walk out with my necklace and a watch for Rafaele, and I announce that I'm done for the day.

The final tally is one point one million dollars.

Inside, I'm doing a little dance complete with pirouettes and high kicks. I can't *wait* to see my husband's reaction.

CHAPTER 16

RAFAELE

JUST AS I pull up to my uncle's house for a meeting with him and one of my capos, my phone rings with a call from my accountant. "Don Messero, your wife is... Well, how do I say it... You see, she's—"

"Get to the point, Carmine," I drawl.

"She's spending a lot of money, sir."

I frown at the phone. "I don't pay you to monitor my wife's spending."

"Of course, sir. I was just doing your books when I saw the transactions go through in real time. I thought it was my duty to call you. We're talking about a large sum."

"How much?"

I can hear him swallow on the other end of the line. "She's already spent nearly half a million dollars, sir."

I sit up straight in my seat and eye the clock on the dash. It's two p.m. *How the fuck...*

"Where?"

"Dior, Hermès, Chanel— Oh, another transaction just came in. She's at Bottega Venetta now. That one is forty-eight thousand."

Incredible. Sandro texted me when they left the house at half past ten. My wife managed to spend over half a million dollars in about three hours?

"As your accountant, I'm advising you lock down the card. If I have your permission to call the bank—"

"No."

"No?"

"No, you don't have my permission. Her ability to deploy capital so efficiently is impressive, isn't it?" Cleo's clearly not going to waste a second of our marriage moping about her situation. Not a day has passed, and she's already on the attack.

Carmine makes a surprised sound. "Sir? I'm not sure I understand."

"Leave the card alone. Whatever my wife wants, my wife gets," I tell him and hang up the phone.

During the meeting, I pull up my banking app and track Cleo's shopping spree in real time. She doesn't let up until about five p.m., when I get another text from Sandro telling me that they're on their way home. I wrap up the meeting, say a quick goodbye to my aunt, and get on the road.

When I walk inside the house, Sabina accosts me with questions about some contractors.

"Where's Cleo?" I interrupt.

Sabina frowns. "I'm not sure. I think I saw Tiny bringing some bags into the living room after they returned."

That's where I find her. My wife is perched on a sofa by the window, a magazine in her lap, and a sea of shopping bags stretched out on the floor before her.

Sabina is still talking to me and not paying attention to where she's going. She nearly trips over one of the bags. "Oh my—"

I grab her elbow to steady her. "Careful."

The house manager gasps as she takes in the scene before her.

Cleo yawns, sits up, and reaches for the small red box on the coffee table. "Welcome home. I've had *such* a long day."

The room is so full with her things, I can't even see the carpet underneath. She must have been waiting for me to come back so that she could see my reaction. I keep my expression carefully neutral as she hops over the bags and stops in front of me.

"Guess what?" she asks.

"What?"

There's a wicked glint in my wife's eyes as she shoves the red box at me. "I got you a gift."

I take it out of her hand.

Cartier.

Ah, yes, the last stop on her rendezvous today.

The expression on her face suggests she's hoping to piss me off with her spending spree. What my wife doesn't know is that I don't give a flying fuck about her spending my money. I have plenty to spare. She'd have to establish a relationship with a yacht broker to really make a dent in my net worth. But I'm not going to make it clear just yet that all her effort was wasted. She's glowing with barely suppressed excitement, and it's fucking adorable.

I fix my face into my usual cold mask and open the box.

"It's a tourbillon in a platinum case," she croons. "When I saw it, I immediately thought of you."

I tilt the watch, examining the intricate craftsmanship. "Why's that?"

She drags her fingertip over the edge. "Cold, precise, calculating. Don't those words ring a bell?"

"I'm flattered. You shouldn't have."

She spreads out her arms. "I felt bad getting all of these things for myself and nothing for you. I hope I didn't overdo it."

I close the box with a loud snap. "I got a call from my accountant after lunch."

Her eyes spark. She looks so fucking eager. I don't think anyone has ever been this excited about the prospect of me losing my temper. "Oh?"

"He was very surprised at the amounts on the transactions. You spent more than a million dollars in one afternoon."

She grins. "Oops. I warned you I like to spend money."

"You did." I step closer and wrap my arm around her waist. "I told him whatever my wife wants, she gets."

The smile on her face melts right off. "You *did*?"

"Anything to make you happy." I lift the box with the watch. "Put it on?"

A notch appears between her brows. She takes the watch out of the box and undoes the clasp. I offer her my wrist, and she slips it on.

"You're not angry?" She can't even keep her disappointment out of her voice.

I tighten my arm around her waist. "Why would I be? Looks great," I murmur, glancing down at the watch. We're so close her nose is practically brushing against my jaw. Her breasts are pressed against my chest, and when I look down her shirt, I have to suppress a groan. God, I can't wait to fuck her.

"Have someone bring the bags up to our bedroom," I command Sabina.

Cleo makes a weak attempt to pull away from me, but I don't let her. I hold her firmly in my arms until the maids appear and start taking the bags away.

"A gift this beautiful deserves a thorough thank you, don't you think?" I ask when we're alone.

Her eyes widen. "Hold o—"

I crush my lips against hers and slide my tongue inside her mouth.

Her sweet taste floods my senses. I push my fingers into her copper hair and tighten my fist, making it impossible for her to escape me.

Not that she's trying to. I don't know if it's because I took her by surprise or because her body knows what she wants far better than her mind does, but she melts against me just like she did in the church and lets me pillage her mouth.

Her heat seeps through the fabric of my suit and sets me on fire. She feels so good in my arms. Images of her flawless body flash in front of my eyes, and my cock twitches. I press it against her thigh so that she knows exactly what she does to me.

When a maid reappears, I break the kiss and press my lips to her ear. "Your mouth is the best thing I've ever tasted. But I think I'll enjoy the taste of your sweet cunt even more."

She chokes and then extracts herself from my arms. "Keep dreaming," she stammers, her chest rising and falling with harsh breaths. She picks up a few of the remaining bags and practically sprints upstairs. So eager to get away from me. But I have no intention of letting her go.

"Leave the rest for now," I say to the maid.

I prowl after Cleo, enter the bedroom, and slam the door shut behind me.

She whirls around. "What are you doing?" she demands, no longer in a good mood. Her skin is still flushed from our kiss.

I take my jacket off and throw it over a chair. She notices the guns strapped to my chest and her eyes widen.

I move toward the ottoman, aka her nest, and sink down in the armchair beside it.

"You spent my money," I say in a low voice.

Red creeps up her cheeks. She keeps looking at my guns, like she's worried I'll shoot her. "So you *are* angry. Were you holding back because we had an audience?"

I shake my head. "That black card is yours. Use it as you see fit. You are my wife, and you will never lack anything."

The red turns deeper, and she swallows.

I spread my legs. "But you're going to show me what I paid for." There's no way she bought modest dresses to impress me with her demureness. She wants to play games? Let's see how well she does when I turn the tables on her.

"Now, Cleo," I growl when she doesn't move.

She glares at me but grabs a few bags and disappears inside the bathroom. When she comes out a few minutes later, my fingertips dig into the armrests.

Fuck.

She's in a long-sleeved black dress that covers most of her, but it molds to her banging body, highlighting every curve. Her hair cascades down her shoulders, wild copper curls that nearly reach her narrow waist.

I've never seen a woman as beautiful. Every drop of blood in my body rushes downward.

I lean forward. "Spin around."

She does, slowly showing me her body from every angle.

I drag my thumb over my bottom lip. "Did you buy what you're wearing underneath too?"

She gives a jerky nod.

My fingers twitch. "Then I want to see it."

Tension simmers between us. I challenge her with my gaze and wait to see if she's brave enough to take off her clothes in front of me.

Again.

She did it without hesitation two nights ago, but now she doesn't look so sure. She shifts her weight from one foot to another and blows out a breath.

I arch my brow. *No?*

Her gaze narrows. She reaches behind her, and the soft clicking noise of a zipper being opened pours through the room.

She moves slowly. Carefully. As if she wants to make a point that she's not in any rush to obey my command. She pushes the dress over one shoulder, then the other. Pulls one arm out of a sleeve, then the other.

I have to hold in a groan when I see what she's wearing underneath.

Her bra is a scrap of see-through lace. Her hard little nipples protrude through the thin fabric, and my mouth goes dry at the sight. She shimmies her hips out of the dress, lets it fall to her feet, and takes two delicate steps out of it. Her hands fall to her hips. Her expression is pure defiance.

Fuck me.

I drag my palm over my jaw and drink in her body, inch by perfect inch.

Her eyes glint with something dangerous. She glides her palms over her sides and curls her fingers over the edges of her lace panties before gently hiking them higher on her hips. "Do you like it?"

I know what she's doing with that husky voice and those bedroom eyes.

Torturing me.

And still, I fall into her trap.

"Come here." My voice is a rasp.

She takes a few tentative steps toward me, taking her damn time. I open my legs wider and tip my chin downward, signaling for her to stand right there. Her bare thighs brush against the fabric of my slacks.

I'm so fucking hot that I'm sweating through my shirt.

"Closer."

Her knees bump against the edge of the seat between my legs. I'm not sure I'm breathing, but neither is she.

I lift my hand and pluck the little bow at the front of her panties. Then I tip my head back and meet her gaze. "You want to know if I like it?"

"Uh-huh."

"Find out for yourself."

Her gaze drops to my lap, and when she sees the outline of my hard cock, she goes very still. Her fingers twitch.

I sit back, spreading my legs further to give her better access. Seeing how far she'll take this game.

Her desire to prove she's not a coward wins over her nerves. She leans down, giving me a glimpse of her tits, and cups my erection.

I huff out a breath. Without breaking eye contact, she gives me two slow strokes, and something short-circuits inside my brain. I clutch the armrests, my knuckles white with effort. It's impossible to breathe.

"You seem to like it a lot," she says in a velvety voice. She removes her hand and steps away. It takes all of my willpower not to drag her onto my lap.

She turns around and gives me her back. My gaze drops to her ass.

"Enjoy the view," she says over her shoulder. "That's all you'll ever get from me."

CHAPTER 17

CLEO

THAT NIGHT, Rafaele spends a long time in the shower.

My suspicions about what he's doing in there make my face heat, and when he comes out, I make sure I'm buried deep under my duvet on the ottoman.

I thought I'd done so well today, so why does it feel like I failed? He didn't seem to care about all the money I spent, and somehow the day ended up with me standing in front of him in my underwear.

And touching his cock.

Fuck my life.

The worst part is that I felt an embarrassing wetness gather between my legs when I palmed his erection. He was very hard and *very* large.

I wait until I hear his breathing even out and then I dip my fingers inside my panties. Yep, still wet. I bite on my pillow and get myself off as quickly as I can, making sure I don't make a single sound.

It's a good thing Rafaele is out of the house for the next few days, coming home once I'm asleep and leaving before I wake up. I call Gem and Vale a few times to chat and use the rest of my free time to regroup.

On Friday morning, I read over my plan once again. It had seemed so well crafted initially, but now I'm not so sure. I don't know him well enough to know which buttons to press.

I scratch out the bullet point about bankrupting him. It would take me far too long given how much money he has.

Would he care if I redecorated? It appears he barely spends any time at home. I scratch that one out too.

The dog idea is worth exploring, but I'd obviously have to be the one to take care of it, so I should think about whether I'm ready for that kind of commitment.

I wander into the bathroom to brush my teeth. There's a Post-it note on the mirror in the bathroom.

"Pick you up at 7 pm."

It takes me a moment to clue in. I had forgotten about the dinner. I pick up my phone and send him a text.

> Where are we going tonight?

His response comes a minute later.

> Il Caminetto.

Il Caminetto is one of the hottest restaurants in New York right now, and the rumor is it's funded by mob money. But it's all hush-hush since the owner is a big-shot movie producer, and he's the official face of the restaurant group. If I had to guess, I'd say Rafaele is one of the investors.

Is he hoping to parade me around in front of his business partners?

Apprehension tunnels through me. I hate these dog and pony shows where daughters who are nearly of age and new wives are paraded around like some shiny trophies.

Whenever Mamma brought me to something like that, I always acted like I'd been raised by wolves. Eventually, she gave up altogether.

Maybe I should try the same tactic with Rafaele.

My phone buzzes with another message.

Wear that dress you showed me.

My cheeks heat. God, he's such a bastard. Does he want to torture me by reminding me of what happened, or does he just get off on dictating what I wear? I'm not his fucking circus monkey.

My stomach growls, so I head to the kitchen to get a snack. No need to be hungry and angry. Sabina is sitting in the breakfast nook, doing some work.

She looks up from her notebook and rakes her gaze over me. "You went shopping. Didn't you buy something decent to wear around the house?"

She has issues. I'm wearing a pair of booty shorts and a loose T-shirt. What's wrong with that?

I grab an apple. "Get used to it."

"Your parents didn't raise you right, you spoiled, rotten girl."

I take a bite. "They'd probably agree with you."

"Do you know what they all say about you? The don's relatives?"

"No, but I'm sure you're about to tell me all about it."

"They say that once Don Messero gets tired of your body, he'll toss you away and find himself a real lady for a wife."

For some reason, that stings, even though I know better than to care about what people say about me.

"One can hope," I mutter. Although, I'm not sure how he's supposed to get tired of my body if I won't let him touch me.

She scowls. "If I were you, I wouldn't show my face in public. You're a disgrace."

"And you're a miserable old hag. We all have our problems."

She gasps and starts swearing at me, but I just walk away and go back to the bedroom. I don't have time for her. I need to find my outfit for tonight.

The bloody sheets seem to have made no difference to how people perceive me. Maybe some suspected it was all a fraud.

Well, if they insist on calling me a whore, I'll dress like one. The last thing I want anyone to think is that I give a fuck about their judgment.

I take off my clothes and select one of the couture dresses hanging in the closet. Calling it a dress is generous. It's no more than some rhinestone fishnet material that leaves little

143

to the imagination. Maybe it would be okay with some full-coverage underwear and a tank top, but instead, I grab a black lace panties and bra set from La Perla.

When I take in my reflection in the mirror, I know there is zero chance Rafaele will let me go out like this. But it'll be worth trying just to see the look on his face.

Maybe he'll finally snap and "find himself a real lady for a wife."

Seven o'clock rolls around, and I totter out of the room in a pair of sky-high heels. From the top of the staircase, I see Rafaele lounging on the couch below, his phone in his hand. He got a haircut. He looks all neat and trimmed and fucking *edible*.

No, he doesn't. You don't find him attractive at all.

I take a deep breath and clutch the railing as I make my way down the steps.

His gaze snaps to me when I'm halfway down. I thought he'd look shocked, but the only visible reaction I spot is the slight narrowing of his eyes.

My steps slow. He's going to tell me to go back upstairs and change, and I'd rather not do the full climb back up the steps in these heels.

But he doesn't. Instead, he just goes right back to texting on his phone.

Heat creeps up my neck. Who is he texting that's so important? Well, I can't just hover here like an idiot. I take it step-by-step until I get to the bottom landing.

"Ready?" he asks when I stop in front of him.

"Yep."

He stands, his body casting a shadow over mine, and gives me another distracted glance. "I hope you're hungry."

Suddenly, I'm worried this plan is going to backfire spectacularly.

He offers me his arm and leads me to the garage. There, he helps me into his Bugatti and takes the driver's seat.

"Isn't Sandro going to drive us?" I had assumed Sandro and Tiny would accompany us to the restaurant.

"It's his night off," Rafaele says as he starts up the car.

"We're going to Il Caminetto, right?"

"Yes."

"Are you an investor?"

"I am. The owner is a friend of mine."

I eye him suspiciously. So there are definitely going to be people there that he knows. I can't believe he's letting me go out looking like this.

While his eyes are on the road, I glance down at myself. Indecent doesn't even begin to describe it.

Nervously, I start chewing on my nail. The AC is on full blast, and it's fucking *cold*. Why didn't I have the foresight to at least bring a shawl with me? My nipples are rock hard, protruding through the lacy fabric of my bra. I shiver and rub my arms, praying we won't be stuck in traffic, because I'm way too proud to ask Rafaele to turn the temperature up.

We park in what looks to be the back of the restaurant, and Rafaele helps me out of the car. There's no one around us, but the muffled sound of music filters through the door. It sounds like a live jazz band.

He wraps an arm around my waist, his fingers pressing against bare skin. He must notice how stiff I am, because he asks, "Are you all right?"

I give him a tight smile. "Yep."

He stares at me for a beat, and there's a hint of amusement in his eyes before he blinks it away. He grasps the handle of the door and pulls it open.

A dark and narrow hallway greets us. Rafaele's hand is pressed against my lower back, which is a good thing because I'm on the verge of freaking out.

Maybe I took it too far.

What if he's as calm as he is because he's decided to murder me in front of everyone? The hallway is probably only fifteen feet long, but our journey down it feels like an eternity.

And then we step inside the main dining room. It's spectacular. There's an enormous chandelier in the center, mirrors lining the walls, shiny marble floors, and an air of sophistication.

And...it's completely empty.

I blink. This can't be right. This is the hottest restaurant in the city. People book it three months in advance. But there's no one here except the band, and they're playing a jazz tune...blindfolded.

I choke on my saliva.

Rafaele curls a possessive hand over my waist as he surveys the space around us. "What do you think? The architect really outdid himself, didn't he?"

I'm still processing. "It's empty."

His gaze falls to me. "Did you really think I'd let another man see you dressed like this?" His eyes darken, and he leans down, placing his lips close to my ear. "This body belongs to me. I warned you I don't share."

"But how?" I croak.

"A simple text to the owner telling him to clear the restaurant for tonight."

"And he agreed?"

"He didn't have a choice." He slides his hand into mine, leads me to a table, and pulls out a chair. "Have a seat."

I sit down slowly, my gaze drifting back to the blindfolded band. They're playing like nothing's wrong.

This is insane. My husband might actually be as crazy as I am. I blink at him like I'm seeing him for the first time. "How can they play like that?"

Rafaele takes a seat across from me. "They're professionals."

I have no words.

A satisfied smirk appears on his handsome face. "Let's order. I'm starving."

CHAPTER 18

RAFAELE

THE MOMENT I saw Cleo in that outfit, I saw red. Did she really think I would ever allow anyone to see her looking like that?

Then I understood. She was trying to provoke me again, just like she did when she went on that over-the-top shopping spree. I kept my expression indifferent and quickly made the necessary arrangements. No one would see her showing off the body that I fucking own, and I wouldn't give her the satisfaction of seeing me riled up.

I'm getting increasingly ready for this game to be over. The sooner she understands her antics won't get her anywhere, the quicker I'll get what she's been denying me.

A female waitress comes over, clearly nervous about serving us. She pours us some champagne and does her best to avoid looking at Cleo as she takes our orders.

Before she hurries away, I pull up the camera app on my phone and hand it to her. "I'd like a photo of me and my wife."

The waitress gives me a tight smile. "Of course. Where would you like to take the photo?"

Cleo scowls at me. "That's really not necessa—"

I pull her chair toward me with one hand, lift her out of her seat, and deposit her onto my lap. She makes a strangled sound.

"Right here," I drawl as I curl my hand over Cleo's hip. My palm meets warm skin through the gaps in her dress. "Smile, darling."

The waitress snaps a few quick photos and hands me the phone back before hurrying away.

"I'll send them to you."

Cleo scrambles off my lap. "I don't want them," she snaps.

Her phone buzzes on the table.

"Too late."

She shoves her phone into the purse.

I raise my champagne glass to Cleo. She doesn't reciprocate. Instead, she glowers at me. Her arms are crossed, pushing up her chest in the most alluring way.

I take a moment to admire her body. Her skin is like silk— luminous, soft, unblemished except for a smattering of freckles here and there. So fucking lovely.

So fucking *mine*.

There's a hint of muscle in her arms and shoulders, and since her dress is an abomination that covers nothing, I can see an outline of her abs.

They'll flex beautifully when she's on top of me, riding my cock.

My fingers tighten around the stem of my glass. "Anything wrong?" I ask.

"No," she snaps.

I lean in closer, savoring her anger and frustration. She's losing this game, and she knows it. "Tell me, what are you trying to accomplish with all this?"

She turns up her little nose. "I don't know what you mean."

"Don't lie. The shopping spree. The dress." I make a vague wave. "Is this the kind of thing that worked on your parents?"

When she doesn't answer, I know I guessed right. "Your father is a weak man. When you acted out, he had to hide you away from the world. I don't need to hide anything, Cleo. I can simply bend the world to my will."

Her cheeks redden. "You're way too full of yourself."

"I'm only stating facts." I take a sip of champagne. "If you tell me what you want, maybe I'll give it to you."

Her gaze narrows. "A divorce."

"Anything that's in the realm of possibility?"

"Can't you just send me to live somewhere away from you?"

"What for?"

"So that I can be happy."

"Why would that make you happy?"

"Because I can never be happy here with you. I'm your prisoner. I don't have any freedom, and I don't do well in captivity."

"I don't see how this is any different than what you had when you lived back home."

Her gaze sparks. "Do you think I liked my life at home?" Anguish slips into her tone. "Do you know how often I wished I was born to a different mother? One that didn't try to fit me into a mold that I resented with every fiber of my being?"

I know a thing or two about being forced to fit into a mold by a parent, but unlike Cleo, I allowed myself to be poured right into it. There was no other choice for me. Not if I wanted my mother to survive.

I give her a pointed once-over. "It doesn't seem like she succeeded."

"No," she says sullenly. "But I never got what I wanted either. So we both lost."

"You are my wife, and you belong with me. There's nothing you can do that will make me send you away, so I suggest you stop wasting your time trying."

Something crumples inside her eyes. Hope?

Without thinking, I reach for her knee under the table and place my hand on it. Then I realize what I'm doing. I'm trying to comfort her. I can't remember the last time I comforted anyone.

A prickle of unease spreads over my skin.

No, this makes sense. This might be the quickest way past her defenses, and that's why I'm doing it. She lets me keep it there for a few seconds before she jerks her leg to the side.

I hold back a sigh. So fucking stubborn. "All right. If you could do anything, what would you do?"

She brushes her hair over her shoulder and levels me with a penetrating gaze. "Before I married you, I wanted to go to college."

Sending her to college is out of the question. She'd be a target if she went, and I have no desire to send her somewhere where other men can ogle her.

"What for?"

"To study business. I wanted to be a music manager."

"Music manager?"

"Yes. The people who manage the careers of singers and bands."

"Why that?"

"Because I wanted to help make sure artists don't get taken advantage of. Haven't you heard what happened to Britney Spears?"

"I don't make a point of staying up to date on gossip."

She looks offended. "It's not gossip. She's one of the biggest stars in the world, and for years, her family took advantage of her and controlled her life. If it could happen to her, it could happen to anyone. My friends and I used to go to marches in support of her, trying to bring attention to the situation."

"Your parents allowed you to do that?"

"Yes, after they got sick of my whining. But I would have gone anyway. Britney needed our help."

My lips twitch. Maybe she saw parallels between the pop star's situation and her own.

God, she really is a bit strange. And she's got that youthful idealism. Sometimes I forget how young she is. I was never idealistic, not even at her age. My father showed me the ugliness of the world before I reached puberty. But I like her passion. Maybe there's a way to channel it somewhere more productive.

"I have someone you can help."

"Who?"

"One of my cousins. Her name is Loretta. She owns a custom clothing store, and it's not doing well. I can't keep bailing her out forever. She'll have to close down if she can't turn it around. She's not a celebrity or a musician, but she could use some help."

Cleo's eyes flicker with curiosity. "Really? What kind of help?"

I shrug. "An extra set of hands to help at the shop, and someone with a new perspective on how she's running things there."

She glances down at her lap and refolds her napkin. "Are you sure she'll want me there?"

"She doesn't have a choice. She's got enough money to pay for the next three months of rent, and then she'll have to vacate the space."

"You'd let her fail like that?"

"Failure is the unavoidable stepping stone for success. Me treating Loretta's business like a charity isn't doing her any favors."

Cleo tips her head to the side. "Wait, so you allowed her to start this business?"

"Yes, when I became don. She'd asked my father for permission for years, but he always refused her."

"Why didn't you refuse? It goes against your family's traditions, doesn't it?"

"I don't believe traditions should be immutable. It's been more than a century since my family came to America, and the world has changed since then. With every generation, certain traditions fall by the wayside. And I've seen how women operate in the Camorra now. They are allowed to get involved in the business if they so wish, and many become powerful assets. Why deprive my family of that kind of potential advantage?"

No one in the Cosa Nostra would argue that the Camorristas in Italy have set up a formidable operation, and a lot of that has to do with their willingness to adapt their methods to the changing world instead of blindly sticking to tradition.

I smooth my hand down my tie. "If a woman comes to me and has a plan for how to contribute to the business, I am willing to consider it. But the situation with my cousin hasn't gone well. I took a risk on her, displeasing her parents in the process. If she can't turn her business around, it will make it harder for me to give other women a chance like that again."

Cleo's looking at me like I've grown antlers.

I'll admit, the arrangement with Loretta is an experiment that's on the verge of failure. She's unmarried and her parents don't like that I allowed her to delay getting paired off to someone, but I wanted to give this a try. When Loretta approached me initially, I thought she had what it took to make the business a success. But it's been nearly a year since she opened the shop, and things are not looking good.

I top off Cleo's champagne. "So? What do you think?"

She picks up the glass and takes a long pull. "I know what you're doing. Helping your cousin isn't the same as going to college, no matter how you present it to me."

I lean back and cross my arms over my chest. "The way I see it, you have two choices. Spend the rest of your life being miserable and wishing for something you can never have, or you can attempt to make the most of the hand you've been dealt. I already said I have no intention of keeping you caged. The only cage you're in is the one you've got in your own head."

She drains the rest of her champagne and mulls that over. I wait. I think I managed to get through to her.

At last, she gives me a stiff nod. "I'll try to help."

Finally. "I'll let her know to expect you on Monday morning."

Something unexpected happens. Cleo smiles at me.

It's not a full-blown grin, but it's enough to make something shift inside my chest.

A warm feeling washes over me. And as I'm admiring how that smile lights up her whole face, the window shatters.

CHAPTER 19

CLEO

EVERYTHING HAPPENS QUICKLY. One moment, I'm wondering if maybe Rafaele isn't exactly who I thought he is, and the next, I'm on the ground.

Someone is shooting up the restaurant.

"Fuck," Rafaele growls, his body pressing down on top of me. "Stay down." He's already got a gun in hand, and he's looking past me, trying to spot our attackers.

On the other side of the restaurant, the band trips over each other as they rush to flee through the emergency exit behind the stage. I'm about to yell at them to get down when one of them is shot in the back of his skull. His brain splatters everywhere.

Oh God. I squeeze my eyes shut as bile rises up my throat. I'm never going to unsee that.

More gunshots ring out, sounding closer than before.

The thought I might meet the same fate as that musician in a few minutes makes me shake uncontrollably.

"Cleo, look at me." There's no fear in Rafaele's voice.

I crack open my eyes.

His gaze is hard, and he looks completely in control of himself. "I'm going to get us out of here. As long as you do exactly what I say, you'll be safe. Do you understand?"

My ragged breath puffs out against his lips. "Yes."

"Good." Rafaele snakes an arm around my waist and rolls us toward the closest wall. I clutch onto his strong body, fear and adrenaline mixing inside my veins as gunshots ring out around us.

When my back hits the wall, he lets go of me and moves to a crouching position with his gun at the ready. The expression on his face sends a shiver down my spine. That's the expression of a man who first killed at age thirteen. One who will happily kill again now.

"Crawl behind the bar." He nudges me with his free hand. "I'm going to take them out."

My lungs constrict. "What? We're splitting up?"

"Go, Cleo," he growls.

His eyes meet mine, and it's like someone pressed the mute key on the chaos around us. My mind quiets for a brief moment.

"Stay down, no matter what you hear," he says, his voice ringing in my ears. "Got it?"

I give him a shaky nod. "Okay."

157

He waits until I'm safely behind the bar and then springs into action. My stomach does a somersault when he throws himself into the center of the dining room and starts firing back.

What is he doing? There's nothing between him and our attackers.

A few screams ring out. Rafaele runs to a table and flips it, using it as a shield. I hope it's thick enough to block the bullets raining down on him.

He peers around the table and takes a few calculated shots. I like to think I hear someone grunt in pain every time he fires, but that's probably just my imagination. Then he runs forward and disappears out of my field of vision.

I can't see what's going on. Time slows to a glacial pace. I chew on my nails. Is he okay?

That groan. Did that sound like him?

The gunshots are farther away now. Funny how a few minutes ago, I hoped they would stop, and now I'm hoping they won't. At least if they're firing at each other, it means Rafaele is still alive.

I can't believe he's trying to fight back on his own. I can't see how many men are shooting, but he's definitely outnumbered.

My chest tightens.

He's going to die.

Fuck.

I can't just sit here while he's putting his life at risk.

We need backup. And if anyone's going to call for it, it's me.

I glance across the room. My purse with my phone is on the ground a few feet away from where my chair fell when the shots first rang out. If I get it, I can call Sandro.

Fear wraps its icy fingers around my stomach.

I can do this. We need help. Rafaele won't be able to hold them off for long by himself.

Before I can talk myself out of it, I dart out from behind the bar and lunge for my purse. My body slides along the marble floor and sharp pain blooms along my belly.

What is that?

There's no time to check. Ignoring the pain, I snatch my bag off the ground and crawl back to my hiding spot. My hands shake as I take out my phone and dial Sandro.

"Hello?"

"Get to Il Caminetto right now. We're getting shot at."

"What? Fuck. Okay, I'm on my way! I'm not too far." He hangs up.

I drop the phone to the ground and realize it's gotten eerily quiet.

Heart-crushing fear seizes me. Is Rafaele dead? He must have run out of bullets. He only had two guns on him.

The backs of my eyes prickle. Stupid idiot. We could have tried to escape out the back together.

Someone is walking toward me. The sound of their deliberate steps resonates through the room, growing closer and closer. I press my back against the bar and jerk my knees close to my chest.

Ow!

I glance down at myself and my heart drops. There's blood *all* down my front.

Was I hit by a bullet?

Oh no. No, no, no. Was I shot? I must have been.

I'm so pumped up on adrenaline, I didn't even feel it.

The footsteps halt. "What the *fuck*?"

I yelp, my gaze jumping to Rafaele. Relief floods through me. He's all right. Somehow, he's got less blood on him than I do.

He sinks to the floor beside me, his jaw clenched and his face pale, and clutches my shoulders. "Why are you bleeding?" There's a strange waver to his voice.

"I don't know." My throat tightens with panic. There's so much blood. "I think I was shot."

Rafaele growls a curse and pulls out a knife.

I grasp his arm. "Tell Gem, Vale, and Vince that I love them."

He ignores me, his expression a mask of pure concentration. He cuts through the glimmering cords of my dress and pushes them aside to expose my belly.

My gaze jolts back up to his face. I don't want to look at the wound. I can't. I'm going to be sick.

"Rafaele," I breathe.

He grabs a cloth napkin from the bar and starts gently prodding my stomach.

"*Ouch.*"

"I'm sorry," he says gruffly. "I need to clean up the blood so that I can see what's going on."

I'm dying, that's what's going on. How many times did I say I'd rather die than be a mob wife? Now, here I am, less than one week into my marriage, bleeding out on the floor of a restaurant, and I feel like an idiot.

I *don't* want to die.

"You're not as horrible as I thought you'd be," I squeeze out.

Rafaele doesn't answer. He's so focused on what he's doing, I'm not even sure he heard me.

"Maybe if we had more time," I whisper. "Maybe if I got to know you better..." I don't know what I'm trying to say. Everyone says you're supposed to have clarity on your deathbed, but I'm more confused than ever. I reach for his wrist and wrap my hand around it.

Finally, he lifts his gaze to mine. There's no coldness in it. Just relief.

"You're going to be fine."

I shake my head. He's in denial. He couldn't defend me, and made men don't know how to handle failure.

"I'm dying." My voice is weak. I use the last of my strength to cup his cheek. "Don't let my death haunt you for the rest of your life. You did the best you could."

His lips twitch. "You're not dying." He presses a kiss to the inside of my wrist. "Who knew you were so dramatic."

My brows furrow. I don't understand. "What? But I'm bleeding. I feel faint."

"Flesh wounds. You somehow got shards of glass in your belly, but they're not very deep. A lot of people feel faint when they see blood if they're not used to it." He kisses my palm this time, ignoring that it's covered in my blood. "How did this happen?"

Is he serious? I glance down at myself even though I feel like I might puke. There's no bullet hole. Only glass.

"I-I slid along the floor to get my purse so that I could call for help."

He huffs an annoyed breath. "Why would you do that? I had the situation under control."

My cheeks grow warm. Everything grows warm. "I didn't know that. I thought they were going to kill you!"

"It was just three guys. Two are dead and one got away." His eyes flicker with amusement and something softer that steals the air out of my lungs. "You were worried about me."

Worried? Was I worried? Yes, I was. But now I'm not worried. Now I'm just embarrassed.

"I didn't want to die here with you," I mutter. "I was only worried about myself."

He shakes his head, his lips lifting at the corners. "You said I wasn't as horrible as you thought I was. And what else were you trying to say? Something about us having more time?" He leans down and kisses my forehead. "Don't worry, we've got all the time in the world, *tesoro mio*."

His treasure.

A cocktail of emotions fills my chest. "Don't call me that." I try to shove him away, but he shushes me, his expression once again turning serious.

"Stop. You shouldn't move too much, or you might lodge the glass in more. We need to get you cleaned up."

The doors to the restaurant burst open, and men with guns stream in, led by a frazzled-looking Sandro. "Boss!" He jogs over to us. "You two okay? Nero is on his way."

Rafaele covers me with his jacket. "My wife is hurt," he says to Sandro as he lifts me off the ground and cradles me to his chest. "One of the shooters got away. Clean this mess and find him."

Sandro rakes his gaze over me, but he can't see the mess on my stomach under Rafaele's jacket. Still, his jaw firms. "We'll get him."

Rafaele's grip on me tightens. "I want him brought to me alive so that I can carve his body into pieces after I find out who he works for," he says, his voice dangerously low.

Ice threads through my insides. If I were the attacker who got away, I'd be shitting my pants right about now.

"You got it," Sandro says and rushes away.

Rafaele's cold blue eyes drop back to my face. Cold on the surface, but there's warmth inside their depths.

Feelings surge through my chest, raw and unwelcome. There's no fighting them back. I want to look away, but I can't move a muscle. He holds me captive with his gaze, peering so deeply inside of me that I'm certain he can read each one of my traitorous emotions as if they were written on a page. Nerves crawl beneath my skin. I'm not sure what

I'm more nervous about—getting all that glass out of my skin, or what will follow.

Because I can already feel an impending change between us, the way one sees the ocean swell and knows there's nothing that will stop the coming wave.

CHAPTER 20

RAFAELE

I RACE DOWN the freeway with Cleo lying on the reclined seat beside me.

Every time I look at her pale face, rage pulses inside my veins. I will destroy whoever is behind this attack, and I won't give them a quick death.

The image of Cleo covered in blood flashes in front of my eyes. I can't blame her for saying she got shot—she was in shock, probably still is—but my chest got really fucking tight when I thought her life was in danger, and I didn't like that.

I didn't like that at all.

Instead of seeing it purely like a problem that needed to be solved, I saw it as...something else.

"How are you doing, *tesoro*?"

"Stop calling me that," she grumbles.

Well, at least she's well enough to talk back to me. I grab my phone and dial Doc's number. Her wounds didn't seem deep, but he'll need to treat them and give her a full physical.

"Hello?" It's his assistant who answers.

"Put Doc on the line," I order.

"He's in the operating room, Mr. Messero," she says. "I'm sor—"

"It's not a fucking request."

There's a beat of silence before she says, "Okay, one moment."

I tap my fingers against the wheel as I wait.

"Mr. Messero? What is it?"

"I need you to come over."

"I'm in the operating room."

"I know. Doesn't matter."

"I'm in the middle of a—"

"I don't give a fuck. Get someone else to take over or let them die, for all I care. My wife is hurt. We'll be home in twenty minutes, and you better be there waiting for us." I hang up. Annoyance pulses at my temples.

"Rafaele?"

I turn to look at Cleo. "What?"

Her eyes are wide. "Are you insane? I don't want an innocent person to die because of me."

"Trust me, if it's Doc working on them, they're far from innocent."

There's a line between her brows. "I can wait."

"Five minutes ago, you thought you were dying, and now you think you can wait to get your injuries treated? No, you can't. You're bleeding and in shock."

Her brows rise up her forehead. I realize that my voice is raised and my heart is pounding inside my chest. I crack my neck and swallow past a foreign tightness in my throat. What the fuck is wrong with me?

"It's my fault." The words are pouring out of me. "I should have let Sandro drive us. I made us a target." I shut my mouth and clutch the wheel tighter. Cleo could have died tonight. All it would have taken is one well-aimed shot.

I suck in a deep breath. Why am I thinking about what-ifs? We're safe. She's safe. I need to calm the fuck down.

"You said it was his day off." Her voice is quiet.

I grind my teeth. "I lied. I told him I didn't need him tonight because I didn't want him seeing you in that dress." I can't even look at her as I say those words. I'm supposed to protect her. Instead, I got her hurt.

She doesn't say anything for the rest of the drive home. Maybe she's processing how I've failed her. The thought lodges a knife inside my gut.

When we pull into the garage, Sabina and one of the maids are already waiting for us.

"Where is Doc?" I ask as I help Cleo out of the Bugatti.

"In your bedroom," Sabina answers. "He's waiting for you."

I brush past them with Cleo in my arms and take her straight upstairs.

Doc's already got all of his supplies laid out. "Put her down here," he says, pointing at the bed. He adjusts his glasses. "What happened?"

I lay Cleo down and lift my jacket to show him the wounds.

Fuck, they look awful. "She cut herself on some glass. I don't think the cuts are deep, but there's a lot of them."

Doc tsks. "All right. Let's get these cleaned up and see if she needs stitches."

My head pounds. I don't understand what's wrong with me. This is far from the first time I've been shot at, but I've never been this shaken up. I glance down at my hands. They're covered in dried blood.

Her blood.

I take a step toward the bathroom. I need to wash this off. "I'll be right back," I say gruffly.

In the bathroom, I scrub the mix of dirt and blood off my hands and roll up my sleeves. Most of the blood on my shirt also belongs to Cleo. I fucked up. As a husband and as a don. I should have been more careful. Guilt surges back into my consciousness. I clench my jaw against it.

No.

I don't have the luxury of feeling guilty. Feelings have no place in the life of a don. I learned that a long time ago.

My breathing deepens. Slowly, I push all the useless emotions out of my mind until all that remains is a blank canvas. A canvas where I can paint whatever I want.

When I come out, Doc is rummaging in his bag. "She's got eleven lacerations on her stomach. A few will require stitches and might result in light scarring. She also appears to have a concussion."

I rewind what happened in the dining room inside my head. Now that I've calmed down, it's easy, like watching a movie. "She fell hard to the ground at one point. When I first heard the shots, I acted on instinct and pulled her down."

Doc takes out a syringe. "Well, you probably saved both of your lives by doing that. I'm confident Cleo will make a full recovery."

The tension in my shoulders eases. "Good."

He sits back down on the edge of the bed. "I'm going to get the glass out and clean your wounds."

Cleo presses back against her pillow. "What's that?"

"Just a local anesthetic."

She swallows. "I don't like needles."

"If I don't numb you, it'll hurt a lot more."

She looks at me like she's hoping I'll tell Doc not to inject her. I can't do that. He needs to treat her.

"You'll be fine. It's just a few shots," I say.

My dismissive remark doesn't land well. Hurt flashes in her eyes, but then it's gone. Her gaze shutters. A prolonged silence fills the room, and I feel like the shittiest husband in the world.

What the fuck am I supposed to do?

Doc clears his throat. "Maybe it would help if you sat beside Cleo."

I clench my jaw. Of course. She needs to be comforted. I can do that. It's my duty, isn't it? I walk around the bed, climb in on the other side, and wrap my arm around her shoulders. She stiffens for a moment before she relaxes into my touch.

"Ready?" Doc asks.

She stares at the syringe. "No."

I run my thumb over her upper arm. "Don't look at the needle. Look at me."

She huffs a breath before she obeys. Our eyes lock. She's so close that I can count her freckles. She looks tired and worn out, but she's still fucking stunning.

My wife.

My gaze drops to her lips. The doctor is saying something, but I can't hear him over the whooshing inside my ears.

Kiss her.

Cleo sucks in a breath. "Ow."

I tear my gaze away from her face and down to her belly.

"Just one more," Doc says. "Okay, done. Now, I'll sew you up." He pulls out a needle and some medical thread.

When Cleo sees them, her eyes widen. "I've never had this done to me before," she says, sounding panicked. She presses into me. "Oh fuck, oh fuck, ohhhh—"

Doc squeezes one of her wounds shut and pushes the tip of the needle into her skin.

Cleo jerks. "Fuck! That hurt!"

I have to bite back a curse aimed at Doc. My nerves are stretched taut.

"I haven't even pierced your skin," the man says.

"I'm pretty sure you did."

Doc blows out a frustrated breath. "This is going to take a long time if you keep jumping every time I bring the needle close to you."

Do something. "Do you want me to do it?" I ask.

Slowly, she turns to look at me. "You've done this before?"

"Yes. Many times." Sometimes, I don't have the luxury of having Doc a fifteen-minute drive away. I've lost count how many times I've had to stitch myself or Nero up.

I ease my arm from around Cleo and get off the bed. "I'll take it from here, Doc. It'll make my wife more comfortable. Why don't you go downstairs for a bit?"

He nods. "I'll be back in fifteen to check on how you did."

I take Doc's spot and pick up the needle.

Cleo squeezes her eyes shut. "I feel like such a coward."

"A lot of people are scared of needles."

"You're not. You're not fazed by any of this, are you? You were so steady back at the restaurant."

Is that what she thinks? I didn't feel very steady when I saw her lying on the ground covered in her own blood.

I shake off that uncomfortable thought and refocus on the task at hand. "Take a deep breath."

She scrunches up her face. "I think I'm going to throw up."

"You're not. This will only take a few seconds. Breathe, Cleo. I know you're strong enough to handle this."

She darts her hand out and wraps it over my knee before giving me the smallest of nods. "Do it."

I bring the needle closer and pierce her skin. She winces but keeps breathing deeply like I told her to.

"Good girl," I murmur. "Just keep breathing."

The pace of her breathing speeds up. Her fingernails dig into my leg, but I don't show any sign of pain. If she needs to use me as her stress ball, she's more than welcome to do it.

I work as fast as I can to sew her up. It only takes me about ten minutes before I'm snipping the last thread.

I put everything away on the nightstand. "All done."

Slowly, she peels her eyes open. "Thanks."

What is she thanking me for? "I'm the one who got you into this mess."

She stares at me and swallows. "It wasn't your fault," she says. "Don't blame yourself. I forced your hand by showing up to dinner in that dress. If I hadn't, we would have been driven by Sandro, and the hitmen probably wouldn't have attacked if the restaurant had been filled with other patrons."

I place my hand over hers and lace our fingers together. "I liked that dress."

Surprise slips into her expression before it morphs into wry amusement. "Admit it, you're glad it's ruined."

"Not at all." She looked sexy as hell in it. "I'll buy you a replacement, and next time, you'll wear it in the privacy of our own home." I lean closer. "Without anything beneath it."

Finally, some color returns to her cheeks.

The door opens, and Doc reappears. "How are we doing?"

The simmering tension around us bursts like a balloon. I let go of her hand and stand.

"Take a look."

He comes over to examine my work and then gives me a pleased nod. "Good. The concussion is my main concern. I'd like to keep an eye on her for the next few days."

"Keep your phone close. If her condition worsens, I want you on hand."

"Very well." He leaves and shuts the door behind him.

I drag my fingers through my hair. I need a shower, a strong drink, and a good eight hours of sleep, but for now, I'll settle on just the first. I unbutton my shirt and toss it in the hamper.

Cleo gasps. "You're hurt too."

I glance down. It takes me a moment to realize she's talking about my arm. There's a shallow wound where a bullet grazed me on my biceps, but I barely feel it. "It's a scratch."

"Let me see," she demands stubbornly. "Come here, or I'm going to come over to you."

"Stay still," I growl.

It really is nothing. The only annoying thing is that the cut bisected one of my tattoos. A dark, hooded figure levitating over a bed of bones.

My father.

Cleo's eyes roam the wound and the image beneath it. "Your tattoo is ruined."

I shrug. "Adds character, don't you think?"

"Do you need me to stitch you up?"

"I think you might cause more damage than the bullet."

Her cheeks turn pink. "Rude. Well, at least get the doctor to do it."

"It's fine. I can do it myself in the bathroom."

She purses her lips but doesn't argue.

In the shower, the water runs pink for a while, but I know the cut isn't anything to worry about. I press my palms against the wall of the shower and let the water run down my back.

She's fine. The doctor will make sure she has a smooth recovery. There's no logical reason to worry at this point.

There's nothing logical about wanting to punch a wall either, but here I am. Why the fuck am I so riled up? I grab a bar of soap and scrub at my skin. *Get it together, Messero.*

When I come out of the bathroom, Cleo has changed into a T-shirt, and she's lying stiffly on the bed. Her gaze darts to me, and her eyes widen when she realizes I'm only wearing a pair of boxers.

I wonder how she'd react if I walked over to her and kissed her right now.

She wouldn't push me away. What happened tonight chipped at her walls. Maybe even brought them down completely. But I don't feel like playing our game tonight. Not when she's weak and vulnerable.

"I'll sleep on the ottoman," I offer, dragging my fingers through my wet hair.

She shakes her head. "You're injured too."

"I told you it's nothing."

"Rafe." Her jaw firms. "The bed is huge." She reaches across and pulls back the duvet on the other side. "Just get in."

I stare at her for a long moment. She doesn't back down.

All right. If she insists, I'm not going to fight her about it. I walk around the bed and climb in. A moment later, she turns off the light and darkness wraps around us. Soon, her breathing slows and deepens. I lie there for a while, staring at the ceiling and revisiting old memories that made me who I am. Memories of my mother and my father. Memories of that lamplit bedroom and my bare feet against the smooth hardwood floor.

I'll stop when you stop your whining, boy.

I exhale a heavy breath and shut my eyes.

CHAPTER 21

RAFAELE

I SLAM the car door shut and inhale the crisp morning air that's mingled with the scent of the river. Today's going to be a long fucking day, and I woke up wanting to burn off some energy before I get started.

It's been three days since the attack, and the whole fucking thing's been harder to shake off than I anticipated. Probably because we still have no idea who's pulling on the strings.

Nero pulls into the parking lot of the gym in his black Jeep and waves at me through the window.

We walk into the building, the only ones here since it's not even six a.m. The owner, Mike, is sitting behind the check-in desk, doing something on his computer, and he waves us in without coming out to chat. He knows the only time we're here this early is if something's up.

I start warming up on a bag. "Any news?" The need to end whoever shot up Il Caminetto has been churning inside my chest ever since the incident occurred.

The two men I killed were freelancers, assassins for hire who work for anyone willing to pay them. They were professionals, and their business model relies on discretion. Not that we haven't tried to trace them, but so far, we've gotten nowhere.

Nero jabs at the bag beside mine. "I've got four of our best guys looking, but there's nothing so far."

"Who the fuck would try a move like this? My initial guess would be Ferraro, but he's usually far more subtle."

"I doubt it's Ferraro," Nero says, jumping away from the swinging bag. "I've spoken to Joe since it happened, and they seem more willing than ever to put a truce in place. They heard about the shooting, and Joe was quick to deny any involvement."

"You trust him?"

"I do."

I glance at Nero. He's good at getting an accurate read on people, so I have no reason to doubt his assessment, but if not Ferraro, then who?

"The Bratva might still be holding a grudge about us not allowing them to invest in the restaurant," Nero says.

"That wouldn't surprise me, but I doubt they'd risk bringing war to their doorstep over one deal."

"Their power is growing. I heard they've managed to push their way into the racetracks in Jersey."

"I don't give a fuck about that. As long as they're not pushing up against Garzolo's territory, they can do as they please over there."

Nero lands a few shots against the bag. "Speaking of, I paid him a visit yesterday."

Garzolo is one of the obvious suspects, especially after our last interaction. "And?"

"He was at his house in the Hamptons with the wife. They had a party. Plenty of witnesses. None of them saw him take a single call. Everyone said he looked at ease."

"We should keep a close eye on him. If this is his work, he'll try again." I tip my head in the direction of the ring. "Let's spar."

We climb under the ropes and get in position.

"How the fuck did they know Cleo and I would be there?"

Nero jabs at me, but I easily step out of the way. He's bigger than me, but I've got speed as my advantage.

"It had to be someone at the restaurant or Andres," he says. "They were the only ones who knew you'd cleared the place and that you'd be in the dining room practically alone. Whoever is behind this wouldn't have risked attacking if it had been a full house."

I bounce on my feet, looking for an opening. "I trust Andres." The owner of Il Caminetto isn't someone who'd ever go behind my back. He knows better than that. "He wouldn't try anything like this. You talked to the staff already?"

"Yeah. They all seem good."

"What about the band?" I throw a punch.

Nero ducks. "I haven't talked to them yet, but that's a good idea. As far as I know, they play there often. I'll reach out."

I hold his gaze as we circle each other. "Good. Keep me posted."

His jaw flexes. "I'm sorry, Rafe. I should have more by now. I know this is important. We'll find the bastard responsible for it, I promise you."

I grunt in response and nearly clip him in the chin.

He jumps back. "How's Cleo?"

"Recovering." We've slept in the same bed ever since the attack, so I guess there's at least one good thing that came out of it.

But I haven't pushed it any further. *Yet.* As soon as she's feeling better, I'm going to bring our little game to a quick close.

"She's still getting headaches, so the doctor recommended another few days of bed rest." This time, my punch lands against Nero's kidney, and he sucks in a harsh breath. I give him a second to recover before I land two more punches against his ribs.

"Fuck, Rafe," Nero grunts, backing away.

I lunge forward again, swinging my fist at Nero's head. He ducks and pivots to land a hard punch against my ribs. I grunt but don't falter, quickly recovering and landing a few more hits on Nero's gut. We continue sparring until sweat's pouring down my face and my muscles burn with exertion.

I'm supposed to drive up to Albany right after the sparring session, but when Nero and I finish, I get an inexplicable urge to see my wife.

I climb into my car and look out at the Hudson River. My head is way too fucking wrapped up in her.

It's only gotten worse since the attack. When I saw Cleo bleeding on the ground, it felt as if someone had wrenched my ribcage open and pressed the cold, unyielding barrel of a gun right against my heart. She couldn't die. The possibility of her being gone had rooted me to the spot, spreading fear through me. I can't remember the last time anything affected me like that.

I roll my shoulders and turn on the car. This is ridiculous. I should just go to work. But at the light, despite my best intentions, I turn in the direction of the house.

Fuck it. I'll check on her, make sure she has everything she needs, and then I'll get back to work.

Ten minutes later, I'm walking through the front door. I head directly upstairs, not bothering to take my coat off. This will only take a few minutes.

The door to our bedroom is cracked open. I'm about to step inside when I hear it.

"Stupid whore."

My hand stills on the door handle.

"I always knew you'd bring havoc into this household. Don Messero should have let them kill you. He would be far better off without you."

What. The. Fuck.

That voice coming from inside the bedroom belongs to my house manager, Sabina. The old woman's been with the family for decades. She sure as fuck has never spoken to me like that.

Cleo mutters something in response, something that sounds like, "You'd probably declare the day a holiday, wouldn't you?"

She sounds so unbothered. Like she's used to it.

"Do you know how many women would kill to be in your position? To be married to our don. He deserves a real lady for a wife. A woman his family can respect and admire. Instead, he has you. You worthless, pathetic slut."

There's a ringing sound inside my ears. I push the door open wider and watch as Sabina walks closer to where Cleo is sitting in bed. My wife looks bored as Sabina slams a plate of food onto her nightstand. "Here. I hope you choke on this."

What the fuck is happening here? She did *not* just utter those words. And then the vile bitch does the unthinkable. She tosses a spoon at my injured wife. It hits Cleo's chest, bouncing against the duvet. Cleo calmly reaches for it and places it on the nightstand by the plate.

Rage clamps down on my lungs. "What the *fuck* did you just say to her?"

Cleo's eyes snap from Sabina to me.

"Don Messero," Sabina gasps. "I—"

I march over to them, putting myself between Cleo and the old cunt, and pick up the spoon.

Sabina's wide eyes drop to it and terror blooms across her expression.

"I will carve out your tongue and ram it down your throat for speaking that way to my wife," I growl. "Apologize right now."

She turns as pale as a sheet. "I'm so sorry."

"Not to me," I grind out. "To. Her."

Sabina swallows and volleys her gaze to Cleo. "I apologize, Mrs. Messero."

"You're done. Fired. Get the fuck out." My throat is so tight with anger, I can't even get a full fucking sentence out.

She takes a few steps back. "Sir, I was hired by your grandmother."

"My grandmother is dead, and you'll be too if you don't remove yourself from my sight this very second. You have fifteen minutes to pack your belongings and get the hell out of my house."

She just stands there, staring at me like I'm not making any sense.

"GET. OUT!" I roar.

She jumps. Her eyes dart between Cleo and me and then she flees.

My chest rises and falls with rapid breaths. *Calm down.* I can't. How fucking *dare* she?

"Rafe."

I turn to my wife. Cleo stares at me, her cheeks bright red.

"What was that?" I hiss. "Why didn't you say anything? If I knew she behaved that way with you, I would have fired her a long time ago."

She swallows nervously and clutches the duvet. "It doesn't matter," she says quickly. "I'm used to it."

My vision narrows. "Used to it?" I grind out past my teeth. "What the fuck does that mean?"

She flexes her hands. "How do you think my parents spoke to me?"

My fists clench. I want to kill Stefano Garzolo. He might not have hit Cleo, but that doesn't mean he hasn't harmed her in other ways. That piece of shit. He and his wife taught Cleo that she isn't worthy of respect. That it's okay for a *fucking servant* to disrespect her.

The floor tilts. The urge to drive over to Garzolo's house right now and shove a knife through him swells in my chest.

"That. Ends. Now." My voice is a low rasp.

She sucks in a shaky breath, tears filling her eyes. "I don't care how people talk to me. Their words don't affect me."

"They affect *me*."

Even though they shouldn't. Even though it normally takes a lot more than a few words to make me angry. I've managed to keep a cool head with a barrel pointed at me, but seeing my wife disrespected is apparently enough to get me going.

The realization spills ice into my veins. Unease wraps around me. It gets worse when I register Cleo's penetrating gaze.

"Why?" she whispers.

The answer is automatic. "Because you're mine. No one gets to speak to my wife that way."

The unease starts to melt away. Being a don means enforcing respect. That's all I'm doing here.

Cleo gives me a bitter smile. "Because when they insult me, they're insulting you?"

"That's right."

Her face becomes pinched, and she looks away. I get the sense that I've said something wrong. I sit down on the edge of the bed and grab her chin with my hand. A tear slips down her cheek.

"That's enough," I growl. "They don't deserve your tears, *tesoro*. They don't deserve to breathe the same air as you. The next time anyone talks to you that way, I will kill them."

She pulls my hands away and looks down at her lap. "Okay."

I frown. She doesn't sound okay. "Cle—"

She slides down the bed, pulls the duvet up to her chin, and turns away from me. "I'm tired. I think I need a nap."

The clear dismissal stings. Some foreign emotion pulses inside my chest, insisting that I stay here with her, but I shove it away.

She wants to be alone. I should let her. She needs to rest.

I rise to my feet and look at her for another moment before I move toward the door, the air around us heavy with things unsaid.

CHAPTER 22

CLEO

A FEW DAYS after Sabina's firing, the doctor gives me the all clear. Rafaele doesn't seem thrilled when I tell him I want to start working at his cousin's business right away, but with the doctor's permission, he has no excuse to keep me at home.

When I wake up the morning of my first day at work, Rafaele is in the shower, and I have a text from Gemma.

> How are you doing?

She's been checking in with me every day since the attack.

> Much better. My cuts are healing, and my head is fine. Rafe is finally letting me go to work.

My phone buzzes with her response a minute later.

> Rafe?! Sounds like you two are getting cozy. How is he?

I'm not sure what to text back to her. A week ago, I would have written an essay about how much I hate my husband, but how can I possibly rail against the man who nearly took a bullet for me? The man who volunteered to stitch me up when I was scared? The man who didn't get angry when I tried my best to piss him off, but who absolutely *lost it* when he heard Sabina being a huge bitch to me?

He fired that horrible woman on the spot. I can still barely believe it.

It's been almost a week since we started sleeping in the same bed. With every night that passes, the space between us seems to shrink. And I can't stop thinking about kissing him again.

I drop the phone and press my palms to my face.

I'm softening for him. Doing the thing I promised myself I'd never do.

What about my plan? I haven't even looked at that scrap piece of paper since the attack. I'm not sure if I have it in me to continue with any of it. Not when Rafaele is starting to seem a lot less like my jailer and a lot more like a man I could possibly be falling for.

I curse under my breath.

He's winning.

He's winning because he's got me right where he wants me, and I have to keep reminding myself of the life I'll never be able to live because of him. Of the fact that he's ruthless, and clever, and knows just how to turn this situation in his favor.

It shouldn't matter that he protected me. Yes, if it had been my father and me in that restaurant, dear Papà would have used me as a human shield, but Stefano Garzolo is hardly the standard I should compare other men against.

Rafaele had to protect me because he would have looked weak if I died, and his path to becoming the boss of the Garzolos would become more complicated.

But he seemed genuinely concerned for my well-being. Or he's a very good actor. When he saw me bleeding on the ground, I swear he seemed worried. More than worried.

Tortured.

I drag my palm over my lips. I don't understand him, and I don't know how to handle the version of him that seems to actually feel something for me. Is it real or an illusion? What if this version of Rafaele disappears the moment he sleeps with me?

The bathroom door opens, and Rafaele comes out in only his dress pants.

Fuck me.

I should be used to the sight of his body by now, but I'm not. My skin heats, and my heart pounds a little faster.

"Nero will drive you to work."

"Why?" I ask from where I'm lying in bed. I'm trying very hard to keep my gaze on his face and not his body.

I'm failing.

Muscles ripple beneath his tattooed skin, and I can't look away.

"Because I want him to," he says as he puts on his dress shirt.

I swallow. "Why not Sandro and Tiny?"

"They're helping me search for whoever is behind the attack, and they've been working long hours. I don't want Sandro driving you when he's tired."

"Doesn't Nero have more important things to do?"

Rafaele meets my gaze in the mirror as he does up the buttons, hiding his eight-pack from my view. "No."

That one simple word sets off a flutter inside my belly. Nero isn't just some soldier. He's Rafaele's consigliere. The most valuable member of his team. And Rafaele is assigning him to me. The flutters multiply. He's treating me like I really am his treasure.

His pride hangs on his ability to protect you, remember?

But what if it's more than that?

He breaks our eye contact and takes his jacket off the back of a chair. The fabric of his shirt stretches over his broad shoulders as he slips the jacket on.

"He'll pick you up at nine."

"I'll be ready."

He walks over to me and gently lifts my chin with his fingers. My pulse picks up speed. Is he going to kiss me? That's what normal married couples do, isn't it? Kiss each other before they go to work in the mornings.

Only we're not normal. We exist in a different galaxy from "normal."

Still, my eyelids flutter as he leans down and brings his face closer to mine.

"Is there something else you're ready for now that you're all better, *tesoro*?" he asks, his breath coasting against my lips.

I can feel my panties grow wet even as disappointment spreads beneath my skin. There it is. He's waiting for me to declare surrender and hand him his prize.

I jerk my chin out of his grasp. "I don't know what you mean."

His gaze sparks. "Are we just going to pretend you didn't spend the last few mornings salivating over my body?"

A bucket of cold water breaks right over my head. I rip off the duvet and push past him as I get out of bed. "Fuck you."

"You will. Very soon."

I whirl around, ready to find something to throw at him, but he's already halfway out the door.

He leaves, but the ghost of his touch remains branded into my skin.

Nero's waiting in the foyer when I come downstairs in my first-day-at-work outfit. I decided to optimize for comfort, since I don't really know what Loretta will have me do all day, so I'm wearing a pair of wide-legged jeans, a green blouse, and some sneakers.

Nerves dance beneath my skin. I want today to go well.

Nero looks up from his phone and takes stock of me. "You actually don't look too bad."

I cross my arms over my chest. "Gee, thanks."

He laughs and drags his palm over the scruff on his chin. He's nearly as tall as the doorway behind him. Today, he's dressed down from the usual black suit I'm used to seeing him in. Instead, he's wearing a pair of jeans, a gray T-shirt, and a black leather jacket. "I meant it as a compliment. Heard you got banged up."

"Felt like a pretty backhanded compliment."

He slides his phone into his jacket pocket. "You always assume the worst of me."

"Always? We've spoken like...twice."

"Yes, but our first interaction was so insightful. I feel like I really got to know you." He opens the front door and waves me forward.

I step out and breathe in the crisp March air. "You mean when you and Rafaele pulled me off the side of the road like two barbarians?"

Nero unlocks the car and opens the door for me. "It was the beginning of your beautiful love story."

I can't help but snort as I slide into my seat. "Oh yes, because all love stories involve kidnappings, being forced into marriage, and dates that end in a hailstorm of bullets."

He grins. "The ones that aren't boring do."

I put on my seat belt while he comes around and gets in on the other side.

"Well, maybe some of us like boring."

He starts the car. "Yeah, but not you." He smirks at me, like he genuinely believes he knows all about me.

I clench my teeth and decide that I'm over this conversation.

But Nero is not. "So, how are things going with you and Rafe?" he asks as we pull out of the driveway.

He's trying to sound way too casual.

"Fine."

"You warming up to him? He's not as bad as he seems at first."

I groan. "Is this why Rafaele assigned you to me? So that you could make a case for him on the drive over?"

"No. He asked me to do this because he's worried about you."

"He doesn't worry about anything or anyone." It comes out bitter. I'm annoyed about this morning and how I actually wanted Rafe to kiss me...until he ruined it. Is there some pathetic part of me that's hoping this marriage might work? I really am a colossal idiot.

Nero shrugs. "That's what he'd like to believe, but his actions indicate otherwise. Heard he fired Sabina because of something she said to you."

"Yes, well, apparently my existence has been reduced to being an extension of him. He takes any offense against me very personally."

"You really don't get it, do you?"

I glance at him. "Get what?"

"Sabina's been with the family for four decades. And he fired her without even thinking it over. Rafe thinks *everything* over."

I shift in my seat. "What are you implying?" That Rafaele acted emotionally for once?

"Nothing. I'm just making observations."

"Just observe the road."

Nero huffs a laugh and turns on the radio. He cycles through the stations until he finds one playing hip-hop, and then he bops his head along with the song. A puff of air escapes my lips as we get onto the highway. My perception of Rafaele is shifting like a kaleidoscope. I don't know what to make of my husband anymore.

When the song ends and the commercial comes on, Nero turns down the volume. "You know, there's at least one other thing Rafe did quite impulsively."

I glance at him. "What was it?"

There's a knowing smile on Nero's face. "Agreeing to marry you."

CHAPTER 23

CLEO

WE PULL up in front of a brick building in the Lower East Side. "We're here," Nero says. "Sit tight. I'm going to come around to help you out."

"That's really not neces—"

He's already climbing out and slamming his door closed.

I sigh and try to clear my head. It's my first day at work, and I need to focus on that instead of psychoanalyzing my husband, but Nero managed to confuse me even more. That was probably his intention.

The consigliere walks me to the front door of the shop and presses on the doorbell. "I'll be nearby. Call when you're ready to go home."

"You're going to wait around all day?"

"Just until Sandro gets here to keep watch so I can grab some lunch." He gives me a very male grin. "I've got a friend in the area."

I roll my eyes. "Just when I thought you might be more than a barbarian in a suit."

"Wouldn't want you to think too highly of me. Rafe might get jealous."

The lock turns and a woman opens the door. She must be Loretta. Her hair is the same color as Rafaele's—black with hints of hazel in the light. She and Nero share a quick embrace and greet each other in Italian, but the consigliere doesn't stick around. He pats my shoulder as he brushes past me and walks back toward his car.

Loretta's attention moves to me. She gives me a slow once-over and pops her gum. "You looked different at the wedding."

I shrug. "Left the diamonds at home."

She doesn't laugh, and the expression on her face is not exactly friendly. She must be younger than Rafaele since she's still unmarried, but the heavy makeup she wears makes her look older.

The wind picks up, and she tugs her sweater tighter around her.

I peek inside the shop over her shoulder. It's filled with bolts of fabric, and there's a crooked mannequin in a skirt and no top by the register.

"Are you going to invite me in?"

Her eyes narrow. She pops her gum again and then moves aside. "Come in," she says.

I follow her inside and take in the dusty shelves. The place smells of mothballs and old leather. The register is near the front, and there's a small desk in the back corner with a laptop, a printer, and a stack of invoices. Another desk beside it holds a sewing machine.

Loretta leans against the register. "Rafaele must really want me to fail if he sent you here," she says, her tone riddled with mistrust.

Okay, rude. My jaw hardens, but I don't take the bait. "What's going on with this place?"

She gestures vaguely at the space around us. "Not enough customers. I bought up all this stock more than a year ago, and it's been sitting on the shelves ever since. These are good fabrics. High quality, not the kind of polyester crap you see in stores these days. I thought there'd be demand for it, but it looks like everyone just wants to buy off the rack."

I glance around again. "Do you have a catalogue?"

She shakes her head. "I have pictures of what I've made in the past. You can look at them over there." She points toward the desk at the back.

I spend the next few hours poring over the photos. There are a ton of them, dating back as far as five years ago.

It's clear Loretta is an exceptional tailor. The intricacy on some of the pieces rivals that of high-end fashion houses. But it's not hard to see why someone would become over-whelmed. There are so many options here, and so many different styles. It's almost impossible to choose.

I put the photos back in the boxes they came from and walk over to Loretta. She's working on a skirt at the sewing machine. "Have you thought about creating a collection of styles? Maybe changing them out every season?"

She doesn't look up from her work. "The vision for the shop is to create one-of-a-kind pieces. Everything custom-made."

"You can still do customizations. People can select the fabric, buttons, make small adjustments to the styles. But it would help them understand what they can get from you."

"Whatever they want. That's the point."

"Sometimes too much choice is overwhelming. Not everyone is a clothing designer. There are plenty of people who want high-quality clothes, but only a small subset of them know enough about fashion to tell you exactly what they want made."

Loretta looks at me, her eyes narrow. "That's not in line with my vision."

"Well, your vision isn't working. Why not try this?"

"Because I'm not going to redo my entire business plan based on an idea you just pulled out of your ass. What do you know about this? I've been working on this business for two years. You showed up two hours ago, and you're already telling me what to do. Do you think you're smarter than me?" She scoffs and shakes her head.

My walls surge right up. "Why are you being like this? I'm trying to help you."

"You spit on everything my family stands for. Tradition. Honor. Virtue." She shakes her head. "You get married to my cousin, and the first thing you do is spend his money. What? You don't think we heard about that? You're spoiled and vapid. I don't need your help. I knew this was a waste of my time."

Frustrated, I grab my purse and march out of the store. Rafaele might be manipulating me, but he's right about not letting people talk to me like that. The wind nips at me as soon as I step outside. It's barely past lunchtime, but Nero's already back here.

He sees me from the car and frowns. "Done already?" he asks as soon as I get in.

"Yes." I can feel his gaze probing the side of my face.

"How did it go?"

"I don't want to talk about it."

A beat passes. "Look, Loretta can be a bit prickly. Don't take it personally."

Yeah, right. Everything she said to me felt pretty fucking personal.

I sniff. "I'm not."

"Wanna talk about it?"

Frustration rings deep inside my bones, so I take it out on Nero. "Are you my driver or my therapist? Can you just take me home?"

I force myself to look at him and immediately feel guilty for snapping like that.

But Nero just shrugs. "All right. Your mother called. Wants to see you."

"Why?"

"Maybe she's worried about you after the attack."

That's doubtful.

"You can say no if you don't want to," he offers.

I don't want to, but I could use a distraction after my disastrous first day. I'm not in any rush to tell Rafaele how poorly it went.

"Fine. Take me there."

The city is gridlocked, and it takes us nearly an hour to get to my old house.

When we arrive, a servant I don't recognize opens the door.

"Mrs. Garzolo is waiting for you in the living room," he says. "Mr. De Luca, may I offer you some coffee?" He leads Nero away to the kitchen while I go search for Mamma.

Passing through the grand foyer, I briefly note the picture frames on the round foyer table. There are three. One of me and my sisters, one of the whole family, and one of just my parents. They seem perfectly normal, but I know the smiles in them are all forced. Mamma and Papà have always been big on appearances and little else.

I find my mother reading a magazine on the sofa. When she hears me enter, she puts the magazine away and stands. Her gaze scans over me, her nose wrinkling.

I know exactly what she's thinking. My casual outfit is too sloppy. My hair's not sufficiently styled. My makeup is too sparse.

Thank God, I don't have to deal with this every day anymore.

She walks up to me. "I heard you were hurt during the shooting." There isn't a hint of warmth in her tone.

"Why did you want to see me?" I ask, knowing she's not really concerned for me.

She sniffs, probably displeased at how quickly I saw through her facade. "Your father is waiting for you in his office."

Irritation inches along my skin. So it's Papà who really wants to talk to me, but he knew I'd never show up if the invitation came from him.

I clench my jaw. I want to speak to my father as much as I want to go back to Loretta's shop. But I'm already here, aren't I? Might as well see what this is all about.

Papà's office is a place of bad memories. It was here where I saw him hurting Gemma. But I know he'd never dare to raise his hand to me. Not now that I'm married to Rafaele.

I push the door open. Stefano Garzolo is sitting at his desk, a stack of papers before him.

He looks up. "Come in and close the door."

I step inside and take a seat in a chair across from his desk. "What do you want?"

"How's married life?" he asks, a hint of mockery in his tone.

My eyes narrow. "Did you summon me here so that you could rub it in?"

An insincere smile cuts across his face. "Not at all. I want to know if Rafaele is treating you well."

Better than you ever did. Married life is growing on me, but my father is the last person in the world I'd confess that to, so I say only what he expects to hear.

"I gave up my independence and freedom. I can never go to college like I wanted to. I will never have the career of my dreams. How do you think it's going?"

He nods, his eyes flashing with satisfaction. My stomach curdles. It's like he gets off on thinking I'm miserable.

"Well, maybe you don't have to spend the rest of your life with Messero," he says slowly.

I frown. What is he talking about now?

He brushes his palms over the desk. "I want to make you an offer."

"What kind of an offer?" Outside, a raven croaks like a bad omen. My eyes dart to the window in time to see the bird fly by.

"My retirement plans have changed," my father says. "I've decided five years isn't enough for me to do what I'd like to do as don of our family."

"And what is that exactly?" As far as I can tell, he's spent decades lining his pockets, hosting parties at La Trattoria, and acting all-important.

There's a reason he went to jail—one of his capos turned on him and spilled the beans to the feds. Why? Because my father got greedy. He kept asking for bigger and bigger cuts and squeezed his own men too tightly.

"I want to finish getting rid of the rats, rebuild my ranks, and bring the Garzolo family into a new era. New businesses, new partnerships, new points of leverage." He steeples his hands in front of him. "It'll take some time, but the future is looking bright for Garzolos."

Quickly, I start to put it together. What he's saying is that he has no intention of letting Rafaele become his successor.

"You want to stay on as don."

He lifts a shoulder. "I'm fifty-four. My father retired at seventy. I've still got plenty of time to bring our family back to the top of the food chain in this town."

"Rafaele will never allow this to happen. You made a deal with him. He gave you five years."

Papà nods. "Which is why Rafaele needs to go."

My blood runs cold.

Of course. I should have known Papà would want to have his cake and eat it too. Use Rafaele to get himself out of prison and then find a way to get rid of him before his five years are up.

Anger kindles inside my chest.

"Why are you telling me this?"

"Your husband is an impenetrable fortress. I've tried to find his weaknesses, to find some way to get leverage, but so far, I've found nothing. He's got all his capos under his thumb. They all say he's a control freak, that he doesn't feel emotions and cares about no one, that he can kill anyone and anything around him if they get in the way of his plans. They're all fucking terrified of him."

A chill runs through me. Rafaele would never hurt me. Or would he? Am I being naive thinking that my famously brutal husband won't ever show that brutal side to me?

I push the thought away. "What do you want me to do about it?"

"Help me find something that I can use against him. There has to be *something*. You're in his house, in his bed. Eventually, you might learn things about him that no one else knows."

My eyes widen. I can't believe this. "You want me to *spy* on him?" I laugh. "You're crazy to think I'll help you."

My words don't faze him. It's as if he expected me to say just that.

"Don't do it for me. Do it for yourself. If you help me take him down, I'll give you your freedom."

I scoff and shake my head. "Yeah, right. What does that even mean?"

He leans back and crosses his arms over his chest. "I will formally disown you. You can go live with your sisters in Italy or move anywhere you want. Help me, and you can live your life as you wish."

My breath hitches. It takes me a moment to convince myself I heard him say those words. He just offered me the one thing I've always wanted.

Freedom.

A way out of this life and this world.

My father's expression turns triumphant. "What do you say?"

There's no way he means it. Is he really this desperate? Desperate enough to try to make a deal with *me*?

I shake my head. "You expect me to believe you after you just told me you plan on breaking another deal you've made? I don't trust you. How can I be sure you'd let me go if I help you?"

His lips curl into a sneer. "Your mother and I tried to make you into a palatable human being, but we clearly failed. You're a fucking nuisance. I'm happy Rafaele took you off our hands, and I sure as hell want *nothing* more to do with you after I get rid of him. I'll put you on a plane and hopefully never see you again."

A bitter taste floods my mouth. He knows trying to flatter me would have done him no good. I wouldn't believe him.

But this I believe. My father hates me as much as I hate him. If he kills Rafaele, I'll be a widow with a questionable reputation. I'll be of no use to him.

His words echo through my head. *If you help me take him down, I'll give you your freedom.* He wants me to join him in betraying Rafaele. To help him find a way to murder my husband.

My limbs feel numb.

Even my dreams aren't worth that price, are they?

I shouldn't be entertaining this. I'm tempted to laugh in his face and call him an idiot for letting me in on his plan. To see how he'll react when I tell him I'm going to go straight to Rafaele with this information.

But another part of me holds me back. The part that wants to at least consider the possibility of being with Gemma and Vale. Of being free of all of this.

"I'll think about it," I say.

The words taste like poison on my tongue.

CHAPTER 24

CLEO

THE NEXT MORNING, I wake up with my back pressed against a heater.

It takes me a moment to realize that's my husband. I remember falling asleep very aware of the six or so inches of space between us, and now they're gone. Erased by the pull between our bodies in the night.

My fingers twitch against the bed sheets. Rafaele's breathing is slow and steady, but I know what he sounds like when he's asleep, and he's not asleep now.

Instead of pulling away like I should, I flex my spine, pressing my hips slightly backward.

It's an infinitesimal movement. The kind people make in their sleep. The hardness that presses back against me would be enough to jolt anyone awake.

My breath hitches. I know he heard it. He probably felt the tiny jump I made against his chest.

A large hand slides over my hip, dragging against the fabric of my nightgown and setting off a pleasant buzz beneath my skin. His movements are slow and languid, as if we're in a dream. He pushes me forward until my front is pressed to the mattress and my face is half buried in the pillow. My hard nipples make firm contact with the bed, and I groan lightly from the pressure.

Rafaele touches his lips to the side of my throat and licks at my heated flesh. I stifle a gasp, a moan. His fingers dig into my hip, his thumb pushing down against the swell of my ass. His lips move to my nape and then drift lower, traversing down my spine. Wet kisses against each vertebra that I feel between my legs.

I ache for more.

I squeeze my eyes shut, swept away by the sensations he's creating inside my body.

And that's when a tiny devil lands on my shoulder and whispers into my ear, *"If you help me take him down, I'll give you your freedom."*

My eyes snap open.

Fuck.

The conversation with my father comes rushing back.

I elbow Rafaele in the ribs and nearly tumble to the floor in my haste to get away from him. He catches me as I'm about to roll off the side of the mattress, his hand a vise around my waist.

Our gazes meet for the first time this morning. His is dark and hungry and laced with frustration. Mine, wide and anxious and so fucking *caught*.

I haven't decided what I'm going to do—if I'll take my father up on his offer or not. But the mere memory of his words floods me with guilt.

Papà wants Rafaele dead. And I'm sitting on that information instead of telling him.

"Let go of me," I whisper.

He does. I land on my feet inelegantly, dart into the bathroom, and lock the door behind me. My heart thumps a panicked rhythm inside my chest. The thought of working with my father makes me sick, even if it would be for my benefit. Stefano Garzolo doesn't deserve to be don.

And Rafaele doesn't deserve to die.

He's killed countless people. He is a symbol of everything you hate. Everything you've wanted to escape from.

I turn on the shower, set the temperature to ice-cold, and step inside. A violent shiver runs through me when the water hits my skin.

I need more time. More time to get to know Rafaele. More time to convince myself there's a real human hiding inside the brutal man. And I need more time to figure out what I want out of my life.

Because for the first time since I can remember, no clear answer comes.

An hour later, Rafaele and I sit having breakfast together. It's the first time we've done it since we got married.

A maid comes out with a pot of coffee and refills my cup. Rafaele is on his phone, but when she leaves, he puts it face down on the dining table and turns his attention to me.

"How did it go yesterday with Loretta, *tesoro*?"

I reach for the sugar and add a spoon to my coffee, taking my time with it. "Not well."

His face darkens. "What happened?"

I don't really want to talk about it, but I doubt he'll drop it. I exhale a breath. "She made it clear she doesn't think I can help her. She's not interested in listening to my ideas."

"Why's that?"

I take a sip of my coffee. "She's right. I don't know anything. I've never run a business. I've never tried to save a company. Maybe if I'd gone to college, I would know how to save a failing business, but the way it stands, she's probably better off without me."

Rafaele shakes his head. "Trust me, you don't learn business by going to college. You learn by trying things, failing, and learning from your failures. You think anyone taught me how to run this enterprise?"

"Didn't you learn from your father?"

A shadow passes over his expression. "My father taught me cruelty. He taught me how to be brutal and how to instill fear in people. He had no patience when it came to teaching me anything else."

This is the first time Rafaele has said anything to me about his father. He never talks about his family. Not even his mother or his sisters.

Curiosity stirs inside of me. "What about your mother? What did she teach you?"

His jaw hardens. "We're talking about you right now."

"Well, what about me?" Frustration seeps into my tone. Why is he pushing this so hard? I was the one who made a big deal out of having a job. He should be happy I'm giving up on the idea. "As you've already seen, I'm good at spending money. I'm not good at making it."

"I didn't think you were a quitter."

"Now you're trying reverse psychology?" I stand up, no longer hungry. "It won't work. I won't go back there. Loretta thinks I'm spoiled and vapid, so why should I bother with her?"

He grabs my wrist and rises, his body casting a shadow over me. I gasp as he corners me against the edge of the table.

"You lean into people's lowest opinions of you because you think it gives you power. It doesn't. You know what gives you real power? Proving them wrong."

I swallow against the bitter truth in those words. "Stop it," I whisper.

"Stop what?"

"Stop trying to get me to change. I'll never measure up to whatever ideal wife you have in your head."

He raises his hand and brushes his knuckles over my cheek. His face is just inches from mine, and my gaze drops to his lips. The lips I've thought about kissing again. Some part of me hopes that the next time we kiss, it'll be different. That my stomach won't flip, my nerve endings won't fire.

"How do you know the ideal wife in my head looks any different from you?"

Blood rushes in my ears, and that's when I know that I'm screwed. Because suddenly, my marriage doesn't feel like a rigid cage. It feels like a steep cliff in the night, illuminated by the moon and the stars. I've been standing on its edge ever since I walked down the aisle. And now, I'm falling.

I've never belonged anywhere. I've gotten so used to being the outsider. The disappointing daughter. I've never been anyone's ideal. Ever. And hearing him say that to me, even if it's a calculated lie, it breaks something open inside of me.

He dips his head lower. "Why did you run from me this morning?"

I don't know what to say. I don't know what to *do*. Just thinking about my father's offer feels like a betrayal. To win back my freedom, I'd have to go against Rafaele. Two weeks ago, I'd have done anything to be free, but I lack that same conviction now.

He curls his hand around my throat and forces my chin up until our lips are millimeters apart. "Why do you keep fighting this?"

Yes, why?

Would it be so bad to give in to the sparks and the electricity?

His lips brush against my own. "You want this."

Yes, but I used to want other things too. A life where my existence wasn't reduced to being a mobster's wife. A life where I could chart my own course. A life of possibilities. I used to be able to visualize it all so clearly.

But with him this close, my vision is all blurred. He confuses me. Is that his intention?

Using every ounce of my willpower, I turn my head to the side. His breaths are sharp puffs against my cheek.

"I'll go back to Loretta's," I whisper. I pull his hand off me and escape upstairs.

I'm lost. More lost than I've ever been before. And I have no idea how to find my way back.

~

The next day, I'm on Loretta's steps, and I'm a nervous wreck.

Rafaele's right. I can't give up after just one try. I wanted to manage famous musicians, but I can't even figure out how to work with a woman who's now my family?

Ugh. It's pathetic.

Nero dropped me off again, but this time, I insisted that he didn't walk me to the door. I didn't want to talk to Loretta with him as a witness. He's probably watching me from the car and wondering why I'm just standing here.

Swallowing hard, I lift my finger to the doorbell. I rehearsed what I'm going to say at least ten times on the drive over, but I feel like I'm going to forget it all as soon as I open my mouth. I squeeze my eyes shut and press the button.

A few seconds later, Loretta's face appears on the other side of the glass. Her eyes widen with surprise for a split second before they turn weary.

I give her an awkward wave. It's sunny today, and I'm sweating beneath my jacket from heat and nerves.

She pushes the door open and steps out. "What are you doing here?" she asks carefully.

I shove my hands into the pockets of my hoodie. "I think we started on the wrong foot."

Her eyes dart to Nero's car behind me. "Am I in trouble? I'd expected Rafaele to call me yesterday to tell me off for kicking you out."

"I don't think he's going to do that."

Slowly, her gaze moves back to me. My fists clench inside my hoodie. I've never had to do this before—try to win someone over. In the past, when someone didn't like me, I'd just think, fuck you, I don't like you either. And I'd act like an asshole. But Rafe's right. That's not power. That's giving up.

"Look, you're right," I say. "I don't know anything about your business. I shouldn't have waltzed in here and started doling out advice like I know what I'm talking about."

Loretta's cheeks turn pink. I don't know what she's thinking, but at least she's not shooing me away.

"I want to learn. Let me shadow you today and see how you do everything around here. I'll do anything you tell me to. Help you however you'd like. You're the boss, all right?"

Loretta glances at her feet like she's embarrassed. "Not a very good boss, I'm afraid," she mutters. "I shouldn't have said those things to you. It was rude of me."

It was pretty rude, but at least she's woman enough to admit it. That's more than most people ever do.

"It's okay," I say. "So we both fucked up. People make mistakes, right? Why don't we start over?"

Loretta stares at me for a moment, considering my offer. "Okay. But you listen to everything I say and do exactly as I tell you."

I grin. "Yes, ma'am."

A slow smile appears on her face. "Then let's get to work."

CHAPTER 25

RAFAELE

IT'S PAST MIDNIGHT, and my office is bathed in darkness. A single antique desk lamp illuminates the space, casting shadows onto the wooden bookshelves.

I like working in the dark. I find it easier to focus. And I really need to focus if I want to get to sleep in the next hour.

It's not like me to procrastinate, but it's been a long week, and I'm drained.

We've still got no new leads on who's behind the Il Caminetto attack. With the trail growing cold, I'm getting less and less optimistic we'll get to the bottom of this anytime soon.

On top of that, an issue with my capo in Rochester kept me in the city for longer than I would have liked. We captured a Bratva informer who's been doing surveillance on us to find out which businesses pay us protection. My left hand still fucking aches from hitting his thick skull.

Maybe getting his body back in a suitcase will make the Russian pakhan realize he should stay the fuck out of our state.

Last night, when I got back home after being gone for four days, Cleo was sitting cross-legged on the couch in the living room with her computer in her lap. The moment she saw me, the lines of concentration in her forehead softened, her eyes widened, and her lips quirked up. She missed me.

"You're back," she said, those two words underscored with relief.

A strange feeling passed through me. One I couldn't name. The sensation started at the center of my chest and spread with every step I took toward Cleo. She watched me approach, pulling on her bottom lip with her teeth, and asked me about my trip.

Instead of answering her, I leaned down and kissed her. It was chaste. *Sweet*. It was probably just my exhaustion muddling my head, because in the moment, I didn't want to fuck her. All I wanted was one simple kiss from my wife.

She didn't pull away. She leaned into me like it was exactly what she wanted too.

And that tiny movement was everything.

I rake my fingers through my hair. I almost have her. By now, I've realized that the way past her defenses isn't through her body, but through her mind.

Tesoro mio. So sharp on the outside, but she's all soft inside. How did I not see it earlier?

She craves for someone to accept her for who she really is. Acceptance is one of many things her parents never gave her. She hasn't been enough for them her whole life. They told her she is flawed, wrong, undesired.

But I desire her. Her flaws give her character. She is just right for me.

I might never be able to love her—my ability to love was ruthlessly trained out of me—but I can appreciate her. It will be enough for her, because it will be more than anything she's ever gotten before. She won't know the difference. How could she?

Our game is almost at its end. She put up a far stronger defense than I anticipated, but with each passing day, I chip at it bit by bit.

I'm a patient man.

I've been repeating those words so often in these last few days they feel like a prayer. It's only a matter of time before she finally surrenders to me, and I can declare checkmate.

I was right all along. Cleo is a puzzle, one I've nearly managed to solve. And when I do, she won't occupy so many of my thoughts.

The tension will dissipate. The intrigue will be over. And my mind will be calm again.

Nero was wrong. He thought she would unmoor me. That she would make me lose control. But no matter what my consigliere thinks, I've stayed in control the entire time we've been playing. And that's the way it'll always be.

There's a knock on the door. I glance up from my laptop. Since it's late, the staff has been dismissed for the evening. A shiver of anticipation rolls down my spine.

"Come in."

My wife appears in the doorway, a stack of papers in her arms. She's dressed in the same outfit I saw her in this morning—a white blouse and a pink skirt that stops mid-thigh. Her copper hair is loose, cascading over her shoulders.

She's so beautiful.

"What is it?" I ask.

She leans against the doorjamb. "I need your help. Do you have time right now?"

I tear my gaze away from her bare thighs and nod. "Of course."

She comes inside, closing the door behind her. "Loretta and I have started planning on how we can repay all of her debts." She puts the stack of papers on my desk. "I've called most of her creditors today asking to put repayment plans in place that will give us some breathing room."

Things between my cousin and her must be going well. "That's a good idea."

"There's one creditor that won't give us an extension for some reason. It's the fabric supplier and starting next week he's refusing to deliver any more stock until the debt is repaid."

"How much is it?"

"A hundred thousand dollars."

I lean back in my seat. "How long will it take Loretta to pay it back?"

"We've implemented some changes to how she runs her business, and I think we'll see things start to turn around quickly. Assuming her sales double, she'll pay him back in six months. If they triple, it'll take four months."

"Do you have numbers to back this up?"

She pulls out a USB from her pocket and slides it across the desk. "The financial model and all of our assumptions are here."

I take the USB and plug it into my laptop. When I open the Excel file, it's an effort not to show my surprise. "You made this?"

She sits down across from me and nods.

"How?"

"A lot of hours watching videos on YouTube."

This financial model is better than most of the ones my capos show me whenever they have a new idea. I've lost count of how many times I've been promised there was no way for me not to make a return, only to look at the numbers and realize the idea is a dud.

I scroll through the spreadsheet and spend a few minutes playing with the assumptions. Everything Cleo said about the repayment timeline checks out.

I look up at her. "I'm impressed."

She rolls her eyes. "What? Did you think I was a moron? I'll have you know math was my best subject in high school."

That's news to me. "It was?"

"I was nearly top of the class."

Interesting. I lean back in my chair. "Are you asking me to pay this?"

Her back straightens. "No. I'm not here to ask you for money. I already sent this to the supplier, but they won't budge. I was hoping you could look at the contract and see if there's anything there we can use. I'm apparently much worse at reading legalese than I am at the numbers."

"Is that what this is?" I nod at the stack of papers.

"Yeah."

I pull the papers toward me. "Let me take a look."

Ten minutes later, I have no choice but to deliver bad news. "There's nothing in the contract that will help."

Her face falls.

"But I know this supplier. The owner is Gino Ferraro's cousin. We're invited to have dinner with the don at his house next week."

"We are? Since when?"

"Since a few days ago. I'd like you to join."

Her eyes light up. "Okay. I can talk to him about this then."

"Good idea." I glance back at the business model. "The six-month projection looks good, but I think there are some problems with your long-term view."

"There are?" She stands up and comes to my side of the desk.

"Take a look." I toggle to the correct sheet and walk her through my logic.

She bends at the waist and reaches for my laptop. I catch a whiff of her floral shampoo.

"Hmm." She nibbles on her bottom lip. "It's possible I used the wrong numbers for the cost per square meter. I guess that should go down the more fabric we buy."

I lean back in my chair and glance at her ass. Her skirt's ridden up, nearly high enough for me to see her panties. My hand twitches. I've given her space after she fled from me that time in bed.

Be patient. Let her come to you.

But she did come to me, didn't she? She's here, late at night, the house empty.

"Do you think I should decrease it by ten or twenty percent?" she asks.

She might push me away if I touch her. But I need to fucking touch her. I lift my hand and wrap my palm around the back of her thigh.

She sucks in a low breath. I wait. Give her time to adjust or to shove my hand off her the way she's done so many times before.

But seconds pass, and she doesn't.

This emboldens me. I move my fingers in a light caress against the inside of her thigh. "I think fifteen is a good guess."

Goosebumps erupt over her flesh. She types in the new number. "Done." Her voice is hoarse. "Any other feedback?"

"You should probably increase your marketing expenses in Q4." I inch my hand higher, stopping when I reach the edge of her panties. "Once you pay off the debts, you'll want to double down on growth."

"Okay."

Slowly, I start to move the tips of my fingers back and forth along the edge of her underwear. Her skin is so soft and warm here.

Her elegant throat bobs. "By how much?"

I shift in the chair, my cock straining against the fabric of my slacks. She still hasn't pulled away, so I go farther. To the damp lace fabric covering her pussy. To the valley that molds to her slit. She gasps and squirms against my hand.

"Ten percent." My voice drops an octave lower. The lace grows more and more wet with every swipe of my thumb.

She's frazzled now. She mistypes the numbers, deletes them, types them in again. Her hands are shaking.

"I think I need to—"

I increase my pressure, and she chokes on her words.

"Need what?" I slide a finger under the lace.

A satisfied groan rumbles inside my chest. Drenched. My wife is fucking drenched for me.

"I should increase the he-headcount." She's panting now. "We'll need to hire someone to help with the marketing." The sentence comes out in one breath.

Her wetness coats my digits, and there's so much of it. My dick weeps at the thought of sliding through all this wet, warm heat.

I draw a circle around her clit. "Good idea."

With a shaking hand, she adjusts the numbers and then slams the laptop shut. A puff of air escapes past her lips, and she lets her head fall forward.

Slowly, I rise out of my chair, brush her hair over her shoulder, and bring my lips close to her ear. "Do you want me to stop?"

The air fills with the sound of her heavy breathing. Anticipation tightens inside my gut.

She swallows. "No."

I press a kiss to the side of her neck, my body buzzing with triumph. "Good girl." She whimpers. "I'm going to feast on you, *tesoro*. You've kept me so fucking starved."

I roll my chair until it's directly behind her, sit down, and lift her skirt.

I groan.

Red lace panties stretched over a firm, round ass. So fucking perfect. I hook a finger around the fabric and pull it aside to examine her.

Fuck me. Her cunt is dripping down her inner thighs, and it's the best thing I've ever seen. That pussy is made to be eaten.

I shove the panties down her legs and make her step out of them.

"Put your elbows on the desk."

She's trembling, but she does as she's told. Her perfect, glistening cunt is right where I want it—in front of my face.

I wrap my hands around her legs and pull my chair closer, and then I spread her open. Gently, I run the pad of my thumb over her little asshole, and then I dip it inside her folds. So tight and warm. I lean in and drag my tongue over her wetness.

"Oh God," she moans.

Her taste floods my senses. Fuck, I've waited for this for so long, and it's somehow even better than I imagined. I lap at her, pushing her thighs apart, pushing my tongue deep inside of her, pushing all her fucking reservations out of her body with every slow swipe.

"You taste so fucking good," I growl against her as I push a finger inside of her.

A shiver runs through her. She's strangely quiet, with the exception of her throaty moans. I have to remind myself that this is new to her.

Right?

I pull away from her, and she whines at the loss of my tongue.

"How many men have done this to you?"

"What?" She glances at me over her shoulder, her cheeks red and her eyes hooded.

"How. Many. Before. Me?"

She huffs a disbelieving breath. "Rafe, right now?"

"Tell me."

She tugs on her bottom lip. "A few."

Possessiveness cuts through my haze of lust. "After I make you come, you will write down their names."

She holds my gaze. "Why?"

"So I can kill them all."

Her wetness gushes over my hand. I look down. "Fuck, you like that, don't you?" I curl my finger inside her.

She gasps. "Shut up."

"They ever make you this wet?"

Her brow arches. "They never took a break to chitchat, so at least they had that going for them."

This smartass. "You're going to pay for that." Before she can bite back some snappy retort, I pull my finger out and run my tongue over her.

Her moans turn more frenzied when I press my fingers against her clit and start drawing tighter and tighter circles around it. She drops her forehead to the desk. Her pussy starts clenching. She's close. I wish I could see her face when she comes.

I pull back while my fingers keep moving in faster and faster circles. The view is spectacular. Round ass, dripping pussy, and her little pink skirt bunched around her waist. I palm my cock through the fabric of my pants. "That's it, *tesoro*. You have no idea how good you look like this."

She mewls something unintelligible and comes apart.

I lean forward and suck on her opening, letting her juices flood my mouth.

A groan spills past my lips. My fingers dig into her thighs, and I keep her there until I get my fill.

It takes a while for her legs to stop shaking. Slowly, I let go of her and push my chair back. I'm too worked up to take her to the bedroom. I want her to unzip my pants, take out my cock, and impale herself on it.

She pushes off the desk and turns around, her cheeks red and her chest rising and falling with rapid breaths.

I stand up and anchor one hand on the desk beside her, my wrist brushing against her waist. Her hooded eyes meet mine. I lean down and claim her lips.

For her sake, I hold myself back. The kiss starts off slow and mellow. She's relaxed after she just came so beautifully for me, and her body melts against mine.

I cup her breast and groan into her mouth when I realize she's not wearing a bra. Her back arches as I tweak her nipple through the thin fabric of her shirt. The thought of finally being able to explore her body for as long as I wish weakens my knees.

This fucking woman.

She breaks the kiss when I lower my hand to her damp inner thigh and cup her bare pussy. Her eyelids flutter, and her tongue darts out to lick her bottom lip. I grab the back of her head and kiss her again.

This time, it's not gentle. I tug and bite and thrust my tongue inside her mouth, rubbing it against her own. She doesn't back down.

She kisses me back.

Intense. Needy. Perfect.

Slowly, I push one finger back inside of her. She makes a surprised noise that I really want to hear again, but before I can get anywhere with that, a buzzing sound cuts through the air.

I glance down at where my phone is lying on the desk behind Cleo. The screen shows Nero's name.

Why the fuck is he calling me this late?

I don't care. Whatever it is, he can deal with it. But it keeps fucking buzzing.

I tear my mouth away from Cleo with a groan. "Fuck. I have to take this." I grab the device and bring it to my ear.

Cleo's eyes widen. "Are you serio—"

"What is it?" My fingers are still inside my wife's pulsating cunt. I nestle the phone between my shoulder and my ear and press a hand over Cleo's mouth.

She shakes her head, bucking against me, but I pin her to the desk with my thigh.

"We need you at 37 Ringold. Caught another Bratva fucker sniffing around a construction site."

I curl my fingers inside of Cleo, pressing against her G-spot, and she stops fighting. She makes a muffled moan against my hand.

"Who's with you?" I remove my hand from her mouth, grab my phone, and mute it. "Are you going to come for me again, *tesoro*?"

Cleo's green eyes flash with outrage, but there's enough lust in her gaze to almost mask it.

"Jeremy and Vinny. We think this guy might be a higher-up. Someone might come looking for him soon."

Irritation buzzes beneath my skin. I don't want to go torture this fuck. I want to drive my cock inside my wife's tight cunt and hear her moan my name. I want to make her mine. I unmute the phone and put my hand back over Cleo's mouth. My fingers thrust in and out of her, hitting just the right spot. Her eyelashes flutter. She digs her nails into my biceps.

"Are you coming?" Nero asks.

"I was about to until you called," I say under my breath. Cleo snorts against my palm.

"What's that? Can't hear you."

Honestly, fuck my life.

"Yes. I'll be there," I snap. I'm a don, not a teenage boy. I can wait a bit longer.

I hang up the call and press my thumb against Cleo's swollen clit. She grinds her hips against me, her body seeking its release. My hand moves from her mouth to tangle with her hair. "Come for me, *tesoro*," I growl. "Let me see it."

She sobs, her green eyes hooded. "Oh fuck." And then she tosses her head back and rides her climax, wave after wave.

I stare at her, drinking it all in. The drama of her orgasm plays out across her pretty face, and I can't look away.

Something warm spreads through my chest at how good it feels to please her. But it's over all too soon.

I pull on her hair until our foreheads touch. "I have to go," I say against her lips. "But when I get back, we're going to finish what we started. This game is done. You're mine, Cleo. Do you understand? You're. Fucking. *Mine*."

CHAPTER 26

CLEO

Rafaele doesn't come back that night, and in the morning, I get a message from him saying he needs to go to Syracuse for some meetings.

I wonder if it's hard for him to be away from me after what happened, the way it is for me. All morning, I amble around the house and pretend to be a functioning human being instead of a needy, lust-filled mess. A movie of what happened in my husband's office won't stop playing on repeat inside my head. I imagine what it looked like for him, to see me splayed on his desk with my pussy presented to him like it was dinner.

He ate me like a gourmet meal.

An insistent heat pulsates in the pit of my belly. I have to swap my underwear once or twice. I even consider texting Rafaele that to torture him a bit the way he's torturing me, but something holds me back.

Something.

As if I don't know exactly what it is. The bitter taste of my father's offer is right there, lodged beneath my tongue.

If Rafaele hadn't left right after he made me come, I would have let him take it all the way. I would have slept with the man my father wants to kill. The man my father wants me to *help* kill.

After lunch, I step out onto the terrace and brace my palms on the stone railing. A cool breeze brushes over my skin. At the edge of the property, tall pines sway in the wind and whisper secrets. I suck in a lungful of fresh air, expanding my chest until it's full, and then slowly breathe it out.

It does nothing to calm my anxiety or my racing pulse.

This can't go on. I can't keep going to Loretta's and doing inventory, spending my evenings buried in spreadsheets and ignoring this thing hanging over my head.

My mother asked me to come see her yesterday. I knew what it meant, and because I'm a coward, I didn't go to my old home. Papà wants an answer. And I want...

I think I want Rafaele.

My eyes fall shut. I told myself I'd never surrender to him, but that was when surrender meant defeat.

It doesn't now. The truth is, I don't hate my husband anymore. There's far more to him than meets the eye. He's more than a don, more than a killer, more than my prison warden.

Rafaele works a lot. Unlike Papà, he doesn't just sit in his office and expect his capos to bring him their reports. He goes to their territories, helps them with their problems, and he seems to genuinely give a shit about taking care of them.

My father always thought that was beneath him. All he knows how to do is yell and threaten, but I've overheard how Rafaele talks to his men, and he doesn't need to raise his voice to get them to do something. He's a natural leader, and he has their respect.

And then there's the way he treats me. The way he makes me feel. Like I'm more than just a fuckup. Like I've got something good to give.

I've been written off by everyone in my life, one way or another. Everyone but him.

I cover my face with my palms and finally come to terms with it.

I can't betray him.

Maybe it's a mistake. Maybe I'm allowing myself to be driven by feelings Rafaele may never reciprocate. Maybe. But I've never been one to worry about consequences, have I?

I drop my palms and gaze at the clear blue sky.

I will never be Rafaele's possession.

I will never belong *to* him.

But I think I belong *with* him.

A few more days pass with Rafaele gone. He returns on Friday, the same evening we're scheduled for our dinner with the Ferraros. Everyone knows who they are, but I've never met any members of the family. I'm not sure which family is more powerful, the Ferraros or the Messeros, but they're equally feared in New York.

I'm trying to pick what to wear when my husband strolls into the closet and meets my gaze in the mirror. His is pure hunger. He prowls over to me, wraps his arm around my waist, and presses his lips to the side of my throat. A low buzz appears beneath my skin.

"How was your trip?"

"Too long," he growls against my skin.

"Missed me?" I try to sound casual, but the second it takes him to respond makes my heart stutter.

"You have no idea." His eyes meet mine again. "This dinner couldn't have come at a worse time, *tesoro*. I don't want to share you with anyone tonight."

My body burns under his gaze. He knows. He *knows* I'm done for. If he pushed me down to the floor right here in the closet and said he wanted to fuck me like an animal, I'd let him. There isn't much I wouldn't let him do to me right now. I missed him too. More than I thought was possible.

He glances around the closet. "Picking your outfit?"

"Mm-hmm."

"The Ferraros won't agree to wearing blindfolds willingly," he says in a low voice, his lips close to my ear. "Don't make me force them."

My laugh is breathless. "Don't worry. I've got something at stake tonight too, remember?"

Maybe he doesn't. Loretta's supplier contract is hardly the most important thing he has on his mind.

"I remember." He turns me in his arms so that I face him. "I prepared the revised contract with updated payment terms. All Gino will have to do is get his cousin to sign it."

My stomach flutters. "When did you have the time to do that?"

His hand slides down my back, and there's a subtle smile playing on his lips. "I always make time for things that are important."

My chest constricts. I can't wait any longer. I have to tell him about what Papà asked of me. I've decided I won't help him. Now, I just have to warn Rafaele.

But before I can tell him, he cuts me off with a kiss. The kind that scrambles thoughts and makes nerve endings fire. His tongue brushes against mine, and I forget all about my father. I lean into Rafaele's strong body, dragging my hands over his muscled shoulders, and imagine what it will feel like to have this body moving over me.

Heat stirs between my legs.

Too soon, he breaks the kiss and steps away from me. There's something distinctly unrestrained in his expression, but he manages to blink it away. "We should leave in fifteen." His voice is hoarse. "Will you be ready?"

Tell him.

No, I can't tell him now. Not when I have the convenient excuse of being in a hurry.

I force a smile. "Yes."

I choose a shimmery white dress off the rack and disappear into the bathroom to change.

Twenty minutes later, we're in the car with Sandro. He drives us to Manhattan, straight to a building in Billionaires' Row.

When the private elevator opens, Rafaele and I step inside a palatial lobby with a glittering chandelier and an intricate mosaic floor that depicts swirling fish. Straight across from the elevator is a magnificent water feature—a large slab of stone with water cascading down its surface.

A man in a butler's uniform greets us and takes our jackets before leading us behind the water feature and into the living area.

My eyes widen. The home spans two entire floors. My father's condo a few streets over, which I've always thought of as the height of luxury, suddenly feels incredibly small.

The design of the space has an obvious Asian influence. It's serene and sophisticated, with clean lines, natural colors, and dark furniture.

I catch a glimpse of what might be the best view in the city before my attention is drawn to the man walking over to greet us.

Gino Ferraro, the don of the family. He doesn't look like one of the most dangerous men in New York. With his handsome grin and thick silver hair, he'd fit right in at Bloomingdale's on Christmas, dressed in a red Santa suit, sans the gut. But he's not the first monster I've met in our world who hides his monstrous nature beneath layers of deception.

"Rafaele," he says in a rumbling voice. "Welcome."

He and Rafaele shake hands. "Thank you for inviting us into your home."

"It's my pleasure. And this must be your lovely new wife." He pins his perceptive gaze on me. When I offer him my hand, he lifts it to his lips, and the coarse hairs of his white beard brush against my skin.

"I'm glad we could make this happen. Let me introduce you to my boys."

His sons are standing in the corner by the floor-to-ceiling windows that overlook Central Park like three dark sentinels, their black suits in stark contrast against the beige crane-patterned wallpaper.

Whatever serenity the decor of this place managed to create is immediately erased. I don't think there's anyone who'd ever feel at peace in the presence of these men.

One after the other, they turn toward us. Each one deadly. Each one undeniably handsome. Beautiful monsters. This world is filled with them.

Gino leads Rafaele and me toward his sons, and the collective force of their attention makes my throat go dry.

"This is my eldest, Cosimo," Gino says, gesturing at the tallest man in the group.

Cosimo Ferraro could have been a movie star if he wasn't a mobster. Not that he had much of a choice, which makes it even more of a tragedy. Men who look like him, with flowing hazel hair and piercing blue eyes that rival those of my husband's, don't belong amongst us mere mortals. They're meant to be idolized by the fawning masses.

He sizes up Rafaele, his eyes lingering on the exact spots where my husband is hiding his weapons beneath his suit. The fact that no one asked Rafaele to disarm when we first walked in likely means they're all carrying.

A nervous shiver runs down my spine. This is a friendly dinner. Let's hope it doesn't end the way our dinner at Il Caminetto did.

Cosimo coolly greets Rafaele and barely spares me a look before Gino steers us to the next man. "This is Alessio."

The Ferraro's famed enforcer. His long hair is tied back, showing off the scar that runs across his temple. A smaller one cuts through his left brow. Tattoos cover his hands and his neck, and when he shakes my hand after Rafaele's, I make out the letters on his knuckles. *MORE.* My gaze drops to his other hand. It completes the phrase. *MORE PAIN.*

My blood cools. Jesus. Is that what he promises the men he tortures if they don't give up their secrets?

"And this is my youngest son. Romolo."

I tear my gaze away from those tattooed letters and turn to the last brother.

He's the only one who smiles at me, even if it doesn't quite reach his eyes. "Call me Rom." By the time he turns to Rafaele, the smile is gone. "Messero," he says, a bite to his tone. "I have to admit, I didn't think we'd ever see you walk through these doors."

Everyone knows about Rom Ferraro.

A long time ago, when I was scheming how to ensure I would be eliminated from the marriage circuit, I considered arranging a meeting with Rom. His reputation as a womanizer is unmatched by anyone in our circles. Just being seen in the same room as him while unsupervised used to be enough to start a scandal.

Rumor is he's grown up in the past few years, but tales of his conquests still filter through the mouths of my father's men.

Rafaele gives Rom his signature icy stare. "Likewise. But times change."

Rom's lips tighten. "Yeah, they sure fucking do."

"Language! You know better than to speak like that when you're in this house, Rom."

Everyone turns in the direction of the voice. It belongs to a statuesque, silver-haired woman who must be their mom. She walks over, her perfectly straight locks swishing back and forth with each step, and she gives me a smile that wraps around me like a warm, cozy blanket.

Some tension in my shoulders disappears. Somehow, I just know this woman will make sure no blood is spilled tonight. She hugs me, pulling me tightly against her chest, as I catch a whiff of her refined perfume.

"Cleo Messero." Her eyes sparkle with warmth. "I'm Vita. How are you, my dear? I hope they didn't bore you with their manhood-measuring contest. That's how these boys always are. What are you drinking? Wine? Whiskey? A strong martini? Alcohol is always the answer on nights like these." She places a hand on my back and steers me toward the bar.

Gino clears his throat. "Vita."

She glances back at him. "Yes, my love?"

"There's one more guest," Gino says, giving his wife an indulgent smile.

She tsks. "Ah, that's right."

"Hello, daughter."

Ice pours into my veins. Slowly, I turn toward my father.

"What are you doing here?"

"I invited him," Gino says, coming to stand by Papà's side. He's wearing an is-there-a-problem-here smile as he gives Rafaele a pointed look. "After all, you've joined your families, so I thought it would be best if we all sit down at the table."

"Good to see you, Garzolo," Rafaele says, seeming unfazed by this turn of events, but I can't say the same for myself. Is Papà seeking an ally in Ferraro to take down Rafaele? I doubt Ferraro would work with someone whose word clearly means nothing, but what do I know?

My father stops before me and leans down to press a kiss to my cheek. "We need to talk," he whispers in my ear.

I know what he wants to talk about, and he won't like what he hears.

We sit down at the oval dining table, and Rafaele brings up the issue with the contract before we've even finished the first course.

Gino waves his hand dismissively. "Done. My cousin Ricardo has always been a stickler on issues like this, but I'll take care of it."

"I appreciate it," I say automatically. Rafaele squeezes my hand under the table, but I'm too tense to feel relieved.

The dinner proceeds without a hiccup, and the conversation flows easily with the help of Vita's friendly presence.

The Ferraro matriarch is very different from my mother. She seems so kind and lovely, and there's no mistaking the adoration in Gino's eyes whenever he looks at her. She tells us the story of how she and Gino met. She was a fashion model, and he sat in the front row for one of the shows she walked. He asked her manager for her number and proposed a week later.

"It was a whirlwind romance," she exclaims. "Took a while for his family to warm up to me, given that I'm not Italian.

"But she eventually won them over," Gino says. "Very few can resist my wife's charms."

God, they're cute together. And here I thought all mafia marriages were miserable. The way they're looking at each other, I get the sense they still fuck like bunnies.

"Rafaele, I'd like to have a word in private," Gino says once we finish our dessert. "Why don't you join me for a drink on the terrace?"

Rafaele nods before turning to me and lowering his voice. "You okay on your own for a while?"

"Of course." I nudge his thigh. "Go."

Rafaele and Gino leave. Vita offers to show me some of their Japanese artwork, and we look at the paintings for a while before I have to excuse myself to use the bathroom.

"It's just down that hall," Vita explains.

I do my business, wash my hands, and dab some cold water on my neck. Anxiety crawls over my skin. And it's justified, because my father corners me as soon as I come out.

He backs me against a wall. "Have you thought about my offer?"

I wince. His breath reeks even worse than his desperation.

"Give me some space," I say, pushing at his chest.

He backs away slightly, his beady eyes narrowed and his forehead shiny. Nervous? He's right to be worried. He won't find an ally in me, or anyone else who possesses an ounce of sense.

"We don't have a lot of time, Cleo," he growls. "I'm waiting on your answer."

My fists clench. "I won't help you."

His reaction is immediate. A hiss comes out of his mouth, and then his forearm is against my neck, and my back is being slammed against the wall.

I gasp from the sudden pain, my veins blazing with shock. I expected him to be angry, but I didn't think he'd turn aggressive.

"Did you tell him I asked, you stupid slut?"

I claw at his arm. I can't get enough air. Just when dark spots start to appear in front of my eyes, he lets go of me.

"Did you?"

I back away from him, rubbing my throat. My brain struggles to catch up with what just happened. He's dangerous.

"Don't ever do that again," I say, unable to keep my voice from shaking. "No, I didn't tell him. But I won't help you. I don't want *anything* to do with you."

He snarls. "I should kill you right here so that you won't run your mouth to him."

I straighten my back and force myself to stay calm. "I'd like to see you try. If I'm dead, Rafaele will make sure you're carried out of here in pieces."

I brush past him, but he seizes my forearm and jerks me back. "Whatever he told you to turn to his side is a lie. You'll be miserable with him. He's not a good man."

"And you are?"

His hold on me tightens until he's practically crushing my bones.

"Ow, stop!"

"You'll regret this decision."

"Let go of me."

"You've always been such a fucking disappointment," he hisses.

"Want to know what I find disappointing?" a cool voice drawls. "Your utter lack of manners, Garzolo."

Papà releases me at once. I whirl around to see Cosimo standing at the end of the hallway studying us. His appearance somehow feels a lot more menacing than all of Papà's threats.

He crosses his arms over his chest and props a shoulder against a wall. "Save the domestic dispute for when you're in your own home."

"My daughter and I were just catching up," my father says, a tense smile on his face.

"We're all caught up," I mutter.

That earns me a sharp glare, but at least Papà keeps his mouth shut. He hurries past Cosimo and disappears around the corner.

Cosimo studies me as I walk toward him. "He's a real piece of work," he says when we're shoulder to shoulder. His gaze drops to my arm. "Something tells me your husband won't be thrilled about that."

I pull down my sleeve. "I'm fine. Please don't say anything to Rafaele." He'd lose it.

Cosimo stares at me for a long moment and then nods. "Not my business."

I brush past him, knowing there's no way to undo the decision I made.

Tonight, I will have to come clean to my husband.

CHAPTER 27

RAFAELE

Gino and I walk out onto his terrace, and he leads me toward a rectangular pool full of koi. The fish are apparitions in the dark water, coming to the surface for only a few seconds before they disappear again.

"They don't get cold in the winter?"

Gino follows the movement of one with his gaze. "They're resilient. The pool is deep enough for them to swim near the bottom even when the top freezes over."

"They can live under the ice?" That sounds like a claustrophobic nightmare.

"They can." A smile pulls on his lips. "Impressive, isn't it? One of my earliest childhood memories is sitting by a koi pond with my mother and watching them swim. She'd take me to the Japanese garden in Brooklyn and tell me the tale of the koi that climbed up the waterfall. A Japanese legend. The fish that managed to overcome the challenge of swimming upstream in a waterfall became a fearsome dragon. She'd say to me that no matter how impossible it felt to navigate a given situation, pushing through would make me stronger."

A bitter taste floods my mouth. I can't remember ever having moments like that with my mother.

Father didn't like her spending a lot of time with me, so he kept us apart for most of my childhood. She was always with the girls, and I was cared for by a rotating menagerie of nannies, none of whom ever stuck around for long. When I turned eleven, he sent Mamma with the girls to the house in the Hamptons. By then, I was glad she left. It meant she'd be safe from him.

"She sounds like she was a good mother."

"She was. She left us too soon." Gino clasps his hands behind his back and wanders over to the edge of the terrace.

Only a thick sheet of glass and a black railing prevent a gust of wind from throwing us off the side of the building. Central Park sprawls below us, a dark gash in the sea of concrete and skyscrapers.

Gino drags his hand over his beard. "I'm curious... How did your father explain our tense relationship to you?"

"He said it was because he killed one of your uncles." He always claimed it was an accident, but knowing my father, that was probably a lie.

Gino exhales a low laugh. "Of course he'd give you that reason. He probably believed it himself." He places his hands on the railing. "My father had eleven brothers. He got along with about half of them. One of them, he choked with

242

his bare hands over an argument that had something to do with a car his brother borrowed without asking for permission. Another was so brutally humiliated by my father on multiple occasions that he hung himself. We are a complicated family. The uncle your father shot was frankly irrelevant."

I glance at him. "Then what really happened?"

"As I'm sure you've realized being inside my home, I have an affinity for water. But your father... He loved fire. Did you know that even before he killed my Uncle Aldo, he burned one of my warehouses down to the ground on a cold night in December?"

Fire.

A memory scurries through me.

My father used to burn the faces of the men he interrogated. He'd grab them by the scruff of their neck, drag them to the fireplace, and shove their face into the flames. When I was a kid, he'd sometimes make me watch. I had repressed that memory for years.

Gino continues, "I'll never forget it. It was Christmas Eve ninety-one. You weren't even born then, were you? I was with my family, and Vita had prepared a feast. I can still remember that giant roast turkey. It looked like it was taken straight out of a commercial on the Food Network." He chuckles. "I couldn't wait to try it. I think I ate one bite before I got the call. They shouted that a warehouse was on fire. I had to leave the dinner to go check it out. Vita looked like she was going to kill me, but we had about twenty million dollars' worth of product in that warehouse, and back then, that was a lot for my family. By the time I got there, there was nothing left to salvage. The fire burned everything to the ground."

Yeah, that sounds like my father. He liked to destroy things.

"I walked through the smoking rubble and found a charred corpse. A guard. We only had one that night because we thought no one would dare try something on *Christmas*?" Gino sounds incredulous. "None of us are upstanding citizens, but for men like us, family means something."

I purse my lips. My father was first and foremost a don. For him, family wasn't even in the top ten of his priorities. He cared about me in his own twisted way, but when it came to my mother and my sisters... He treated them like possessions devoid of thoughts and feelings. He wasn't the kind of man who'd ever have any empathy for another man's family. For all his rigid rules and traditions, he spit on all our family's core values.

He respected only one thing—strength. Which is why he loathed dying a weak man.

I turn to Gino. "Let's not keep our families in this decades-long standoff over something that happened before I was even born. Let me repay you for the damage my father caused."

He lifts his shoulder. "I appreciate the gesture. I do. And maybe we can start there. But I can't promise that it will be enough, because it wasn't just my business that was harmed that night."

Foreboding slithers down my spine.

"You're married now. One day, you might disappoint your wife the way I disappointed mine that Christmas, and if you love her, maybe you'll find it just as difficult to forgive the man who caused that disappointment." His gaze leaves me, moving back to the Manhattan skyline. "That year was hard on Vita. I was away a lot, always working, always trying to grow the business. We were newlyweds, and she was adjusting to a world that was completely new to her. I tore her away from the life she had, a life where she was successful and independent and happy, all because I promised I'd make her happier, but that year, I failed on my promise."

I take a sip of my whiskey. Gino might be the only don in this city married to an outsider. I can see why he thought Vita was worth the trouble. Even now that she's older, she is a strikingly beautiful woman. His affection for her is blatant. He doesn't try to hide that he worships her.

How strange. Isn't he afraid someone will use her against him one day?

"Cosimo was one. Vita was already pregnant with Alessio. She spent all evening with our baby, both of them waiting for me to return so that we could enjoy that moment with our little family. But I didn't come back until the morning, and I brought bad news." He sighs. "That lone guard was Vita's cousin, Andy. Andy was ostracized by the rest of her family for being an addict. But Vita never gave up on him. She helped him get clean, and she even got him a job with me. She invited him to spend Christmas with us, but he wanted to work, wanted to be busy on the night when those with messed up families feel most alone. Imagine how it felt for me to tell her that he'd died."

Fuck. My jaw clenches.

I wonder if my father knew the man's identity. Probably. He was exceptionally good at finding other people's weak spots.

"Vita struggled for a while. My boy seemed to act differently toward me too, even though he was far too young to understand what had happened. Seeing how I hurt them broke my heart." He draws a loud breath through his nose and exhales with a shake of his head. "Not much gets to me like that."

Emotions flicker across his face in quick succession. Disappointment, pain, grief...

I shift on my feet, uneasy. He's opening up to me, leaving his feelings bare for me to see. His love for his family. His love for his wife. His need to protect them. Doesn't he know doing this is a sign of weakness? You don't reveal your soft spots to a rival. Even better, you don't develop soft spots at all.

When he meets my eyes, there's a clear warning in his, the kind that can't be misunderstood. He's telling me that if I ever hope to establish peace between us, I have to stay the fuck away from him and the people he loves.

I smooth my hand over my tie. I'm not a fan of apologizing for my father's many sins, but the situation warrants it.

"I'm sorry. I know my father never apologized to you, and hearing it from me won't carry the same weight, but I want you to know that I *am* sorry for the harm he caused you."

It appears it's the right thing to do. Gino's gaze flashes with a hint of respect. "I can see you're sincere, and I appreciate it."

He brings his glass of whiskey to his lips and finishes it off. "Let's keep this conversation going. We should touch base week to week. The threat of the Bratva isn't one we should ignore, and it will serve everyone if the two big players in the city are a united front."

Good. This is progress. "I agree."

He pats me on the shoulder. "We should go back."

I look toward the room, searching for Cleo on the other side of the glass. But I don't see her anywhere.

CHAPTER 28

RAFAELE

I REENTER through the sliding doors and glance around the room. Vita and two of her sons are by the bar cart having a heated discussion about something.

Where's Garzolo? More importantly, where is my wife?

The staccato of her heels reaches my ears before she pops out of a random hallway. Cosimo is a few steps behind her. My eyes narrow. What were they doing there together? And why does she look so flustered?

I cross the room. Her steps slow when she sees me approach.

"What happened?"

"Nothing." She says it too quickly, and her cheeks are flushed.

An ugly suspicion blooms inside me. "Where were you?"

"In the bathroom."

"Why was Cosimo following behind you?"

She crosses her arms and huffs an annoyed breath. "Because I was sucking his cock."

My vision darkens at the edges. *What the—*

"God, I'm joking," she snaps. "Relax."

"Bad joke," I growl.

She shakes her head and looks around the room like she's searching for someone. "How much longer until we can get out of here?"

What is going on with her? "We can leave now."

We say our goodbyes and leave the condominium. Cleo won't meet my eye on the elevator ride to the parking lot.

My jaw clenches. "Cleo."

"What?" she asks the floor.

For fuck's sake. I corner her against one of the mirrored walls and lift her chin. "What's going on with you?"

She drops her gaze to stare at my chest, clamping on her bottom lip with her teeth.

I nudge her chin higher, forcing her to look at me. "Answer me."

"Drop it," she breathes.

"No."

The elevator door opens. She pushes past me, hurrying into the lot, but I'm right behind her.

I grab her forearm. "Cleo—"

She winces like I'm hurting her. I know I'm not. My grip is firm, but not enough to be painful. I pull her sleeve up and see a handprint on her forearm. A hot wave of anger rolls through me.

He. Hurt. My. Wife?

He's a fucking dead man. I disengage the knife strapped to my wrist, letting the handle slide into my waiting palm, and start walking back to the elevator. I'm going to slice off the hand Cosimo used to do this. And then I'm going to feed it to that fucking koi.

"Rafe! What are you doing?" Cleo shouts after me.

"Gonna cut him."

There's a gasp and I hear her heels clacking against the concrete floor as she tries to catch up to me. "He's already gone! You can't just walk back into Ferraro's home with a knife! What's wrong with you?"

I halt. "Who's gone?"

"My father." She comes around me, blocking my path.

My thoughts rush to catch up. "Your *father* did this to you?"

"Who do you think?" Her eyes widen with realization. "You thought it was Cosimo? *No*. He got Papà away from me."

This doesn't make any sense. "Why would your father do this to you? You told me he never laid a hand on you."

"He didn't!" She shoves her fingers into her hair and huffs out an anguished breath. Her gaze flickers with whatever she's refusing to tell me. "Rafe, please. Just calm down."

Calm down? Only then do I clue into the fact that I'm panting like an enraged bear. My pulse is pounding so hard

I can hear it inside my ears. My palm is hot around the handle of the knife. Every muscle in my body is tense, ready to strike.

It's happening again. This is how I felt when I saw Ludovico trying to force himself on her in my club. How I felt when I saw her bleeding on the ground in Il Caminetto.

Out of control.

I give my head a shake, Nero's warning coming back to me loud and clear.

I've seen how she gets under your skin.

Fuck it. I don't give a fuck about any of that right now. All I know is that I'd do anything to protect her. Anything. And if that means killing her father so he can never touch her again, so be it.

She grabs my wrist and tries to pull me in the direction of our car. "Please. Let's just get into the car and go home."

"Cleo, tell me what is going on. Why would your father do this?"

She sniffs.

I force myself to take a deep breath. "You know you can tell me anything, right?"

She grimaces. I study her face. Her eyes are wide and, God fucking help me, *guilty*. I know that look so well I'd recognize it on anyone. But if her father hurt her, why does she feel guilty? And why isn't she answering me?

Cleo hates her father. She wouldn't stay silent to protect him. But she'd stay silent to protect herself.

Whatever she sees in my expression makes her let go of my arm. She takes one step back, then another.

Alarm bells are ringing in my head. "What did you do?"

Her cheeks are flushed. "Okay. Listen. I can explain."

I start to advance on her, my suspicions confirmed. "Do you know how many times people have said that to me? I'll let you guess how those conversations usually end."

She backs away from me. "Two weeks ago, Papà made me an offer."

I match her step for step. "What kind of an offer?"

"He..." She swallows. "He asked me to spy on you."

My body freezes. A deep pit opens in my stomach, filled with razor blades and ice.

"To what end?" I grind out.

Her eyes fill with tears. "He wanted me to find a weakness so that he could get rid of you."

I can't help but laugh. This is too good. Garzolo, that fucking backstabbing snake. I should have known a man like him can never be trusted. But this was really his best plan? Get his daughter involved?

My eyes narrow on Cleo. She makes me feel like I'm going crazy. Did I really just think I'd do anything for this woman? That's not how this works. I know that's not how this works.

I'm a don, and my first duty is to my position, not to her. But she is my wife, and she is supposed to be fucking loyal to me.

A tear slips down her cheek. "I didn't do it!"

My stomach swoops with relief, but it's short-lived as I rewind our conversation. "Two weeks ago? You've been sitting on this information for two weeks?"

She presses her lips together, trying to hold back her emotions. Emotions I don't fucking understand, because the way it seems to me, I should be the one upset here.

I advance on her. "Did you find anything? Did you spot any weaknesses?"

Her pulse pounds against the side of her neck. She takes another step back. "You don't have any."

"You and your father aren't on good terms. He must have offered you something in exchange."

"He did. He offered me freedom. I wouldn't have to marry anyone else. He said that after he managed to kill you, he would disown me, and that I could go to Italy to be with Vale and Gem."

Go to Italy? In what fucking universe would I allow that to happen? Oh right, the one where I'm dead.

The thought of her living a life without me somehow triggers me far more than anything else she's just said. My anger pulsates beneath my flesh, my vision narrows, my breaths come out short and quick. There isn't enough oxygen in my lungs.

This is a possibility she considered for *two fucking weeks*?

Cleo tries to take another step back, but there's nowhere to go. Her calf hits the edge of our car, and she yelps as she loses her balance.

I eat up the space between us with two long strides and force her back against the car door. Above us, a fluorescent light flickers. It's the only movement in the empty garage.

Did I bring this on myself by being so lenient with her? Has she forgotten who she married?

She glances at the hand I've got pinning her shoulder, exposing her neck to me. I lift my knife and press the cool blade against her delicate throat. She stiffens. Sucks in a breath.

Sandro's head pops out on the driver's side. "Boss?"

"Get the fuck back inside."

A beat passes before he does as he's told.

I move my hand from her shoulder to her chin and turn her face toward me.

My wife stares at me with her piercing green eyes, the color of emeralds. Who knew they could hide so much deceit inside their depths?

"He offered you a good deal," I whisper.

She licks her lips. "Everything I thought I wanted."

"And tonight, you told him no?"

"I told him no."

I lean closer. "Took you two fucking weeks to do it, though."

When she swallows, a part of her neck brushes against my blade.

You know what's infuriating? Even now, with my knife pressed to her throat, she doesn't seem scared. Upset, yes, but not scared. Like she knows I'd never harm her, even

254

after what she just confessed. And she thinks I have no weaknesses?

"What finally made you decide not to turn on me?"

Another tear slips down her cheek, but she doesn't answer.

I press in, my hips pinning hers. "Hmm? What was it? The jewelry, the money, the staff that's at your beck and call?"

Slowly, she shakes her head. I have to pull my knife back a few millimeters so that she doesn't cut herself on it.

"Was it the way I ate your cunt a few days ago?"

She bites down on her lip and shakes her head again.

I'm so close, our noses are practically touching. "Then what the fuck was it?"

She exhales a broken breath. "It's the way you see something in me. Something that no one else does. Around you, I'm not just a fuckup that needs fixing."

My chest caves in. Something inside me wavers.

A sob escapes her. "I should have told you earlier."

Glistening eyes. Wet cheeks. Parted lips. I know guilt, but I know sincerity too. It skims off some of my anger, turns the temperature down.

"You shouldn't have even considered it. Your father is a fucking idiot, and his plan would have never worked. You should have known that."

"I'm sorry. I'm so sorry."

I lower my knife, tuck it back up my sleeve, and open the car door. "Get in."

She slides inside, keeping her gaze on me the entire time. I follow after her and slam the door shut.

Sandro looks at me in the rearview mirror, his jaw tense and his skin as pale as a sheet. "Where to?"

"Home."

Cleo huddles on the other end of the seat, her pink-rimmed eyes glued to me. I look away from her. We drive through a maze of skyscrapers, and I attempt to settle down, but ten minutes later, I'm still buzzing.

She didn't do it.

But she thought about it. She imagined her new life without me in it.

She chose you.

A growl tears its way out of my throat, and I grab her, pull her on top of me, shove the skirt of her dress up so that she can straddle my thighs.

Her wide eyes meet mine. She looks like a deer in the headlights, unsure about whether to stay still or try to run.

I shove my hand into her hair and kiss her. It's rough and raw and dominating. Meant to stake a claim. Meant to remind her who she belongs to.

She chose you.

Her mouth parts for me. My tongue slides in. I bite on her lips, pulling on them with my teeth. I kiss her until we're both panting, until my anger mixes with arousal, the kind that makes one burn.

I'm furious with her, and I'm so fucking hard.

She chose you.

Cleo brings her hands to my chest, her right palm over my pounding heart. I pull them off me. Why should she know how she makes this damned thing race?

I guide her wrists behind her and press them to her lower back. I dip my other hand into the pocket on the back of Sandro's seat and pull out one of the zip ties I always keep there. I'm still kissing her as I wrap the tie around her wrists. Pull it tight.

She rears back, her lips puffy and her cheeks pink. "What are you doing?"

Sandro's gaze flicks to us in the mirror. We make eye contact for a split second before he swallows and looks back to the road.

"You called me your jailer. Maybe it's time I start acting like one."

Her mouth parts in shock. Her arms flex as she tests the restraint, but it's no use. She's at my mercy now.

"Take it off." Her voice shakes.

"No."

I drag my gaze over her body, down to where I can see the triangle of her underwear peeking out. My thumb brushes her slit through the fabric. She whimpers. I do it again. And again. Until she's shaking, struggling to stay still.

She glances over her shoulder like she's worried Sandro's watching us. He can't see anything from the angle he's at.

I dig my fingers into her thighs and lean forward, pressing my lips to her ear. "I should fuck you right here and have you bleed all over the seat. Maybe I'll ask Sandro to clean it up afterward."

I expect her to curse me, but she doesn't.

When I lean back, indignation burns inside her eyes. Like she knows I'm not this, that I'd never do this, and that I'm not fooling her, so why am I saying it? Just to hurt her? The way she hurt me? My chest spasms.

No, nothing hurts you.

She leans forward and kisses me.

This time, it's different. Soft. Apologetic. Conciliatory.

I turn my head, ending it. I'm not done being angry at her.

"I want to punish you," I whisper.

"Then do it," she whispers back.

CHAPTER 29

CLEO

Rafaele stares at me over the low hum of the car's engine and the barely there song playing on the stereo. The silence clogs my throat, but I don't dare break it. We hit a speed bump. I bounce in his lap and make contact with something hard.

My tongue darts out past my lips, and his gaze dips to my mouth.

The air in the car feels more charged than the sky before lightning strikes.

See the problem with not thinking about consequences? It's how you end up in the back seat of a car with your wrists zip-tied, lips raw, and heart aching.

I should have known he'd get angry about how long it took me to tell him the truth, but I needed that time to sort through my feelings. I'm taking a huge leap of faith here.

His hands, big and warm, are on my thighs. He traces the edge of my panties with his fingertips. I don't think he even realizes he's doing it. He's so far gone inside his head. The tendons in his neck are taut, and his jaw hasn't unclenched since I whispered into his ear.

Is he thinking of the ways he'll punish me?

"What will you do to my father?" I ask, if only to pretend like I'm not buzzing with anticipation.

My husband is a killer. I should be scared of what he'll do to me. But it's not fear that's making my pussy clench. There's a dark promise inside his gaze, the kind that makes me think of tangled sheets, bite marks, and filth muttered against my ear.

"He will die, but I'm done talking about him tonight."

I nod. I guess, so am I. What happens to my father now is out of my hands. He dug his own grave.

The car glides to a smooth stop.

"We're here," Sandro says.

Heat travels up my neck in a wave. I don't know how much Sandro saw or heard, but I know it'll be a while before I can bring myself to look my driver in the eye again.

"No need for you to come out," Rafaele instructs, his gaze on me. "Go home, Sandro."

"Yes, boss."

Rafaele lifts me off him, pulls the skirt of my dress back down, and opens the door.

He helps me out and wraps a hand around my biceps. The zip tie digs into my wrists as he walks me up the front steps. Behind us, the car starts, and Sandro drives off.

Rafaele unlocks the door and gives me a light shove inside. The house is silent. The staff are gone this late in the night. There's no one here but us.

Even if I scream, no one will save me.

The door locks. I feel that harsh click reverberate deep inside my gut. A tendril of fear licks over my nape, but it's swallowed by another wave of heat.

Rafaele stops us in the middle of the foyer and turns me around with a tug on my arm.

The moonlight makes love to the sculpted lines of his face, tracing his furrowed brow, strong jaw, and sharp cheekbones. He lifts his hands to the neck of my dress and curls his big fists around the fabric.

I can guess what he's about to do, but the *rip* that pours through the air still makes me suck in a harsh breath.

I'm not wearing a bra. My breasts pop out. Rafaele's gaze drops to them. He pinches one nipple hard enough to sting. Pain tangles with pleasure. My boobs are achy, begging to be touched and sucked and fucked. When he moves to the other, cupping it completely with his palm, I moan.

Something cruel pierces through his expression. He removes his palm and meets my eyes. Darkness flickers on the edges of his gaze.

"On your knees."

Sparks run straight to my clit. I go down inelegantly, nearly tipping over, but he stops me from falling with a fist in my hair. I gasp from the harsh pull on my strands, from the way he forces my head back so that I'm looking up at him.

Possession swirls inside the dark-blue waters of his eyes. One hand still in my hair, he undoes his belt and pulls it out of the loops. He throws it to the ground, the buckle clanking against the marble floor.

I glance down and see an outline of his cock straining against his slacks. Shivers erupt over my spine as he pulls down his zipper, reaches inside, takes himself out. My mouth waters at the sight of him. He's long and thick, with veins running up the shaft. Pre-cum glistens at the tip.

I've done this before a few times, but I was always in charge. Not now, though. Now, he's going to take whatever he wants.

My clit pulses with the thought of that thick cock inside my mouth. How well will I please him?

He steps closer, wraps a hand around himself, and drags the swollen tip over my puffy lips. "I want you to remember this the next time you're tempted to imagine a life without me. You're mine. Do you understand? No one else will touch you like this. No one else will come inside of you. No one else will fuck your throat like I'm about to. All those things are my fucking privilege, Cleo. And I will kill anyone who conspires to take that privilege away from me."

His fingers tighten in my hair, and his cock bobs against my lips.

Sweat breaks out over my skin. This is meant to be degrading, but I guess I'm into that, because my panties are drenched.

He tugs me toward him. "Open up."

The second my mouth parts, he slides himself inside. Salty and male and very *large*. I close my lips around him and suck. He makes a few shallow thrusts, letting my mouth get familiar with him.

I flatten my tongue and press it against the underside of his cock. A groan rumbles deep inside his chest.

That sound is so hot it makes my eyelids flutter. Waves of heat crash over my skin, making every nerve ending fire. Even the sting of the hard marble floor against my knees seems erotic.

He pushes in deeper, until his head touches the back of my throat. Until I gag and choke and writhe on the floor before him.

"Fuck," he grunts, pulling back to let me catch my breath. I suck on air, but he only gives me a second before he thrusts back in, his fist firm in my hair.

He picks up his pace. It's rough and hard and overwhelming, but I don't fight it. It's shocking how easy it is to give him control. To let him use me however he likes.

My wrists flex against the zip tie. I do my best to relax my throat muscles. The next time he thrusts, he goes even deeper, so deep that the tip of my nose brushes against the trimmed hair at the base of his cock. My eyes water, and when I glance up at him through my wet eyelashes, he groans and pulls out until only the head is in my mouth.

I suck on it and swirl my tongue against the sensitive spot underneath.

Suddenly, he pulls me off him. "You're too fucking good at that," he mutters like he's annoyed.

He shoves his cock back inside his boxer briefs and lifts me by my hair until I'm back to swaying on my heels, my makeup ruined and my dress ripped halfway down the front. His gaze sweeps over me like he's admiring his work.

There must be something wrong with me, because despite my aching throat, I love how pleased he looks.

I clench my thighs together, desperately searching for relief that isn't there. I want him to touch me, God, I'd do anything for him to touch that spot between my legs.

But he's in no rush. He untangles his fingers from my hair and fondles my breasts. Like I'm a toy on display for him to play with. His thumb circles my nipple, making it hard before he moves to the other.

"Exquisite," he mutters to himself. "You're exquisite."

I sway. "Rafe."

His eyes jump to mine. He breaks me apart with his gaze, layer after layer, until it feels like he's staring right into my soul. My eyelids lower in a slow blink. God, I can't believe I'm about to say this.

"You win," I whisper. "I'm begging you. Please fuck me."

A shudder goes through him. He takes me by the waist, lifts me over his shoulder like I weigh nothing, and takes me up the stairs, down the hall, and into our bedroom.

The next thing I know, I'm back on my feet, my front pressed against the wall by the bedroom door. Warmth seeps into my skin where his big hand wraps around my tied wrists. He lowers to his haunches behind me and tugs on the leather shoe strap wrapped around my ankle. One stiletto comes off. He moves to the other. His touch is featherlight against my skin, and I'm so damn turned on that I moan in response.

He stands. There's a rustling sound, like he's taking something out of his suit. I turn my head to check what's happening, but the only thing I see is a flash of metal before the left strap of my dress snaps.

Oh my God. He's cutting off my dress. It takes him another second to cut the other strap, and then my dress is no more than a puddle at my feet. He tucks the knife away somewhere where I can't see and presses his front against my back.

I don't protest when his rough hand slides down the front of my thighs and forces my legs apart. I don't protest when that same warm, big hand pushes its way inside my panties. And I definitely don't protest when he thrusts one thick finger inside of me and growls, "So fucking wet for me."

I am. I'm ready for this. I *need* this.

One finger becomes two, and with it comes a pleasant stretch.

"You have no idea how tight you are," Rafaele murmurs, his breath hot against my neck. "Tighter than I imagined whenever I fucked my fist thinking of you."

My core quivers. "Did you do that often?"

He sides a hand around my front and cups my breast. "Nearly every day. Before I married you, that is."

My head lolls back, bumping against his chest. "And afterward?"

He curls his strong fingers inside me, hitting a spot that makes me gasp. "Too often to admit. Every time I woke up and saw you on the other side of the room, on the other side of the bed. So fucking close, and yet so far." He dips his head, pressing his lips to my neck. "You have no idea what you've done to me."

Teeth press into my flesh. First lightly and then harder, until pain sparks. I whine, and he decreases the pressure. His tongue darts out, and he licks the mark he's undoubtedly left.

The wet sound of his fingers fucking my pussy floods through the air, becomes more and more obscene. I don't care. I don't care about anything anymore. I want him to keep touching me. I want to come. God, I want to come so bad.

"Oh God. That feels so good. Fuck, Rafe—"

He moans and grinds his erection against me. He keeps thrusting his fingers in and out of me, and it's good, it's *so* good, but it's not enough.

"Lick me," I plead. "Please lick me."

And then I'm on the bed, and he's ripping off his jacket and rolling up his sleeves, like he's about to get into all kinds of dirty things.

He kneels on the ground, rips the panties off, shoves my legs apart, and drags his tongue over my folds.

My bound hands dig into my lower back. I arch my body, pushing myself farther into his face. He wraps his arms around my thighs, keeping me in place, and sucks on my clit, flicking it with his talented tongue until I'm hanging on by a thread. The pressure builds, and builds, and builds, and then I come apart.

Oh, how I come apart.

My thoughts are scrambled words on a whiteboard, and the orgasm wipes them clean. There's nothing but ecstasy. Nothing but the pleasure pumping through my body.

I gasp and roll my head to the side. I'm panting, trying to catch my breath.

A thumb brushes against my lower lip. Fingertips trace my jaw. A hand wraps around my neck. When I open my eyes, Rafaele is above me, his hair disheveled and his eyes pitch-black with lust. He tightens his hand around my throat and presses his lips down on mine.

My own taste floods my senses. I moan into his mouth, rolling my hips against him. My clenched fists dig into my lower back, but I barely register the discomfort.

More, more, more.

He pulls back and stares down at me. There's no anger left in his face, just lust. I guess he took all of the anger out on my throat earlier. He moves his hand from my neck to my forehead, brushing away the red strand that's fallen into my eyes.

"If you want me to stop, now would be the time to say it."

Something sparks inside my chest. I shake my head.

Slowly, he breathes out. "Are you on birth control?"

"Yes." I snuck out and got an injection, just in case, when Papà was trying to set me up with Ludovico. It should last at least a few more months.

He nods and climbs off me.

I'm expecting him to take off his clothes, but instead he snakes one arm around my waist and flips me to my front. Disappointment wafts through me. This is how he wants to do it?

There's a cold lick between my wrists, and the zip tie gets tighter before it snaps.

Oh. He freed me.

The knife lands on the carpeted floor with a dull thud.

I roll to my back and stare at him as he takes off his clothes. His deft fingers make quick work of the buttons of his shirt. He pulls his arms out of the sleeves, the muscles in his shoulders and chest flexing with the movement. The pants go next, together with the boxers. My gaze dips to his abs, the V-below, then lower. I swallow. Somehow, he looks even bigger than before.

This might hurt.

He gets on the bed, settles his weight between my legs, wraps one palm around my thigh, hiking it up higher. I run my hands up his muscled chest. He's burning up. So am I.

His cock presses against my center, and he wraps his fist around it, guiding it where it belongs. He pushes into me slowly, stretching me, hurting me. I choke from the sudden pain and claw at his back until I tear his skin.

"I'm sorry," I breathe, knowing that I'm making him bleed too.

"Do what you need," he rasps.

He stops before he's fully in. Tears sting in the corners of my eyes, and I squeeze them shut so that I don't cry.

His hand disappears from my thigh and moves to cup my cheek. "Cleo. *Tesoro*."

I blink at him, barely seeing him through my blurry vision.

"Stay with me." He swipes his thumb over my cheekbone. "Breathe through it."

I do. I focus on taking in air until he leans down to kiss me, and then I focus on the way his mouth fits against mine. He kisses me for a long time. So long that the tightness in my center starts to unravel. So long that I part farther for him. He fills me all the way up, and a moan pours out of him.

It's so fucking sexy that it makes electricity dance over my skin. He kisses me while he fucks me, tenderly, reverently. Soon, I forget about the pain. It disappears, gets replaced with pleasure. I wrap my legs tighter around him and dig in my heels. He picks up speed and drops his head to suck on my neck.

"You're squeezing me so tight," he mutters against my skin. "You feel so fucking good, Cleo. You're perfect."

His words set me off. A familiar pressure builds inside of me, ratcheting up with every smooth stroke. He changes the angle of his hips, and it feels even better, more intense. My eyes roll to the back of my head, and then my orgasm is crashing through me.

"Oh fuck," he growls as I flutter around him. His body grows taut, every muscle prominent and hard. I scrape my nails down his chest and watch his face morph into a grimace. His cock jerks, and he spills inside of me with a guttural groan.

For a while, we stay tangled with each other. I press a kiss to his chest. He brushes his fingers through my hair. I don't know how much time passes, but it's enough for him to start softening. Eventually, he lifts himself up on his hands and pulls out with a hiss.

Warm liquid trickles out of me. He stands up, his gaze latching onto my pussy, and he looks at it for a prolonged moment, his chest rising and falling with hard breaths. "I'll get a towel."

I sit up and glance down between my legs. There's a reddish-pink stain on the white sheet. But this one, no one will see.

No one but us.

CHAPTER 30

RAFAELE

I WAKE up to sunlight glaring directly into my face.

God, why is it so bright?

I groan and try to dodge the light by turning away, but my arm is weighed down by something.

It takes me a second to process that something is my wife. She's here, nuzzling against my chest instead of lying on the other side of the bed. One of her legs is slung over my hips, her curly hair is tucked beneath my chin, and her arm is wrapped around my waist.

A satisfied smile tugs on my lips as images from last night come flooding back in. She finally gave in to me. Finally begged. Finally came to terms that she's fucking mine.

It's enough to make me forgive her for hiding her father's plan from me for two weeks. She probably tried to talk herself into going against me, but in the end, she couldn't do it. In the end, she realized that she belongs with me.

I tug Cleo closer and drag an absentminded hand down her bare back. Her skin is so smooth. She shifts against me, her leg brushing against my already hard cock.

I want to fuck her again.

And again.

Hearing her moan my name sounds like a perfect start to my day.

My phone buzzes on the nightstand. I bite back a groan and reach for it, doing my best not to disturb Cleo. It's an incoming call from Nero. Ugh. I have to take this. I texted him after Cleo fell asleep and told him to find Garzolo. I wanted that cockroach in my torture room before the sun was up so that I could give him exactly what he deserved. Carefully, I untangle myself from my sleeping wife, duck into the bathroom, and close the door.

"Did you get him?"

"Garzolo is gone. No one's seen him since he left the dinner."

Fuck. I grip the phone tighter. "His driver?"

"Garzolo drove to Ferraro's on his own. His guards were a few blocks over in his penthouse, but he never returned. He must have been afraid Cleo would tell you what he asked of her and thought it best to skip town."

Damn it.

I should have set Nero on Garzolo as soon as Cleo told me about his plan, but my head was somewhere else. That was a stupid move. I should have known that Garzolo was a flight risk. This is going to turn into a mess once his family starts asking about his whereabouts.

"If we can't find him in a few days, I'll need to step in to stop this from escalating."

"How are you going to explain this to his family? They might suspect foul play."

Of course they will. Their don disappears right after sitting down with me and Ferraro? Doesn't take a genius to put two and two together.

If Nero had caught Garzolo, I would have roughed him up and demanded he tell his capos he's taking his retirement early in exchange for his life. He'd do it, the fucking coward. I'd have given him a few weeks before I disposed of him for good. But with him just gone, this becomes more delicate. If the Garzolos think I killed their fucking don, his capos might turn on me.

"The family is mine. They all know I'm Garzolo's successor, and now that I'm married to Cleo, no one will dare question my right to assume command if he's skipped town."

"If you move in too soon, it won't look good."

"Let's give Garzolo five days to come back and face me like a man. If he doesn't, schedule a meeting with all his capos so that we can get this moving."

"Got it."

I hang up and rake my fingers through my hair, feeling irritated. What was I thinking? All of this could have been avoided if I'd set Nero on Garzolo quicker. I roll my shoulders, trying to get rid of my building unease.

Last night, I wasn't acting like myself. I was too fucking focused on deflowering my wife. Well, I've done it now. Bloody sheets and all.

Does that mean my life can finally go back to business as usual?

I thought getting what I wanted from Cleo would free me from this obsession. But where's the relief? Where's the mental clarity I was hoping for? It's not here, that's for fucking sure. Even now, after I've just screwed up with Garzolo, my head's still preoccupied with Cleo. A part of me wants to skip work and stay in bed with her all day.

Jesus. Fuck.

I open the tap and splash some cold water on my face.

When I imagined myself with a wife, I always had a clear picture of what that marriage would look like—comfortable companionship with some sex sprinkled in. I'd appreciate her, and she'd respect me. We'd put on a united front in public and keep a healthy distance from each other in private.

After all, nothing good comes from getting too entangled with another person. Especially for someone in my position.

But this? This is not that picture, at all.

I need to figure out how to stay in control of myself as far as she's concerned, or one day, I'm going to do something really fucking stupid. Something far worse than giving Garzolo a twelve-hour head start.

Maybe I just need a few weeks to fuck this obsession out of my head.

I drag my thumb over my bottom lip. Yes, that's it. I'm going to fuck her until I tire of her. Until I can evict her from the space she's inhabited in my head like an illegal squatter. Now that our game's done and she's spread her legs, the intrigue is gone. It won't take me long to get back to safe ground. I'm sure of it.

I take a cold shower. It helps. By the time I start toweling myself off, my mind is firmly back on work matters.

I need to divert some resources from Albany to New Jersey so that we can do a proper search. Garzolo could not have gone far. No doubt he's only retreated so that he can come up with a new plan to get rid of me. He'll need allies for that, which means we need to put tails on all his closest buddies. Eventually, he's bound to pop up somewhere.

I pull on some clothes and return to the bedroom. Cleo is up, her red hair tousled and messy, and her lips fixed in an adorable, sleepy pout.

I walk over to her and kiss her. It's meant to be a peck, but before I know it, my tongue is in her mouth, she's sucking on my bottom lip, and her fingers are playing with the buttons of my shirt. I break the kiss with a frustrated groan and take a step backward.

Work. I need to work.

She gives me a puppy-eyed look. "Where are you going?"

To shoot myself in the head, because that's apparently the only way I'm going to be able to get her out of it.

I tug on my collar. "Your father is gone."

This jolts her awake. She sits up, holding the sheet to her chest. "*What?*"

"He fled during the night. We're looking for him now."

"He must have realized I'd tell you the truth eventually," she mutters as she slips out of bed, naked as the day she was born, and heads toward the closet. It takes every ounce of my self-control not to drag her back to bed.

She comes back out dressed in a black silk robe. "I can write down all the places he might be hiding."

Surprise flickers through me. "You'll help me hunt down your father?"

"He wants to kill you. He's my enemy as much as he's yours at this point."

A tight fist squeezes around my heart. She's trying to protect me? That's not her job. That's never been anyone's job. Ever.

She walks across the carpet until she's standing right before me and tips her head backward to look me in the eye. My nape prickles. Can she see how she weakens me? How she makes me waver in my convictions?

Her arms slide around my waist, and she pushes up on her tiptoes. The inches between us disappear as I lean down and kiss her. Again, it turns into something more. Something that makes my chest feel light and heavy at the same time. Emotions swell under the surface, threatening to burst out, and even though my gut is screaming "Danger! Back away!", I don't listen to its warning.

It's only when I jerk her against me and she gasps in pain that I remember myself. I break the kiss. "Are you sore?"

Her lips are swollen and pink. She shifts her weight between her feet and winces. "Yeah. A bit."

"Go take a bath. Relax. I don't want you going to Loretta's today."

"It's the weekend."

"Right."

She sighs and looks down at my tie. "But you have to go," she says, sounding disappointed.

Don't make this harder than it already is.

I cup her cheek and give her another kiss. "Send me that list. I'll see you in the evening."

I walk away from her, one painful step after another.

That night, Cleo is already in bed when I come home covered in blood.

Her eyes widen. "Oh my God." She springs out of bed and rushes over to me. "We need to call Doc."

I shake my head, exhaustion pulling on my eyelids. "No. It's not mine."

She halts, and I brush past her into the bathroom where I quickly take off the bloody shirt.

It was a bad day.

We went to all of Garzolo's usual spots, and no one's seen him since last night. Then Nero and I went back to Il Caminetto and talked to the staff again. By that point, I was sure it was Garzolo who ordered the hit on us.

One of the band members saw us come through the door and took off. Nero and I caught him a few blocks away and took him to one of my warehouses, where he broke immediately and confessed he'd been on Garzolo's payroll ever since the restaurant opened up, acting as his eyes and ears.

He heard Garzolo disappeared and freaked out as soon as he saw us appear, sure that we were onto him.

We got the confirmation we needed, but I wasn't in a forgiving mood. He had a slow death. Then we got a call that a few Bratva thugs were trying to rob one of our restaurants outside the city. Nero and I raced over along with a bunch of our men, but we got there too late. The owner was dead, as was his daughter. It took us four hours to hunt down the fuckers that did it.

Unfortunately, the things we did to them didn't help the owner and his daughter.

"What happened?"

I look up, meeting Cleo's gaze in the mirror. I hadn't even realized I'd been leaning against the vanity for the last few minutes, staring at the sink.

"Later." My voice is a hoarse whisper from shouting commands at my men.

I push away from the sink, take off the rest of my clothes, and walk into the shower. The water runs pink as I wash off the blood that managed to leak through my shirt. I'm so fucking drained that I can barely find the energy to scrub myself with the soap.

The girl was only sixteen. She was helping her dad at the restaurant after school, bussing tables and doing dishes. Rage simmers inside my gut. Those Bratva fuckers are too bold. The pakhan doesn't seem to care how many men he loses in these reckless raids. This truce with Ferraro needs to become public soon. A strong show of a united front will go a long way in scaring the Russians off.

When I come out, Cleo's sitting on the edge of the bed waiting for me. She stretches out her arms. "Come here."

I do. I walk into her embrace and lean forward to capture her familiar scent. I'm too tired to do anything, but when she pulls me down on top of her and opens up her thighs for me, my cock grows hard. She's wearing just a nightgown, no panties, and sinking into her is the easiest thing ever. She takes a sharp intake of breath.

My chest clenches when I realize my mistake. "Fuck. I'm sorry. You're sore."

"I'm fine." She tightens her hold on me, her pussy gently clenching my stiff cock. "Just go slow."

I kiss her and roll my hips, drawing the motion out until she relaxes. Her eyes pierce through me, flickering with concern and arousal and something so vulnerable that I can't bear to hold her gaze. I bury my face against her neck and suck on her skin, leaving bruises on her. Marking her as mine.

She moans a short while later, and when I reach between us and strum her clit, she unravels beneath me. The sounds she makes are enough to take me over the edge with her.

After we get cleaned up, she cuddles up to me and asks again what happened. I try to find the words. Try to come up with a way to say it. But all I can see is that girl lying in a pool of her father's blood, her eyes wide and glassy. There's a scratch at the back of my throat. She didn't deserve to die. But deaths like hers happen all too often. A tithe to the gods that rule our brutal world.

I count to ten and push the feelings away. Lock them up in a box, hide it under my childhood bed. That's where they belong—the same place I used to hide when I was scared and weak. I'm not that boy anymore.

"Bratva attack," I say gruffly, tucking Cleo's head under my chin. "Go to sleep."

She stills, the air around us growing cold. I fall asleep, knowing I disappointed her with my dismissal.

And knowing that I'll disappoint her again.

CHAPTER 31

CLEO

ONE WEEK FOLDS INTO ANOTHER, and soon we're in the middle of April, and my father still hasn't been found.

By now, everyone is aware of Stefano Garzolo's disappearance. Everyone except for Gemma. Vale and I decided we wouldn't say anything to her. She doesn't need to concern herself with the whereabouts of our piece of shit father when she's busy growing a new human inside of her.

Rafaele assumed command of the Garzolos in my father's absence, and he's busier than ever. I see him far less than I would like, which is why when I walk into the dining room one morning and find him there having coffee, my insides perform a happy little jig.

"What are you doing here?" I ask as I take the seat across from him.

He peers at me over his newspaper. "Decided to work from home today. Heard Loretta's forcing you to take a day off. Said you've been working too hard."

It's been a busy few weeks at the shop. Loretta's taken my suggestions to heart, and our catalogue for the new season just came out. Orders are up, debts are down, and we've even managed to find some money to hire a crew to repaint the store.

"She's working just as hard," I tell him.

"It's her business. She's supposed to be. You're not."

I take a sip of orange juice. "I like helping her. It's better than just sitting alone at home."

I've thrown myself into work so that I don't ruminate too much on Rafaele's absences. He's always gone during the day. At night, he returns to our bed late enough that we only have time for one thing.

The sex is good. More than good. My husband seems to have made it his mission to learn every subtle nuance of my body. Even on nights when he appears exhausted, he's never too tired to make me come. Never too drained to spread my thighs and feast on me until I see stars.

There's one problem though. He won't talk to me. Not really.

I've given up asking him about work on the days he seems distracted. He refuses to open up to me about whatever is bothering him. But even on days he seems okay, as soon as the conversation veers past small talk, he shuts down. He distracts me with his kisses and his body and keeps me at a distance I don't know how to bridge.

Rafaele's expression softens. "I've been gone a lot."

I study his handsome face. Papà told me Rafaele doesn't feel emotions, but that's not true. He feels, but he keeps every one of those feelings inside. Hidden from everyone. Me included. Sadness pangs through me, even though it's stupid. I shouldn't be so bothered by this...this...lack of emotional intimacy.

I have a husband who treats me well and who fucks me well. He's letting me work. He's letting me do whatever I want as long as I obey a few rules that I don't even mind anymore. This is more than I ever could have hoped for when it comes to this marriage. I should be happy with the hand I've been dealt. But there's something in me, something I don't fully understand, that longs for more.

"You're here now." I smile. "So what are you planning on doing all day?"

His gaze sparks. "You."

I arch a brow. "Oh? Bold of you to assume I'll clear my calendar for that."

A small smirk unfurls across his lips. He stands up and walks around the table until he's behind my chair. His hands fall to my shoulders and begin to knead them. "What will it take, *tesoro*, for you to make some time for me?"

"Hmm." Damn, that feels good. My eyes flutter closed. "It's morning, so it's too early to be wined and dined."

He applies more pleasure, working a low moan out of me.

"Maybe a gift," I breathe.

His lips brush against the shell of my ear. "How fortuitous. I already bought you a gift." He nips on my earlobe with his teeth. "I think you'll like it a lot."

A frisson of excitement runs down my spine. "What is it?"

He straightens back up and pulls out my chair. "Come."

I leave my breakfast untouched and follow him to his office. Once inside, he closes the door and locks it.

"Take off your panties," he commands as he walks over to his desk.

I arch a brow. "Shouldn't I get the gift first?"

He throws me a heated glance. "You'll get it in a moment. Take off your underwear, *tesoro*."

This man. So bossy. I reach under my dress and shimmy out of my underwear under his watchful gaze.

When they're off, he nods with approval. "Good. Remember the first time I made you come in this room?"

"How could I not?"

His lips quirk. He pats the surface of his desk. "Come here and bend over just like then."

My core clenches. What is he planning? Some kind of reenactment? And where is my damn gift?

I huff an annoyed breath but do as he says, coming to his side of the desk and lowering onto my forearms.

His knuckles lightly brush against the back of one thigh as he lifts up the skirt of my dress. "So wet already," he murmurs, dragging a finger through my folds.

My lips part on a gasp, and my back arches in response to his touch. "Is the gift an orgasm? I feel like that's cheating."

His fingers disappear. "It's not an orgasm. You're very impatient."

"Yes. You should know this by now."

He makes a low chuckle. "Today you'll get a chance to work on that particular skill."

What?

"Stay there. Just like that," he says in a low voice.

I hear a drawer open and then close. Now I'm really curious. I try to look over my shoulder, but a hand appears around my neck, preventing me from moving.

Something slick and cool rolls down the crevice of my ass.

I gasp. "What is that?"

"Lubricant."

Again, *what?* My brain is still trying to catch up with what's happening when something smooth and firm prods against my back entrance. Tingles erupt over my skin. "Rafe, are you doing what I think you're doing?"

The pressure doesn't disappear, but he doesn't increase it either.

"What do you think I'm doing?"

"Sticking things up my butt."

He snorts a laugh. "You catch on quick."

"What exactly are you trying to put up there?"

"I got you a toy."

I drop my forehead to the surface of the desk with a thud. "Oh my God. This is my gift, isn't it?"

"Don't you want to test it out?"

"Please tell me it's smaller than your cock."

He huffs with amusement. "Yes. Significantly."

He moves the toy in a tight circle, spreading the slickness around my asshole, massaging it almost. An unexpected jolt of pleasure travels through me.

"Anal is not something I had on my agenda for today," I mutter, even as I lean back into him. A part of me is very curious and very turned on.

"Do you trust me?" he says in a low voice laced with arousal.

I bite down on my lip. He's never done anything to me I haven't enjoyed... "Yes."

"Good. Take a deep breath and relax."

The pressure increases until it turns slightly uncomfortable, and then it's gone. "Breathe," Rafaele instructs. "It's in."

Tentatively, I clench my cheeks. I can feel there's something there.

Rafaele wraps his palms around my shoulders and guides me back up until my back is pressed to his front. "Today, I'm going to take your ass," he says, his lips brushing my ear. "I'm going to own every part of your body."

I clench again, trying to get used to the strange sensation. There's a foreign pressure inside me, but it's not as notice-able as I would have expected. "Who says I'll let you?"

"Oh, you'll let me." He takes a step back. "Actually, you're going to beg for it, just like you begged me for everything else."

I turn around to face him, my cheeks hot and my pussy pulsing with excitement. "Keep dreaming. Now what?"

An all-too-satisfied smirk graces his lips. He slides his hand into the pocket of his slacks.

Click.

A gasp tears its way out of my lungs. *Holy shit.* The toy is vibrating inside of me.

I anchor my palms against the desk behind me so I don't tumble to the floor. The sensation isn't like anything I've experienced before. I can feel the vibration in my ass and my core, and somehow, even in my clit.

I blink at him against the dizzying wave of pleasure that envelops me. "What the fuck. You're playing dirty."

His smirk grows. "Can't handle it?"

My body quivers. "I. Can. Handle. It," I grind out, trying my best to pull myself together. I move my hips, trying to escape the sensation, but it's impossible. My chest rises and falls with heavy breaths, drawing Rafaele's attention.

His eyes darken, and he reaches out to fondle my breasts through the fabric of my dress. When he tweaks a nipple, I feel like I might explode.

"Doing all right?" he coaxes, his expression all decadent amusement. "Or are you getting hot?"

I'm burning up. "Not at all."

"How long do you think you can last?"

"Not sure. Long." There's pressure building inside of me, but not the kind that'll ever find release without some additional help. I can see how this will quickly become maddening.

He leaves my breasts alone and drags his hand down to my belly, letting it hover just over my pubic bone. I try to grind against him, but he keeps it just inches away from where I really want it.

Torture. Pure torture.

"Well, I have to get some work done," he drawls even as he turns up the strength of the vibrations with the remote in his pocket. He makes an attempt to lead me out of the room, but I plant my feet against the floor and refuse to move.

"No."

"No?" He turns up the setting once more.

I make a wanton moan. "Are you crazy? How long do you need to work for?"

He stifles a laugh. "I'll just be thirty minutes."

"Thirty minutes?" I shriek. "I'll take care of it myself in those thirty minutes."

His gaze flashes with warning, and he wraps his hand around my throat. "Don't you dare."

"Ten minutes," I squeeze out.

"Fifteen."

"Fuck. Fine."

He drops his hand and gestures at the sofa. "You can wait there."

"I'll stand."

"As you wish."

The bastard sits down at his desk like he's not actively torturing me, and opens his laptop. He looks like he doesn't have a care in the entire world. In the meantime, my body breaks out in a sweat. The vibrations just keep going and going, taunting me with the promise of pleasure. I shift my weight from one foot to the other and bite on the inside of my cheek. There's a steady pulse inside my clit, needy and begging for attention.

I eye the clock on the wall. It's been a minute? Only a minute?

If I want to do this for another fourteen, I need a distraction. Even shuffling over to the bookshelf is agonizing. I gulp down air and try to move my body in a way that doesn't make my problem any worse than it already is.

When I make it close enough, I grab the first book I see and open to a random page.

"He thrust into her, his throbbing member as hard as a steel pipe. Desiree moaned wantonly, 'Yes, yes, Jeremiah! Fill me with your seed.'"

"What are you reading?"

I slam the book shut. "Smut. Why do you have *smut* in your office library?"

"Ah, you must have found my deceased aunt's old collection. She lived in this house for a few years. Lovely woman."

"Sorry to spoil your memory of her, but she was a total perv." I shove the offending text back onto the shelf. The last thing I need right now is to be a fly on the wall for Desiree and Jeremiah's night of passion.

I grab another book, this one with a safe title—*A Comprehensive History of Geopolitics*—and open to chapter one.

The clock counts down at a snail's pace. About halfway through, shivers start to cascade through my body. Drops of sweat trail down my back and soak my dress. I'm swaying, sucking down air while the pressure in my core builds and builds. I clutch my book tighter and read the same sentence over and over again. Finally, we hit the fifteen-minute mark.

Rafaele stands up, an envelope in his hand. "I just have to drop this at the mailbox."

I toss the book aside and throw my body between him and the door. "Don't you *fucking* dare."

Amusement dances in his eyes. "What's the magic word, wife?"

"Please," I beg. It sounds like a sob. "*Please.*"

He presses me against the door with his muscled body. The impact nudges the toy against a spot inside of me that makes me whimper.

"Please what?" he asks in a husky voice.

I look at him through my eyelashes. "Please make me come."

He brushes a strand of hair behind my ear oh so gently, like he's not the most evil man on earth. "What else?"

I swallow. Damn him. "Please fuck my ass."

He grins. Butterflies explode inside my belly. "That's my good girl. I'll gladly fuck your pretty little ass."

Before I know what's happening, he's carrying me out of his office in his arms. I squirm in his hold, chasing that high that's just out of reach. My body buzzes, every nerve ending at the ready, and when we finally make it to the bedroom, there isn't a thing in the world I wouldn't let Rafaele do to me.

He tosses me on the bed and flips me on my stomach. "Get on your hands and knees."

I quickly slip out of my dress and obey, baring my ass to him. Slowly, he pulls on the toy.

"Oh fuck," I moan as he thrusts it in and out of me a few times. I need more, so I reach between my legs and press my fingers against my clit.

The toy disappears. Rafaele pulls my hand away and holds it firmly against my lower back.

I cry out in protest. "Why?"

"Because you'll come when I say you can come." There's the sound of his belt buckle coming undone.

He snakes one arm around my thighs and pulls me toward him until my feet are hanging off the edge of the bed. A moment later, he slides his cock inside my pussy. I nearly choke at the sudden fullness. He starts thrusting and reaches around to strum my clit. I groan. *Yes, finally.* His fingers move in tight, perfect circles at just the right speed. The pressure inside of me expands until I'm fisting the sheets and moaning his name. He thrusts into me, going fast and deep and hard, making me writhe until my orgasm explodes through my body. I fall off the edge into the abyss, my body spasming with harsh waves of pleasure.

"Oh God," I groan.

Before I can even catch my breath, he pulls out of my pussy and prods against my back entrance. My eyes spring open as he starts to push inside. He's definitely bigger than the toy.

I clutch the sheet. "Holy shit." The stretching sensation is back, and it's a lot more intense. On the edge of barely manageable even in my post-orgasm haze. I do my best to breathe through it.

Rafaele grunts behind me. "Fuck. So tight."

I whimper as he goes deeper.

He stills, digging his fingers into my hips in a possessive hold. "*Tesoro*, are you okay?"

"Fine," I squeeze out, trying to focus on relaxing my muscles.

Rafaele drags a firm knuckle down my spine. "Is it too much?"

I press my forehead to the bed and let my head loll to the side. "Give me a few seconds."

He moves his hands to my ass cheeks and starts to massage them. Soon I can feel the remaining tension uncoil inside of me.

"Keep going," I tell him.

He pushes in a few more inches and groans. "That's it. You almost got it. Fuck, you look gorgeous."

His words send a fresh wave of arousal through me. Sweat drips down my neck. Everything feels deliciously dirty. I rise up on my palms and press back into him until my thighs meet his.

"Fucking hell," he mutters.

I expect him to start moving, but he stays still. Waiting for something. "How is it, *tesoro*? I want you to enjoy it as much as I am."

Warmth slides through my entire body. "I might if you start moving sometime this year."

He chuckles, gives my ass a firm smack, and begins to thrust. I arch my back, meeting his movements with my own.

He groans. "Fuck. You take it so well, Cleo. I wish you could see it."

I imagine his thick cock sliding in and out of my tight little hole and moan at the image. I want to see it too. A brilliant idea comes to me. I *can* see it.

My phone is on the nightstand, a few feet away. I shift and manage to reach far enough to grab it. "Rafe," I moan. "Call me from your phone."

Rafaele's movements slow and then stop. "Fuck, okay," he says hoarsely.

He pulls out while I place my phone on the bed in front of me. There's some rustling as he fishes his phone out of wherever it is.

A few seconds later, I pick up his video call.

The image of his hard cock spayed across one of my ass cheeks makes me groan.

"Watch," Rafaele growls as he wraps his hand around his length and presses the head against my hole. Slowly, so fucking slowly, he enters me, and it's all I can do not to come right then and there.

"Oh God," I moan as he fills me right to the hilt.

He holds the camera slightly above, giving me a full view of my ass and back. And then he starts to pump.

Watching him fuck me on video is like having sex on steroids. My body tingles everywhere, and all traces of my earlier discomfort disappear. Now, it just feels good. Really fucking good.

Rafe smacks my ass again, his groans growing louder.

"I'm close," he grunts. "You're gonna come for me one more time, *tesoro*. You've earned it."

He reaches around and presses his long fingers against my clit before giving it a flick.

That's all it takes for me to explode. I writhe against him as my orgasm wreaks havoc inside my body, struggling to keep my unfocused gaze on the screen.

His camera work gets sloppier as he fucks me harder and harder. I can tell he's losing control.

"Fuck, Cleo. *Fuck*."

At the last second, he pulls out, and I watch him come in long spurts all over my ass and back. He ends the call and throws his phone on the ground.

I moan and splay out on the bed. He collapses beside me, cheeks red, forehead sweaty, and lips parted as he takes deep gulps of air. I'm utterly breathless. Boneless. Buzzing.

Somehow, Rafe manages to get up a short while later. He returns, and I feel something warm and wet drag over my skin. He wipes me down and presses a kiss to my right butt cheek. I peer over my shoulder at him, and he's giving me a reverent look.

"Jesus, Cleo. That was…" He clears his throat, seemingly at a loss.

Satisfaction flickers inside of me. "I know." I turn onto my back and pull him down beside me.

Soon enough, sleep tugs on my mind. Why not take a nap? I press up against Rafe and let out a happy sigh.

This is good. This is easy. This is all you need from him.

But as I drift off, that tendril of longing for something more flutters deep inside my chest.

CHAPTER 32

RAFAELE

I HUFF as I deadlift a barbell off the ground. My muscles ache, and my body's just about ready to be done with this workout. I usually get my exercise at the boxing gym with Nero whenever time allows, but I woke up this morning feeling restless, so now here I am, down at the home gym doing rep after agonizing rep. I'm pushing myself even though I know I'll regret it tomorrow when I'm sore all over.

Right now, this is good. The intensity, the pain, and the effort are all ideal distractions from the fact that I'm worked up over a dream.

A fucking dream.

What am I, five?

I drop the weight with a loud thud. Good thing I built this place in the basement, so I don't have to worry about anyone hearing me. The house is designed for maximal privacy, especially down here. There are three separate sections to the basement, with three different access points. One leads down to the gym and steam room, the other to the cigar room with the jewelry vault, and the third to my torture room.

I haven't used the last one since my wedding to Cleo. It doesn't feel right to bring that aspect of my work home anymore. It's not that the torture room isn't secure—no one's ever managed to escape from it—but why take a risk I don't need to take? I've got plenty of other places to take people. And if anything happened to Cleo because I brought someone dangerous to our house...

I close my eyes.

"Rafe! Help me!"

I'm in Midtown, eating a hot dog, when I hear her voice. I whip around, trying to find her, but it's impossible to spot her in the dense lunchtime crowd.

"Rafe! I'm right here!"

My heart jumps into my throat when I finally see her. Cleo is crying, a gun pressed to her head. A man in a black hoodie, the hood obscuring his face, is holding her. I sprint toward her, but no matter how fast I run, I don't get any closer. The hooded man pulls her farther and farther away. Frustration and fear hammer inside my chest.

"Cleo!"

And then I can't see her anymore. She's gone. All I can hear is her voice, her begging, her crying. And then a gunshot slices through the air.

My eyes snap wide.

Fuck. Why am I replaying the dream again? It's bad enough that I woke up gasping, my hands searching for my wife.

The moment I touched her, my body shook with bone-deep relief. And it felt like all the progress I'd made over the past few weeks had been erased.

Our relationship had just started to fit into acceptable boundaries. I'd stuck to my plan when it came to her, focusing on the physical aspect of our relationship and living practically every night between her legs.

I haven't slept much, but I've fucked every hole and licked every inch of that magnificent body, enough to have it all memorized in clear detail.

My desire for her hasn't waned, but I'm learning how to handle the lust. I do my best to forget about it during the day and indulge in the night. With a few exceptions—days when I want her so badly that I skip work despite my best intentions—I was succeeding. My head was clearing. I've been able to stay focused on my work.

The Garzolos moving under my command have served as a convenient reminder why I need to stay detached from everyone, including my wife. Not all Garzolo's old capos are happy with me coming in as their new boss, and they're sniffing around for weak spots, trying to figure out how they can get leverage on me. I've spent my life trying to make sure that leverage doesn't exist.

There's nothing I'm not willing to lose to protect my rule. But in that dream, losing her felt worse than anything in the entire world.

I exhale a heavy breath.

It was a fucking dream. I don't need to get this worked up over it.

I grab a towel and turn toward the shower just as the door to the gym opens and Cleo walks in. My gaze sweeps over her. Her copper hair is pulled back into a tight ponytail. She's dressed in a blouse and a pair of jeans, ready to go out. Her eyes spark as she takes in my sweaty, shirtless form.

"What are you doing here, *tesoro*?" I ask, tossing the towel over my shoulder.

She bites her lip, her gaze flickering from my abs to the barbell on the floor. "I didn't even know this was down here. You've got an indoor pool tucked away somewhere as well?"

"No, but that could be arranged."

A smile tugs on her lips. She walks up to me and drags her nails lightly over my bare abs, sending a shiver through my body. "You know, Gem's spent years trying to convince me to go to the gym, but this view might be what finally does it."

The appreciation in her tone is good for my ego. I'm normally immune to flattery, but apparently not when it comes from my wife.

I cup her cheek and press our lips together. Her mouth opens immediately, and she slides her tongue against my own. There's none of the hesitation, none of the resistance from the day of our wedding.

She really is mine.

The dream echoes in my mind. I want to forget it, to push it aside and focus on Cleo and the present moment, but it lingers like a bad taste in my mouth.

I pull away. "You off to work now?"

She tucks a strand behind her ear. "I'm going to go to Loretta's after my doctor's appointment."

A doctor's appointment? Concern flares inside of me. "What's wrong?"

"Nothing. I just need to get another birth control shot. Unless you want to start getting cracking on that heir," she adds, a teasing smile on her face.

My stomach dips. She's joking. I know it. But that doesn't stop a tsunami of emotions from crashing into me.

Having a kid with her...

My heart rate picks up speed.

Producing an heir is expected of me, but it's always seemed very far away. Fine in theory, but in practice... I blink and peer into Cleo's eyes. *Tesoro mio,* pregnant. Just the thought of it makes protectiveness surge inside of me.

I don't think I'll make a good father. How can I be a good father if protecting my power, my position, has to always come first? And how can I stay emotionally detached from a woman who'll one day become the mother of my child? *Fuck.* I mean, many men have done it. My father being the prime fucking example. But I sure as hell don't want to be like him.

I take a step back, overwhelmed. I don't know how to handle this conversation.

Cleo's smile falls. "Rafe, I was kidding. I'm definitely in no rush to pop out baby Messeros. It was just a joke."

"I know." My voice is strained.

"Then why do you look like you're about to have a heart attack?"

It takes everything—*everything*—to fix my expression into a neutral mask. "I'm fine."

"Are you?"

"I said I'm fine."

She frowns, her perceptive eyes seeing past the mask even though they shouldn't. "Something's wrong. Talk to me."

"I have to get to a meeting. I should hop in the shower." I give her my back. "Good idea on the birth control."

I leave her and take the quickest shower in history. My skin feels like it's crawling off my bones. I need to get the hell out of the house. Good thing I brought my clothes down here with me. I change into them and leave the house without bumping into Cleo again.

Nero's waiting for me in a car outside. "You all right?" he asks once I get in. "You've got a weird look on your face."

"It's nothing. What's the plan for today?"

A beat passes. He turns the car on and pulls out of my driveway. "The guys at Oyster Bar called me earlier. They finally got the money..."

I tune him out. My father was a real monster. The kind that's unusual even in our world where cruelty is a necessity. He turned that cruelty inward, toward me, toward Mamma. He might have turned it onto my sisters too if Mamma didn't have the foresight to send them to a school abroad. They didn't want to go without Mamma. They begged to stay, begged me to convince our parents to keep them here, but I couldn't do that. For their own good, I couldn't.

The day they left, they told me they hated me and Papà. Will my kids hate me too?

301

"They asked to see you so that they can be sure we're all—"

"Do you think it's possible to be a good father and a good don?" I interrupt.

Nero glances at me, brows furrowing. "I don't know. You're the one who had a don for a father."

"It sure as fuck wasn't possible for him." Nero doesn't know the details of what happened back when I was a kid, but he knows I never loved my father.

"At least your old man made your family rise to the top," Nero says. "Look at Garzolo. That idiot's shit in both areas."

"What about Gino Ferraro?"

Nero blows out a breath. "Who knows. It's hard to tell with him, but his sons aren't exactly poster boys for sanity, are they? Alessio seems to have more than a few screws loose. And I don't think Romolo's got anything but tits and ass floating in his head."

I grunt. "So you're saying it's impossible."

"I don't think it's impossible, but I think it's hard. Most don't bother trying. You know how it is, Rafe. Kids are pawns until they knock over the king and take his place."

He's right. The mob's all about family, but somehow, we all end up screwing those around us. Thing is, I don't want to have a fucked-up family with Cleo. But what's the alternative? None of this fits into acceptable lines.

Nero clears his throat. "Why are we talking about this?"

"Cleo brought up kids."

He laughs. "Fuck, you two are crazy. A few weeks ago, she hissed and bared her claws whenever you got too close to her, and now she wants to have babies with you?"

"It's not like that. She just mentioned it offhand."

He shrugs. "Then forget about it. That's a problem for tomorrow, and tomorrow might never come."

I grunt. Again, he's right. I can't worry about the future. I've got enough shit to deal with right now. But the uncomfortable feelings that came up from this discussion stay with me for the rest of the day.

CHAPTER 33

CLEO

ANOTHER MONTH PASSES in the blink of an eye, during which Rafaele and I fall into a comfortable rhythm.

No, that's a lie. A rhythm, yes. Comfortable? Maybe for him.

On paper, things are going well. He's been around a little more this month. We've gone on dates, attended dinner parties, and even went to a gallery opening together. When we're together, I never feel like I bore him. He's a great listener, and whenever I have some problem at work, he gives me thoughtful advice. I enjoy his company, and I think he enjoys mine. But as soon as I try to pierce the armor he wears, to move beyond facts and logic, I hit resistance.

Every time he shuts down a conversation or pulls away, I have to remind myself not to be greedy.

The problem is...I *am* greedy. With each passing day, my feelings for him grow. They pulse inside my chest, a cocktail of longing, affection, and desire. And I want more from him. I want to know what Rafaele is thinking when he looks at me with those piercing blue eyes. I want to know what he's feeling when he touches my skin, sending shivers down my spine. I want to know if he feels the same way I do, and whether he wants more too.

I'm falling for him, fast and hard, and I don't know what's waiting for me at the bottom of the drop.

It's Sunday morning, and the house is quiet. I wander onto the back terrace and take a look at the garden. It takes me a moment to realize it's in full bloom. I'm checking the calendar on my phone for the date when familiar footsteps sound behind me. Rafaele wraps his arms around my waist and presses a kiss to my shoulder.

"I can't believe it's July," I say. "Do you know my birthday is in a week?"

"Of course, I do." His voice is still raspy from sleep. "How would you like to celebrate?"

I turn in his arms and place my palms on his chest, feeling his steady heartbeat. "I want to celebrate with my sisters."

It's been too long. I miss Gem and Vale, and it's gotten particularly bad over the past two weeks. We talk on the phone often, but it's not the same. I need an in-person heart-to-heart. Desperately. Maybe my sisters will be able to give me some advice on how to navigate this marriage.

I know Rafaele can't be thrilled about my request. As expected, when I lift my gaze to his, he's wearing a pensive look. I can practically see the wheels inside his head turning. Gemma is the woman who walked out on him. There's no way Ras will allow her to travel here alone, so Rafaele will have to play nice with the man who got his ex-fiancée pregnant while she was engaged to him.

And Damiano will insist on escorting Vale. I guess Damiano and Rafe are business partners, so that's not too bad. But if I'm inviting all four of them, I'll also have to invite Mari, Damiano's sister, and her husband, Giorgio, who's Damiano's head of security.

That's a lot of Casalesi mobsters to have in New York at one time. But it's not like Rafe would let me go see my sisters in Italy on my own, and he's too busy with work to take time off.

"I know it might get a bit messy," I say. "But I haven't seen Gemma since she left or Vale since the wedding. That was almost four months ago, and I miss the hell out of them. It would be the best gift ever. A big party with all of them around."

He sighs. "And here I was thinking the thirty-carat diamond necklace I bought at auction last week would be enough."

I grin. "It's a good start, for sure."

A smile tugs at his lips.

"We could invite your sisters too," I offer. "Maybe they could fly down with Vince from Europe together."

The light in his eyes dims. "They're usually too busy to attend anything that's not a wedding or a funeral."

"Why aren't the three of you close?" I ask, trying to sound casual.

He shrugs. "Just how it is."

Frustration pulses at my temples. Rafaele doesn't talk about his mother or his sisters. Why? What happened between them to make their relationships so strained? As his wife, don't I have a right to know about his family history? Why won't he share even that with me?

Maybe he senses my frustration, because he pulls me into him and distracts me with a kiss. When we break apart, both breathless, he tucks a strand of hair behind my ear and says, "Fine. You can throw your party."

Excitement blooms inside my chest, overriding the disappointment. "Thank you."

He smiles again and presses his forehead to mine. "Anything for you, *tesoro*."

I wrap my arms around him and press my cheek to his chest.

Anything? Or just the crumbs you're willing to offer?

I spend the next week calling Vale and Gemma, making arrangements for their travel and figuring out the logistics of the party. The theme is tropical paradise, and since I have no idea if I'll be able to do this again next year, I decide to go all out.

On Wednesday, they deliver dozens of mini palm trees. When Rafaele comes home that evening, he nearly trips over one. On Thursday, the bamboo bars arrive. On Friday, while Rafaele and I are having breakfast, the staff start bringing in the alcohol I ordered.

His brows climb up his forehead. "*Tesoro*, are you trying to get the whole state of New York drunk?"

I give him a wicked grin. "Don't think can keep up with me?"

His eyes darken, and he shakes his head, but he can't hide the amused smile on his face.

On the day of the event, I'm so excited that I practically bounce off the walls. The staff are still adding some last touches to the décor, but the ballroom already looks like Party City exploded inside of it. The mini palm trees are arranged around the perimeter, fruit decorations hang off the ceiling, there's a giant champagne tower on a gold table with a pineapple base, and bartenders are ready to serve every sugary drink you can imagine from behind the bamboo bars.

Rafaele and Nero are chatting in the corner while holding piña-colada-filled coconuts in their hands. They accepted the drinks from me without too much grumbling, but apparently, I took it a step too far with the matching tropical-patterned button-up shirts, because they categorically refused to put them on.

Around three p.m., my sisters finally arrive. Gemma's bump is just starting to show and she's glowing. Vale looks more tanned than the last time I saw her, and her hair is longer than mine, reaching past her waist. I run toward them and envelop them in a hug. "You're here!"

We squeeze each other and jump around in a circle like a bunch of lunatics. Mari stands to the side, watching us shyly, until we pull her into our big group hug.

Damiano, Ras, and Giorgio greet Rafaele and Nero with as much warmth as an icy breeze on a cold winter morning. My sisters and Mari pause our conversation to regard them for a few seconds.

"We all told them to behave, right?" Gemma asks.

"Oh, yeah." Vale tucks a strand of hair behind her ear. "I told Dem I'll murder him if him or Ras ruin your birthday."

Mari shrugs. "Gio won't do anything. He's always well-behaved."

Vale arches a brow. "I'm pretty sure I saw him looking at everyone's home addresses and credit card statements on the flight over. He's researched the entire guest list to death, hasn't he? Memorized everyone's social security numbers? Dug up old family secrets?"

Mari winces. "You know how he is. He doesn't go anywhere unprepared."

"Rafe will probably just glare at them the entire night," I say, noting the frigid look on my husband's face. He must feel my attention on him, because he glances my way, and a bit of warmth slips into his expression.

"C'mon," I say, wrapping my arms around Vale and Mari. "Let's grab a drink."

Soon, the party is in full swing. I introduce my sisters and Mari to Sandro and Tiny and bring them around to the kitchen to say hi to Luca. Then I take them on a tour of the gardens, excitedly pointing out all the flowers that recently bloomed.

I catch Vale giving me a curious look. "What?"

"Nothing. You just...seem happy," Vale comments.

Gemma nods in agreement. "You do. How are things with you and Rafaele?"

"He's growing on me," I say.

"So you like him?" Mari asks.

Like him? It's progressed far beyond that. I let out a sigh and glance between my sisters. I can't believe I'm about to confess that I've thoroughly fallen for my husband.

"Cleo!" A voice calling my name grabs my attention. It's Loretta. She's standing with an older couple in tow. I vaguely recognize them from the wedding. They must be her parents.

"Give me one sec," I say to my sisters before I walk over to Loretta.

"Happy birthday, darling," Loretta says. "You look beautiful. Doesn't she, Ma?"

Her mother gives me a tight-lipped smile that doesn't reach her eyes. "The skirt is a bit short, but what do I know."

I resist the urge to roll my eyes. I may have won over Loretta, but I guess her parents are a different matter. Whatever. I don't care. It's my birthday and my family is here. I'm not going to let this lady ruin my mood.

Loretta frowns. "Ma, don't be rude. I told you Cleo's really helping me with the shop. Why do you have to insult her?"

Surprise bursts through me. I wasn't expecting Loretta to come to my defense.

"I don't know what you mean," her mother says, her cheeks turning pink. "You asked for my opinion, so I gave it to you."

"Huh. You never seem to have those sorts of opinions about other hosts. Or at least you know well enough to keep them to yourself."

"It's okay," I cut in, for once not in the mood to start any drama.

Loretta shakes her head. "No, it's not okay. The only reason I've been able to pay back all of my debts is because of you, Cleo. I won't have my own mother disrespect you like that."

Loretta's father clears his throat, his expression stoic. "Thank you for your assistance. It's been a great relief to our daughter, and we appreciate the interest you've taken in the business. Right, Claudia?"

Loretta's mom sniffs, her entire face flushed. "Of course," she says, clearly embarrassed.

The tension in the air dissipates, and the older couple soon moves on to talk to other guests. I turn to Loretta. "Thank you. I'm touched. You didn't have to do that."

Loretta shrugs. "I'm just tired of this family hating on you. Besides, you've been a good friend to me." She flashes me a small smile before heading off to greet another guest.

I rejoin my sisters and Mari, and Gemma asks if we can go into the house so she can use the bathroom.

"My bladder's terrible these days," she grumbles.

I nod. Better wait until tomorrow to bring up my dilemma with Rafaele. I'll organize a lunch for just the four of us where we can talk without any interruptions.

When we return to the back terrace, Rafaele's mother approaches me. I give the woman a careful smile. She hasn't been around much, but I've seen her at a few of the family events Rafaele's taken me to. I'm not sure where we stand though.

She kisses me on both cheeks. "Happy birthday, Cleo."

"Thank you, I'm glad you could make it. What do you think of the party?"

"It's lovely," she says, a small smile on her face. "I just wanted to talk to you for a moment, if that's all right?"

"Of course."

She leads me aside, away from the chatter and laughter of the party. We stop in front of a small stone bench surrounded by potted plants. She sits down and pats the space next to her.

I brush my skirt under my thighs and take a seat. When I turn to her, her eyes are glistening with unshed tears.

My stomach hollows out. "Mrs. Messero, are you all right?"

She reaches over and squeezes my hands. "Yes, I'm just relieved, that's all. I didn't think I'd ever see my son in love. Thank you."

My blood slows. Why would she say that? "Did Rafe say something to you?"

"No. But I can tell he loves you, Cleo."

She's just making assumptions. An awkward laugh escapes my lips. "I'm not so sure."

She sniffs and gives me a watery smile. "Do you love him?"

Oh God. I haven't even confessed my predicament to my sisters yet, but there's something about how she's looking at me that convinces me to open up. "Yeah, I think I do."

"Have you told him how you feel?"

"No," I answer quickly.

How can I confess my feelings when I have no idea what's going on inside his head? It's too big a risk. Things are good between us. Great, even. I never thought going into this marriage that I'd actually *enjoy* being married. So am I going to ruin everything by pushing for more?

Mrs. Messero seems to read my mind. "You have to be patient with him. He's not good at expressing emotions or even understanding how he feels."

Don't I know it. "Why is that?"

Mrs. Messero glances at her feet. "He had a very difficult childhood."

The childhood that I know nothing about. "Can you tell me about it?"

She grimaces, her eyes still fixed on the ground. Foreboding seeps like rot inside my bones.

"Rafaele was a sweet young boy," she says quietly. "Good-natured, gentle, and curious. Everyone loved him. But his father never saw him as a child, only as a future don."

She reaches inside her purse, takes out a folded handkerchief, and dabs it under her eyes. "Rafe saw things he shouldn't have. His father used to beat me. Sometimes, he did even worse. One night, Carlo was very unhappy with me. I can't even remember why, it was always one thing or another, but he started hitting me. I remember hearing the door open, and it was my sweet boy. I'll never forget the sound he made when he saw me on the ground. It was the most horrible sound I've ever heard."

Blood drains from my face. I'd walked in on a similar scene only a few months ago with Papà and Gemma. Even as an adult, it was a hard thing to process. But to see something like that as a kid?

"When Carlo saw the tears on Rafe's face, he got even angrier. I thought maybe seeing the horror in his son's eyes would make him rethink what he was doing, but it turned out to be the opposite. He grabbed Rafe and shook him. 'Why are you crying, you stupid boy? I didn't raise a crybaby.'"

My stomach sinks. God. And I thought my father was horrible.

"Rafe kept crying. I wanted to go to him to console him, but Carlo pushed me away from my son. He told Rafe that until he learned to control his emotions, he'd keep hurting me."

I cover my mouth with my hand. "Oh my God."

"From then on, he'd drag Rafe into the bedroom while he beat me. Whenever Rafe cried, his father would hit me harder. Carlo taught Rafe that emotion was weakness. Empathy was weakness. Attachment was weakness. He taught him that those things should be repressed and rejected at all cost." Her skin turns a shade of gray. "And it was only when Rafaele managed to w-watch his father h-hurt me...very badly, without shedding a tear that he deemed my boy ready for his training to become made. He was eleven."

Her last sentence is no more than a pained croak. I shift closer to her and wrap an arm around her shoulders. "Mrs. Messero, I'm so sorry. I can't imagine how difficult that must have been. For both of you."

She gazes into the distance, her pain etched into her weathered face. "The sad thing is that it was what saved me. With Carlo's focus completely on Rafe, he let me take the girls to our home in the Hamptons, and we lived there for most of the year. My husband rarely drove down to see us. We had peace there. And when the girls got older, I convinced Carlo to send them to a boarding school in Geneva."

I swallow. It's all starting to make sense now.

A tear streams down her cheek. "But Rafaele paid the price. Carlo molded him into a weapon. Cold, ruthless, withdrawn. I know deep down he still loves us, but he's careful not to show his affection for me, Elena, or Fabi. And how can I blame him? He understood Carlo would see it as a weakness and use it against him and us."

"His sisters don't know?"

She shakes her head. "His sisters were too young. The only thing they remember is their brother being closed off with them whenever they came home. He's always kept them at a distance. They dislike him for it."

"Why not try to mend their relationship now?"

She turns to me. "Some conversations are so difficult to have... Maybe it's better not to have them at all." Emotions flicker in her eyes—pain, regret, and love. Love for her son. A son who was torn away from her by an evil man.

She presses her lips together. "Rafe won't be happy if he finds out I told you. But I want you to know. I want you to understand him."

I nod, my throat tight and scratchy. "Thank you. I think I'm starting to."

She gets to her feet. "Will you excuse me?"

"Of course." I watch her leave, and then I turn toward the setting sun.

My heart is heavy inside my chest. Rafe was forced to become this version of himself all because of his father's twisted agenda. Does he still believe that love equals weakness? The thought makes me ache for him. Maybe I can prove to him that it doesn't. After all, the only reason we're here now is because I was brave enough to marry him because of how much I love my sister. My love for her gave me courage.

And now my love for him does the same.

I let out a breath.

It's time to take another leap of faith and tell Rafaele how I feel.

CHAPTER 34

CLEO

I RETURN to the party and search for my husband. He's standing outside by the bar, surrounded by his capos and their wives. I squeeze past them and take his hand. "Come with me."

He gives me a curious look but doesn't argue when I pull him after me.

I guide him down the illuminated path that leads into the garden and walk along a wall of dense bushes that conceal us from view. I stop, press my back against the foliage, and tug on Rafaele's lapels until there are only inches between his body and mine.

He stares at me, brows furrowed. "What's going on, *tesoro*?"

"Rafe, I have to tell you something." My voice is trembling. I'm acting weird, jittery from the adrenaline and everything else.

His eyes narrow. "Did something happen?"

"No. Nothing bad."

The tension in his shoulders eases. "Then what is it?"

"I just...there's something I want to say." It comes out as a whisper. God, I sound completely terrified.

What if he rejects me? What if he says he doesn't feel the same? That he'll *never* feel the same? I don't know. But I can't keep doing nothing. That's not who I am. I take a deep breath.

Suddenly, understanding flashes across his expression.

My heart drops. Oh no. I think he just guessed what's coming. There's no time left to waste. I have to tell him. "I I—"

His lips crash down on mine, silencing me.

A fracture appears inside my chest. Maybe I should pull away, but I don't. Instead, I whimper and pull him closer.

He wraps his arms around me and holds me tightly. He bites and tugs on my lips, sliding his tongue in and out, his body hard and hot against me. We break apart, and then he's back. He won't give me more than a second to catch my breath.

I'm not an idiot. I get it.

He doesn't want to hear what I have to say.

The backs of my eyes prickle, but I push the feeling down. It's not hard, not when his hands are under my top now, hot and possessive, and he's tweaking my nipples and making my skin buzz. I moan into his mouth, and he falls to his knees before me, hikes up my skirt with one palm, shoves my wet panties aside, and drags his tongue over my burning flesh.

I let out a broken gasp. Yes, this is good. This is easy. Him giving me pleasure, and me accepting all that he's willing to give.

What if that's all he'll ever give? Is it enough? Forever?

I give my head a hard shake, ignoring the pinch from the twigs poking against my scalp.

"Hold your skirt. I need both hands."

I clutch onto the fabric, and he spreads my legs apart a few inches farther, giving himself better access. He pulls down my panties and shoves them into the back pocket of his slacks.

He licks my opening and then moves back up to my clit. I shudder when he sucks it into his mouth, moan when he swirls his tongue. Heat blankets my body. I slide my fingers into his hair and hold on to him as he brings me closer and closer to the edge.

Suddenly, his mouth is gone. He pulls me down to the grass, his movements harried, desperate. His face appears above me, wet with my juices.

"Why did you stop?" I pant.

"I need to be inside you," he grunts, undoing his tie and pulling it off his neck. He balls it up and stuffs it into my mouth. I make a muffled sound.

"Shhh. I don't want our guests to hear your screams."

The only warning I get is the clank from him undoing his belt buckle, and then he shoves into me with one hard stroke.

A scream tears its way out of my throat, muffled by his tie. My eyes roll to the back of my head. I'm so full, so stretched.

"You okay?" he asks, his chest rising and falling with harsh breaths.

I press my heels into his thighs, urging him to move. I'm right on the edge again, my orgasm within reach. He doesn't need more encouragement. He starts thrusting, soon settling into a relentless rhythm against my G-spot.

So damn good. My eyelids flutter. He pulls the neck of my dress down and wraps his mouth around my nipple, tugging on it with his teeth. "You going to come hard for me, *tesoro*? You better be quick. Someone might wander down to the garden. You know I'd have to kill anyone who saw my birthday girl getting railed."

I sob against the wave of pleasure that crashes into me. My climax bursts, every nerve ending firing, every bit of oxygen removed from my lungs.

His cock slips in and out a few more times before he groans and spills inside of me. "*Fuck.*"

I clutch onto him. Above us, the sky is full of twinkling stars, and one of them cuts an arc through the darkness.

He removes his tie from my mouth and stares down at me. His breaths come out as pants. His blue eyes shimmer with something, something he can't voice, something he may not even understand.

I sit up and fix my clothing into place. He plucks a leaf out of my hair and kisses my forehead. "I made a mess out of you."

I laugh softly. "Yeah." In more ways than one.

This was meant to be a distraction, but the three words are right there again, ready to spill out. Something holds me back. Maybe it's the fact that he can look at me like that, like I'm the most precious thing in the world, while keeping so much from me.

Why hasn't he ever confided in me about the horrors he's lived through?

Doesn't he trust me?

Doesn't he see by now how far I've fallen for him?

The morning after the party, I wake up hungover. It's worth it, because last night. Was. A. Blast.

Around ten, after Luca brought out my cake, most of the guests I didn't know very well left, and then the real party started. Someone brought out a karaoke machine I didn't know we owned, and everyone sang me "Happy Birthday." We did rounds of shots. I'm pretty sure there's a video of Vale and me dancing on a table. And most importantly, all of our men somehow managed not to kill each other. By the end of the night, Gemma convinced Ras to put on one of the themed shirts I bought, and he drunkenly told everyone he loved the little parrots on it. I grin at the memory and snuggle up against Rafaele.

His body shifts. "You awake?" Rafaele didn't seem that drunk last night, but his voice still has a rasp to it.

I turn my face up to him. "Yeah."

He looks tired. "I just got a call. There's something I need to take care of." He gazes down at me and brushes his fingertips over my lips. "I'm sorry. I wish I could stay in bed with you all day."

A butterfly appears inside my stomach. Then I remember how he cut me off last night, and the butterfly disappears. He wouldn't let me tell him that I love him. Why?

Because he doesn't feel the same, and he doesn't want you to ruin everything.

My throat tightens. Maybe he needs more time. His mom told me to be patient.

I force a smile. "Don't apologize for being a good boss. I'll see you tonight."

After Rafaele leaves, I have breakfast in bed and watch a rom-com for a bit before I finally decide to get my ass up. I told Loretta I'll be in today since we're receiving a big shipment of fabrics, and she'll need help doing inventory. And Gemma, Mari, Vale, and I are meeting for a happy hour at a restaurant nearby. I want to take full advantage of having them here, and I also desperately need some advice.

A half hour later, I step inside the shop. The bell we recently installed rings above my head. "Loretta?" I call out. "It's me."

She comes out of the bathroom looking a little green. "No need to shout."

I grin. "You okay?" When Rafaele dragged me upstairs, she was singing karaoke in the living room while hanging off Nero's arm.

"Drank too much," she says in a harsh whisper. "And my voice is completely gone."

I burst into giggles. She rolls her eyes and gives me the middle finger. "Don't laugh at my misery. It's all your fault, you know. I can't even remember how many shots you poured down my throat, you little she-devil."

"I don't remember you complaining."

She groans. "You're a bad influence."

We get to work. The delivery is a big one—hundreds of rolls of fabric that need to be catalogued and put in the right place. Our hangovers make it even more difficult, but we power through, fueled by coffee.

Around one, we take a quick break for lunch. Sandro walks us to the deli, and he's looking rough too.

"Can you not park in my customer parking?" Loretta asks. "You're scaring people off sitting there looking all glum."

"I don't look glum," he protests. "I'm just reading the news."

"Well, read it on the other side of the street, will you?"

"Fine," he grumbles. "I'll move the car when we get back."

We have our lunch and get back to work. Later in the afternoon, my phone buzzes in my pocket. I check the screen. It's a text message from Vale.

> Something's wrong with Gemma. Ras is driving her to the hospital right now. I'm almost at the corner of Clinton and Rivington—come quick.

My stomach drops. What? Was there an accident? Is it the baby?

I grab my purse and dart out of the shop. Loretta calls after me, but I ignore her. My feet hit the pavement, and I'm off running.

"Cleo!" Sandro shouts from somewhere behind me and a car door slams.

I ignore him too. My sneakers slap against the street as I sprint to the location Vale mentioned in her message. The thought of Gemma being hurt or of her losing her baby nearly makes me stumble. This can't be happening. Not when Gem is finally doing so well.

My lungs burn from exertion. I don't think I've ever run this fast. I cut across the street, and cars grind to a stop and honk all around me. I sprint to the corner Vale said she'd be at. There's a black limo waiting there. The door of the car opens, and I throw myself inside. It shuts right behind me.

"What happened?" I pant. It takes a moment for my eyes to adjust to the darkness inside the car.

When they do, it isn't Vale staring back at me.

It's Papà.

He smirks. "Hello, daughter."

Something pricks against the side of my neck, and then everything goes black.

CHAPTER 35

RAFAELE

I'M ABOUT to drive home after sorting out a situation with one of the concrete businesses that pays us protection money, when my phone buzzes. An unknown number shows up on the caller ID.

I pick up. "Hello?"

"How are you, Rafaele?"

My blood ices over. Garzolo. He's finally decided to make contact, and he sounds too fucking cheerful for a man in hiding. A bad feeling swirls inside my gut.

"Where the fuck are you?"

He chuckles. "You sound stressed. Must be hard running two families at the same time. Ah. Well, you won't be busy with that for too long now."

"What do you want?" I growl.

"What do I want? The question, actually, is what do *you* want? Your wife dead or alive?"

My pulse skitters. He's fucking with me, but my hands still strangle the wheel. "Reconsider what you just said."

"I'm afraid that's just what it is, my boy. If you want Cleo back, you'll do as I say."

He's bluffing. He has to be. Cleo is at work, and Sandro knows better than to leave his post. There's no way Garzolo has her.

"You're lying." I put him on speakerphone and pull up the locator app I use to track Cleo's phone.

"Go ahead. Check for yourself," Garzolo drawls, guessing at what I'm doing.

Her dot isn't showing up. I tap on her name. Tap. Tap. Tap. Nothing changes.

She's gone.

A glaze of cold sweat breaks out over my skin. "If you touch a hair on her head, I'll kill you."

"Come to this address within the next twenty minutes. 9001 Hopkins Road. I want this over with quickly."

"Let me talk to Cleo."

"She's somewhere else. Somewhere you'll never find her. Bring one fucking soldier with you, and I'll give the order to kill her. You come alone. You understand?"

I can barely hear him over the blood rushing inside my ears. I brake sharply, causing cars to honk behind me, and do a U-turn.

"Careful," he says with a chuckle. "Don't get yourself killed on the way here."

I'm going to tear his throat out with my bare hands.

"She's your daughter."

"She's a nuisance. She's always been a fucking nuisance."

"Garzolo—"

He hangs up. My hands are shaking. He has her. He *will* kill her if I don't go to where he is. How the fuck did this happen?

I jam my finger at the screen and call Sandro. As soon as the line connects, I shout, "Where *the fuck* were you?"

"Boss, I'm sorry, she got away from me! She fucking sprinted out of the shop and jumped into a car before I could get to her. I chased after them, but I lost them after a few blocks."

Cleo got into the car willingly? What the hell did Garzolo do to lure her to him?

Blood drains out of my face. What if she's changed her mind about helping her father? Maybe she got sick of me and decided she'd rather be free. Maybe seeing her sisters made her realize she would be happier living with them instead of me.

I drag my palm over my face.

No.

No, she wouldn't do that. Not after last night when she almost told me she loved me. I couldn't let her say it. What was I supposed to say back? That she confused me, mesmerized me, drove me crazy?

I can't love her. It's forbidden. Wrong.

"What should I do?" Sandro asks, sounding more than a little panicked.

"Get Vinny, Jeremy, and Tiny. Wait for Nero to call you." I hang up and call my consigliere as I take an exit off the highway and program the address Garzolo gave me into the GPS.

"Rafe?"

"Garzolo has Cleo. He's threatening to kill her if I don't go and meet him. He's going to try to kill me."

Nero sucks in a breath. "That fucking piece of shit."

"Get the search going. We need to find my wife."

"It'll be like looking for a needle in a haystack. We don't know the location of Garzolo's remaining safe houses."

He's right. We've been searching for Garzolo for months, and he's well aware of it. Everything that we could have found, we've already found. "Call De Rossi. Ask for his help. His wife will force him to do it. This is her sister we're talking about. Maybe that computer genius he's got working for him can help us."

"On it. What about you?"

"Forget about me. Call me once you have something."

I hang up and try dialing Garzolo on his old number, but he doesn't pick up. My thoughts race. If Nero can't find Cleo's location, I have to put my trust in Garzolo and hope he lets her go once I get to him. But Garzolo has proven himself to be a liar again and again.

I tug on my tie to loosen it. My throat is dry. I need to find a way out of this. I need to get her back.

Ten minutes later, Nero calls me again. "You're not gonna believe this. Giorgio thinks he's found her. Apparently, we should have asked him for help when we were looking for Garzolo because the guy's got all of Garzolo's properties mapped out. He just finished scanning the camera feeds near them and one of the cameras has a car that looks like it could be one of Garzolo's out front."

"Where is it? New Jersey?"

"No, a warehouse in Brooklyn. I'm on my way. I'll be there in fifteen minutes."

"What's the address?"

"59A South Bleeker Street."

I grab a pen from the console and write the address down on an old receipt. "Call Sandro. He's on standby."

"Already did. I'll get there before the rest of them. Are you coming?"

"I have to go to Garzolo." I won't risk him ordering his men to kill Cleo if I don't show up.

"Good luck. I'll get her, Rafe. I promise."

I hang up and pull up the address Nero gave on my GPS. It's close to Ferraro's territory.

Are they working together? No, no way. Ferraro would never align himself with a snake like Garzolo, not when the man's willing to kill his own fucking daughter to get what he wants.

I pull up Ferraro's number and press dial without a clear plan. I don't know what I'm going to say. I'm not thinking clearly. I'm fucking desperate.

He picks up on the second ring.

"Gino." I clutch the wheel tighter. "I need your help."

"Rafaele? What's going on?"

"Garzolo reappeared. He kidnapped my wife, and he's using her to get to me. He's got her in some building on the border of your territory. Nero is on the way, but it'll take a while for the rest of my men to get there. We don't know what he's walking into, and he needs backup."

"Ah, fuck. You want me to send my guys there?"

"Do you have someone nearby? She's at 59A South Bleeker Street."

"I'm checking now. Give me a second."

My heart is hammering inside my chest, and a drop of sweat rolls down my back. I've got to get Nero some help.

Gino comes back on. "I should be able to send someone."

"Cleo can't be harmed. Do you understand?"

"I get it, but Rafaele—"

"Whatever you want in exchange, you'll get it."

There's a beat. "You sure you want to write me a blank check like this?"

It's something I have never done before, but there's no other choice. I have to save Cleo. "Yes."

"All right. My nephew Michael is doing his rounds not too far from there with one of our guys."

"Thank you, Gino."

I hang up, race past a red light, and dial Nero again to let him know.

Busy signal.

I try again.

No luck. He's probably organizing our men, but I need to let him know about the backup Ferraro is sending so that he knows what to expect.

I should have run this by him before I called Gino.

Mistake after mistake. I look down at my hands. If I lift them off the wheel, they'll shake.

Nero calls me back when I'm minutes away from the address Garzolo gave me.

I pick up. "Nero, Ferraro is sending some of his men. Watch out for them."

"Rafe? Rafe, I can't hear you."

I pull my phone away from my ear and glance down at it. The signal's shit, and the GPS says I'm right where I'm supposed to be.

"Damn it." I hang up and park the car. I'm typing out a text to Nero, hoping that'll go through, when there's a loud knock on the window. I look up at a barrel pointed at me through the glass.

"Get out," a voice orders. "Nice and slow."

I put the phone down and get out of the car. The warehouse where Garzolo must be waiting looms a short distance away.

Three guys surround me, guns at the ready. "Move," one of them barks, jerking his head in the direction of the entrance.

I have no idea what I'm about to face here. The parking lot is empty. Garzolo's guys must have parked out the back. How many men does he have with him? I could take these three down—they haven't even taken my weapons—but for all I know, Garzolo's got another twenty inside with him. I start walking with them.

What the hell does Garzolo want? If he just wanted to kill me, one of his men could have done it by now. He must want to talk. Why? I pass through the entrance of the warehouse and glance around.

Ten more men. All armed.

Garzolo walks out from behind a shipping container, gun in one hand and a knife in the other. "Right on time." He looks way too fucking pleased with himself.

"Where's Cleo?"

He smiles. "First things first. Drop your weapons to the ground and kick them over."

I take my guns from the holster strapped across my chest and slide them over.

"All of your weapons."

I pull out three knives and slide those over too.

"Good," Garzolo says, his gaze twinkling with premature triumph. His men keep their guns pointed at me.

I spread my arms. "I'm here. Let her go."

He chuckles. "I have to admit, I'm a bit curious. My daughter isn't someone who inspires much loyalty. What is it about that awful girl that made you show up? I wasn't even convinced she'd be good enough bait."

I bare my teeth. How fucking dare he talk that way about her? "She's mine."

"Ah, I understand." He drags his palm over his white beard. "It's a matter of pride then. What kind of a don would you be if you couldn't even protect your wife?"

"Garzolo. Let. Her. Go."

He smiles again. "I will, once you give me what I want."

"Fucking get to it then."

"You know, all of this could have been avoided if you'd just moved a little slower in that restaurant. Instead, you had to make my life difficult."

That fucker. So it was he who hired those hit men. "What life? Your life is about to be over."

"No, my life is just beginning." He shakes his head. "I want to know what you have on the district attorney. Must be something big for him to drop the charges against me. Give me the leverage you've got, and then we can get this over with."

Of course. He wants to know how I got him out of jail so that he can kill me and still have it as insurance. A guy like him doesn't know how to stay out of hot water.

"You're an ungrateful piece of shit."

He snickers and shakes his head. "I don't want to be here all night, Rafaele." He pulls his phone out and dangles it from his hand. "One call. That's all it will take for Cleo to die."

Rage and fear twist inside of me. How did I end up in this position?

"I'm going to ask you one more time. Think carefully about your answer. What do you have on the DA?"

My heart races. As soon as I tell him, he'll kill me. If I keep my mouth shut, maybe I can buy myself some time. Find a way out of this mess. But that will mean risking Cleo's life. I have no idea if Garzolo will really make that call. He's fucking crazy.

I swallow past my dry throat. This is what my father trained me for. I spent years learning how to keep everyone at a distance. How to detach from my emotions. How to use that ruthlessness to my advantage.

The right thing would be to refuse him.

Garzolo watches me. A drop of sweat trails down my back.

He presses dial on his phone.

"Fine!" I break, my control slipping through my fingers. I squeeze my eyes shut, feeling something shatter inside of me. "The DA's got an indentured servant that he's been hiding for years in his home."

Garzolo's eyes flash with victory. "How very awful of him." He lifts his gun, pointing it at my face. "Guess I'll have to pay him a visit soon."

I stare down the barrel.

And then a shot rings through the air.

CHAPTER 36

RAFAELE

I BLINK. Somehow, I'm still alive. Garzolo is crouched on the ground shouting commands at his men, and there's gunfire all around me.

I duck and glance over my shoulder.

De Rossi and his consigliere, along with two more men I don't recognize, are storming the warehouse. I huff out a breath. I might actually make it out of this alive.

Staying low, I run toward where my guns are lying discarded on the floor. I snatch them up and find cover behind the closest storage container.

Five against fourteen.

Not fucking bad.

I take aim and start firing, picking off Garzolo's men one by one. De Rossi and his guys fight like demons raised straight from hell. Sounds of gunfire and screams ring through the air. Ras appears and takes cover beside me. He exchanges shots with one of Garzolo's guys, and when he runs out of bullets, I take aim and get the man between the eyes.

"Fuck, nice shot," Ras says, reloading his gun. "You okay?"

"Fine. You and your boss have perfect timing. Where's Garzolo? We need him alive. I've got plans for him."

"Yeah, you and the rest of us," Ras mutters. "Over there." He nods toward a pile of boxes at the back of the warehouse. "I saw him running."

I glance around. Damiano's men are keeping Garzolo's guys occupied, and it looks like they've got it.

"I'm going to make sure he doesn't get any farther," I say to Ras and run toward the boxes. A bullet grazes me, but I ignore it.

Breathe in, breathe out, breathe in—

My back slams against the wall. From this angle, I can see him. Garzolo's huddled in the corner, crouching with his gun raised while his men are dying.

Coward.

There's a look of sheer panic etched onto his face. Blood runs onto the ground from his leg. He must have been hit when the fighting broke out. It takes him a while to notice me approach. He yelps and tries to shoot, but I'm on him too quickly. I force him down to the ground, knock the gun out of his hand, and press the barrel of my gun to his temple.

"You're going to pay for what you've done," I growl.

The gunshots around me die down. The fighting is over. Footsteps sound behind me, and Ras and De Rossi appear at my side.

"Not so fast," Ras growls. "This cockroach deserves to die slowly."

De Rossi nods. "Very fucking slowly."

They're right.

I stand up, keeping my gun pointed at Garzolo. I lift my foot and step on where Garzolo's leg is shot. His bone makes a loud crunch, and he screams out in agony. It's music to my ears. But it's not enough. Not even close. I want him to suffer. I want him to feel the pain and fear Cleo felt when we were getting shot at by his men at Il Caminetto. Bloodlust makes my vision darken at the edges.

Then I remember—Cleo is waiting for me.

Fuck. I have to go to her.

I turn to De Rossi. "Did they get my wife?"

"I don't know," he says. "I sent Napoletano there to help Nero, but I haven't heard from him yet."

He sent Napoletano to Cleo but the two of them came here? "You should have gone there too."

"We saved your life, asshole," Ras snaps, his gaze fixed on Garzolo. "Go to her. You can thank us by leaving him to us."

He wants to deal with Garzolo? I size the two of them up. I suppose if there's anyone who wants Garzolo to suffer as much as I do, it's them. They won't show him mercy, not after everything Garzolo has done to his other two daughters. Garzolo abused Gemma and married Valentina off to a madman before she escaped and met De Rossi. This vermin deserves everything that's coming to him.

Cleo is still out there, and I have to go to her.

I give Ras a nod. "Fine. He's yours. Savor it."

Ras's eyes flash with dark excitement. He pulls a knife out of a holster strapped to his arm and walks up to Garzolo.

"You have no idea how long I've been waiting for this," he croons at the man.

I leave them to it. De Rossi bumps my shoulder with his fist as I walk past him.

The last thing I hear as I step out into the parking lot is Garzolo's ear-piercing scream.

It's a twenty-minute drive to get to the address De Rossi gave me. I try Nero, but he doesn't pick up his phone. I've never been an anxious person, but right now, I'm a ball of fucking sweat. My skin prickles with discomfort, and I can't seem to get enough air. I have to trust that Nero saved Cleo.

My thoughts churn. I can't seem to hold on to a single thread. My reliable friends—clarity, rationality, common sense—have abandoned me. Everything in my head is disorganized, impossible to piece together. It's unnerving. As if I'm in a trance.

Finally, I get there. It's another warehouse, smaller than the one I just left. I park by a car I recognize as Nero's, leave the engine running, and jump out. Something desperate and terrified claws up my throat as I sprint toward the entrance.

If she's been harmed, I'll burn this city to the ground.

The scene inside the warehouse isn't as bloody as the one I just left. Three bodies lie on the ground, none of the men mine, and I rush past them, my gaze desperately searching for Cleo. I spot Nero and Sandro. They're arguing loudly with a guy I vaguely recognize as one of Ferraro's. They hear me and turn.

"Where is she?" I shout.

Nero points to the left, and that's when I find her.

Cleo's huddled on the ground by a knocked over chair, someone's jacket wrapped around her. She's staring at the ground, eyes wide, like she's in shock.

De Rossi's guy, Giorgio, is kneeling beside her, saying something in a low tone.

My lungs expand.

She's alive. She's safe.

Slowly, she lifts her face, and her gaze meets mine. A fracture appears inside my chest at how vulnerable she looks. I rush over to her, fall to my knees beside her, and pull her into my arms.

She makes a low sob. "Rafe."

"*Tesoro*. Are you hurt?" I can hardly recognize my own voice.

"No." She shakes her head, holding me tightly to her. "I'm okay. Is my dad…"

"Dead." Or he's well on his way there. "He'll never harm you again."

She sobs again, and I rock her in my arms. My throat tightens, and everything feels so overwhelming and so fucking *raw* that a new wave of panic claws up my chest.

The memory of my mother's pained screams pierce through my head. I squeeze my eyes shut for a long moment and then open them.

I can hear Sandro and the other guy still shouting at each other, but Nero is here now. He's standing just a few feet away with Giorgio.

They're both staring at me with strange expressions on their faces. Like they don't know who they're looking at. Like the Rafaele they know is gone, and in his place is another man. A man who's allowed himself to be consumed with fear. A man who's been brought to his knees. A man who's weak.

A don must never look weak.

What's happened to me?

What the fuck am I doing?

Throwing away my reputation, the one I've spent a lifetime building, right here on this dirty fucking warehouse floor?

I let go of Cleo and get to my feet. I am not that man. I *cannot* be that man, or everything I have will be lost.

"Are Garzolo's men all dead?" I ask Nero.

"Yeah," my consigliere says. He wipes his palm over his mouth. "But we have a problem."

"What happened?"

The dark-haired Ferraro who was arguing with Sandro appears in front of me and shoves against my chest. "This fucking fool," he shouts, pointing at Nero, "shot Michael. My cousin. The don's nephew. Do you fucking idiots understand what you've done?"

Fucking fuck. "Nero, is that true?"

Nero gives me a guilt-ridden look. "It was an accident."

The guy sneers. "You better pray he makes it."

I put a hand on his shoulder. "Calm down. What's your name?"

"Emanuele."

"Where is your cousin?"

He jerks his head in the direction of a man lying on the ground. Tiny and Sandro are beside him, pressing rags to what looks like a gunshot wound to his gut.

"I didn't know they were coming," Nero says, his voice hoarse. "I thought he was one of Garzolo's men, and I just fucking shot him. It was chaos. I was trying to get to her."

Fuck. It's my fault. I never warned him the Ferraros were coming.

"We already called Doc," Sandro says. "He's on his way."

I walk over to where the man is lying on the ground. The guy's pulse is still there, but weak. He's bleeding out.

Nero kneels beside me. "Rafe, what were the Ferraros doing here?"

"I called them. Asked them to help."

"Why would you do that? I had enough men."

I open my mouth and then shut it. There's no good answer. I panicked and made a mistake. A big one. If Michael dies, there will be a war.

I stand up and take a step backward. Everything is falling apart. How is it possible that in less than an hour, I've lost control over everything? We didn't even need Ferraro's men. Nero had it covered. Why did I think it was a good idea to involve them in this?

No, I wasn't thinking at all. I was desperate to save Cleo.

I didn't even consider the potential consequences of my rash decision. I let my emotions take control of me.

Bile rises up my throat. Nero was right after all. She did manage to get under my skin.

She is my living, breathing weakness.

Tires screeching outside. Everyone pulls out their guns, but it's just Doc. He runs through the entrance of the warehouse, his medical bag in hand.

"Over here," Nero shouts.

While the doc's checking Michael out, I walk back to Cleo. She's still on the ground, watching everything with wide tear-stained eyes, but she's visibly calmer. I offer her a hand to help her up, but there's this angry buzz beneath my skin.

"Tell me what happened. Start at the beginning."

She wraps her arms around herself. "I got a text from Vale saying Gemma was hurt and that she'd pick me up from work."

Giorgio clears his throat. "I took a look at her phone. Garzolo used Valentina's old US phone."

I want to laugh. So fucking obvious. Garzolo didn't have to try very hard at all. He'd waited for the best opportunity, and it presented itself when Cleo's sisters came to town.

How could she have fallen for it?

My gaze narrows on her. Fury throbs through my body, heating me from the inside out. "I told you to never go anywhere without your guards."

She winces. "I'm sorry."

"Why didn't you ask Sandro about it?"

"I didn't think—"

My fists clench. "That's right, you never fucking think."

She jerks like she'd been slapped. God, I want to slap her. I want to shake her for being so goddamn reckless. She bridges the distance between us, tries to reach for me, but I turn away.

Hurt flashes across her face. "Rafe?"

The heartbreak in her voice pierces through me. This can't go on. I am a don first and foremost, and I cannot be with a woman like her.

A hurricane.

I was a fool to think I could tame a hurricane. A fool to let myself get attached to her. This is why there was never supposed to be anything but lust between us. There's too much at stake.

"Get her out of here," I say to Giorgio. "Take her to her sisters."

Giorgio nods, but Cleo shakes her head. "No. I want to go home with you," she pleads.

"I won't be home for a while." My voice is pure ice. "I have to clean up this mess. If you want to wait there for me alone, be my guest."

Her eyes fill with tears, and I can't fucking stand to see it.

I walk away from her, trusting Giorgio to get her home safely, and with each step, I shove my feelings for her down.

CHAPTER 37

RAFAEL

IT TAKES three hours to bury the bodies and get the warehouses cleaned up. In the meantime, Nero, Doc, and Emanuele take Michael Ferraro to the hospital for treatment so he'll have the best chance of making it out of this alive.

I'm nearly home when I get the call from Nero.

I pick up. "Speak."

"He's dead."

My heart freezes mid-beat. Just our fucking luck. Why is it that some assholes are seemingly impossible to kill, but this kid goes down with one damn bullet? I rub my forehead with the heel of my palm. This is bad.

"Get out of there right now and go somewhere safe."

"Doc is still with me."

"Ask him if he's willing to stay until Ferraro's men come. I'll call Ferraro and explain the situation."

A beat passes. "Rafe, he'll want me."

I clench my jaw. Ferraro will demand vengeance. There's no doubt about that. "I know. Let me talk to Gino. Where's Emanuele?"

"With his cousin. Saying his goodbyes."

"Leave now. Destroy your phone. Next time you call me, use a burner."

Nero lets out a heavy sigh. "Will do."

I park the car outside the house and go straight to my office, my mind running over my limited options.

Can I deny Nero shot him? Impossible. There's a witness. We should have killed Emanuele earlier and claimed both of them died in the gunfire. I sink into my chair and drag my hand down my face. I might have thought of that on the spot if I'd been in control of myself instead of flailing like an idiot and losing my mind over my wife.

It's too late now. Emanuele's probably already told Gino what happened. The only thing I can do is fucking pray Gino will forgive Nero for making an honest mistake.

Gino picks up my call right away. "My nephew is dead, killed by your consigliere, after I went out on a limb and sent him over to help you." The anger in his voice is palpable.

"Gino, it was an accident. Nero didn't know your guys were coming. I didn't have time to call."

"Your incompetence is not my fucking problem." His voice booms over the speaker. "If you weren't in control of the situation, you shouldn't have asked for my fucking help."

He's right. He's *fucking* right. In retrospect, I can't believe the reckless stupidity of my actions. It was pure desperation. Devoid of logic and reason.

"Truly, I'm sorry."

"Fuck your sorry. You think that sorry is going to matter to Michael's mother? And do you even realize how this makes me look? I agreed to help you as a gesture of good faith. I thought we really had a chance to put the feud between our families behind us once and for all. There's only one way to make this right, and you fucking know it."

My blood runs cold.

"I want to see Nero's body by tomorrow morning. If you're not man enough to kill him, I'll do it myself."

I get up and walk over to the bar. "Look, let's not overreact. Let's talk about this."

"There's nothing left to talk about, Rafaele."

I splash some whiskey into a glass. My hands are shaking. "Let me compensate you for your loss. How much would fix this?"

"I don't need your money."

"Territory then. I'll give you my assets in Manhattan. You can run them as you wish."

"This isn't about that," Gino snaps. "This is about you learning a lesson I would have thought you learned a long time ago. You don't put another don's men at risk like this. I

347

won't ever work with you if you don't make this right, do you understand?"

The alcohol burns my throat. I want to roar in frustration. I can't risk a war with the Ferraros when I'm still trying to get a handle on Garzolo's family and trying to fight back the Bratva. My resources are spread thin. There's a good chance they'd squash us. How the fuck did I allow this to happen?

"Nero's gone," I grind out. "It'll take me longer than that to find him."

"You can find him, or *I* will. And trust me when I say his death will be far quicker if you do it."

"Gi—"

He hangs up.

I stare at the phone screen for a few seconds before I throw my glass across the room. It hits a bookshelf and shatters. Next goes the paperweight, straight through the mirror. Then I shove every piece of crap I've got on my desk onto the floor. Papers fly everywhere, but it doesn't help. Nothing fucking helps.

"Fuck!"

Nero. He wants *Nero*.

My consigliere. My friend. The man who's stood by my side since we were kids. The man who's put his life on the line for me whenever I've asked him to do it, doing whatever I've fucking asked of him. The man who's been unfailingly loyal to me. And in my moment of weakness, I set him up. I did him fucking dirty.

The door to my office opens, and Cleo appears.

"Get out," I growl.

She pauses, her hand on the door handle, but then her lips firm into a line, and she steps inside. "No."

I glare at her, feeling like all of my organs are shriveling up. "Not now, Cleo."

She ignores my warning. She casts her gaze around the mess inside my office, her brows pinching in concern. "We need to talk."

I don't have time to talk. I've got the most powerful don in New York waiting for me to deliver the body of my consigliere to his doorstep.

This woman is my ruin. And she doesn't even realize it.

She approaches the desk, her expression worried. "Rafe, I'm so sorry. I know what I did was stupid, but when I thought Gemma was in trouble... I just wasn't thinking. I thought something had happened to her or the baby. I just..." Her eyes well up with tears. "I panicked."

"Why didn't you call me first?" I demand. This could have been avoided if she hadn't taken her father's bait. If she'd just fucking used her brain.

Funny how the exact same criticism can be thrown right back at me. I wasn't thinking when I called Ferraro. And now my consigliere has to pay for my mistake. Rage pulses inside my chest. I've never hated myself more than I do right now.

She's done this to me. Made me into someone not worth the responsibility I've been given. Made me into a weak, impulsive, *emotional* man.

This can't go on.

I have to end this or everything I've worked for, everything I've bled for, will burn to the ground at her feet. My heart shreds apart inside my chest.

"I promise this will never happen again," Cleo says brokenly.

"You're right." I look past her at the broken mirror hanging on the wall, at my fractured reflection. "It won't, because we're over."

There's a beat.

"What?" Her voice is a harsh whisper.

"You wanted a divorce." I look down at my desk, unable to look at her, unable to be near her. "Congratulations. You're getting it."

"What are you talking about? That was *months* ago. Things have changed. You know that."

"I'll get my lawyers on it."

"We can work through this," she pleads. "Come on, it was one mistake. We can make this right again. Don't tell me you'd throw all of this away over one damn mistake!"

She doesn't get it. My life was fine before I met her. Everything was steady. I could control my reality, bend it to my will, enact anything I wanted. And now? There's only mayhem. The reins are slipping out of my hands, and she's the one pulling on them.

"I cannot be the don I need to be with you around." I manage to keep my voice free of emotion. "You need to leave."

She rushes to me, her footsteps loud against the hardwood floor. She takes my arm. "Rafe, stop. You're acting crazy."

"You made me fucking crazy!" I roar, shaking her off. Our gazes clash. "Do you know how badly I fucked up when I thought you were about to be killed by your father? When I thought you were in danger, I couldn't fucking think straight. I still can't think straight with you around me."

A broken sob escapes her, and a tear runs down her cheek. "I love you."

I force myself not to look away. To take in this moment. I know I won't ever hear those words again. I don't fucking deserve them.

"That's unfortunate," I say harshly.

She sucks in a breath. "I know you love me too, damn it."

"I don't love *anyone*." I step away from her.

"I know about your father! That he made you watch while he beat your mother. She told me."

My stomach hollows out. Mamma told her?

Not everything. She'd never tell her everything.

"He was a sick man," Cleo whispers.

If only she knew how sick.

"And he was wrong. Emotions don't make you weak. Love doesn't make you weak."

Oh, but it does. Its roots penetrate through cracks, destroy walls, crumble strong foundations. I don't recognize myself anymore.

I need to undo this.

"Was he wrong? I don't think so. The only thing that's wrong here is me and you."

Her eyes widen with disbelief, as if my words don't make any sense.

"Rafe—"

"You'll leave with your sisters today. I want you out of this house. It'll take me a few days to clean up the mess you caused and get the papers in order. I'll mail them to you in Italy."

"You can't do this." Cleo reaches for me again.

I tear my arm out of her grasp and move toward the door. "I've said everything I have to say."

"Where are you going?" Her voice cracks, and God, how that hurts me.

"To figure out some way that today doesn't end with my consigliere dead."

"Why would he die?"

I halt. Slowly, I turn around to face her. "Because I called Gino Ferraro for help when I knew you were in trouble, but I didn't have time to warn Nero. Nero shot one of Ferraro's men by accident. The don's nephew. He's dead. Now, Ferraro wants Nero *dead*."

Blood drains out of her face. "No, no, he—"

"Ferraro expects me to deliver Nero's body in the next twelve hours. All because of you and your recklessness."

Shame floods through me as soon as that sentence leaves my mouth. The truth is, it's as much my fault as hers. No, it's more. I am the don. My people are my responsibility, not hers. But I need her to leave. I need her out of my house, out of my mind, out of my heart. I need her gone.

"No. *No.*" She covers her mouth with her hands, tears cascading down her cheeks. "You can't do it. Nero can't die because of me. Rafe, please. Please tell me—"

I turn on my heel and leave. I can't hear her voice anymore. Can't look at her face. Not if I'm going to be able to do what needs to be done.

CHAPTER 38

CLEO

I COLLAPSE onto my knees right on the floor of his office, my face wet with tears, my entire body shaking. How can this be happening? Gino Ferraro wants Nero dead because of me.

Nero. Rafaele's closest confidant and friend. His consigliere.

I squeeze my eyes shut and let out a low moan. There's an insistent ache inside my chest that expands until I feel nothing but pain. Footsteps sound outside the room, drawing closer and closer. The door creaks open, and there's a gasp.

"Cleo!"

I don't have the strength to even raise my face toward Vale. She runs over and crouches down beside me, placing her hand on my back.

A moment later, Gemma's there too. She pulls out a tissue from somewhere and starts dabbing it against my face. "What happened?"

"He... He wants a divorce." My voice breaks.

Vale gasps. *"What?"* She and Gemma exchange a look. "Oh, Cleo. Let's get you off the floor, okay? And then you can tell us everything."

They help me up and lead me toward the leather couch on the other side of the room. I feel like I'm about to shatter.

"It's over between us," I whisper.

Gemma's eyes are wide and disbelieving. "There's no way. He's angry, but he'll calm down and realize that's ridiculous."

I shake my head. They weren't there when he said those words. There wasn't a hint of doubt in his tone. He meant them. "He wants me to go to Italy with you and wipe his hands clean of me."

Vale heaves a pained sigh. "Does he know that you love him?"

I never told them that I love him, but there's no point in denying it. It's fucking obvious. I sniffle, feeling like the biggest idiot in the world. "He knows. It doesn't matter. He doesn't want me after the mess I caused."

Gemma scrunches up the tissue in her hand. "What mess? You're fine. Everyone is fine."

"No." My lips waver. They don't know the kicker yet. "Nero killed one of Ferraro's men by accident. Now Gino Ferraro wants retribution." My chest feels tight, like it's about to cave in on itself. "He wants Rafaele to kill Nero."

Gemma's mouth falls open. For a moment, no one speaks.

"That's insane," Gemma says eventually in a hushed voice. "Nero is his consigliere, and Gino must know it wasn't intentional."

"It doesn't matter. Rafaele has been trying to make peace with the Ferraros for a long time, and this jeopardized the whole thing. *I* jeopardized the whole thing." I squeeze my fists so hard my nails pierce my skin. "I'm a fucking idiot. It didn't even occur to me that the text could be fake. I just dropped everything and *ran*."

Vale wraps her arm over my shoulder and pulls me closer. "But how can he blame you for acting like that when you thought Gemma was in danger? You were scared and worried. Most people would have reacted the same way you did."

"And how is it your fault Nero shot a Ferraro?" Gemma shakes her head. "None of this makes sense. I don't understand why he'd push you away."

Because he doesn't think I'm worth all this. Did I ever really believe he'd think I'm good enough? No one else ever has. All those things he said to me about being his ideal wife were probably just to get me into his bed.

I give my head a shake. No, even in my current state, I know that isn't true. This was more than sex. Things were going well between us.

Maybe Rafaele thought they were going *too* well.

When he told me he didn't love anyone, he uttered "love" like it was a dirty word.

I wrap my arms around myself. "He said he can't be the don he needs to be with me around. Even if he does feel some-

356

thing for me, I don't think he wants to. He won't let himself love anyone."

Gemma shakes her head. "He's making a huge mistake. Why don't you try to talk to him again?"

His words echo inside my brain. *I've said everything I need to say.*

"He's gone. He's trying to figure out what to do about Nero. He told me he wants me out of the house, and that I should go to Italy with you."

Vale's expression crumples. "Oh, Cleo. I'm sorry."

I wipe my nose with the back of my hand and huff out a breath. Should I try to talk to him one more time? No, he made his position clear. But what if he just needs a bit of time to cool down?

I huff bitterly at the thought. Rafe needing time to cool down. Who would have thought we'd end up here?

"I want to rest for a bit. I'm exhausted." I get up from the sofa. "Will you stay here until I talk to him again?"

"Of course," Gemma says. "We'll be in the living room. I'll go ask Luca to bring you a snack."

Food is the last thing on my mind, but I nod anyway. "Thanks."

Upstairs, I make it to our bed and fall onto it face first. My soul hurts. Everything hurts.

When I woke up after my father jabbed me with a sedative, I was scared and disoriented. I didn't know what was going on, and it was awful. But somehow even that felt less horrible than this. If Papà's men had killed me, at least I would have died with a clear conscience. But now? How can I live with Nero's death on my hands?

There has to be something Rafaele can do to stop it from happening. He's clever and capable. He has to find a way to keep Nero alive.

There's a knock on the door.

"Come in."

Luca comes in with a tray of food. When he sees my puffy face, his expression falls. "I'm sorry, signora."

"It's okay, Luca. Just put that over there." I gesture at the coffee table by the ottoman.

Just before he leaves again, he pauses by the door. "It'll be okay. This too shall pass."

I give him a weak smile. I'm not even sure he knows what's at stake, but I appreciate him trying to make me feel better. "Thanks, Luca."

He leaves, and I pick a bit at the food. I haven't eaten since lunch, but I'm not hungry. How can I be when my stomach is in knots?

An hour passes. I stare at my wedding band. I should take it off. Leave it on the nightstand for Rafaele to find when he gets home. I wrap my fingers around it.

Take it off.

Do it.

I can't. I sigh and tip my head back. *Fuck.*

My phone is a few feet away from me on the bed. I pick it up, pull up my texts with Rafaele, and write a message.

> When will you be home? Can we talk?
> Please?

I press send. The house is quiet, but there's blood whooshing inside my ears as I wait for my husband to respond.

His message comes a minute later.

> There's nothing to talk about. I don't want to see you there when I'm back.

My vision blurs with tears as I type back.

> Please tell me you won't do it.

Three dots appear on the screen.

> I don't have a choice.

I squeeze the phone in my hand until pain blooms inside my palm, and then I hurl it at the floor. "Damn it!"

It's over. There's no way back from this.

I fly into the closet, jerk a suitcase off the bottom shelf, and fling it open. Things go inside—clothes, jewelry, whatever—and then I slam it closed and zip it up.

Vale must hear the commotion, because she comes into the bedroom at the same time I drag my suitcase out of the closet. Her gaze falls onto my bag. "Are you all right?"

I shake my head, tears dripping down my face and onto my shirt. I can't remember the last time I cried like this. "I need to get out of here. Please, just get me out of here."

She rushes over. "Come on."

Vale's driver takes Gemma, Vale, and me to the hotel in Manhattan where they've been staying. My temple pressed against the glass, I close my eyes and try to calm down, but as soon as I replay Rafaele's words, my throat tightens, and I start crying again.

I can't believe it's over.

When we walk into Vale's suite, Damiano and Ras are there waiting for us. Giorgio is sitting in the corner, his hands steepled as he watches everyone from afar.

"Where's Mari?" Valentina asks.

"In our suite," Giorgio says, his gaze flashing with pity as he takes me in. "She tried to wait up, Cleo, but I told her to get some sleep. We have an early flight tomorrow."

Vale shoots me an apologetic look. "I'm sure we can postpone it if you don't want to leave just yet."

I shake my head. "What's the point? There's nothing left for me here. What hope is there for Rafaele and I when I'm the reason he's about to lose his best friend?"

My voice cracks on the last word, and Vale pulls me against her chest. "Shhh. It'll be okay, Cleo."

"No. It won't." I press my face into her shoulder, staining her clothes with my tears. I've never felt more helpless in my whole life. Not even when I was walking down the aisle toward Rafaele, when I was sure marrying him was the worst thing that could possibly happen to me.

Wasn't it?

If we hadn't gotten married, none of this would have happened. If only he could have seen into the future when he agreed to take me instead of Gemma... He never would have agreed.

I disentangle myself from Vale, suddenly overwhelmed with her touch, overwhelmed with everything. Panic claws up my throat, and that's when my gaze lands on Damiano. My sister's husband wears a somber expression. Damiano is a don too. He's powerful, smart, resourceful. The only reason he helped Rafaele today is because I'm Vale's sister. Beyond that, he's got little skin in the game. He can keep a clear head. Maybe he can think of a way out of this.

I cross the room and stop before him. "Rafe's going to kill Nero because of me. Damiano, can't you do something? Please."

My sister's husband looks at me with compassion I wasn't sure he possessed. "Cleo...it wouldn't be right for us to interfere. We're guests here."

"Please." My voice rings with desperation. "Rafaele is your business partner. Him losing his consigliere can't be good for business. I'm begging you."

Damiano turns to Vale, who's giving him a pleading look that mirrors my own. He sighs. "All right. I'll give him a call. But I can't promise anything."

A flicker of hope appears inside my chest, even though I know it's far-fetched. Damiano, Giorgio, and Ras walk out of the suite into an adjacent room and close the door.

"Let's sit down," Vale says, leading me to a chair. "I'll make some tea. They have peppermint here. Your favorite."

Vale walks over to the small kitchenette, and Gemma sits down in the chair beside me, taking my hands into hers. "We'll get through this. No matter what, okay?"

"I don't know how I'll live with myself if Nero dies." I thought Nero was an arrogant ass when I first met him, but he's grown on me over the last few months. All he was doing was trying to protect me from my father's men. How can he die for that?

"It's not right for Rafaele to do this," Gemma says angrily. "Blaming the situation with Nero on you isn't fair."

"Nothing about this life is fair," I spit out.

A barbed wire of anger wraps around my heartbreak. This is why I never wanted to marry a mobster. This is why I tried so hard to escape the life I was born into. There are no winners in this world. Everyone loses eventually.

Vales comes over with the tea, and I take the mug from her.

"Careful, it's hot."

It is, but I welcome the burn. It's the only thing that keeps me from spiraling deeper into my dark thoughts. We drink our tea and wait for the men to come out. There's nothing else left for me to do. Their muffled voices filter through the door, but I can't make out what they're saying.

After what feels like forever, they finally emerge. My breathing slows until it stops entirely. I can see the answer on Damiano's face before he even says a word.

"I'm sorry," he says roughly. "It's out of our hands."

CHAPTER 39

RAFAELE

THE THIRTY-MINUTE JOURNEY to the address where Nero is waiting is pure agony. Sandro is behind the wheel. I asked him to drive so that I could devote all of my brain power to finding a way out of this mess. But we're nearly there, and I've got nothing close to a solid plan.

Gino doesn't want anything I can give him. He wants to teach me a lesson, maybe the same one he wanted to teach my father but couldn't.

Don't fuck with my family.

I should have never gotten him involved in this mess. I still can't believe how poorly I thought everything through.

That woman. She short-circuited my brain.

But what's done is done. I shouldn't think about her anymore, certainly not now when I've got bigger problems on my hands. She's safe with her family, while I'm still trying to find some way out of this.

We pull into the driveway of a rickety-looking house with peeling white paint and a front yard full of weeds. The number on the door says fourteen. I knock—three times, then two. For a while, nothing happens. Then I hear a chain jingle and the lock turn. Nero appears, gun in hand. For a moment, I wonder if he's considered just shooting me. He must suspect what's coming. But he lowers his gun and waves us through the door.

Sandro and I step inside in silence. Nero locks the door and leads us to a living room with two sunken-in couches and a scratched-up coffee table. The place is a dump.

Nero sits down, making the couch groan. "Have you talked to Gino?"

I take a seat across from him. "Sandro, see if you can make some coffee."

He gets the hint and leaves. Nero gives me a weary look, like he knows I wouldn't need privacy if I had any good news to deliver. No, there's little good about any of this.

I drag my fingers through my hair. "Gino wants you dead."

Nero's expression turns frozen.

"He's furious at how this ended with his nephew. He wants me to make it right. I offered him money. I offered him territory. He said no."

My consigliere is completely still. He doesn't even blink. I'm not sure he's breathing. He just stares at me from under his thick brows, an air of disbelief swirling around him.

"Fuck, Nero. Say something."

A beat passes. Finally, he huffs a bitter laugh. "For the first time in my entire life, I've got nothing."

And neither do I. I'm supposed to be the guy with the solutions, but all I see are problems coming at me one after the other.

"Tell me, if you don't make it right, what will happen?" Nero asks.

"He'll do it himself. And if he can't kill you, he'll declare war. He'll start by trying to turn the remaining Garzolos to his side. I haven't had enough time to prove myself to that family, and not everyone's thrilled with having me as their don. He won't have to work hard to find allies. Gino Ferraro isn't Stefano Garzolo. He's intelligent, and he's got his three sons to do his bidding. It will get bloody."

Nero's gaze gets even darker. "Sounds like a mess."

"It is a fucking mess."

He swallows. "You're thinking about doing it then?"

Aggravation slithers down my spine, followed by shame and a healthy dose of disgust. "Of course, I'm thinking about it." I have to. I'm a don, and that means making impossible choices.

"Fucking shit." He swipes his hand over his lips. "Somehow, I managed to convince myself over the years that you care just a little about me."

"I don't want to do this, Nero," I growl. "But I can't ignore all the logical downstream effects if I don't do what Gino wants."

The coffee table goes flying toward me. I jump to my feet, pull out my gun, and point it at him. The air around us crackles with tension.

"You and your fucking logic," he spits out, his eyes ablaze with anger and hurt. "I don't want to hear it. I don't need to know how you'll rationalize this." He advances until the barrel of my gun presses up against his chest. "Do it, Rafe. Just fucking do it. I can tell you want to. It's the *logical* thing to do, isn't it?"

My index finger hovers above the trigger. Seconds tick by.

It *is* logical. But it feels so fucking wrong that I can taste bile coming up my throat.

"I thought you'd finally changed," Nero whispers. "Because of the girl. Because of your *wife*."

That word triggers a flood of memories.

The way I kissed her at the altar. The way she looked at me when I told her it was over. The way my chest spasmed when she said those three fucking words.

"You were right," I whisper back. "I never should have gotten involved with her."

He curls his hand over the barrel, keeping it steady. "I don't blame her for this. You shouldn't either." He leans even closer, his gaze piercing through me. "At least she showed you what it feels like to be human."

Something is lodged inside my throat. A pressure builds behind my eyes.

Do it. Pull the trigger. I trained you for this.

At thirteen, I listened to my father's words.

But at twenty-seven...I don't.

I jerk the gun out of Nero's grip and lower it. Surprise and then relief flash in his eyes. I turn away from him and cross the room, putting some distance between us. A headache blooms inside my skull. I want to claw my fucking brains out.

Some minutes pass before Nero asks, "Why didn't you do it?"

I shake my head, refusing to meet his eye. "I don't know."

He huffs. "So what now?"

"We've got time. It's not morning yet."

Nero checks his watch. "Five hours until sunrise. Until Ferraro sends his army after me. How do you want to spend them?" He spreads his arms and laughs, but it's humorless. "Not much entertainment around here. I might be able to find us a deck of cards."

My pocket starts vibrating. I place my gun on the coffee table and dig the phone out of my jacket.

"Ferraro?" Nero asks.

I stare at the caller ID. "No. It's De Rossi." Why is he calling? Is Cleo with him by now? Not wanting to torture myself by wondering about it all night, I pick up. "Is she with you?"

"Yeah. We're leaving with her in the morning."

A heaviness settles inside my chest, but I ignore it. "Good." The words taste like ash on my tongue.

"We heard what Ferraro wants."

I grunt in response.

"Are you with Nero right now?"

"Yeah."

"Have you figured a way out of it?"

I stare at the gun on the coffee table between Nero and me. Since I'm not going to kill Nero, Gino will. Or at least he'll try. And how many more will die as a result?

My jaw clenches. "No. Why are you calling me?"

"Cleo asked me to see if I can help somehow. She's inconsolable."

An ache appears inside my chest. I crack my neck, forcing myself to ignore the sensation. "I'm all fucking ears. Ferraro expects to see a body tomorrow. If he doesn't, he will declare war. Many will die."

Gino told me he had an affinity for water, but he won't hesitate to let New York City go up in flames.

De Rossi makes a thoughtful noise. "You said Ferraro wants a body."

"Yes, a body," I answer.

Hold on. A beat passes. "Doesn't have to be Nero's body," I whisper more to myself than to De Rossi.

Across the room, my consigliere looks up at me.

"Let's talk it through," De Rossi says. "I'm putting you on speaker. Ras and Giorgio are here too."

I start pacing. "Right. Garzolo had a few big guys with him. About Nero's size."

"He did. We could get them back for you."

If De Rossi brings me the bodies... "I could make it look like a fire. Make them unrecognizable."

"Gino will want the remains," De Rossi says. "He'll want to verify it himself."

"Yeah. He'll check the DNA. Nero's been swabbed before, and Gino has contacts inside the police who'll be able to run it through the database."

"I can update the records they have on file," a deeper voice says, one I recognize as Giorgio's.

I frown at the phone. "Are you sure?"

"It won't be a problem," he says, not a hint of uncertainty in his tone. "But you'll still have to figure out what to do with Nero. He won't be able to show his face around here ever again."

I glance at my friend. He's got his elbows on his knees, his palms cupped in front of his face.

"He'll have to disappear," I say.

Nero holds my gaze.

"I can't send him to any of my safe houses in the state," I say. "Too risky."

"No, he has to leave New York," Giorgio says. "I suggest sending him a few states over. Somewhere quiet without any mob presence. He can't be spotted by anyone who could report back to Ferraro."

Nero must pick up on what I'm proposing, because he gets to his feet, clear protest in his eyes.

Nero in a small town? What the fuck is a big-city guy like him going to do somewhere quiet on his own? He's not going to like this, but he doesn't have a choice. Not when the alternatives are death or war. I need to make sure he doesn't come back, no matter what. But how?

Sandro picks that moment to walk through the door, two cups of coffee in hand. My gaze latches onto the driver. The kid's got no family. He's in his early twenties. And he owes Nero and me for pulling him out of the street racing scene where he would have crashed and broken his neck sooner or later.

I'll send Sandro with Nero.

He'll keep Nero from doing something stupid like coming back here as soon as things quiet down.

"Grab two of Garzolo's men," I say into the phone. "Sandro is going with Nero."

"Sandro the driver?"

"Yeah."

Sandro and Nero exchange a what-the-fuck look.

"All right," Giorgio says. "Ras and I will grab the bodies and bring them to you. I'll get a DNA sample from one of them, run it through as soon as we get back to Italy, and swap with Nero's record," Giorgio says. "That way, if anyone runs anything through the system, they'll get the confirmation they're looking for."

I nod to myself. This is going to work. "We need to move quickly. Can you leave right now?"

"Yes," Ras says. "Damiano will stay here to keep an eye on the women. If we all leave, they'll get suspicious. How far are you from where we buried Garzolo's men?"

"About forty-five minutes." I rattle off the address we're at now.

"We'll be there in about two hours. Be ready with a few tanks of gasoline."

It won't take much to burn this place down, but we need to make sure the bodies are unrecognizable. "Will do."

"Rafaele." It's Giorgio again.

"Yeah?"

"No one but us can know about this," Giorgio says. "Not even the women. The more people who know, the bigger the risk. Nero and Sandro can never come back."

I swallow. "I know." The rest of the world must think I killed my consigliere. They must believe it. I hang up and turn to Nero and Sandro.

"Rafe, what the fuck are you planning?" Nero growls.

"You're going to disappear. Both of you."

Nero narrows his eyes. "What does that mean?"

I bring him and Sandro up to speed, and when I finish, Nero's glowering at me.

"I'd rather die like a consigliere than be sent away to some shithole where I'm a nobody."

"You won't be a nobody to Sandro."

My driver blows out a breath. Unlike Nero, he doesn't argue. "Never thought retirement would be in the cards for me this early. I'll need to find some hobbies," he says.

"You'll need to find a job. The two of you will need to blend in wherever you end up."

"Sandro, shut up," Nero growls. "We're not going anywhere."

"You'd rather die than get a demotion?" I ask.

"It's not a demotion. You're sending me into fucking exile."

"Yeah, well, I think that's a lot better than the pit of hell you were about to land in."

I see a flash of amusement in his eyes before he reins it in. "You're a fucking asshole. I can't believe this is what I get for the decade I've given you."

I place a hand on his shoulder. "I'm doing this to keep you alive. I'm your don, and this is an order."

He grinds his jaw.

"We don't have time for negotiations. This is happening. Sandro, we're going back to my house to pick up documents for you and Nero. Then we have to get some gas."

"Got it, boss. I'm ready when you are."

Nero spreads his arms open. "And what am I supposed to do?"

"Stay put and think about your nice new life."

He shakes his head. "I saw an old bottle of bourbon in the kitchen. Maybe I'll drink myself into a stupor before you come back."

"Just don't do anything stupid," I tell him, already halfway out the door.

When we get back to the house two hours later, Ras and Giorgio are there with Garzolo's dead guys. They're lying on the floor and still covered in a lot of dirt.

Nero crouches beside the larger one, eyeing him skeptically. "So this is supposed to be me?"

Giorgio nods. "He's about the same height and has a similar bone structure."

"I think the other guy looks more like Sandro than this one looks like me."

"He'll do. Even if they suspect something, the DNA test will put their suspicions to rest." Giorgio glances out the window. "Sun will rise soon, so we should get moving."

I walk over to the two bodies. The one who's supposed to be Nero has a bullet in his head. The other guy's chest is shot up. "I'll say Nero convinced Sandro to turn to his side. We got into a shootout, and I had to kill Sandro too."

"And you set the house on fire?" Giorgio asks. "You'll have to explain that too."

"Heard a siren in the distance. Didn't have time to drag both of them out and had to cover my tracks."

Ras nods. "Not bad."

"We've got four cans of gasoline," I say. "That'll be plenty."

"Here." Giorgio tosses Nero his car keys. "Take my car. It's a rental, so you'll have to dump it somewhere. Buy a new car, and use your fake ID."

I reach inside my jacket and take out a plastic baggie with two California IDs and a few thick wads of cash. "This should be enough for a few weeks."

Nero nods. "I've got a few offshore accounts. Can I assume those are safe to access through the dark web?"

"Should be fine, but remember, you can't be flashy," Giorgio says. "And use a VPN."

"Yeah, I'm not a fucking idiot." Nero glances at Sandro. "You ready?"

My driver shrugs. "As ready as I'll ever be, boss."

I walk up to Sandro and shake his hand. "Keep an eye out for him. Don't let him do anything stupid. Remember, you two have to blend in and stay under the radar."

He nods. "Will do."

I move toward Nero. "We had a good run."

My consigliere embraces me and gives my back a hard slap. "You'll always be my brother, even though you're an asshole. And Gino Ferraro will die one day."

"He will," I promise him. But even when he does, Nero won't be able to come back. Not with Gino's three sons still around. They'll always remember the man who killed their cousin.

This is goodbye.

Nero and Sandro walk out, and Giorgio, Ras, and I get to work. We pour the gasoline everywhere, until the house smells toxic and everything is doused in the fluid. I grab a rag from the back of my car and wipe my hands clean, watching as Giorgio flicks on his lighter and sets a rolled newspaper aflame. He carries it over to the house and tosses it through the front door. Within minutes, the entire building is on fire.

We stand there for a while longer, witnessing the destruction. Out of the corner of my eye, I notice Ras looking at me.

374

I sniff. "Your boss and you two did me a solid. I won't forget it."

He nods. "We know. But we didn't do it for you."

My jaw clenches. Of course. They did it for Cleo.

Take care of her.

The words are right there, begging to be set free, but I don't say them. My throat is too tight to get them out. We shake hands, say goodbye, and I get into my car to drive home.

It feels like I've been up for three days straight. When I get back to the house, I stagger into our bedroom. Her scent fills my nose, and I glance around, half expecting to see her.

But she's gone.

I told her to go, but there was a part of me that hoped she wouldn't listen.

A part that I'm going to have to bury.

I sit on the edge of the bed, prop my elbows on my knees, and hang my head between my shoulders.

Funny how one's life can change in the span of a single day.

CHAPTER 40

CLEO

A WEEK AND A HALF LATER, I sit down for dinner with everyone in Vale and Damiano's home in Casale Di Principe. I stare at my hand-painted dinner plate. It's beautiful. A blue and white pattern with birds, flowers, and leaves. It reminds me of the plates we had at my wedding.

I've grown up a lot since that day.

The months of my marriage made me realize something about myself. Something that feels like a fundamental truth. The kind that once you see it, you can't unsee it. It follows you everywhere, a lens through which you perceive your past in an entirely new light.

I always thought my defiance and constant rebellion were proof that my parents didn't get to me the way they got to Gemma and Vale. I never bought into their shit. If they wanted something from me, I'd do the opposite. I knew how to ignore their expectations, how to spit on their vision for my future. I thought that made me strong.

It was after I went back to Loretta's after she first kicked me out that the truth dawned on me. Standing there on her doorstep and humbling myself before her...*that* was hard. Rebelling against my parents was easy. It made me feel better about myself. It was something I leaned into when I felt like I was crumbling inside.

So really, I'd been lying to myself for years. My parents *did* get to me. Deep down, they made me feel worthless. To them, I always was and always will be worthless. They broadcasted that message with their every word and action, and I'd believed it. No matter how I'd lie to myself or pretend otherwise, I'd believed it.

It was because of Rafaele that I started to believe something else.

He fed me a new narrative about myself. A reframing of my existence. And it felt good. Boy, it felt *good*. Which is maybe why it hurts so bad now that I know it was all a lie. He didn't see my worth either. I was a plaything, an amusing fixture in his rigid life. Until I was no longer fun. It was so easy for him to say goodbye.

I glance up and catch my sisters exchanging a concerned look. Since we arrived here, they've given me the space to... I don't even know what, to be honest. Grieve?

Yes, that's the right word.

The man I loved broke my heart.

My marriage has collapsed.

And Nero...

I suck in a deep breath.

Nero is dead.

"Mamma called me today," Gemma says. "She's selling the house. She wants to live in the Hamptons full time."

Vale nods. "That's probably a good idea."

"She asked if we want to get any of our old things."

"I'm good," Vale says. Like me, she'd rather gouge her eyes out than spend time with our mother.

But Gemma's too kind. She sighs and moves her food around with a fork. "I don't know. I was thinking about going there for a bit to help her."

Vale frowns. "She's got plenty of help, trust me. All of our aunts and cousins. And if there was ever a time for Vince to step up, it's now."

Gemma looks unconvinced, but Ras reaches over and wraps his palm around her wrist. "Peaches, you've got to focus on yourself and our baby. You don't need to solve everyone else's problems, remember?"

The tension in Gemma's forehead eases. She gazes at her lover and gives him an adoring smile. "You're right. We still have lots of work to do on the nursery."

"I can't wait to see it," Mari says. "The little outfits you showed me last week gave me serious baby fever." She glances at Giorgio, who's sitting beside her. "Who knows, maybe your son will get a cousin in a few years."

Giorgio gives her an indulgent smile while Damiano chokes on his wine.

"Mari, you're nineteen," her brother says.

"I'm nearly twenty," she says. "Gemma's only a year older."

"Having children is a big decision. You shouldn't do it on a whim."

Vale snorts a laugh. "Isn't that word for word what I said to *you* the other night when you were getting a bit ahead of yourself?"

Damiano's mouth slams shut.

Mari chuckles. "Hypocrite."

"*Anyway*," Gemma interjects, an amused smile on her face. "I for one can't wait until we have a bunch of kids running around here."

The staff come out with the next course, and the conversation gets diverted to something else, but I retreat inward. A vision of a young dark-haired boy with blue eyes smiles at me, and a painful pang of longing echoes through my chest.

God, what's wrong with me?

I used to hate the idea that I'd be expected to have kids with my arranged husband. But knowing that Rafaele and I will never have a family fills me with sadness now.

I get out of my seat. "I've got a headache. I think I'll go lie down." The backs of my eyes sting, and I don't want the floodgates to open at the dinner table. Although it wouldn't be the first time this week.

Vale glances at me, the worry clear in her expression. "You sure?"

"Yes. I'll see you all tomorrow." I flee up to my room, hoping they won't hear me cry.

The next morning, the door to my bedroom flies open, jolting me awake.

Gemma strolls in. "No more moping." She throws a leather duffel bag onto the bed and walks over to the window to pull back the curtains, letting bright light hit me right in the face. "We're getting out of town."

"What?" I ask groggily, shielding my eyes against the sunlight with my palm.

"You heard me. Pack your things. We're going away for a girls' weekend."

I yawn, my gaze drifting to her protruding belly. "You're pregnant."

Gemma shrugs. "So what? I've still got plenty of time. Plus, we're not going far."

"Where are we going?"

"Amalfi Coast. Vale booked us this incredible spot near Positano with a private beach. The pictures look incredible."

"Amalfi? Isn't that far?"

"Only a few hours from here. We're leaving in an hour." She pokes me through the duvet. "Seriously, get up. This is happening."

I pull the duvet over my head and groan into it. "No. Leave me alone."

She rips the blanket off me. "No can do. This isn't you, Cleo. It's time to move on and embrace your new life."

I cross my arms over my chest and glare at her. She just stares right back, fierce determination inside her eyes. Yeah, I'm not getting out of this.

I untangle myself from the blanket and slip my feet into a pair of fuzzy slippers Vale got me the day we landed in Italy. "Okay."

Gemma's face lights up. "Okay?"

"I said okay!"

She jumps up and makes a loud whoop. "Hell yes. Come on, I'll help you pack. We're going to have so much fun. This weekend, you are moving the *fuck* on."

A few hours later, the duffel is full, and I'm ready to go. Gem and I go down to the living room where Vale and Mari are already waiting. Their men hover beside them, looking less than thrilled about us leaving.

Giorgio, Ras, and Dem follow us out of the house like a litter of puppies.

"If you feel even a little bit unwell, ask Ignazio to drive you to the hospital," Ras says to Gemma.

She shoots me a look. She's mentioned a few times how Ras is overly anxious about her pregnancy. I think it's sweet.

"Don't worry, I will." She gets on her tiptoes and gives him a kiss.

Damiano scans us over and shoves his hands into the pockets of his slacks. "Are you sure you don't want us to join you?"

"Yes, we're sure," Vale says. "Like I've already explained a dozen times, this is a girls' weekend."

"I don't like that you'll be there unprotected."

"You're sending a car full of bodyguards with us." She waves at the second SUV that's parked just behind the car we're about to get into. "I'm not even sure who they're protecting us from, given you're the big boss now."

And given that Papà is gone. It's crazy to think that my own father tried to kill me. Even knowing everything I knew, I didn't think he'd go that far. If there's one person I'm not grieving, it's him. Stefano Garzolo was a bad man, and the world can breathe easier without him.

"If they get too zealous, I will tell them to back off." Vale is still talking to Damiano about the guards. "Got it? I'm praying they packed some clothes to blend in."

"Okay, baby," he says, sounding strained. "Just be careful."

His displeased expression makes me snort a laugh. These men are ridiculous. And so damn in love. A flicker of envy appears inside my chest as I watch Damiano wrap his arms around Vale and pull her into a kiss. I look away, my lips tightening into a line.

What's wrong with you? Are you really jealous of your sisters? You should be happy for them.

I am happy for them. But I'm also jealous. How can I not be when I almost had what they have, but I lost it?

My throat constricts. It takes all my willpower to push the feelings away. My sisters have already done so much for me, and I don't want to worry them anymore. All of this crap inside my head is mine and mine alone to deal with.

The guys help us with our bags—we've definitely packed way too much for three days—and then stand in a neat little row in front of the house, the three of them looking equally sullen. We wave at them through the window, and we're off.

CHAPTER 41

CLEO

THE DRIVE to Amalfi is breathtakingly beautiful. Once we get out of Naples and onto the coast, I roll down the car window and let my thoughts dissolve.

Steep cliffs covered with lush greenery plunge into the sea below, and the aquamarine water is dotted with sailboats. Small villages hide behind the bends in the road, built right into the cliffs, seemingly defying gravity. The sun is warm, and the air is just the right amount of humid.

By the time we get to the house Vale rented, I feel lighter. If I just stay focused on the beautiful surroundings, I can almost let go of the thoughts weighing me down.

We squeeze into a small wedge of a parking space just off the narrow main road, and the driver quickly unloads our things. "I'll have to park just up ahead," he tells us. "When you need me, send a text."

The SUV with the bodyguards pulls up next, and the four men help us carry our bags down the steep stone steps that lead to the house. We pause at a small terrace that holds another spectacular view. Vale pulls a set of keys out of her purse and unlocks a creaky wooden door.

"Come on," she says, gesturing for Gemma, Mari, and me to follow her.

Behind the door is a small entryway. We shuffle along it, making jokes about how the guards will get stuck with our big bags because it's so narrow, but when we make it out on the other side, we shut up. It's hard to speak with our jaws on the floor.

I move through the living room toward the view that's framed with a clear arched window. There is no horizon distinguishing sea from sky. The water simply melts into a lighter blue, stretching as far as the eye can see. It is a sublime kind of beauty. The kind that renders you speechless. Gemma wasn't exaggerating. This place is something.

We flit from room to room, oohing and ahhing about the views from every window, checking out the colorful pottery that decorates the house, and admiring the watercolor art on the walls.

Behind a side door in the kitchen, there is a set of steps leading down to a pebbled beach. We climb down them, warning each other to be careful while clutching a rickety wooden railing that's been weathered by water, salt, and wind. At the bottom, we find a few loungers with umbrellas just feet away from the water and a dock with a small boat.

"I feel like I'm in an Italian movie," I say. "This is so cool."

Vale comes to my side and wraps an arm around me. "And now you live just a few hours from all this. You can come back whenever you want to."

I smile down at the water lapping at my feet, but it's a bitter smile. How can it not be when the sky reminds me of the color of Rafaele's eyes? I would have loved to come here with him. We never even had a honeymoon.

Fuck. Why am I thinking about him? What fucking honeymoon? My marriage is over. Even though he still hasn't sent the papers.

He seemed in such a rush to get me away from him, but I've been here for almost two weeks, and the divorce papers that he promised so vehemently haven't arrived. I'm trying not to read into it.

"So what's the plan?" I ask, forcing myself not to ruminate on my soon-to-be ex-husband.

"We've got a boozy cooking lesson booked for the afternoon," Vale says. "It's only fifteen minutes away from the house, but it's a bit of a hike."

Mari gazes at the water, a smile on her face. "Who's up for a swim?"

"Me!" Gemma says, plucking her shirt away from her chest. "I'm boiling."

We grab our bikinis from the house and jump off the dock into the cool water. Gem, Vale, and Mari stay close to the shore, but I swim farther out. There are some small fish around me, and a few boats in the distance, but otherwise, I'm all alone.

I float on my back and close my eyes, letting the sun caress my skin. The waves rock me gently back and forth, and for a moment, I almost feel at peace.

Almost.

I used to find it hard to imagine what happens when you die. I'm not religious, and I don't believe in God, so in the past, my default answer was nothing happens. One second, you're alive, your senses drunk on your surroundings, and the next, the lights go out. But now, that thought makes my skin chill despite the sun blazing above me.

I want to believe there was something waiting for Nero on the other side. Something that made up for the crap hand he was dealt. He died because of me.

Something drips down my cheek, and I realize I'm crying again. I'm so fucking tired of it, but I just can't stop.

How do I stop this heartache?

I roll onto my front, submerge my head under the water, and swim back to the shore.

By the time we finish our swim, it's time to get ready for the cooking class. I pick out a cute green sundress, a pair of platform sandals, and a tiny white purse that's just big enough for my phone.

When I come out of my bedroom, Mari scans me over and gives me a thumbs-up. "You look so cute."

I smile at her. I've gotten a chance to get to know Mari better since arriving in Italy, and she's the opposite of her bossy brother. She's soft-spoken, gentle, and has an air of calmness about her. She's easy to get along with.

"So do you." She's wearing a light-blue skirt, a cropped top, and a few layered gold necklaces.

My sisters appear a few minutes later, and we leave the house with our bodyguards following us. By the time we hike up to the place where the cooking class is, I'm groaning and sweating.

"Oh my God," I croak. "A person needs to train before they attempt those damn stairs. Gem, I don't know how you did it."

My sister gives me a wide grin, looking barely winded. "I'm still doing Pilates three days a week. This is great exercise for the baby."

I shake my head. She's a fitness lunatic. I fan myself with my palms as we walk into the restaurant. We're greeted by the cheerful owner. He leads us to the back and onto the terrace where a bunch of tables are set up with cooking supplies.

Vale pulls me to the bar. "We need wine," she says to the young bartender. "Do you have rosé?"

"Of course."

"Three glasses, please. And one sparkling water for the pregnant lady."

"Let me get it from the fridge," he says with a charming smile.

When he disappears, Vale elbows me. "He's cute."

"I guess." Then I realize where she's going with this, and I roll my eyes. "Oh no."

Vale shoots me an innocent look. "What?"

"Don't even try," I tell her. "Just the thought of men makes me want to vomit at the moment."

She laughs. "All right, all right. I'm just teasing."

"Plus, I'm technically still married," I say. "He hasn't sent the papers."

Vale folds her lips over her teeth. "How do you feel about that?"

"I don't know."

She waits, coaxing me to continue with her silence.

"I guess I'm annoyed," I say. "I don't know what it means. He seemed so eager to end things."

"Are you hoping he changed his mind?"

I don't know what I'm hoping for. Each day, I oscillate between missing Rafaele and wanting to call him just so I can scream at him for tossing me away like I'm nothing. And then there is the guilt about Nero. I feel it the most at night when I'm lying in bed and sleep just won't come.

The bartender reappears with a sweating bottle of rosé and tells us he'll serve it at our table, saving me from having to try to give Vale an answer.

The menu for the lesson is simple—caprese salad, paccheri pasta with fish, and *delizia al limone*, a mini sponge cake filled with lemon custard. The chef demonstrates how to do everything and goes around to check we're doing it right. Despite our wine glasses being refilled frequently, the chef takes it all very seriously, correcting our technique until we're all giggling.

"It's very important!" he exclaims, showing us exactly how to roll the pasta dough into tubes.

Mari is the star of the class, and the chef constantly points out that her work is what the rest of us should aspire to. When my sisters and I tell him we're Italian, just like her, he makes a big show of not believing us. We burst into giggles again.

Somehow, we manage to get through the class. The end result isn't pretty, but it's delicious. The chef brings out a new bottle of wine, accepts our thanks, and leaves us to enjoy our meal. The conversation flows easily. We talk about the art gallery Vale and Gemma are working on opening next year and the artists they've been meeting in Naples. Mari's been trying to buy a painting from one of them for the new vacation home she and Giorgio bought in Ibiza, and apparently, the man's been impossible to get a hold of.

"They can be quite eccentric," Vale says, giggling. "One of the guys we've been talking to will only sell his work if he likes the client's astrological birth chart."

I grin. And I thought Loretta had extreme ideas when it came to her business.

It's interesting learning about my sisters' lives on this side of the world. Can I imagine staying here forever? Doing whatever I feel like doing? I guess I don't have to imagine it. I don't have to wish for freedom. I have it. Almost.

It's just one signature away.

But there's no breathless joy accompanying the realization.

My expression must reflect my darkening thoughts, because the table quiets. Slowly, all eyes turn to me.

"Cleo, do you want to talk about it?" Mari asks gently.

I bite down on my lip. I haven't really talked about Rafaele since I arrived in Italy, even though I haven't stopped thinking about him. Maybe it's time. Maybe letting it out will help.

Plus, the alcohol has loosened my tongue.

"I guess..." I blow out a breath. "I'm still processing how fast it all happened. It's not that things between us were perfect, but I was optimistic about our relationship. I was ready to tell him I loved him, even if he wasn't quite there himself. I was going to take a leap of faith."

Gemma nods. "We all saw how he looked at you on your birthday. Even his poker face couldn't hide the fact that he adored you."

I twist the stem of my glass between my fingers. "And the next day, I made a mistake. One fucking mistake. And it was enough to ruin everything? How is that fair?"

"It's not fair," Gemma says. "And Rafaele had no right to blame the situation on you."

"I mean, it was a fucking mess, but you're right. Why did he blame it *all* on me? It's not like I climbed into Papà's car knowing how everything would spiral."

I leave the glass alone and lean back in my chair. "When we got married, I wanted nothing to do with him. I tried to get him to send me away by doing all sorts of bullshit, but he wasn't fazed by any of it. I kept expecting him to lose it the way Papà and Mamma always did when I acted out—which, let's be honest, was most of the time—but he took it in stride. He listened to me, and he built me up. He made me fall for him." I give my head a shake. "And I was reckless, but that was because I thought Gem was in trouble." I glance at my sister. "I love you, Gem. I'd do anything for you."

Gemma's lips waver. "I know."

Rafaele made me feel like such an idiot for falling for my father's trick, but what right did he have to do that? Couldn't he understand why I did what I did? Apparently not.

"I don't know what you guys think you saw at my birthday party, but Rafaele didn't love me. He's never loved anyone. He doesn't get it." A deep sadness pierces through my drunken haze. He may have felt *something* for me, but whatever it was, it wasn't love.

"Cleo, I'm not sure that's fair," Gemma says quietly. "He put everything on the line for you when he thought you were in danger."

"Yeah, and he obviously decided he never wants to do that again. I'm not worth it."

Not worth losing his consigliere. Not worth putting his kingdom at risk. Maybe no one is worth all that, but I can't help the anger that licks up my veins.

"Well, it's his loss," Vale says after a while.

Mari nods. "Exactly."

I glower at my wine. "Fuck him."

"Yeah, fuck him." Gemma lifts her glass of water. "Cheers to that and to moving on."

We clink our glasses, drink, and open another bottle of wine.

By the time we decide to wrap it up, I'm so drunk, I can't even see straight. But when I fall asleep that night, I still dream of him.

CHAPTER 42

RAFAELE

DESPITE LOSING MY CONSIGLIERE, I somehow manage to bring the situation in New York under control in about a week.

Gino Ferraro comes to see the burned safe house and collects the bodies as expected. A few days later, I get a call from him saying he's confirmed the corpses belonged to Nero and Sandro and that now things are even. Well, they'll be even once I send him the twenty million dollars he asked for, which I do that same afternoon.

The feud between the Messeros and the Ferraros officially comes to an end.

With Vince Garzolo flying to New York and showing his support for me, the Garzolos accept me as their permanent new don. It helps that their old don died because he tried to kill his own daughter. Whoever wasn't convinced Garzolo was a piece of shit before finally gets on board after that revelation.

There are many questions about Cleo and her whereabouts. There, I mostly stick to the truth. She's with her sisters, recovering from what happened.

I tell no one about the impending divorce. In fact, I haven't even called up my lawyer. Every time I dial his number, something holds me back. Something I haven't been able to exorcise no matter how much I push my body at the boxing gym or how much I drink in the evenings.

It's been twelve days since she left. Twelve days since I kicked her out of this house and out of my life.

Our last few conversations are a blur. When I try to remember the details, a gaping hole opens in the pit of my stomach. I'm starting to believe I said things I shouldn't have, and that terrifies me.

I thought that without her here, I'd regain control over my emotions, but despite my face betraying nothing, it's still complete chaos inside my head.

Something broke in me that day. Something I have no idea how to fix.

It's after dinner time, and I wander through the empty house, my second glass of whiskey in hand. My feet carry me upstairs to our bedroom, where I can try and pretend she hasn't left. Her purse is on the ottoman. A T-shirt that she used to sleep in, one of mine, is thrown over a chair. In the bathroom, her makeup is scattered all over her side of the vanity like she was just there, getting made up for an evening out.

Her clothes still hang in the closet. I haven't been able to pack them away. My fingers brush over the soft satin of that black dress she tried on for me. I grasp the fabric and bring it to my nose. There's a faint hint of her familiar scent.

My fist tightens, and I bury my face in the dress and breathe her in.

In. Out.

In. Out.

I do it for so long that I lose it. My senses get accustomed to it and it disappears.

Pressure builds behind my eyes. That's been happening more often in the past week.

The longer Cleo's gone, the less I recognize the Rafaele that told her to leave. I was so angry. So fucking out of control. And now without her here, I'm lost, wandering like a ghost through a house filled with memories.

There's a shallow drawer in the closet where she kept her jewelry. I pull it open and find most of it still there. She didn't take the necklace I got for her birthday with her. Why would she? Why would she want a reminder of me when she can start with a blank slate?

A folded piece of paper is wedged between the velvet insert and the edge of the drawer. I pull it out and unfold it.

"Cleo's plan for ruining Rafaele's life."

There are devil horns above my name. I read the bullet points beneath and huff out an amused breath. At first, it's no more than a chuckle, and then it builds and builds until I'm laughing like a fucking lunatic. She's always managed to make me laugh.

It feels good, and it hurts. *God,* how it hurts.

Eventually, I quiet down. I brush my thumb over her writing and the little doodles she drew on the page. She didn't go through with her plan. She gave up on the first bullet point.

"You did it anyway, *tesoro*," I mutter and take a swig from my glass.

I leave the bedroom and head back downstairs, tapping my glass against the wooden banister as I go down the steps.

Clank, clank, clank.

It's so fucking quiet in here. Has it always been this quiet in this house?

The doorbell rings.

Cleo.

That's an insane idea. She's too proud for that. She'll never come back here, not after how I treated her. That's what I wanted, wasn't it?

There's another knock, louder this time. Why isn't anyone opening the door? Then I remember I dismissed all the staff. I couldn't bear the questioning looks they kept giving me as I roamed the halls. Luca was the only one brave enough to utter her name. He asked if I knew how she was. I roared at him to get out. Roared at all of them to leave for three weeks. As if that will be long enough for me to forget her and glue myself back together.

What a fucking joke.

I turn the lock and open the front door. My sisters stand in front of a black car.

I frown. "What are you doing here?"

"Let us in," Elena demands, tossing her blonde hair over her shoulder with an angry flick of her hand. "You've kept us waiting out here long enough."

I step aside, letting her and Fabi pass.

The second I close the door, Elena whirls around and gives me a scathing look. "You look like shit."

I catch my reflection in the mirror hanging on the wall. She's right. I look like I haven't slept in weeks. Truth is, I don't think I've gotten more than three hours a night since Nero and Cleo left.

"I've had trouble sleeping."

"Yeah, I wonder why," she says, her tone accusing.

Fabi touches my arm. Her gaze drops to the glass in my hand. Worry flashes across her features, and for a second, I think she's going to embrace me.

Thankfully, she holds herself back. We never hug. It's not the kind of affection I've ever welcomed.

"We want to talk," Fabi says. "Let's sit down."

The alcohol is making my brain sluggish. I'm still trying to process the fact that they're here. "When did you get in?"

"We came straight from the airport." She tugs on my sleeve. "Come."

I follow her, feeling like a stranger in my own home. Elena walks behind us. We spread out in the living room. I sink into the sofa and finish off half of my whiskey in one gulp. Fabi and Elena sit down across from me. An expectant air fills the room, the kind that precedes a difficult conversation.

My sisters and I don't have those kinds of conversations though. In fact, we barely talk. They don't like me very much. And I don't know them very well. We're family, but we aren't friends. I'd die for them, but I'd never go to them for help.

I place my glass on the side table. "You said you want to talk. So talk."

Elena clenches her fists in her lap. "We heard what happened to Cleo and her father. We heard Nero is gone."

"Correct."

Fabi swallows "When you say gone, you mean..."

"*Gone* gone."

A stunned silence permeates through the room. My sisters have known Nero for most of their lives, but they weren't close with him either. And yet Fabi starts crying. Elena swears and turns to comfort her. I watch them embrace, Fabi tucking her face against Elena's shoulder.

Must be nice to have someone hold you when you're upset.

I stand up. I don't know what to do with myself. Every movement feels wrong, like I'm an actor on stage but I've lost the script.

"I'll get you some water," I mutter.

Elena shoots me a glare over her shoulder. "She doesn't need water. Sit down."

It's like she wants me to witness this. Why? "I don't understand. You weren't friends with Nero."

"Damn it, Rafe. So what? We still cared for him. And Fabi's not just crying over Nero. She's crying over *you*. He was *your* best friend, wasn't he? Is it true that you gave the order to kill him?"

"Yes." The next part comes easily. It's rehearsed and memorized. "I had to. It was the only way to avoid war with the Ferraros."

Fabi pulls away from Elena and sniffles. "It's so horrible. How are you feeling? Are you all right?"

How do I explain the mix of anger, sadness, and regret inside of me? I don't know how to put it into words.

"Of course, he's all right," Elena snaps. "He doesn't care about anyone but himself. One day, he nearly loses his wife. The next day, he kills his consigliere. Tomorrow, he'll execute some poor bastard for looking at him wrong. It's all the same to him, Fabi. He's just like our dad was. Empty."

"Stop it," Fabi begs. "You're being cruel."

"Cruel?" Elena demands. "I'm not the cruel one here. I'm stating facts. Aren't I, Rafe?"

I meet Fabi's teary gaze, and it touches me somewhere deep. A place I've tried to ignore so fiercely and for so long, but I don't think I can ignore it anymore.

Sinking back down on the sofa, I hang my head. I've never felt more alone.

"Cleo is gone," I rasp. "I told her I want a divorce." It's hard to speak when my throat is this tight.

"Why?" Elena demands.

I force myself to look up at my sisters. Whatever Elena sees in my expression makes her sneer waver. Her eyes widen. They're the exact same shade of blue as mine.

"Because I can't handle having her around. She made me into someone I was never meant to be. She made me weak."

Elena's brows furrow. "How did she make you weak?"

"She made me feel things. I'm not fucking good at feeling things. I was *trained* not to."

"Trained? By who?" Fabi asks, her voice small.

How could they be this clueless? "Do you think I was born like this?" I ask. "Who do you think?"

A storm is brewing inside Elena's eyes. "If you're asking for pity, you won't get it from me. I saw you there that night."

My head is starting to pound. "What night?"

"The night our father beat our mother," Elena hisses, fury flashing across her features. "It was a few days before Christmas. The last one we spent at the house before we moved to the Hamptons. You were in their bedroom, and he was hurting her, and you just stood there and watched."

What the fuck. She's known all along?

Elena leans forward. "From where I was, I could see your expression. I could see that you felt *nothing*. Your face was blank. It's haunted me ever since. How could you just fucking stand there, Rafe? Our own mother? Did you enjoy seeing it?"

I recoil, stunned. She thinks she knows, but it's clear she doesn't understand what actually happened that night.

So this is why she hates me. By the way Fabi's looking at me, I can tell this isn't news to her. Elena told her.

Whatever grip I had on myself falls apart piece by piece. The weight of the secret I've been carrying all these years is suddenly impossible to bear.

I promised myself I'd never tell them the truth. That I'd protect them from the horrors of our father's depravity. But I can't keep this from them anymore. I need to make them understand that I wasn't born a monster.

I was made into one.

"You've got it wrong," I whisper.

Elena cocks her head. "Did I? Explain it then, Rafe."

I wrap both palms around my glass, my pulse loud inside my ears. "Our father forced me to watch. That time wasn't the first time either. The first time it happened, I was far from calm. I tried to stop him, Elena. I cried and screamed and fought him until he punched me so hard I blacked out."

Fabi winces, listening to me intently. Elena is still glaring at me, her arms crossed over her chest, but a flicker of uncertainty appears inside her eyes.

"Father didn't like that I was so upset about what he was doing to Mamma. I was only ten, but as his successor, I was supposed to be strong, even as a child. So he decided to teach me a lesson. He'd bring me into the room, and then he'd hurt her. If I cried or showed any emotions at all, he'd keep going. He would stop only when I managed to calm down. When I managed to pretend like I felt nothing."

Elena's expression goes slack.

"It took me a long time to be able to do what he wanted from me. Every time I'd start crying, unable to control myself, he'd grab Mamma by the throat and say, '*You see? We can't rely on anyone to save us but ourselves.'* He repeated that phrase to her often. I don't know if it was to taunt her into fighting back, but she never did. Maybe she knew she didn't stand a chance against him, and so she didn't want to risk provoking him any further. But every time I heard it, it made me desperate to prove him wrong. I would gain control over my emotions. I would save Mamma. It took me months."

"Months?" Fabi breathes. "How many times..."

"How many times did he do it? I don't know. Every few days." Too many. It took me too damn long. "The day I managed to keep my mask in place the entire time was the hardest day of my life. He only beat her for fifteen minutes before he stopped. He left her on the floor and walked over to me. He grabbed my chin and turned my face one way and then the other. *'Good,'* he said. *'You've learned.'* I was relieved. I thought that was the end of it and that I'd saved Mamma."

My sisters stare at me in mute horror. They don't realize the worst of the story is still coming.

"But there was one final test." I close my eyes and allow the memory of that gruesome night to unfurl. A wave of nausea hits me, so strong that for a moment I wonder if I'll be able to get the words out. If I even should.

I breathe through it, forcing the sensation down. When I open my eyes again, my sisters' faces are drained of blood. There's no irritation left in Elena's expression. Only dread.

"He raped her in front of me."

Fabi's moan is guttural, filled with raw pain and disbelief. Elena chokes and presses her palm to her lips.

"I barely remember that night—a small blessing. I think I disassociated. Somehow, I managed not to move a single muscle. I stood as still as a statue while our mother tried to be as quiet as possible so that her screams wouldn't upset me."

Fabi starts to cry, her entire body shaking.

"Why didn't you tell us?" Elena whispers.

"Because I couldn't." My voice is hoarse. "There were times when I'd do anything to forget what happened. I hope you never understand firsthand the depth of helplessness I felt while I watched him hurt her."

Elena's gaze flickers with emotions—revulsion, astonishment, regret. She stares at me like she's seeing me for the first time. "This is why Mom always tells us to go easy on you. I never understood how she could defend you after what I thought you did."

"Father broke both of us during those nights. I couldn't look at Mamma without being reminded of how I failed her. She probably couldn't look at me without feeling shame. Shame that wasn't deserved, that wasn't hers to own, but shame that she still carries to this day."

I see it in her eyes when she talks to me. It's a darkness that I don't think will ever go away.

"Our father adored you." Elena's face is as colorless as a blank canvas. "He was proud of you."

"Adored? No. He *was* proud of me. Once I passed his final test, I was finally a worthy heir in his eyes. It was his idea to make me a made man at thirteen. I went along with it because I realized it would help Mamma. With Father's attention focused on training me, he ignored her. He even allowed her to move to the Hamptons with the two of you.

But he never loved me the way a normal man loves his son. He didn't love anyone. And he trained me to be the same."

"I remember the day we left," Elena says. "You didn't seem to care that we were leaving."

I peer into my glass. It's nearly empty. "By then, I knew very well how to keep my feelings hidden."

"So you never lost control of your emotions since?" Fabi asks quietly, her cheeks wet.

"Not for a long time. They were entombed deep inside. Locked away and forgotten. But someone found the key."

Fabi sucks in a low breath. "Cleo."

I nod. "I lost my mind when I thought she was in danger. It's my fault Nero's gone. I made so many mistakes in the time from when I got the call about her being kidnapped to when I was finally sure she was safe. I wasn't thinking straight."

Fabi shakes her head. "You did all that, and then you let her go? Why?"

"Because with her around, I can't be the don I have to be."

"And what kind of don is that? The same as our father?" Elena wipes away an errant tear with her sleeve. "God, Rafe. He was a fucking monster. I've spent more than a decade thinking you were cut from the same cloth as him, but now that you told us what really happened, I can see that I was wrong. You are not him. What he put you through as a child is deplorable, and even with all of his sick 'training,' you would never do the things he did to someone you're supposed to love and protect."

"Of course, I wouldn't."

"Then why are you still measuring yourself up to the ridiculous, fucked-up standard he set?"

Her words press down on me, branding themselves on my skin with a harsh burn. I've rejected many things about my father, but his lessons have stayed with me. I've allowed them to define me.

"Cleo compromises me."

"How? Because she makes you feel emotions? Because she makes you give a shit about something other than strength and power?"

"Yes."

"Then let yourself be compromised. Accept it. Work with it. Get stronger because of it. You know which man fights the hardest? The man who's got something real to lose."

I think back to Gino Ferraro. There was a time when his family was far weaker than ours, but in the past decade, they've managed to surpass us. Only now it dawns on me why that is. He's got people he loves in his life. People he wants to protect.

"Our father tried to stomp out your humanity, but thankfully, he failed. He died without ever having lived, Rafe. Can't you see it? Nothing he had was real." She stands up and spreads her arms, gesturing at the lavish living room, at the house from which our father ran his kingdom. "This? This isn't real. Our father thought he had everything, and yet, how did he die?"

"He died alone." My sisters never came home to say goodbye to him and I didn't force them. Mamma stayed at the Hamptons the entire time he was ill. He was cared for by nurses who hated his guts for speaking to them like they were subhuman.

Elena nods. "He died alone. Despite his millions, he was the poorest man I'd ever known."

My sisters are right. Why would I continue down the path of a man I hated? He may have been the only teacher I've ever had, but I don't have to keep his lessons with me any longer. I can choose my own path as don.

Elena studies me. "I'll admit, I thought the marriage between you and Cleo was another soulless match, much like our parents'. But I'm starting to think otherwise."

Fabi's lips form a sad smile. "What you have with Cleo *is* real. Isn't it?"

Slowly, I rake my fingers through my hair. I thought being with Cleo would end with me losing it all. But I was wrong.

I lost it all when I sent her away.

I love her. Fuck, I'm a fool.

I place my elbows on my knees and press my forehead into my palms. A moment later, the sofa dips. My sisters appear beside me, one on either side of me. For the first time I can remember, they wrap their arms around me and hold me tightly.

The ache in the back of my throat spreads through my chest. Slowly, hesitantly, I return their embrace. "I've made a terrible mistake, haven't I?"

"You can fix it," Elena says against my hair. "Go after her."

Can I? Can I undo all the damage I caused when I was trying so hard to deny my own feelings that I showed no concern for her own?

Elena pulls back and looks me in the eye. "Tell her what you told us and allow yourself to feel all the pain that comes with that. Open up to her the way you finally opened up to us."

I only wish I'd done it sooner instead of waiting for so long. My relationship with Elena and Fabi suffered terribly because I refused to be even a little vulnerable around them.

I squeeze Elena's shoulder, grateful for her support. "I'm not sure it will be enough."

Fabi slides a comforting palm down my back. "Don't you think that if anyone knows what it's like to have a messed-up dad, it's her?"

There's a chance Cleo will understand. I'd be a coward not to take that chance.

It won't be as easy as just showing up and telling her I'm sorry.

But that's a good place to start.

CHAPTER 43

CLEO

After two days of relaxing on our girls' weekend, we're about to get on the road back to Casale di Principe. I climb inside the car with a full belly and an Aperol-spritz-fueled buzz from the lazy late lunch at a restaurant that served the best pasta I've ever had.

"This trip was a great idea," I say with a smile.

Gemma grins at me. "Yeah?"

"I feel a lot better."

She squeezes my hand. "You look better. You've even got a bit of a tan."

I glance down. My legs are golden from the two afternoons we spent on the pebble beach below our house. I've never had girls' trip like this, and it was everything I didn't know I needed. I'm already thinking about when we can do the next one. It got my mind off Rafaele—briefly—and I feel closer to my sisters than ever.

I let out a sigh. Maybe everything will be okay after all. "Let's come back again this summer."

"We will." Gemma hands me her phone. "Here. Queue up the next song."

The four of us take turns with the playlist, blasting music through the open windows of the car, and the two-hour drive back passes in no time. We drop Mari and Gemma off at their homes first and then the driver takes Vale and me back to her and Damiano's house.

When we walk through the front doors, Damiano is pacing the foyer. He's on the phone, but when he sees us, he quickly wraps up his call. He strides across the floor and takes Vale into his arms. A grin unfurls across her face before he kisses it off her lips.

Jeez. You'd think we'd been gone for weeks instead of two days.

I look away, giving them some privacy and trying to ignore the pang inside my chest.

"How was the trip?" Damiano asks some moments later, having finished with the passionate make-out session.

"Amazing. We had a lot of fun," my sister responds. "How were things back here?"

"Ah. They were...interesting." There's a strange note to his tone that makes me glance at him. Damiano's gaze moves from Vale to me, and his expression turns wary. "Something arrived here for you, Cleo."

Trepidation snakes up the inside of my belly. "The divorce papers?" I crouch down to remove my sandals, conveniently hiding my crumbling expression. "Good. I'm ready to sign them and move on with my life."

Damiano clears his throat. "Not quite."

The sound of steady footsteps reaches my ears, coming from somewhere up ahead. I'm getting the second sandal off when a pair of patent leather dress shoes appears in my field of vision. I recognize those shoes. Trepidation morphs into disbelief. I swallow. There's no way.

"Hello, Cleo."

Pressed black suit pants, gleaming leather belt, crisp white dress shirt, a triangle of tanned, tatted chest peeking from within. I stop before my gaze reaches his face.

For a few seconds, all I can do is breathe.

What is he doing here? He said it was over. Did he come just to break my heart again? To make sure it was sufficiently crushed under his heel?

No, he's too pragmatic for that. If he wanted me to hurt some more, he could find a way to do it from New York. So why did he come? Did something else happen? Did something change? A pathetic flicker of hope appears in my chest. I crush it immediately.

No. Don't go there.

Rising from my crouching position, I finally allow myself to look at his face. What I see expels the air right out of my lungs.

The entire time I've known Rafaele, even with his grueling work schedule, I've never seen him look more than a little tired. The man is built like a machine, his body and mind honed for performance. But for the first time, I spot cracks in his meticulous facade.

He looks like he hasn't been sleeping well. Slightly ruffled hair, dark shadows under his eyes, and a drawn expression on his face. When our eyes connect, his flash with unmistakable pain.

A part of me I'm not proud of rejoices.

He's hurting too? *Good*.

But it begs the question—why? He was the one who ended it. Ended *us*.

Rafaele's stare burns across my flesh. He clenches his jaw. No one makes a sound. I blink and then whirl around and walk away from him.

～

"I don't want to see him."

Vale clasps her hands in front of her stomach. "He's only asking for five minutes. He's waiting for you in the library."

I stare at my reflection in the mirror as I roughly comb my hair. Whatever peace I found in Amalfi is now no more than a wistful memory. I still can't believe he showed up here. "I have nothing to say to him."

Vale sighs. She opens her mouth and then closes it.

"What?" I snap, annoyed. "Just say whatever it is you want to say."

She shakes her head. "Nothing."

"You think I should talk to him?"

"Cleo, it's your choice."

When I don't answer, she leaves.

I run my brush through my curls over and over until they're gleaming in the light. I thought I was doing better, but one look at him, and I'm a mess. It's not fair. He doesn't just get to waltz back into my life uninvited and reel me back to the miserable place I've tried so hard to crawl out of.

Five minutes later, Vale's back.

"What now?" I know it's not Vale's fault, that she's only playing messenger, but I can't help taking it out on her. I'm so fucking frustrated.

"He says he won't leave until you speak to him."

Anger surges through my veins like poison. That damn asshole. "Doesn't he know better than to make demands? Who does he think he is? We're not in New York anymore. He's a nobody here. Can't Damiano force him to leave?"

Vale runs her tongue over her teeth. "I could ask, if you really think that's necessary."

I take a steadying breath. No, I don't need Damiano to solve my problems for me. I slap my brush on the vanity. "Fine. I'll speak to him, but only so that he'll leave all of us the hell alone."

I stomp downstairs, march through the hall, and fling the library doors open. He's standing by the window, his palms linked behind his back.

"*What* do you want?"

At the sound of my voice, he turns around. The flash of relief in his blue eyes only makes me angrier.

"You have five minutes," I hiss, closing the doors behind me.

He scans me over, taking his time like he's drinking me in. "How are you?"

"You know, I was doing okay until you showed up."

He flinches, and it bolsters me. I'm so angry with him for being here, for bringing all of my raw, painful feelings back to the surface. "I hope you brought the papers, although I'm not sure why you chose to deliver them in person. For future reference, this area is covered by FedEx and DHL."

"I wanted to see you." There's a hint of something desperate in his tone.

"Oh? The last person *I* want to see is *you*." I fill the last word with as much venom as I can muster.

A tremor runs through his cheek. "Please, Cleo. Can we talk?"

"Isn't that what we're doing?"

He moves his jaw back and forth. "I deserve your anger. I said things I shouldn't have."

"Well, it doesn't matter now, does it?"

"It does matter." He reaches for me, and my body buzzes with anticipation. It still craves his touch. Misses it. But my mind knows better. I jerk back, putting more space between us.

"Rafaele, why are you here?"

His arm is still extended in the air. His fingers twitch around nothing before he lowers his hand back down. "I want to fix this. I've realized a lot of things since you left."

My heart crawls into my throat. For a long, tense beat, I think he might say the words I wanted to hear so badly from him before everything went to shit. But then I catch myself. Of course, he won't. That's not who he is.

"Just send me the fucking papers," I whisper. "Or do you really hate me so much that you want to keep me guessing when they'll finally arrive? I want to move on." I show him my hand. "I want this fucking ring off my finger."

We both look at my wedding band at the same time.

I left the emerald engagement ring in New York. It wasn't intentional—I just wasn't wearing it to work the day I got kidnapped. I rarely wore it to work because I had to lift a lot of boxes, and I didn't want to risk damaging it. But I never took my wedding band off. For the last few months, whenever I glanced at it, something akin to pride fluttered through me. But not anymore. Now when I look at it, it just hurts.

There's nothing stopping me from taking it off. I don't know why I've waited. It's not like I needed his permission to do it.

I wrap my fingers around the metal and pull.

Rafaele makes a pained grunt, deep from within his chest. His face flashes with torment, and then he's right in front of me, wrapping his hands around mine, stopping me from removing the ring. "Don't. Just don't. I'm begging you."

I struggle for a bit, trying to twist myself out of his hold. His one hand is big enough to engulf both of mine, and he wraps his other hand around my waist. My body is pressed against him, and I squirm and pant, shock crackling through me at how fiercely he's fighting me.

"Let go of me. I don't want to be near you."

His hold on me loosens, but he doesn't release me. "Please, Cleo. Hear me out. I made a mistake pushing you away. I don't want a fucking divorce."

He's too close. I can count each one of his eyelashes.

"Let go of me, or I'll scream."

Reluctantly, he drops his hands away. I back away. One step. Two steps. Three. The backs of my knees bump against the sofa.

Why should I let him stop me from doing this? I try again. The ring gets stuck around my knuckle, and for a moment, I worry I won't be able to get it off after all, but another hard pull, and it slips off. I throw the ring at Rafaele.

"No, Cleo—"

It bounces off the center of his chest. Falls to the floor. Rolls back toward my feet.

Panic and agony skate across Rafaele's features. He moves quickly, dropping to his knees before me and folding his hands around the ring, like he's afraid I'll pick it up and aim for the window this time.

He looks up, his expression so devastated it sends a wave of shock through me.

I watch, stunned, as he leans forward and presses his forehead to my belly. "Please, Cleo," he whispers hoarsely. "Put it back on. Don't do this."

My throat constricts. The anger inside me wavers like a candle flame in a gentle breeze. I can't believe he'd go this far.

He wraps one arm around my hips, pulling me closer. His lips are against my shirt, pressing a kiss right above my belly button. "It belongs on your finger, *tesoro*."

The endearment feels like a stab right through the heart. It reminds me of everything we had and lost. "How *dare* you?" I hiss. "Do *not* call me that."

His hand flexes against my hip. "Okay. I won't." He exhales a heavy breath and glances up at me again.

I don't recognize him. Who is this person? What has he done to the proud man I married? A man who wouldn't even beg God if it meant getting on his knees?

He takes my hand and puts the ring inside it. "Please."

Pity blooms inside me, pity and something else that's not as easy to describe or understand. I've tried to harden my heart to him, but I haven't succeeded yet. There are parts that are still soft, still tender, and they're weeping.

I'm trembling as I slide the ring back on. "I'm only doing this so that you'll leave."

The torment in his face eases. "I'm so fucking sorry."

"What are you sorry for?"

His hands slide over my jeans, down the backs of my thighs. "For treating you like a liability. I shouldn't have shut down and pulled away when you needed me the most. It wasn't right to blame you for what happened with Nero. It was my fault. I was the one who lost it. I was the one who made mistakes."

His words exhaust me. I sit down on the edge of the sofa and hang my head. I don't want to talk about what happened anymore. I've spent two weeks trying to come to terms with everything, and I was nearly there before he showed up here uninvited.

"It doesn't matter," I say weakly.

He places his palms on my knees. "I should have accepted the fact that I was developing feelings for you instead of running away from it. I kept you at a distance, and I know that must have hurt."

I shake my head. "Don't."

"I was in denial for the months we were together. If I hadn't been, maybe I could have learned how to process my emotions better. Instead, I did everything I could to pretend that I was in control of the situation. I was a coward."

I shove his hands away from me. "*Stop it*. You don't have feelings for me. You said it yourself, and I heard you loud and clear. I don't want to listen to this anymore."

When I stand up and step around him, he reaches for me again. His hand brushes against my calf. "Cleo, please. Don't do this."

I move toward the door. "Do *what*?"

He gets up. "Give up on us."

"Why would I give another chance to a man who is incapable of love? I deserve better than that, Rafe."

He opens his mouth to say something, but I'm done. I can't do this right now, not when my heart is about to splinter. Without giving him a chance to respond, I walk out of the room.

CHAPTER 44

RAFAELE

DE ROSSI IS STANDING JUST outside the library. In my haste to go after Cleo, I nearly run into him. His eyes move to Cleo's retreating form before he levels his gaze back on me. "I don't think she wants to talk to you right now."

"I know." When I first saw her, she looked at me like she wanted to incinerate me, like I was something unholy that had crawled back from the dead.

"What now?"

Great fucking question. I rake my fingers through my hair. I'm not going back to New York. I lost the first battle, but I came here prepared for a long war. I'm not giving up.

"Let me stay here for a few nights."

De Rossi drags his tongue over his teeth and shakes his head. "Cleo made it clear she doesn't want you here."

I bite on the inside of my cheek, tamping down the strong urge to tell him to fuck off. He didn't have to let me into his house, but I managed to convince him. Barely. It won't take much for him to rescind that permission.

"I still have things I need to say to her."

"Why didn't you say them, then?" he asks, his voice razor sharp.

I was supposed to but she ran from me before I could.

When she took off the ring, I lost it. It felt so utterly wrong that I knew I'd do anything to get her to put it back on, and so I did. I got down on my knees for her, begged and pleaded and prayed. It worked. Thank fuck, it worked.

That ring is a symbol of everything we were, everything we still can be. I want her to think of us whenever she looks down at it.

I have to convince her I'm worth another shot.

Tomorrow, I'll try again.

"If you want to win her back, you're going to have to try harder," De Rossi says firmly. "She's hurt. Thanks to you, she blames herself for what happened with Nero."

"Believe me, I know. I fucked up."

He stares me down even though we're the same height. "I can't tell her the truth about Nero." He looks like he wants to say more, but he doesn't have to.

He can't tell her about Nero, but I can.

That would require me to trust Cleo fully. I know De Rossi, Ras, and Giorgio know how to keep a secret. They wouldn't be where they are today if they didn't, and it's in their interest to protect their business partner. They'd gain nothing from ratting me out to Gino.

Cleo's never had to guard information like this before, and she's angry. Knowing the truth might only make her angrier. I've let her believe Nero is dead for weeks. I would be putting my fate and the fate of my family in her hands.

Am I willing to risk everything to get her back?

My father would never do something like that, but my sisters are right. I'm not him. I can be a better man than the one who raised me.

"Give me a few days. If I can't get through to her in that time, I'll leave."

De Rossi blows out a breath, contemplating the request.

What the fuck am I going to do if he says no? Find a hotel nearby? Show up here every day until Cleo agrees to see me again? She'll probably ask De Rossi to set his guard dogs on me. Hopefully, it doesn't come to that.

After a while, he nods. "Fine. There's a guest bedroom down the hall from the library. I'll tell someone to bring your things."

"I'll do it."

He turns to leave, and I call after him. He halts. There was a time I'd rather cut out my tongue than say the next two words to him, but now it seems like a small price to pay to be allowed another chance to win Cleo over. "Thank you."

His jaw tightens. "Three days, Messero. That's all you get."

The next morning, I walk into the dining room around eight a.m. feeling uncomfortable in my own skin. I didn't sleep well, I don't like being De Rossi's guest, and I just want my fucking wife back. But my frustration isn't helpful, so I shove it away.

Valentina is sitting alone at the table, a cup of coffee in one hand and a book in the other. She hears me enter and shoots me a cold glare. "If you're hoping to see Cleo, you'll have to wait. She doesn't have breakfast until much later."

"I know. She lived with me for four months, remember?"

Valentina purses her lips. I pull out a chair and sit down. A maid appears and comes over to fill my coffee cup before asking what I'd like to eat. I request two hardboiled eggs and a side of smoked salmon. The maid leaves, and Valentina stands up, tucking her book under her arm.

"Be very careful," she warns. "If you upset her, I will kick you out. Cleo is my sister, and I will not allow you to mess with her."

"I don't think there's a way around upsetting her. We have difficult conversations ahead of us."

Valentina's eyes narrow. "You're lucky she's not very good at hiding her feelings from me. If I thought she was truly over you, I wouldn't hesitate to make you leave. But she's not."

I sit up straighter. Her words inject a much-needed dose of hope into my veins. "What do you—"

She shakes her head. "I'm not helping you win her over. That's on you. Damiano told me he gave you three days. Use them wisely." She stalks away.

"I'm planning on it," I mutter to the empty room.

That's why I'm here this early. I don't want to take the chance I'll miss her when she comes down. If all I have are

420

three days, I'm going to be around her as much as I can. We need to talk and I have to find some way to make her listen.

I finish my breakfast and down a few cups of coffee while I wait for Cleo to wake up. Just before ten, she shuffles into the dining room in an oversized T-shirt dress, her hair tousled, and her mouth open on a yawn. The sight hits me right in the chest. This is how she used to look in the mornings when she woke up to say goodbye to me before I left for work. My gaze drags over her body, all the way down to her exposed legs.

Where did she get that tan? What has she been doing in Italy? The thought of her lying in a bikini on a beach, her perfect body on display for anyone to see, sends a surge of possessiveness through me.

When she sees me, she halts. Her expression goes from neutral to dismayed before settling on reluctant. "You're still here."

I press my napkin to my lips. "I am."

I'm half expecting her to turn around and walk out of the room, but she surprises me by taking a seat across the table from me.

"Who's running things while you're gone?" she asks, her voice clipped.

"Alec."

"Oh, I remember him from my birthday party." She reaches for the bowl of fruit salad. "He's one of your capos."

"He's been promoted to my underboss." I didn't have an official underboss until now because Nero always played the part of my second-in-command.

Cleo's gaze darts to me. "I'm surprised you trust him enough to run things while you're here."

I do, and I don't. Alec is loyal and smart, but he needs more experience before he can even come close to the standard set by Nero. A few weeks ago, leaving him in charge of my family would be unthinkable, but I didn't even hesitate to do exactly that two days ago. The only thing that mattered was getting here. Getting to Cleo.

"I didn't have a choice."

She scoops some fruit onto her plate. "You always have a choice. You can go home."

"*You* are my home."

She halts, her spoon midair. Pain flashes across her expression, like my words physically hurt.

"If you keep saying things like that, I'll have no choice but to ask Damiano to kick you out," she whispers, putting the spoon down, her gaze on her plate.

"I can't. Not until you and I finish our conversation."

Her lips purse into a thin line. "Rafaele, honestly. What are you hoping to accomplish? There's no path forward for us."

"I disagree."

"Do you think I can just forget that you tossed me away at the first sign of trouble?" she says harshly, trying to mask her hurt with anger, but she doesn't quite succeed.

I stand up and walk over to sit in the chair beside her. She stiffens when I place my hand on her forearm, but she doesn't pull away.

"A lot went wrong that day. I couldn't handle the thought of you being hurt, and I acted in ways I regret."

She stares at my hand. "That's not all it was. You reacted very differently when I got hurt when we got attacked at Il Caminetto."

"Yes, but that was before—"

Forest-green eyes flit to me, a question written in them. "Before what?"

My pulse skitters and I swallow. It feels like every word coming out of my mouth is critically important. I've sat in many negotiations where that's been the case, but this is the first time I've been this fucking nervous.

"At Il Caminetto, I was in control. I knew I could protect you. But when I got the call from your father, I had no idea where you were or who you were with. I didn't know how to find you. I couldn't trust your father to keep his word, and yet I couldn't ignore his demands. I couldn't be in two places at the same time. It was torture to imagine you being hurt while there was nothing I could do. It's why I called Ferraro. I was desperate."

A tiny bit of sympathy seeps into her expression. "You were?"

"Yes. And I didn't know how to handle it. I never learned how to process my emotions. I only learned how to shove them away and pretend they didn't exist. That's what I had to do to survive my father. It's what I had to do to make sure my mother survived him too."

She frowns, a line appearing between her brows.

"The sheer intensity of my feelings for you overwhelmed me," I continue. "It was like being hit with a tidal wave and being dragged away by the strongest current you could possibly imagine. I retreated somewhere safe." I drag my palm down her forearm and take her hand. "I'm not saying this to justify how I treated you, Cleo. There is no excuse. But I think if I want there to be a path forward for us, I have to be more open with you."

Surprise flickers inside her gaze. I curl my fingers between hers. She lets me, but she doesn't return the gesture.

"I talked to my sisters about you. About everything."

"What did you tell them?"

"The truth about why I am the way I am." I clear my throat. "It was far overdue. You said my mother told you about what happened when I was a kid?"

Cleo nods. "She did."

"I don't know what specific details she shared."

Her face softens. "She said your father beat her and forced you to witness it. If you cried, he'd keep going. He made you learn how to lock your feelings away."

"Did she tell you about the rape?"

She pales. "What? No."

It doesn't surprise me that Mamma didn't tell her that part. A prickle of resistance appears in the back of my head at sharing our secret with one more person. Even though our relationship is irreparably broken, my mother has always held out hope for me. And I know she would understand my reasons for sharing this information with Cleo.

"My father raped her in front of me. Forced me to watch."

Cleo's mouth falls open. She squeezes my hand hard. "Oh my God. Our wedding night..."

"I..." There's an ache in my throat. "I decided a long time ago that I'd never be like him. I would never hurt the people I'm supposed to protect. Ever."

Tears well up in Cleo's eyes. I want nothing more than to pull her against me and kiss those tears off her cheeks, but I restrain myself. I haven't earned that yet.

"But I did. I hurt you with my actions and my words."

She curls her lips over her teeth and muffles a sob.

I squeeze her hand tighter. "I know that I'm broken. I *know*. But I need to tell you what I should have told you a long time ago. The feelings I have for you are bigger than anything I've ever experienced. They used to terrify me and make me feel out of control, but not anymore. I'm ready to embrace them. Until I met you, I never realized how much of me died in that dark bedroom. But then you waltzed into my life and showed me what it's like to truly be alive. And now I can never go back to how I was before."

She heaves a breath, her eyelashes fluttering.

My heart is beating so hard it threatens to break through my ribcage. "Cleo, when I look at you, I see the entire universe. It took losing you for me to understand that you are everything to me. There might have been a 'before' you, but there is no 'after'. I can't function without you. I can't sleep, I can't think, I can barely fucking breathe. Without you, I exist in a horrible dark place that's devoid of everything that makes life worth living. Please come back to me. I love you."

A tear escapes and carves a path down her flawless cheek. I catch it with my thumb and slowly brush it away.

Her breathing turns ragged, and my gaze drops to her parted lips. I need to kiss her the way I need air, but before I even move an inch, she pulls out of my grasp.

She stands up, pushing her chair back with a loud squeak, and turns to leave. "I have to go."

No.

I rise out of my seat. "Please don't run away from me."

She halts and slowly looks at me over her shoulder. "Rafaele, I need some time to think. This is a lot. Give me space. Please."

What am I supposed to say to that? "Cleo—"

Before I can come up with anything, she shakes her head and slips out the door.

I rake my fingers through my hair.

She said she needs space...but she didn't ask me to leave again. That's progress, isn't it? I might be getting through to her. But if I push too hard, she might pull back again.

I sink back down in my chair and drag my hands over my face. She wants space? Then I have to give it to her. I'll give her whatever she wants. Because I'm not the one calling the shots anymore.

She's in control.

CHAPTER 45

CLEO

RAFAELE TOLD me he loved me. His admission pulses inside my chest and seeps warmth into my veins as I rush upstairs after our conversation. I lock myself in my bedroom and make an honest attempt to untangle my thoughts and feelings.

Now that I know the full truth about what happened with Rafaele's father, I can understand why Rafaele is the way he is. The thought of what he had to witness as a young child sends nausea churning through my gut. What he and his mother went through is horrific. I sometimes forget that our world isn't only heartlessness toward women, but toward men too. No one is born a killer. One way or another, they are forged by their environment and by the people around them.

Rafe was visibly uncomfortable when he shared the full story with me. I could tell it was difficult for him, but he didn't let that stop him. He told me something deeply private, deeply vulnerable about himself. How many times did I wish he'd open up to me? He finally did it.

And it didn't feel like some tactic just to get me back. It felt genuine.

He really wants to fix this. To fix *us*.

Do I?

Longing snakes through me. I wanted to comfort him just now. To hug him, to kiss him, to say that everything will be okay. I managed to hold myself back though, because for once, I thought about the consequences of my actions.

If I jump back into this too quickly, driven by my raw emotions, I might regret it later on, and I don't want to have any more regrets. I have too many already.

I curl up on the bed and scroll through the photos I have of us on my phone. There's not many, but the few that are there make my chest clench.

The photo he asked the waitress to take of us at the Il Caminetto dinner. I look pissed as hell in that one. There's another photo I snuck of him right before we headed to dinner at the Ferraros'. He's glancing at me from under his brows as he's fixing a cuff link, a hint of amusement in his expression. There are a few from my birthday party. A posed photo I got Vale to take of us on the terrace. A selfie from the afterparty. He's smiling, looking at me instead of the camera.

Cleo, when I look at you, I see the entire universe. It took losing you for me to understand that you are everything to me.

That flicker of hope comes alive inside my chest again. Only now, instead of stomping it out, I allow the memory of our conversation to feed the tiny flame.

I spend the rest of the day in my room, avoiding everyone, and I have my dinner brought to me. Vale comes knocking as I'm getting ready for bed.

"Do you want to skip the concert tomorrow given everything?" she asks as she peeks inside.

Shit. I completely forgot we had plans to go out. A band we both like is playing in Naples, and she got us tickets. We've been looking forward to this, and I don't want to back out just because Rafe showed up. What am I going to do for the next few days? Hide in my room and think about him nonstop? Maybe it'll be good to get out of the house and have a distraction for a few hours.

"I still want to go."

Vale's smile is careful. "If you're sure?"

"I'm sure."

She takes one step inside and closes the door behind her. "Do you want to talk about it?"

"I just need some time to think about everything. Rafaele is really trying..." I sigh. "He told me he loved me."

Vale's expression softens. "About time."

"I know, fucking finally, huh? But is it too late?"

"I don't know. Do you still love him?"

Do I? There's a thick layer of hurt on top of whatever other feelings I have for him, but I can't deny that he's managed to get past it. Somewhat. But I'm not sure that his change of heart is enough to fix our relationship. He might say he loves me now, but that doesn't erase the fact that his consigliere is dead because of what happened.

Nero. Dead.

It still doesn't feel real.

A prickling sensation appears behind my eyes. "I don't know if it matters. Even if I still love him, I am the reason his best friend is dead."

Vale comes over to sit down on the edge of the bed and wraps an arm around me. "Cleo, that is the world we live in. You know that."

I lean my head against her shoulder. "It's why I've always wanted to get away from all of this. The nonstop heartbreak and pain. And I'm almost there. I can do whatever I want now that I'm in Italy. Do I really want to give all that up for another chance with Rafaele?"

That's the real choice I have to make. Say goodbye to him and start a new life in Europe or go back to the life I know in New York. The life I used to hate before I married him.

Vale sighs. "We don't get to choose what life we're born into, but we all have the ability to find our own path if we're willing to pay the price. I had to be brave enough to escape Lazaro and leave New York. I didn't leave our world, not completely, but I found a corner of it that works for me. Damiano is a don, but he's also the love of my life."

"But don't you think it would be so much better if you and him were just normal people?"

"Do I sometimes wish I didn't have to worry about whether he comes home alive after a trip away? Of course. But I also recognize that he wouldn't be the man he is if he was removed from all of this." She huffs and smiles. "And I really like who he is."

Rafaele, no longer a don? It's impossible to imagine. The man was born to lead. And the truth is...I admire that about him. He's got men who rely on him and a family that thrives under his leadership. He would never leave that behind, and I could never ask him to do so.

So if I choose him, I have to embrace all of it. No more rebellion, no more resistance, no more denying the reality of my situation. I would have to be *all in*.

I press a kiss to Vale's cheek. "I think I need to get some sleep. My head feels like it's about to explode."

She gives me another hug and gets up. "Take the time you need. I won't let him rush you."

The next day, my breakfast magically appears in my room before I even ask for it. Damn, Vale is well on her way to getting the sister of the year award. I eat my eggs and toast and drink my coffee while sitting by the window and watching birds make a nest in the tree in the backyard.

Around midday, I hear Rafaele's voice outside my door.

"Can I talk to her?"

"She will come to you when she wants to," Vale says firmly.

"Will you tell her I'd like to see her?"

"I will, Rafaele. Can you stop hovering by her door like a ghost and go downstairs? My staff don't know what to do with you."

I lift my hand to my lips. He's been hovering outside my room? I tiptoe toward the door and press my ear against it. There's the sound of retreating footsteps.

Vale did the right thing shooing him away, because I still don't know what I want to do.

Do I miss him? Yes.

I miss his touch, and his kisses, and the way he looked at me like I was the most precious thing in the world. But will we ever get that back given everything that has happened?

I'm not sure.

When six p.m. rolls around, I start getting ready for the concert. My suitcase is still lying open on the floor. I never really unpacked when I arrived here. I dig through the clothes I brought and pull out a forest-green dress I haven't worn yet. It's low cut with a bow right below my chest, billowy long sleeves, and a flowy skirt that reaches my mid-thigh. I let my hair out of its braid and swipe on a bit of makeup.

When I'm finished, I walk up to the mirror and do a twirl. I'm a bit overdressed for a rock concert, but that's just because I feel like it. It's definitely *not* because I want to look good in case I bump into Rafaele downstairs.

He's not there anyway. I walk into the empty living room and ignore the small twinge of disappointment.

Vale appears a short while later. "Ready?"

"Yes. Your husband isn't here to send you off?"

"He and Rafaele are talking business in his office."

Oh. I swallow and paste on a smile. "Let's go then."

We get into the car waiting outside for us and arrive at the venue accompanied by a driver and two guards. When we arrive, the opening act is already playing. We head up to the VIP area and grab a couple beers.

"This band's great," Vale says, her head bopping along to the music.

The VIP area quickly fills up with more and more people. Our guards are standing off to the side, close enough that they'd be able to reach us in no time if needed. I turn back toward the stage and focus on the music.

Are Damiano and Rafaele still talking to each other back at the house? I wonder what they're discussing. With Nero gone, Rafaele will have to make a lot of changes to how he runs things.

Frustration zaps through me. Ugh. I came here so that I *wouldn't* think about him, but here I am, thinking about him all the same.

A prickling sensation spreads over my neck, like someone's watching me. I turn my head and lock onto a pair of ice-blue eyes on the other side of the VIP area.

CHAPTER 46

CLEO

MY HEART PICKS UP SPEED. Rafaele pushes his way through the crowd and stops when he's right in front of me. The sight of him makes my breath catch.

He's dressed down in a pair of black jeans and a light-blue button-up shirt that brings out the color of his eyes. Without a jacket, there's no hiding the hard outline of his shoulders or the breadth of his muscled chest. I stare at his thick neck and the tanned skin peeking out from under his shirt, and swallow.

Fuck, he looks good.

The tired air he had around him when he first arrived is gone. The only sign of the toll our time apart has taken on him is the light bags under his eyes, but they do nothing to detract from his handsomeness. A familiar heat appears between my legs, and I want to scream. It's not fair that he still has that effect on me.

He drags his gaze over me, letting it linger on my chest and my bare legs. When he refocuses on my face, there's a simmering hunger in his eyes. A hunger I know all too well.

"What are you doing here?" I breathe.

His jaw clenches. "Damiano told me you went to a concert. I was worried."

Inside me, butterflies flutter. "Worried? Our guards are here."

"I don't know them, so I don't trust them," he says roughly, shooting the guards a skeptical look.

Vale groans from somewhere behind me. "Here we go. You know, we somehow survived the past two weeks without your interference."

Rafaele ignores her comment and turns his attention back to me. "There are a lot of people here."

Amusement tugs on my lips. "I know, Rafe. It's a concert."

He clears his throat. "Yes. A difficult place to secure. You can never have too many guards in a place like this."

It's like he's trying to give me a reason not to ask him to leave.

I bite on my bottom lip. I should tell him to go home and that he has no right to be here, but I...don't want to. It's endearing how out of place he looks right now, even though he clearly tried to fit in by wearing casual clothes.

"Have you ever been to a rock concert?"

He rakes his fingers through his hair. "No."

"Well, lucky you. The headliner is about to come on."

He checks the time, bringing my attention to his wrist. He's wearing the watch I got for him, and for some reason, that makes my chest clench. "Yes, any minute now."

Just then, the guitarist walks on stage, and the opening notes of a song stream through the air. The crowd goes nuts when the band opens with one of their most popular songs, surging around me. I cheer with the rest of the audience, but I don't miss the way Rafaele moves to stand behind me, his body acting as a shield to prevent anyone from bumping into me.

The music pounds in my ears, the beat pulsing through me like a living thing. I try to keep my attention on the stage but my awareness is fixated on Rafaele. He's close enough for me to feel the heat of his body. Every time he brushes against me, I want to press back into him. It's like we're two magnets, unable to resist each other's pull. An ache builds low in my belly.

He brings his lips close to my ear. "You look stunning." His hands slide over my hips and then settle on them with a possessive grip. I have to bite back a moan. He's testing my boundaries and I should push him away, but I don't. God, it feels good to have him touch me. His warmth seeps through my dress and into my skin.

I close my eyes and let myself get lost in the moment, the music, the sensation of his body against mine.

I don't want to lose this. But what future can we have together with Nero's death hanging over us?

A crack appears deep inside my chest, and the emotions I've tried to keep under control surge through me. The backs of my eyes prickle. I need to figure this out. I can't keep living in this state of limbo, one foot in and one foot out.

I turn around in his arms. There's longing etched across his face. "Let's go outside," I say.

Rafaele nods and takes my hand into his. He easily carves a path through the crowd and brings us outside to the smoking area. It's empty since the headliner is still playing.

I breathe in the cool evening air and look up at the night sky. It's a full moon.

Rafaele stops behind me. "Cleo?"

The way he says my name brushes over my skin like a caress. "What do you think?" I ask.

"About what?"

"The show."

There's a beat. "It's fun. Just like most things are when I have you close to me."

My vision blurs. Is he even aware of the bittersweet pain that he inflicts with those words?

"Most? Not all?"

"It's not fun when you're right here but you won't talk to me."

I turn to face him. "Then you know how I felt in the months we were married."

A shadow passes over his expression. A moment passes before he responds, like he's letting my words sink in. "It wouldn't be like that anymore."

"No?"

"No." He takes a step forward, then another, until I'm backed against the fence and his body is pressed up against mine. I tip my head back. He lowers his face toward me, his nostrils flaring on a breath as if he's trying to capture my scent. My nerves buzz, and it's a struggle to breathe.

I miss him. I want him. But I'm still not convinced jumping back into our marriage is the right thing. I steel my spine and push at his chest until he reluctantly takes a step back.

"Look, I'm glad you've realized the damage your father caused and that you seem ready to start working through it. But maybe you'd be better off trying again with someone else. Someone you don't have all this baggage with."

His gaze narrows. "I don't want anyone else. I want *you*."

I clench my fists. "How can we repair our relationship when I'm the reason your best friend is dead?"

Reluctance flickers in his eyes. "Cleo—"

"No, really." My guilt comes back in full force, pressing down on my lungs. "Nero's death will always be a dark mark on our relationship. *Always*. It's not something we will ever be able to forget."

And it's not just my guilt. It's the knowledge that Rafaele was able to go through with it. He killed his best friend. Or at the very least, he gave the order for someone else to do that. How in touch with his emotions can he really be if he went through with it?

They grew up together. They were close.

He's barely mentioned Nero since coming here. Why won't he talk about him? Does he even care? Was it easy for him to go through with it? No, it couldn't have been easy. Before I left New York, I saw how torn up he was. Maybe he hasn't brought it up because it's simply too painful to remember.

438

I shake my head. "You're rushing into this because you're grieving your friend. People act irrationally when they're grieving."

Rafaele blows out a breath and drags his hand through his hair. "I'm not grieving. Not in the way you think."

I frown. "What is that supposed to mean?"

Rafaele stares at me, a strange look in his eyes. He swipes his palm over his lips. "Nero isn't dead."

What?

Blood comes rushing through my ears, drowning out the muffled music around us. "What...did you say?"

"Nero isn't dead. You're not supposed to know this. You can't say a word about this to anyone. Not even your sisters."

The world around me blanks. I can't believe what I'm hearing. "Rafe, what the hell?"

"He's not dead."

I stare at him in shock. "Where is he?"

"Gone. He'll be in hiding for the rest of his life. But he's alive."

"How did this happen?"

"I suppose because of you. You asked De Rossi to call me, didn't you?"

"Damiano knows about this?"

Rafaele nods. "Damiano, Ras, and Giorgio know. They're the only ones. And now you."

An astonished huff spills past my lips. I feel like I was just abducted by aliens and plopped into an alternate reality. I press my palms against my face and take a few deep breaths, trying to settle the emotions warring inside me. Relief at Nero being alive. Exhilaration at being freed from guilt. Anger at having been deceived.

When I drop my palms, Rafaele is studying me warily.

"Explain."

"I couldn't kill him. I don't know what I would have done if De Rossi hadn't called. I couldn't think. My head felt like it was on the verge of exploding. I'd lost you, and I was about to lose him, and it was all my fucking fault. I was crumbling under the weight of everything. Nero told me to do it, to just shoot him, and even though I knew it was the only sure way to deescalate the situation, I couldn't pull the trigger." He shakes his head. "When De Rossi called and we started talking, I got an idea. I could make it look like Nero died in a fire. We got two bodies—two of your father's guys that we killed at the warehouse—and we put them inside the safe house."

"Two?"

"One was supposed to be Nero. The other, Sandro."

My jaw drops. "What?"

"Sandro left with Nero. I needed someone with Nero to make sure he doesn't come back."

This is nuts. "Okay, then what?"

"We burned the safe house down, and Giorgio hacked into the police records to swap the DNA data they had on Nero to match that of the Garzolo guy we said was him."

Oh my God. My heart races. Nero is alive. "It worked?"

He nods. "Gino bought it. We have a truce, although things between us are still tense. They have to be. Gino wouldn't believe that I'd just forget he made me kill my closest friend. Cleo, Nero doesn't blame you for any of this. He said that to me just before we said goodbye. I think he'd want you to know."

It's like a dark veil has been lifted from my eyes. My throat is dry, but relief blooms inside of me. "You couldn't kill him."

A sad smile appears on Rafaele's face. "I couldn't kill him. I always said I'd do whatever it takes to defend my rule, but I was lying to myself. I'm not my father. He didn't love anyone, and he thought that gave him power, but if that's what power means, I don't want it."

"What do you want?" I whisper.

Rafaele crosses the short distance between us and wraps his arms around me. His gaze—so bright, so *vulnerable*—pierces through me. "I want to make you deliriously happy. I want to give you everything. When I first agreed to marry you, I thought I'd tame you. I was so confident, so sure you'd pose no challenge to me, but I was *so* damn wrong. I didn't tame you. You are the one who conquered me—thoroughly and completely. I am not the man you married, not anymore. But if you give me a chance, I will be the husband you deserve."

A sob escapes me. I press my cheek against his shirt, and he tucks the top of my head under his chin. His palms travel up and down my arms, comforting me. He smells so damn good.

Like home.

I wrap my arms around Rafaele's waist and allow my body to melt against his. A satisfied grunt rumbles deep inside his chest, and he holds me tighter. The last of my hesitation fades away. We stand like that until the concert ends. Until the doors open and people come flooding outside. Until the moon kisses the horizon and a sprinkle of rain touches my skin. My vision is blurry, but my chest is light.

Rafaele pulls back just enough to search my face. He drags the pad of his thumb over my cheek, his eyes full of warmth. "I love you, *tesoro*. Please come home with me."

I rake my fingers through his hair as my stomach does a flip. I don't think I'll ever tire of hearing him say those words. He stares at me like I'm the most important thing in the world, and I realize in that moment that I believe it.

For the first time since he arrived in Italy, I smile at him. "Okay. I will."

Relief floods his expression, and he doesn't waste a second before he leans down and claims my lips in a kiss.

EPILOGUE

RAFAELE

When the sun rises the next morning, I feel like a completely different person. I went from being a miserable bastard to being the luckiest man in the world. Cleo is coming back to New York with me. There's a weird stuttering inside my chest at the thought of having her in my home again.

Our home.

I plan on telling her she can redecorate all she wants. We'll even get a damned dog if it makes her happy, but under the condition that the creature will make no attempts to keep me away from her.

My bag of clothes is sitting by the closet, so I pull on a shirt and a pair of pants and leave the guest bedroom in search of my wife. I tried to convince Cleo to spend the night with me after we came back from the concert, but she refused, telling me she wanted to take it slowly. My stomach sank with disappointment, my body not at all onboard with that idea.

Still, I knew I couldn't push her last night. She'll come to me when she's ready.

I'm ten feet away from her room when the door opens, and she pops out in a black tank top and a pair of cut-off jean shorts. I have to hold back my groan. Fuck, she looks good enough to devour.

She sees me and smiles, but it fades when she notices the expression on my face. I must look like a predator eyeing its prey.

I walk up to her, trying to act normal and failing. My fists clench. I want her so fucking badly. I can't believe the nonsense I told myself about getting bored with her. That's never going to happen. I'm obsessed and I'm always going to be fucking obsessed.

Cleo's eyes follow me, and when I stop right in front of her, they drop to my lips. The smattering of freckles across her nose is more prominent from the sun she's been getting here. I want to kiss each one of them. I want to run my fingers through her hair and feel the softness of her skin. I want her writhing beneath me, begging me to fuck her. My dick jolts at the visual.

She bites on her bottom lip. "You're staring."

"I know." I raise my hand and brush a strand of hair behind her ear.

Her eyes grow hooded, and she leans into my touch. "Kiss me."

My skin buzzes. I press my lips to hers, possessive and hungry. Her hands go around my neck, her fingers tangling in my hair as she opens her mouth to me. I groan at the feel of her tongue teasing mine and lose myself in her sweet taste.

We announce our reconciliation shortly after.

Everyone's over at De Rossis' for brunch, and when Cleo breaks the news that she's coming back to New York with me, there's a full gamut of reactions. Valentina's eyes narrow on me in a skeptical glare, Gemma gives me a pleased smile, and Mari lets out a breath of relief.

The men manage to hide their feelings better, with the exception of Ras, who opens his big mouth and says, "Are you sure, Cleo? If you want to ask us to dispose of him, now's the time to do it."

"Why's that?" I drawl. After what happened with Nero, my opinion of the fucker has marginally improved, but maybe that was premature.

"You're here alone and defenseless."

"Defenseless? I could take you down with this butter knife if I wanted to."

Ras snickers. "What are you waiting for then?"

"For the mood to strike."

Cleo clears her throat. "Okay, enough."

"He started it," I mutter, shoving some eggs in my mouth.

"What are you, five?" Ras asks.

This fucker. "Put your dog back on his leash, De Rossi."

Gemma reaches over and places her hand on his forearm. "Ras."

He grins. "Look, I'm just making sure he can handle the heat if he's really joining the family."

"I am most certainly not joining your family."

Cleo gives me a pointed look. "You are, Rafe. This is my family. So you've just acquired three annoying brothers."

"I would prefer not to be included in that unflattering category," Giorgio says, methodically cutting into a piece of tomato.

Cleo gives him an amused look. "Okay, two annoying brothers and Giorgio."

I sigh. Fuck me. I really am stuck with these Casalesi idiots now, aren't I? Not only because of Cleo, but because of Nero too.

After all, few things bring people closer than a secret.

"I suppose I'll have to get used to it," I say with a resigned shrug. "As I once told my accountant, whatever my wife wants, my wife gets."

"Oh?" Valentina peers at me over her cappuccino. "Do I sense a good story?"

"You never told them?" I ask Cleo.

Her cheeks turn an alluring shade of pink. It reminds me of another part of her body that's an alluring shade of pink. "No," she answers.

"Ah." I dab my napkin against the corner of my mouth. "It all starts with this list."

Cleo's eyes widen. "You know about the list?"

"I know about everything, my darling. I found it just the other day."

"I'm lost," Gemma says, her arms resting on her protruding belly. "What list?"

"Cleo's plan for ruining Rafaele's life," Cleo and I say at the same time.

There's a beat, and then everyone bursts out laughing.

"Seriously?" Valentina asks. "We're going to need to hear the rest of it."

Cleo giggles as she recites the rest of the list before jumping into the story about her attempt to bankrupt me. I sip on coffee and observe my stunning wife for a long moment before glancing at the rest of the people around the table. The mood is light, and laughter filters through the air. A warm feeling settles inside my chest.

Maybe this family isn't so bad after all. One day Cleo and I will have our own family. This time, there is no fear accompanying that thought. No panic. No hesitation. Only breathless joy.

CLEO

The list story distracts Ras from egging on Rafe any further, and we manage to wrap up brunch without anyone's blood being spilled.

Phew. I was getting worried for a hot second there.

Even now, as everyone settles in the living room, I observe the Casalesi men. For all their bickering with Rafe, they've got more in common than they realize. For one, they're all huge, handsome, and hardheaded. They're all extremely

447

protective of their women, of course. And despite being who they are, they've got a moral code they follow. Their word means something, and they don't hurt people just for the sake of it.

None of them are like my father or Rafaele's father, and that gives me hope. Hope that under their leadership, this world we're all in might not be so bad after all.

Who knows, maybe with time, these four mobsters might actually become friends.

"*Tesoro*?"

I blink, snapping out of my reverie. Rafaele is standing in front of me holding two mimosas. He hands one to me. "Care for a walk around the property?"

I take the glass from him. "What are we celebrating?"

He gives me a crooked smile. "Us."

We tap our glasses together, our gazes locked on one another. Something vulnerable flickers in Rafaele's eyes before he blinks it away.

I still haven't told him that I loved him. A mass of tangled emotion pulses through my chest at the thought of trying to say those words again after what happened last time. But things are different now. Rafe's changed, and so have I. We've both realized what's important to us and what we're willing to do for the people we love. I have more faith in us than ever.

We step outside and make our way toward the trees at the back of the property. The backyard slopes downward, so when we reach the lawn behind the tree line, no one inside the house can see us.

A light breeze brushes over my skin. It's a gorgeous summer day. I lie down on the grass, and Rafe does the same beside me. Above us, a flock of birds peppers the clear blue sky.

I find his hand and tangle our fingers together. His skin is warm and rough, and suddenly, I want nothing more than to feel that roughness elsewhere. When he turns to his side to face me, I can tell he's trying to disguise his hunger, his need, but it's no use. Not when that same need pulses deep inside of me.

He raises himself on one elbow and leans over me. His mouth hovers above my own. "I want you, *tesoro*."

A grin tugs on my lips. "I want you too."

His expression becomes pure rapture. He pulls off my shorts and settles between my legs, his movements smooth and sure. His fingers trace me over my underwear, setting off sparks across my skin. When he moves my panties aside and drags his tongue over my seam, my back arches off the grass.

Too long. It's been too long.

He makes me come with his tongue before he drapes his body over me and rolls his hip, his length pressing against my still buzzing core. I moan. His muscles vibrate with tension as he licks and sucks on my neck, his palm wrapped around my breast, and his fist in my hair.

The weight of him is delicious. I squirm against him, meeting his thrusts, until I can no longer take it. I need him inside of me.

I widen my legs and pluck the side of my lace panties. "Rip them off."

He does. Effortlessly. I reach between us, undoing his belt buckle, and shove his trousers and boxers down. There's nothing left between us but heat. He lifts up on his forearms and looks down at me as he pushes inside, inch by inch, filling me so damn well. I arch my back and moan. His thrusts are slow and decadent, and his eyes glimmer with so much emotion, it's almost too intense for me to bear.

This isn't just sex. He's making love to me.

And suddenly, the words I was so scared to say earlier come spilling out of me. "I love you."

His movements still. My pulse picks up speed. His blue eyes pierce through me, and there's not a hint of ice inside them now.

My breath hitches. The mask is gone. All that's left is raw vulnerability.

Slowly, a smile unfurls over his lips. "And I love you. You are perfect, my darling. You are the best thing that's ever happened to me."

Our gasps and moans echo through the air, masked by the wind and the trickling fountain nearby. We both find our release as my nails dig into his strong back. "Promise me you'll always be like this with me. That you'll never pull away from me again. Or I swear, Rafe, I'll write up a new plan."

He presses his lips to the spot right below my ear and chuckles. "*Tesoro*, you're never getting rid of me. I promise. I am yours, and you are mine. Forever."

~

BONUS SCENE

Cleo & Rafe go on their honeymoon! To get the bonus scene just scan the QR code:

FALLEN GOD DUET: PREORDER BOOK 1

Nero's spin-off story is coming in 2024 and it will be told in a duet. You can preorder the first book right here.

JOIN GABRIELLE'S GALS

Talk about When She Loves with other readers and get access to exclusive content in Gabrielle's reader group!

ACKNOWLEDGMENTS

The Fallen is the series that changed my life and if you're reading this, it means YOU helped make that happen. A huge thank you for reading my books and for trusting me to give you a story worthy of your time. Your support means everything. The Fallen might be over, but I will continue to write in this world because it simply refuses to let me go. I hope you stick around for Nero's book. I've had his story in my mind for a very long time and I'm so damn excited to write it.

To Mr. Sands—you are my biggest supporter and the love of my life. Thank you for all that you do. I couldn't have written this book without you.

To Skyler—you're there anytime I get stuck, anytime I'm freaking out, anytime I'm excited about a scene I wrote. Thank you for being the best critique partner in the history of critique partners. I truly am so grateful for you.

To Heidi—you are the absolute best. I've learned so much from you and I couldn't have asked for a better editor.

To Becca—you are one of the most creative people I've ever met and having you to brainstorm and bounce ideas around has been an absolute game changed to my process. Thank you for sharing your brilliance and for being so supportive.

To Maria—thank you for this GORGEOUS cover and for everything else that you do to help make my vision for my books and my brand a reality. It is always such a pleasure to collaborate with you.

And last but not least, huge thanks to all of my writer friends—you know how you are. You inspire me daily.

Love,

Gabrielle